# THE
# DYING
# CRAPSHOOTER'S
# BLUES

# THE DYING CRAPSHOOTER'S BLUES

## DAVID FULMER

HARCOURT, INC.

ORLANDO   AUSTIN   NEW YORK   SAN DIEGO   TORONTO   LONDON

Requests for permission to make copies of any part of the work
should be submitted online at www.harcourt.com/contact or mailed to
the following address: Permissions Department, Harcourt, Inc.,
6277 Sea Harbor Drive, Orlando, Florida 32887-6777.

www.HarcourtBooks.com

Library of Congress Cataloging-in-Publication Data
Fulmer, David.
The dying crapshooter's blues/David Fulmer.—1st ed.
p.   cm.
1. Police—Georgia—Atlanta—Fiction.   2. Gamblers—Fiction.
3. Atlanta (Ga.)—Fiction.   4. Jewel thieves—Fiction.   I. Title.
PS3606.U56D75   2007
813'.6—dc22      2006016221
ISBN-13: 978-0-15-101175-9   ISBN-10: 0-15-101175-3

Text set in Sabon
Designed by Cathy Riggs

Printed in the United States of America
First edition
A C E G I K J H F D B

*In Memory of Thomas R. Mertz.*

*1946–2006. A brother.*

*"Mr. Williams was his name—Jesse Williams. See, he got shot here on Courtland Street. And after getting shot, I'd taken him home, sick from the shot. And so he gave me this request. He said that he wanted me to play this over his grave. That, I did."*

—BLIND WILLIE MCTELL,
AS TOLD TO EDWARD RHODES IN 1956

# THE
# DYING
# CRAPSHOOTER'S
# BLUES

# ONE

From down the alley, a voice cut through the falling night like a honed blade.

Sharp whispers were not such an odd thing in the shadows off Decatur Street, nor was it so strange when two shapes abruptly animated and split apart, like stage actors who had just heard the call to places. Swept by the swirling wind, they kept their faces hidden and disappeared in opposite directions. Then it got quiet again.

Central Avenue was on fire. The gambling and sporting houses along the street that stretched south from the rail yards pulsed with light and motion this December night, as men who were low on funds tried to win some in advance of the holiday, and those who had received something extra in their pay envelopes went looking for a woman and a drink to spend it on. Coarse laughter rumbled over the sounds of tinny brass and clunking pianos from the horns of Victrolas. Though shades were drawn, there was no doubt what kind of commotion was going on inside the houses. It looked to all the world like a typical Saturday night on Atlanta's scarlet boulevard.

And yet a certain unease was hanging about, a guest in a bad humor. The veteran rounders sniffed the air like dogs catching a bad scent. Sports who knew better snarled at each other over card tables, and fisticuffs broke out left and right. In the upstairs rooms, the sporting girls bickered back and forth, hissing with venom. The whiskey in the speaks tasted a little raw even for moonshine, and too many of the gamblers couldn't get a decent hand or make the dice roll their way to save their souls.

Still, the action on the avenue never missed a beat on this, one of the last Saturday nights before Christmas. Those who believed the rumors that business was going to be shut down after the first of the year bet harder at the tables or ponied up for lookers who had all their teeth and spoke in complete sentences instead of one of the homely and sullen country girls who did it for a half-dollar and never smiled. No one with sense could deny there was something in the air.

On this same night, less than two miles distant, the Payne mansion was splendid in its annual yuletide glory. Every window glowed with festive light, and the ten-foot blue spruce trees on either side of the front door were festooned with little globes inside which cheery candles flickered. Even the tall wrought-iron fence that surrounded the corner property was draped in ropes of holly. Indeed, the massive two-story brick in Greek-revival style with solid columns at its portico had been decorated with such élan that the society scribblers would fairly swoon as they filled their columns with the kind of fawning attention to detail that would make their readers think they had been there. The charity Christmas party was such an event that every year brought rumors that certain unexplained deaths among the affluent class had actually been suicides over being left off the guest list.

The night had brought a bustle of excitement that rippled in and out the heavy front doors with the guests, dressed to the nines, the women aglitter in gems and swathed in gowns from the

Davison and Neiman stores, and the gentlemen stiff in tuxedos of inky black. Music from an eight-piece orchestra was barely audible over all the gay chatter and clinking of glasses.

Outside, a line of automobiles stretched along the Euclid Avenue and Elizabeth Street curbs in four directions. There was not a single Model T in their number; indeed, it appeared that a parade of luxury models had come to a stop: Duesenbergs, Wintons, Chryslers, Whippets, Cords, and a dozen other marques, their nameplates basking in the glow of the streetlights. Chauffeurs were de rigueur, of course, and so Negroes in fancy livery stood around stamping their feet and clapping their gloved hands against the cold. Every few minutes, a pint bottle of homemade whiskey would appear, make a round, and go back into hiding.

Local wags would note that half the automobiles had either been parked there purely for show or had owners who were impossibly lazy, as their homes were within a few minutes' stroll.

Inside the house it was such a hectic event, with so much frantic activity, that no one paid attention when one of the colored maids passed a slip of paper to another, who gave it a quick read and with an absent smile folded it into her apron pocket.

The second maid, dark skinned and sharp featured, made her way to the door that led from the bustling, overheated kitchen to the basement stairs. Keeping her face intent, as if on a pressing errand, she stepped through the door and closed it behind her. She lingered in the basement only a minute and was not missed.

The party bubbled merrily on until the stroke of midnight, when tradition demanded a toast. This year, the glasses were raised to the great city of Atlanta, to those upstanding citizens who had made such generous donations to the Christmas fund, surpassing the previous year's, and finally to new mayor John Sampson for his exemplary efforts in maintaining their safety and protecting their interests. With that, the couples in their tuxedos and furs began to take their leave. The foyer rang with hearty farewells as the guests went out the door and down the walk to their waiting automobiles.

It was when the last of the wraps were being collected from the second floor that Mrs. Charles Payne stepped into the master bedroom and noticed a zebrawood jewelry box that had no business being out sitting atop the dressing table. Lifting the lid, she found it empty, cleaned of a half-dozen pieces of her best jewelry. She let out a gasp and called faintly, then louder, and one of the maids ran down the hall and down the stairs to fetch her husband.

# TWO

The crack of the pistol echoed and died and the gray wisp of smoke from the barrel drifted up into the December night.

Officer J. R. Logue stared openmouthed and bleary as the body folded and collapsed onto the cold sidewalk. He had never shot a man before. It wasn't that hard. He rolled that curiosity through in his addled brain as he turned around and stumbled into the darkness of Gilmer Street.

In the silent wake of the shot, Little Jesse Williams lay on the hard concrete waiting for the angels or blue devils to come claim his bad luck soul. When a tortured minute went by and none appeared, he managed to crawl across the rough concrete to the facade of the Hong Luen Laundry and, with a jagged groan, propped himself against the bricks next to the door, his numb legs stretched out before him.

The slug had gone through his coat, vest, and shirt, and settled like a hot stone below his rib cage. He watched with dull eyes as the blood dribbled out to pool in his lap and then trailed onto the sidewalk. Though he had guessed it might someday come to this, he'd always imagined it would be some big-legged woman's jealous husband rather than a drunken rednecked cop who ended it. That part was his fault; he had played a bad hand, and now he was paying for it.

Tilting his head back to look up at the dim stars, he felt no anger and no sadness. He knew as well as anyone that life for a black man was short and hard. There was so much trouble and toil and so many ended up the same way. Jesse smiled through the pain, thinking how much that sounded like the refrain of an old gutbucket song. The truth was that Little Jesse Williams had chosen to gamble all his days, and now his last deal was going down.

He knew where he was heading. He had seen the bodies laid out on cooling boards and had stood at more gravesides than he could count. He had listened to sweet-voiced choirs offer up their solemn hymns of grief and had heard blues shouters cry out about this man's evil spirit or that woman's loving heart. Now it was his turn to see what all the fuss was about.

He pictured the inscription on his stone: JESSE LEE WILLIAMS, 1896–1923. REST IN PEACE.

All this drama was waylaid when a black man named Robert Clark stepped out of Lynch's Alley. He had been lingering there with the last half inch of whiskey in his pint when he heard a white man's loose voice call out. The words didn't make sense until the crack of a pistol shot brought a second of clarity. Robert peeked out, his eyes going wide, then drew back and waited before stepping from the shadows again.

Crossing over a silent Courtland Street, he heard a rough moan and saw the body flopped against the storefront. As he edged closer, a head came up into the glow of the streetlamp, and he caught sight of a familiar face, fox-sharp, medium brown, wicked-eyed, and now cleaved into halves of light and shadow.

"Jesse!" he cried. "Goddamn! Lookit you!"

When Little Jesse turned, his coat fell away to reveal the dark, wet patch that had stained his vest and fine silk shirt.

Robert said, "Goddamn, boy!" He nearly put a toe into a

tiny puddle of blood that had gathered on the sidewalk and re-
coiled in a staggering hop.

"Did you see it?" Jesse grunted. "You see what he done?"

"I didn't see *nothin'*!" Robert's voice shook and he looked
around, feeling his heart thump. Of all times for the street to be deserted. He crouched down, his eyes rolling side to side as he tried
to get his brain to tell him what to do. He jerked around at the
sound of an automobile. A Chevrolet touring car rounded the corner two blocks north and motored along the other side of the
street, the engine gurgling and fenders wobbling against the frame.
It passed without slowing. The avenue once again fell oddly quiet
for this part of town, in the middle of the rambunctious triangle
formed by Edgewood Avenue and Decatur and Peachtree streets,
and on a Saturday night to boot. It was spooky, and Robert was
wondering if it would be best to just leave Little Jesse in God's
hands. He didn't want any part of a man's dying, and he couldn't
do him any good, anyhow. All the same, he couldn't abide Jesse's
haint walking around his bed in the middle of the night, payment
for deserting him during his last minutes on earth.

As if echoing Robert's nervous thoughts, Jesse said, "Feel like
I'm fixin' to die." He groaned again and his eyes fluttered and
closed.

Robert couldn't tell if Jesse had just that second passed, and
he wasn't of a mind to stick around to find out. He was in need
of another drink and tried to pull from his memory the number
of the house on South Bell where the old conjure woman sold
shorts of corn liquor out her kitchen window. She was known as
a kind soul who couldn't say no to a Negro in need. With a jerking motion he stood up, turned away, and started back across the
street.

Just as he reached the safety of the dark alley, he was startled
by a young man moving along the sidewalk from the direction of
Warren Street.

"Willie!" Robert jumped back a step.

Slender and just under medium height, with skin the color of caramel, Willie McTell carried a big boxed guitar slung across his chest, as if ready to play at a second's notice. Blank, up-staring eyes marked him as blind, and yet he made his way at a steady, unfaltering pace, as if guided by some other kind of sight. Even at that early hour, within shouting distance of the first light of dawn, he was dressed nattily, his suit clean and pressed, his white shirt buttoned to the chin, and his tie knotted precisely. Though the weather was brisk for mid-December, he wore his overcoat open. A slouch hat perched rakishly on a close-cropped head.

Willie could hear the frantic edge in Robert's voice, and he caught the rank scent that came off his body, all the more sour with fear. "What are you doin' out here?" he said. "What's wrong?"

"It's . . ." Robert's hand jerked. "It's Little Jesse."

"What about him?"

"He's back there on the corner. Been shot."

Willie heard the way Robert was shuffling his feet, ready to bolt. "Shot?" he said. "By who?"

"I don't know!" Robert said, too loud for the empty street.

"Is he dead?"

"Don't think so. Maybe."

"Are you going for help?"

"I'm just . . . I'm just *goin'*. He . . . he's . . ." Robert threw up his thin arms and, jerking around, hurried off.

Willie listened to the footsteps patter into silence before turning to cross the intersection. He tapped the curb with his toe, then stepped onto the sidewalk and inclined his head a few degrees. "Jesse?"

A second went by and Jesse opened his eyes. "Hey, Willie," he said, and coughed weakly.

Willie said, "What happened, boy?"

"Shot."

"How bad is it?"

"It ain't good." Little Jesse's voice was as dry as a leaf.

Willie paused, taking in the sounds and odors that inhabited the air around him. Jesse was drawing breath in pained little grunts. The smell of blood rose up from the wound, sickly sweet and heavy, overpowering a cheap cologne. Perking an ear beyond the corner, he heard the traffic up on Piedmont Avenue and the faintest rumble of thunder far to the west side of the city. Trains rolled on clacking wheels into Union Depot, three blocks farther south.

There were footsteps approaching, then a voice called, "Look at that!" The steps hurried away; someone else who didn't want any part of this mess.

Unwilling to leave Jesse there like that, Willie stayed put. Little Jesse gasped and grunted in pain, and Willie was trying to decide what to do when he heard the staccato click of heels on concrete. A woman's indistinct voice was followed by a sharper, deeper one.

"Willie?" the second voice called. "Is that you? What the hell's going on over there?"

The two Negroes, one standing, one in a slouch, turned toward the white man—his skin more a copperish tone, to be exact—who was standing a half block up Edgewood on the other side with a young lady on his arm, looking their way. The new arrival was just above short and almost slender, wearing a heavy overcoat over a decent suit that was a little out of style, with a driving cap pulled low over his forehead. The woman was taller than he by an inch or so and as lank as an *S*, her pale face stark against her black hair and dark painted lips and eyes. Bundled in a coat with a fur collar, she hinted at elegant, a contrast to her escort.

"Joe Rose," Jesse said.

He and Willie watched the man break away from the girl to cross the street, moving with the gait of one used to prowling.

The girl followed at a grudging pace, stepping onto the sidewalk twenty paces away to stare at the bloody tableau that was arranged in the blue light of the corner streetlamp.

Joe greeted Willie shortly and stared down at Little Jesse. "Jesus and Mary," he said. "What the hell?"

"Joe," Little Jesse said softly. "Where'd you come from?"

"Lime Row," Joe said. "Someone ran by, said a man got shot and that it might be you." He knelt down and pulled Jesse's coat open to study the black hole and the crimson patch that surrounded it.

"How's it look?" Jesse said, his breath coming short.

"I've seen worse," Joe said. It was true; the blood was seeping rather than gushing out, and the wound was low enough down that it appeared to have missed major organs. Willie laid a clean white handkerchief on Joe's shoulder and Joe took it and pressed it down.

Jesse flinched and said, "Shit."

Joe knelt down the rest of the way, settling on his knees on the hard concrete. "Who did it, Jesse?"

Little Jesse didn't say anything for a few seconds. Then: "*Police.*"

Joe cocked his head. "What police?"

"It was the . . ." Jesse took a breath, let out another soft wheeze. "Sonofabitch name of Logue."

"Why?" Joe asked. "You start something with him?"

"I didn't start *nothin'*," Jesse said. "I was only—" He closed his eyes, gritted his teeth, sighed. "He . . . he walked up and . . . put one in me. Just like that."

It didn't make sense, and Joe stared at Jesse for a few seconds, then looked up at Willie and asked, "You find him like this?"

"It was Robert Clark found him," Willie said.

"Yeah? Where's he at?"

"Gone."

"Gone where?"

Willie shrugged. "Gone. Run off."

"Guess he thought it was over," Jesse wheezed.

"Joe?" The girl had edged closer and was staring at the colored man who was sprawled all bloody on the sidewalk. "What happened? Is he going to be all right?" This was not the way she expected her night to end. Still, even as her painted mouth curled in distaste, her eyes glittered with fascination at the sordid sight.

Joe ignored her for the moment and surveyed the crossing streets. Two men had appeared at the corner of Piedmont, peering their way. A Negro boy who looked too young to be out at that hour was shuffling across Courtland, staring with wide eyes. A Model T sedan passed by, slowing, and the face of the driver turned. Joe knew the streets well enough to understand that if they didn't do something, the word would travel that there was a man bleeding to death on the corner of Courtland and Edgewood, and there'd be a crowd of vultures in no time.

"We need to get him off the street," Joe said. He stood, brushing the grit from his trousers, and beckoned the kid. "You want to earn a nickel, son?" The boy bobbed his head. "Run down to the Diamond Pool Room on Auburn and tell whoever's there that Joe Rose needs them up here. Tell them Little Jesse's been shot. You got it?" The boy nodded again and started off at a trot. "Tell them we need a hack to carry him home," Joe yelled after him.

Willie grinned in spite of the grim business at hand. Joe Rose always seemed to fill the air around him, and without being one of those rough, bullying types, either. Though it was true that sometimes the man's mouth got him into trouble. The last time was down home in Statesboro, and Willie had to talk the both of them out of a rough corner.

The blind man spent a moment musing on Joe showing up like that. But then he usually did appear out of nowhere. Whenever the first snow fell on one of his Yankee haunts, he would

leave for a warmer clime. He never made an entrance that anyone noticed. Like tonight, when he stepped from the darkness
and into the aftermath of a shooting.

And of course there was a girl at his side. That was the other
thing about Joe: He collected all sorts of women. Willie had never
figured it out. Maybe he was handsome, though Willie didn't
think it was his looks. He was just one of those characters who
trailed something that some females couldn't resist. So Willie
knew that pretty much whenever he heard Joe's voice, he'd smell
French perfume, too.

Though he could be loud, he was staying quiet now, watching over poor Little Jesse as the night crept toward dawn.

"Joe?" The woman pulled her coat tighter around her thin
frame. "I'm cold."

"Well, go on up to the hotel," Joe said absently.

"By myself?"

"Go ahead," Joe said. "It ain't but two blocks. Tell them
you're with me. They'll let you in."

She gave him a peeved look, then stared at Jesse for another
moment before turning around and swaying up the avenue in the
direction of Ivy Street.

From his slouch, Little Jesse watched her tail twitch away and
sighed. "I guess I wouldn't mind if that was the last thing I ever
saw."

Joe and Willie snickered and Jesse stirred some more,
groaning.

"Willie," he said, sounding all mournful. "Promise you'll
sing me a song over my grave."

Joe treated him to a wry look. "You can hold off on that,"
he said. "I believe you're too goddamn wicked for one bullet to
finish you."

Little Jesse coughed out a pained laugh. From the west came
a slight rumble of winter thunder. "Listen," he said. "Is that—"

"It's about to start raining, is all," Willie said. "You stay calm."

"Help's coming," Joe told him.

Little Jesse moaned once more, hollowly, and Joe knelt down again and, removing the bloody handkerchief, pulled a clean one from his own pocket and pressed it on the wound. Jesse flinched from the pain, then closed his eyes and let out a long breath.

Whatever had happened on that cold, dark corner, Joe could see that the damage wasn't yet fatal. It appeared Little Jesse Williams would survive at least another day. Otherwise, he would have sent the kid for the hoodoo wagon instead of a hack.

Mayor John Sampson was on his way home from the Payne mansion, bundled along with his wife in the back of the Essex phaeton that was one of the fringe benefits of his office. The mayor and his spouse were spared the whip of the cold air by heavy overcoats, a horse blanket, and the precise engineering of the automobile. The phaeton was tight as a drum, and the heat of the twelve-cylinder engine was efficiently diverted into the passenger compartment.

The mayor felt the glasses of champagne he'd drunk swimming through his brain as he watched the city—his city—pass by the windows.

The Christmas charity marked the end of a sterling year. A dark-horse candidate, he had been elected on a platform of ridding Atlanta of police corruption so rampant that he often claimed that half of the city's criminals wore badges. He had pledged to root out the blight, and so he had, shocking the citizens by actually keeping his promise and demoting his chief of police and chief of detectives, both of whom were dirty, incompetent, or both. In that one move, he made an example of them and a statement that things were going to change.

This bold stroke was lauded from every corner of the city,

and there were whispers of a run for governor almost before he had rightly moved into his City Hall office. The crowd of wealthy patrons at the Payne mansion had greeted him like an untrumpeted Caesar back from the wars. He smiled as he recalled several of the lovelier ladies fawning over him, and the sight of their heavy bosoms jutting under the lights of the chandeliers as gay music swirled in the background.

He was jerked out of his reverie when a police sedan roared up alongside the phaeton with lights flashing. The passenger-side window was open and a uniformed officer was waving urgently.

"Pull over," the mayor ordered, and his driver steered the Essex to the Irwin Street curb. The cop hopped out of the sedan and trotted to the rear window to whisper a message.

The mayor, a pious and God-fearing Baptist, uttered a rare curse before snapping at his driver to turn around and head right back to the mansion, where a cache of jewelry had been stolen even as at least a hundred of the city's most prominent business and political leaders were hailing the new mayor's crime-fighting triumphs.

It had taken less than a quarter hour for the boy to arrive back on the corner with a gang of sharps and rounders from the Diamond in tow. All rough types, they knew to bring clean towels from behind the counter to help stanch Jesse's wound. They stood in a circle, shoulders hunched against the chill, casting furtive glances and muttering oaths.

All of them knew Little Jesse Williams as a gambler, sometime thief, and all-around sport who had been working Atlanta's streets and alleys since he was a kid. Over the years, he had cheated them out of their money and jacked their women, but the man was in such bad shape, maybe even at death's door, that for the moment all grudges were laid aside.

Still, they were to a man deeply superstitious, so there was a collective sigh of relief at the sound of hack wheels on the macadam and the ring of horseshoes on the streetcar rails. An ancient Negro named Henry had been roused from his bed in Thompson's Alley and had hitched his equally aged nag to his hack. The wagon, used daily to haul junk, creaked out of the Edgewood Avenue darkness and drew to a halt at the corner. Henry looked down at the man on the ground with his blank old eyes as the horse huffed little clouds into the cold air.

With Joe directing, the boys gathered round to lift a groaning Jesse into the bed of the hack. Joe and Willie climbed in with him, and Henry snapped the reins. The Negro boy and two of the rounders followed along behind. The rest of them watched the wagon roll off as the first drops of dawn rain began falling on the corner, washing away all traces of Little Jesse Williams's blood.

When Mayor Sampson stepped into the parlor to speak to the Paynes, his face was pink with chagrin. When he came out, it was crimson with anger. At times like this, he wished he was a tall man who could simply tower over a fiasco. He was especially dismayed to find that at least a dozen of the attendees, including some of the city's most energetic gossips, had not yet left, and that there would be no way to keep the word from spreading. He forced his legs steady as he crossed to the telephone set in the foyer. Snatching up the hand piece, he asked to be connected to the home of the chief of police.

Across town, Chief Clifton Troutman sat on the edge of his bed, listening to Mayor Sampson rail at him like he was some schoolboy. After the mayor had hung up the telephone, he sat numbly, trying to figure a way to fix the awful mess that had just been dropped in his lap.

A chilly drizzle was falling by the time they arrived at Schoen Alley, and Joe hopped down to supervise the clumsy business of getting Jesse up the wooden stairs, through the tiny kitchen, and into the bedroom of the apartment that was kept surprisingly tidy by the string of floozies who had reason to be in and out. Willie followed along, his face grim.

The rooms were over a pawnshop, a convenience for any rounder. Once they got Little Jesse laid out on his iron-framed bed, Joe sent someone to find the doctor. Within a few minutes, one of Jesse's women appeared, then a second, the jealous fires in their hearts quieted by the sight of him laid out in such a poor state, drifting in and out of consciousness and moaning in pain. They dabbed their painted eyes with handkerchiefs, though even in their anguish their thoughts went to who might be taking his place.

A little bit later, a trio of sports showed up after a night in the Decatur Street speaks. One of them poked around and found a bottle Little Jesse had stashed. Drinks were poured and glasses raised to Jesse's speedy recovery, though they all guessed he was a goner. The vigil had begun.

With these characters on hand to watch over Jesse, Willie and Joe descended the rickety stairs to the alley, shook hands, and went their own ways, Joe to the Hampton Hotel and Willie home to his room on Alabaster Street to dress for church.

# THREE

O n the stroke of eleven, as the bells tolled to end Sunday services at Peachtree Baptist Church, Detective Lieutenant Daniel Collins was pacing the sidewalk with an umbrella over his head as cold rain pattered on the sidewalk. The doors opened and the congregation began filing down the broad stone steps. Collins craned his neck until he saw a familiar face and gave a short wave.

Grayton Jackson spied him and broke away from his pretty, plump, and chattering wife to make his way down the marble steps and through the morning drizzle, looking odd and uncomfortable out of uniform as he ducked under the umbrella.

The younger man whispered in his ear. Jackson, known simply as "the Captain," kept his blank stare riveted on the wet sidewalk. When Collins finished, he responded with a blunt nod, dismissing him, and then moved to the bottom of the stone steps to wait in a brooding silence for his wife to stop talking and get moving.

Joe opened his eyes to the lonesome bleat of a truck horn on Houston Street and looked up at the familiar delta of cracks on the water-stained ceiling. Before he could come fully awake, he sensed the heat of a body next to him and turned his head slowly, in case there was a shock waiting. He had woken up to some fiercely ugly women in his day. Not that he cared that much; homely faces sometimes came with bodies that were completely lovely, full-muscled hourglasses built for a good time. Anyway, it wasn't like he was some matinee idol. He just needed to prepare himself when it was time to greet his guests in the morning light.

Though not this morning. The woman next to him— *Adeline,* that was her name—was pretty, pale, raven-haired, with long lashes, a delicate painted mouth, and a body as slender as a flower.

Joe knew her type. Though she came from a decent family and had enjoyed a proper upbringing, she smoked and caroused and found shady characters like him to take her to back-alley speakeasies to drink and dance. She had approached Joe boldly the last time he was in town, casting her eye upon him at a speak and then walking directly away from the fellow who had brought her there and right up to him. He dropped a hint that he stayed at the Hampton when he visited Atlanta, and there had been a note from her waiting at the desk when he checked in.

He had taken her to a little club on Lime Row where they offered a trio of a piano, trumpet, and guitar, along with bottles of half-decent gin. Adeline drank like a sailor, danced up a frenzy to the gurgling jazz, and didn't sober up until they came upon Little Jesse Williams lying on the cold sidewalk with a hole in his stomach.

Joe had walked the six blocks back from Schoen Alley in the drizzly half dawn to find her fast asleep in the bed. Normally, that wouldn't stop him from diving between her legs, but he was tired, and the scene on the street, and then in Jesse's rooms, had darkened his mood, so he let her be.

Turning his head to look out the window, he saw that the sky held a deep gray dinge as the rain kept falling. He slipped from under the sheets and moved through the dim light to the sink to splash some water on his face and gaze at the reflection in the mirror.

People meeting Joe assumed right away that he was at least half Indian, which was likely true. After his copper skin, which went from light bronze in winter to the color of an old penny in summer, they noted his glittering black eyes, then his nose, which had curved like a bow until being broken in his first and only prizefight; and finally his smile, which was wide, white, and devilish, as if he was tending to a private joke. The way he got along so well with colored folks was more proof that he was something other than an American white man. Some people, not unkindly, called him "Indian Joe." On the other hand, he'd gotten into bloody fights with drunks who took one look and decided that "Geronimo" or "Chief" was a more amusing moniker. The truth was no one could say for sure what blood ran in his veins, certainly not him.

When he was a kid, he made a game of imagining that his eyes and hair, as black as anthracite, had come from his father, an Italian, or from his mother, an Iroquois. Or that his compact frame was a gift from his Irish father or Greek mother. The planes of his face, round and oddly cherubic for a grown man, could have come from anywhere. Philadelphia was full of immigrants and had its share of Indians, so he could be anything. The nuns at the orphanage hadn't provided any clues, instead weaving a tale about how he'd been delivered to the doorstep like a gift from the angels. They weren't very good liars, and he suspected something bleaker. He never found out the true story. He had left out of that place at thirteen and had been on his own ever since, making his way by work and wits.

Those same wits had served him well. For the past seven years, he had been by profession a thief of goods that were worth the risk of stealing. That meant jewels, bonds, cash, and like prizes. He stole from rich people, because they had the nicest belongings and were often easy marks; also because he took pleasure in it.

The work was not too hard for a careful fellow, and the rewards could be ample.

He fenced the goods and used the money to keep him moving from place to place, spending modestly until his funds got low. Then he'd go looking for the next opportunity, some trinkets just waiting for him to pick up and carry off. Thus he cut an erratic trail from Philadelphia to Baltimore to New York, then from Atlanta to New Orleans to Memphis. Every burglary cop on the eastern seaboard knew his name, and yet not one of them could hang much of anything on him.

It wasn't a cakewalk, though. Get caught filching from a hobo, no one cared. Steal from a citizen of means and they'd move heaven and earth to find and punish you so you'd never forget.

Joe had known a slick sport in Philadelphia named Jack Johnson. "Just like the prizefighter," he'd say. "But I ain't him." As if it wasn't obvious; this Jack Johnson was rosy white. Poor Jack got caught with one hand up the skirt of a certain well-to-do businessman's wife and the other in a box of her jewelry, and you'd have thought he'd committed capital murder on a child. They took care of Jack, all right. Afterward, they said he hung himself in his cell. Joe claimed the body, because Jack had no one else.

There were other risks. A second-story man who went by "Red" for his bright orange hair had climbed a trellis of a Baltimore mansion on his way to cracking an upstairs window when some coot came out of nowhere and snapped a derringer in his face. It took away half his jaw, and the fall off the ladder broke his back. After that, Red lost his mind and children screamed in terror at the sight of him. He drank himself into regular stupors and was found frozen to death in an alley in the brutal winter of 1916.

So there were dangers, which Joe accepted as the risks of his illicit trade. For all the crimes he'd committed, his jail time had been limited to a three-month stretch in Radford. Along the way, he had spent a year as a policeman in Philadelphia and a shorter stint as a Pinkerton detective in Baltimore. It just turned out that he made a better criminal than he did a cop.

He did not suffer pangs of conscience over his crimes, and never had qualms about stripping some rich citizen's home of anything that wasn't red hot or nailed to the floor. It could be truly said that here the nuns had failed. The one other place he displayed no guilt was with women. He had a long and tangled history of loving and then leaving them behind. If they didn't get wise and drop him first, that is. Women out for a thrill were dismayed when they realized he wasn't Robin Hood or Jesse James, just a common burglar. Only one of them understood that at all, and only because she'd done her own share of thieving.

From behind him, he heard the rustle of bedsheets, then a yawn.

"Well, good morning," Adeline purred sleepily. Joe glanced into the corner of the mirror and saw her reflection as she threw back the blankets and stretched in his direction.

They kept the bed frame rattling and the springs shrieking for a good half hour, as her pallid flesh turned pink, then red, and she moaned as if she was in pain, all the while bucking up and down, her arms and legs flailing. When they were finished, she rose unsteadily to her feet, wrapped herself in the blanket, and, with a woozy smile, hobbled out the door and down the hall to the bathroom, her carefully coiffed curls now hanging down in wet rag-doll strands.

Joe heard voices. One of the other guests had apparently been eavesdropping on the racket from their room and now made some lewd comment, to which Adeline, young lady that she was, snapped back a hearty "you can fuck yourself, mister!" The bathroom door slammed shut, shaking the walls.

Joe ran into girls like her wherever he traveled: wild, crude, and with little shame, no matter what the family background. He'd heard people claim it was the Great War that had done it, something about letting loose as the world came to an end. He didn't know about that. He had been over there for the months right before the armistice and had seen it all: the total obliteration of the landscape; the blind, lame, and insane soldiers; the dead bodies stacked high with horrible contortions frozen on the faces of those who'd been gassed. He had felt death passing close by like a cold wind as he spent his days keeping himself alive, all the while never quite believing that he could. He knew he'd never forget it, and yet he still didn't understand why it turned good girls back home into rambunctious harlots.

Joe guessed it had as much to do with the vote. With that right, women started believing that they could enjoy the same abandon as the men, and were making up for decades of corsets, petticoats, and the chastity those devices helped enforce. Crowning all this was a sudden revolt against those pious zealots who had spent the past two decades trying to shove their chosen morality down the throats of one and all.

Whatever the cause, Joe was pleased with the results. Wild girls like Adeline had a yen for dangerous men, especially those who had seen death at close range, and so he had no trouble luring her into his web. She was ready to go. He also knew that once she'd had her time with him and whichever other rounders she could bed, she'd be ready to *leave,* and find herself a decent man so she could settle into the safety of marriage. Though she would remember the likes of Joe Rose to the end of her days.

So much for her. As he stared out at the gray morning, his absent thoughts drifted to Little Jesse and the strange violence that had unfolded on Courtland Street. Whatever had happened on that dark street, Little Jesse was about to pay for it with the last breaths of his life.

# FOUR

The detectives who had been in and out of the Payne mansion since the middle of the night hadn't learned a thing, except that objects that had been stored away in the master bedroom at the beginning of Saturday night's charity soiree were gone when it was over. Pricey jewelry that should have been stashed in one of the wall safes had been taken out for the ladies—mother, daughter, aunts, and several cousins—to pick over as they dressed. The box was placed in the top drawer of the dressing table because no one dreamed a thief would have the gall to slip in and out during the Christmas gala. There had been more than a hundred people in the house. And not just *people;* a fair number of the city's wealthiest citizens were in attendance.

The officers working the case had been instructed to show up in rough clothes, but that fooled no one, as the word had already started to seep out, just as Mayor Sampson had feared.

When nothing came to light by midmorning, Chief Troutman swallowed his bile. Unable to reach Captain Jackson at his house on Plum Street, he sent a message by way of Lieutenant Collins. Though the Captain's methods were sometimes astonishingly brutal and his moods completely unpredictable, it was also true that he could get a case opened and closed faster than any other officer on the force. Still, it was true that he had been passed over when the mayor and Chief Troutman doled out the good jobs, and the chief wondered frankly if he would seize this moment to extract his revenge.

He needn't have worried, because when the Captain finally called back he was cooperative, promising in his blunt way that he'd deliver on the burglary as if it was a foregone conclusion. It was exactly what the chief wanted to hear, and he called the mayor right away to pass on the good news.

The name on his papers was Grayton Jackson, but he was to one and all "the Captain." By most accounts, and for as long as anyone could recall, he had been commonly regarded as a son of a bitch.

He was a good-sized man, right at six feet and topping two hundred pounds on the scale, and tended to walk hunched over, with his arms hanging straight at his sides and his head thrust forward like a pug or a gorilla. His angular face was too thin for his body and a splotchy white. He was square and solid, and whether he was slapping some dirt-mouthed whore in the lockup or perjuring himself in a courtroom to get some worthless nigger or white-trash tramp sent up, he always put his full weight behind it.

His disposition, already sour, had after the chaos following the election of the new mayor gone absolutely acrid. The only time he laughed was when someone spun a joke or a funny story about some hapless person of color: a coon, Chink, dago, or Jew. Then his mouth would stretch and his eyes would squint and he would make a weird hacking sound high in his chest.

He rarely smiled. When he did, it was usually when a superior happened by, and it came on so suddenly that it was as if a switch had been thrown. The transformation from pinched and angry to grinning and groveling was a bizarre sight, and his fellow officers had a good time miming the weird rubbery contortions of his face. On the occasions when former chief Pell made an appearance, the Captain all but rolled over and pissed on himself like some groveling mutt. The instant the chief left, however, he snapped right back to his old self.

Though nobody liked him, it could not be denied that he was an effective law enforcement officer. The cases that crossed his desk were closed, and he was such an ominous presence that Negro parents around the city admonished their children with a warning that the Captain would get them if they didn't behave. Though, like two-thirds of the Atlanta police force, he was a member in good standing of the Knights of the Ku Klux Klan, and shared eagerly in the graft, he was not accepted into the cabal that operated as a second force within the department. Even corrupt and hateful men couldn't stand him, and so he was ignored when the new mayor and new chief started doling out the good assignments. Which had him simmering with a cold fury that radiated from his eyes with a physical force.

He felt a touch of that same bile, a harsh spike of resentment that stuck in his throat when they pulled the Ford to the curb. He sat staring at the wrought-iron gate of the Payne mansion. There he was, a Christian white man saddled with the responsibility of guarding these wealthy citizens from the imprecations of the lower races, and the only time he was welcome at the door was when some of their trinkets went missing.

He let that dark cloud pass and pushed his thoughts into a more positive direction. Who knew what might happen once he closed this case? It could be his moment, as long as he made sure everyone knew he was the hero of the tale. Already seeing the grateful smiles and hearing the praise for a job well done ringing in his ears, he stepped out of the car and into the midday drizzle. With Lieutenant Collins following a step or two behind, he crossed the sidewalk and passed through the tall gate.

The junior officer announced them by dropping the heavy brass knocker that echoed in the chilly air. They were ushered into the house by a Negro butler, short, stout, gray-haired, and serious. He said his name was Nathan and that he had been told to expect them.

As they waited in the foyer, the Captain managed his pique only by keeping his eyes off the appointments and the art on the walls, all of which was of the finest quality. Collins gazed about, murmuring in frank wonder and irritating his superior officer until the Captain glared at him to shut up.

After some minutes went by, a gentleman came out of an adjacent sitting room to introduce himself as Charles Marks, the family's attorney. He was small and precise, in a perfect suit, like a toy man. His bald pate and spectacles gleamed under the chandelier, and his cheeks and chin were as smooth and shiny as an infant's. He kept his voice low, as if he was in church, and he described the prior evening's event and the crime that had taken place.

The Captain took a deliberate pause to pose his lips in a stiff smile, then asked about the possibility of questioning the guests to find out if anyone recalled anything unusual.

Marks cleared his throat as a signal to the arrival at a delicate subject. "The family would much prefer you pursue another course," he murmured. "This problem is discomfiting in a number of ways . . . I'm sure you understand."

Captain Jackson nodded sourly. He did understand. Good lord, yes. The last thing he wanted to do was cause anyone embarrassment! He went about stalling for a few moments, asking useless questions, hoping that some member of the family would wander through so he could display his talents. When none appeared, he gave up.

"What's the possibility that the thief slipped in with the guests?" he inquired.

"That's not likely," Marks said. "It was an invitation-only event."

"Someone could have stolen an invitation. Or forged one."

The attorney nodded toward the butler, who was standing by. "Nathan would know every guest on sight."

"Is that right, Nathan?" the Captain inquired without looking at him.

"It is, yes, sir," Nathan said quietly.

Captain Jackson caught Collins's eye. The detective nodded and addressed the attorney. "Is the entire staff on hand?"

"They're all here," Mr. Marks said.

"What about the help that was hired for the evening?"

"Yes, they're here also," the lawyer murmured.

The Captain said, "How many?"

"Twenty-two."

"Is anyone missing?"

"No, sir," Marks said in his prim voice. "We managed to assemble all of them."

The Captain nodded gruffly. "Then let's have the regular staff first."

Marks gestured to Nathan, who was waiting next to the doorway to the dining room. The gray-haired Negro slid the doors open and spoke a few words, and the house staff filed into the foyer.

There were thirteen in this group, counting the butler, eleven colored and two whites. Nine of the eleven Negroes and both whites were women, ranging from a girl who looked about fourteen to a fat cook in her sixties. Most were in their good clothes, not long from Sunday services. They stood silently under the Captain's frigid stare as he went from one face to the next.

He finished with the last woman and glanced at Marks. "They can go," he said.

Marks nodded to Nathan, who waved a hand. The men and

women dispersed in different directions, and not one of them looked back. Once they were gone, the butler passed along another sign and the temporary staff filed in, eight colored women, the youngest sixteen and the oldest only in her twenties. Most of these women were also in their Sunday best.

Marks handed the Captain a sheaf of papers, explaining that they were the applications that each person had given when they came to work for the employment agency. Jackson had ordered the agent to be roused from bed and carried to the agent's Mitchell Street office to produce the papers that he now held in his hand. He knew the new chief would be finicky about details, and wanted no holes in his investigation.

He went through the sheets, barely glancing over the information. More than half the documents had been completed by the same hand, one person writing on behalf of those who couldn't. When he finished, he raised his head and studied the eight women. Three of them were light-skinned and would be considered comely for those who had a taste for that sort of girl. One was very dark, with a look about her that made her stand out. Though the others were not quite so striking, it was obvious that someone had screened for attractive faces. They stared straight ahead, their gazes blank, except for one who was wearing a smile, looking inexplicably dazed and happy. The Captain's gaze landed on her and stayed.

"She can't help it, sir," the dark-skinned girl said. "She's slow."

The Captain's eyes shifted to the one who had spoken up. Her features were distinctly African, with high cheekbones, slanting eyes, a deep chocolate face, and an earthy, buxom body. He noticed a certain light in her gaze that might have been a challenge or a defense. Whatever it was, she wasn't flinching.

"Your name?" he inquired in his clipped cop voice.

"It's Pearl," the woman said.

Captain Jackson looked past her. "Pearl what?" he asked.

"Spencer."

The Captain's eyes flicked once, though his face showed nothing as he went on to ask each of the other girls for a name and glance at her corresponding sheet.

When he got to the end of the line, he dismissed six of the eight out of hand. They were simple maids for hire who wouldn't have the wits or the will to get involved in a criminal scheme. None of them displayed a guilty look, though who really knew? Negroes were capable of hiding anything. Only the remaining two were worth his interest. The first was the youngest of the lot, the kind who looked eager to please and might do some sharp's bidding. The other one was Pearl Spencer.

The Captain had Collins take her back into the dining room while he spoke to the young one.

They were finished in a few minutes. The girl's name was Sally Frost and, though plainly nervous, she was ready to cooperate. Within her first few sentences, she mentioned church a half-dozen times. There was nothing devious about it; she was a devout Baptist, and a gold cross hung prominently from the chain around her neck. She explained exactly where she had been in the house and what she had been doing throughout the evening. After a few more questions, the Captain told her she could go.

She smiled, thanked him, and went on her way. As she turned to leave, he caught a small gleam in her eye, a look that made him wonder if he had missed something and should have kept her longer. It was too late, though; she was already at the door, and he'd look like a fool in front of Collins if he called her back. He could always find her again if the need arose. And anyway, he was impatient to get to the one remaining.

"All right, let's have her," he said.

The doors slid open, and Pearl Spencer stepped into the room, moving in a cautious way, all watchful, keeping her face fixed in the kind of mask that few white people could read. Of course, the Captain had encountered this sort of facade before, and it always angered him. For all she gave away, she could be thinking about a recipe for corn bread or about cutting his throat with a straight razor.

It made him want to slap the skin right off of her. He had tried that tactic in the past with her kind, only to find an even harder mantle underneath. He knew for a fact that there were blacks who would let themselves be beaten to death before they'd give an inch. Pearl Spencer had that look, though it was displayed without a shred of insolence. She might well have been a statue carved from mahogany for all she was revealing.

At the same time, a certain spark lit up her black eyes as she leaned just a little forward, shoulders back and chest and chin pushed forward. Whether she intended the posture as an invitation, a trick, or an attack was anyone's guess.

The Captain studied her sheet without reading a word, hiding his face as his mind went into a busy jumble. It wasn't the first time he'd come across the name Pearl Spencer. He knew of her by reputation, too. Now, meeting her for the first time in the flesh, he could imagine her in carnal pictures, the type to work a man until he was ground down to nothing, drown him in her juices, and leave him broken into pieces, though with a memory he might not believe. He knew this was true, because like a lot of other white men, he held the secret of having once dallied with a colored woman. Though it had happened a long time ago, the recollection of the girl's raw and primitive power still vexed him. So he wasn't about to allow a creature like Pearl Spencer any ground at all.

That she had been at the scene of the burglary the night before was all the more reason for him to stay on top of her. They waited in echoing silence while the detective stepped into the dining room and came back with a straight-backed chair, which he placed directly behind the black woman.

"Sit," Captain Jackson said, and Pearl sat. It was a ploy he used often, especially with female suspects, another symbol of his power over them. It didn't seem to bother Miss Spencer, though; she stared straight ahead, unfazed. The way she held her body and the odd, fixed light in her eyes had the Captain flustered, and he knew he'd have to take care that he didn't give anything away.

"You know why we're here?" he said, keeping his voice tight.

"Some things got stolen," Pearl said.

The Captain stared at her. "Was it you stole them?"

Pearl blinked up at him. "I didn't take anything, no, sir." There was no brass in her tone; in fact, she sounded almost bored, and the Captain realized that although at his mercy, she was exerting a certain devilish control over the situation.

He plunged on, determined to keep ahead of her. "No?" he said. "Then maybe you were helping someone. You want to go down for hard time? You know what I'm talking about? You'll get tossed in with them bulls in the women's prison. They'll take care of you, but good."

Pearl Spencer listened to this rabid recitation with a puzzled expression, as if the Captain was speaking Chinese. It was all bluster. He had nothing on her and was letting his temper get the better of him while she just sat there, impassive, revealing nothing. Lieutenant Collins observed the exchange with a little surprise and then much interest.

He detected something that he couldn't quite discern brewing just below the surface. The two of them were going around in a strange dance, like onetime sweethearts or former enemies who had a secret history.

"Well?" Jackson muttered. "What have you got to say?"

Pearl shrugged slightly. "Nothing, sir. It wasn't me stole those things."

"You know who did? I'll give you a chance to talk."

"I don't, sir."

The Captain jabbed a finger. "We're going to stay on this until it's closed. Don't think we're not."

"Yes, sir, I understand that," Pearl said in the same unaffected tone.

"So if you have anything, now's the time to tell us."

"I've got nothing to say, sir."

The policeman glared down at her another few seconds, then snapped, "All right, go."

Pearl rose to her feet in a languid uncurling, like rising smoke. She wouldn't meet the Captain's hard eyes as she turned away.

If it had been left there, she would have won the round. But Captain Jackson had something in reserve, and waited until she had reached the dining room door before saying, "Hold on." She stopped. He took a significant pause. "What about Joe Rose?"

For the first time, her front seemed to waver, and the Captain stifled a snicker of satisfaction.

"What about him?" she said.

"You tell me."

Pearl blinked and shifted her weight, hesitating before she spoke. "I know him, yes, sir," she said. "By way of my brother, Sylvester. He works at Lu—"

"I know your brother," Jackson broke in. "And I know Rose, too. I'm going to bet he's back in town. As a matter of fact, this looks like one of his capers. What do you think?"

She didn't have an answer. He let the silence hang for a few seconds; then, looking pleased with himself, gave her a quick nod of dismissal. "I said you can go."

He watched her disappear through the doorway, then turned to Collins and saw an inquisitive stare, exactly what he'd hoped for. He wanted the junior officer to witness his police work. With any luck word of it might get back to the chief, maybe even the mayor. Let them all chew on it as they waited for him to come through and save their hindquarters.

"All right, detective," he said in a voice that was unusually crisp. "Let's have a look upstairs."

Her coat bundled and hat pulled down low, Pearl Spencer walked away from Inman Park and back toward the city, her thoughts in a whirl.

What had transpired in the dining room at the mansion had been like a scene from a movie, played without the cards. She read what was going on behind the cop's blade of a gaze. It was not so much of a surprise how his conniving was laced with the familiar signs of a simmering rage. She had encountered it dozens of times, white men who looked upon her with desire, hated themselves for it, then hated her in turn, which seemed to ignite the hunger all the more . . . and on it went.

It was an old story, and the number of octoroons, quadroons, and mulattoes on the streets of the city was the evidence. What were less visible were the tales of women of color murdered by men who could not face their shame over giving in to their instincts.

As she walked along the morning street, she wondered if the Captain had picked on her simply because of her looks. Even now, some of the men and women she passed glanced, then stared at her. Though her skin was the deep brown of West Africa, her features leaned more to Egyptian: oval face, aquiline nose, slanted eyes. Indeed, with her strong curves, Pearl missed being a stunning work of womanhood only by some rough edges; there were those, and the blades of light that nestled in her black gaze, which could hint at crazy. When she moved, she tended to a certain stalking grace, as if she was hunting something.

She was never one to behave, either. Like an actress changing roles for a show, she could shift from a musing quiet to brash and noisy; from shyly fawning to alley cat wild; from sweet and kind to mean as a snake. When she did domestic work in a house, she would turn almost invisible. Though anyone who bothered to look would notice that she was different.

So much so that she had been able to hold her own with the likes of Captain Jackson right until the end, when he knocked her sideways by throwing out that name, as of course he knew it would.

Now she glanced over her shoulder, wondering if the cop might have her tailed, figuring she would run to him. In fact, she had an urge to do just that: hop on the next streetcar heading downtown and present herself at the door of his room at the Hampton Hotel. She smiled, knowing exactly what would happen if she did it.

But instead of taking that ride, she turned the corner at Jackson for the three-block walk to Lyon Street, knowing she'd find Joe Rose soon enough.

The Captain calmed down after he sent Pearl Spencer away and got his mind on the business at hand. He spent a quick few minutes in the upstairs bedroom of the mansion, then came back down with Lieutenant Collins on his heels.

Mr. Marks was waiting, still alone. Captain Jackson was annoyed that he had yet to encounter any of the family members. Insisting on questioning at least one of them would be too dicey. There was no way his roughhouse, bullying tactics would work in this place. He sensed that he had a good thing going and didn't want to nix it by pushing too hard.

So he explained it to the attorney. "The jewelry box never should have been left unsecured like that," he said. "Any thief with an ounce of sense would know where to look. It probably took no more than two minutes to get up to the room, locate the box, get the goods, and get back out."

Marks shook his head, no doubt used to his clients' foolish behaviors. Though he did seem properly impressed with the Captain's blunt efficiency.

"I supposed they thought they were safe, because their guests are not the type to steal," he said.

"You'd be surprised."

"No, sir, I would not," the attorney said, in a tone of voice that the Captain appreciated.

"Do you have a complete list of the missing pieces?"

Marks reached inside his jacket and extracted a folded sheet of paper. The Captain glanced over it. "What's the value?"

"In the six-thousand-dollar range, depending on the appraisal," the attorney said.

"Did they have insurance?"

"Yes, of course. But they want the jewelry back. They were special pieces."

The Captain folded the paper and handed it to the lieutenant without comment.

"What will you do to recover them?" Marks inquired.

Captain Jackson gave him his best cool gaze. "That doesn't need to concern you. And neither does the apprehension of the guilty party."

"I understand," the attorney said. "Is there anything else?"

"Not at this moment." The Captain turned on his heel and he and Lieutenant Collins headed for the door.


No matter how late or how wild his Saturday night, Willie McTell always found his way to church come Sunday morning. This Sunday, he walked along Old Wheat Street with his Braille bible in his coat pocket and his guitar hoisted on his back. He never traveled anywhere without the twelve-string Stella and the Good Book.

It was a lifelong habit. His mother, God rest her soul, had rarely missed service at the country church back in Happy Valley, down east in McDuffie County. When Willie was nine, they moved eighty miles away to Statesboro, and there was another church, this one in the black-bottom part of town and a bit more prosperous.

She was fervent in her attendance, and as Willie grew up, he came to understand this was partly because she harbored a desperate hope that Jesus might pour down his grace and make her son's blind eyes to see.

His affliction was the cross she bore. As an ignorant country girl of fourteen, she had laid down with the wrong man, a gambler, moonshiner, and guitar picker who had moved on without a glance back, leaving her and then the blind baby boy he had fathered. And God had punished both of them for her sin.

So at the very least, Sunday mornings and Wednesday evenings found mother and son in their customary pew, right down in front. It was there that music first stirred Willie's soul, the sweet and sonorous gospel songs and the wild shouts of emotion from the amen corner, all in praise of God and supplication of his mercy.

That wasn't all he heard, hard as his mother tried to shield his young ears from the other music that was around, what they first called "gutbucket" then "blues." It was low-down, vulgar, sinful, and a raw reminder of the man whose last name they both carried.

Still, she couldn't strike her son deaf, even if she wanted to, and the devil's music was everywhere: on the street corners, at the Saturday markets and fish fries, pouring out from the burlapped windows of the unpainted clapboard shacks at the country crossroads where they sold moonshine by the pint and where all the men and half the women toted pistols or razors. Young Willie was so completely enraptured by what he heard inside and outside the church doors that when a well-meaning Statesboro neighbor gave him an old six-string guitar, the path of his life was set.

His mother tried to take the guitar away for his own good, and he fussed and pouted until she gave in. She taught him every church song she knew in hopes of keeping him on a godly path. It didn't work; with his eyes blinded, he sopped up everything he heard, and along with gutbucket blues, he mastered ragtime, popular tunes, coon songs, and dance numbers. He could play in the dark delta style, rag it all bouncy like Blind Blake and Blind Boy Fuller, or deliver a ballad in the way the singers along the Piedmont did it.

It was his luck to also possess a sweet voice, high and strong and full of texture. Along the way, he switched to twelve-string guitar and found the lush ring and drone suited him all the better. He played fast and loose with dancing fingers, sometimes using a bottleneck or straight razor like they did in Mississippi. He came to believe to his soul that he was as good as anyone around, and no one who heard him disagreed.

So, like his father, now long gone, he played the devil's music for a living. He hoped God would understand, and believed sincerely that a morning in church after a night on Decatur Street was a small payment in the direction of his salvation.

He had even more reason to cross that sanctified threshold this morning. He had felt death's cold shadow creeping around the street corner the night before, and it gave him a spooking he couldn't shake. Little Jesse might be on a slow train to hell, but the poor boy was on his way all the same.

Willie knew Jesse as a wild and reckless gambler who used crooked dice and marked cards. It was little wonder that someone had shot him. He had always expected that either a wronged woman or cheated man would be the one to do him in. Jesse swore it was an Atlanta policeman. Something wasn't quite right about it. Though who knew what kind of trouble followed a fellow like him?

Willie mulled it some more, recalling how Robert Clark had scurried away, wanting no part of whatever had happened.

Robert had to know what kind of juju he was risking by leaving Jesse to die alone. And yet he had bolted from the scene like a scared rabbit.

Passing Pittman Place, Willie turned his thoughts from that sorry business to brighter news. Word had gone around that the Columbia company was sending some folks to Atlanta to make records. Someone had told him about the article in the newspaper stating that the record people would be setting up in the Dixie Hotel on Tuesday, and he planned to be there. He walked on, shuffling through his long list of songs and thinking about what he might play for the people.

Presently, he reached Decatur Street and stopped on the corner to listen for a moment. The broad boulevard, with its markets, barbershops, billiard rooms, and backroom and basement speakeasies, was a beehive of music and motion six nights a week. On Sunday morning it lay as still and quiet as the wake of a parade. All he heard were echoes.

Moving along the street, he took in the squalor that had been left for the light of day: the fetid odors of garbage, manure, and raw whiskey; the taste of the black flaking smoke from the Georgia Railroad Yards; the scrabble and squeak of rats running through the gutters; and the grunts of drunks who had spent the night in doorways. Had he been sighted, he would have seen the terrain rise sharply on the other side of the tracks to a ridge upon which resided the state capitol, its gold dome a heavenly umbrella now half obscured in the gray morning mist.

Willie knew the avenue as well as any other, and his ears guided him to the corner of Hilliard Street and then into Schoen Alley. He counted off the steps to the bottom of the wooden stairs and climbed up, careful to keep his guitar from banging the banister. When he knocked on the door, a woman he didn't know let him in, and he passed through the tiny kitchen, where two or three people were loitering. From the smell of their cheap colognes, he figured them for local rounders, either standing guard or with nowhere else to go.

He felt his way to the bedroom doorway and stopped. Right away, he heard Little Jesse's labored breathing and smelled the dried blood and sour odor seeping from his ravaged innards. The other rounders in attendance spoke up, greeting him, all except for the one sitting in the corner.

Before he could figure out if it was death himself who had taken a seat in the room, he heard Joe Rose's voice.

"Come on in, Willie," Joe said. "We're just waiting on the doctor."

Over the morning hours, the word about Little Jesse had gone around, and as the afternoon began, more people showed up at his rooms. Not a few of the whores arrived still in their Sunday church dresses and hats. Everyone had advice, and not a word of it was worth anything. All stripes of small-time crooks, sports, and rounders came and then went as soon as a bottle was empty. The women, most of whom Jesse had worked at one time or another, came and stayed. One, a thin and homely whore named Martha McCadden, took over tending to the victim. Joe had left word that he wanted at least two men around at all times.

Jesse lay on the bed, gray and sick, drifting slowly through a morphine fog. Among the visitors, he recognized a couple shady characters, though he couldn't quite make out their faces. Then he realized who they were and knew that they would be staying close by so they could escort him home.

A few minutes before one o'clock, a ruckus started outside and someone called in to announce that Dr. Nash was there at last.

There had been some discussion about carrying Little Jesse to a real doctor or to the emergency room at Grady Hospital, a few short blocks from where he had fallen. He refused, rasping out a curse at the suggestion. A bullet wound would instigate a police report, and that could bring all kinds of trouble, not the least of which might be Officer J. R. Logue or one of his cronies coming back to finish the job. Jesse muttered darkly that he'd take his chances.

Weston Nash was a familiar character in the rougher parts of town. Well educated and from a good family, he had fallen under the sway of the powders he prescribed to his patients, then lost his medical license after a botched surgery resulted in a death. When he wasn't answering a call to stitch a razor cut, take care of a hussy's trick baby, or tend to a crapshooter with a police bullet in his gut, he spent most of his time holed up in quarter-a-night rooms around downtown with his solutions and syringes.

On this Sunday, it had taken the better part of the morning for a couple of the rounders to locate him in a George Street flophouse and drag him out.

He now came stumping up the back stairs and into the bedroom, muttering foul curses. Though he was a tallish man, he appeared bent and deflated by his addiction, like a furtive buzzard lurking near something foul. He wore an old suit that was rumpled and dusty and splotched with stains, a shirt that was yellowing at the collar, and a loud tie that hung askew. His face, florid pink with exertion, featured eyes webbed red behind tarnished spectacles and, in spite of the morning chill, his few remaining strands of hair were plastered with sweat to his pink skull. He came in huffing and snorting through his nose like a horse that had been run too hard. When he stopped in the kitchen and opened his black bag, Martha stepped forward and offered to boil the implements.

Willie caught Dr. Nash's odor before he even reached the room: a small cloud of sweat, old cologne, and something ranker. Who knew into what sort of fluids those unsteady hands had plunged lately?

The doctor dropped his bag on the mattress and pulled down the bedsheet to examine the bandage that Martha had fashioned. With a nod of bleary approval, he pulled it away from the wound. Little Jesse grunted over the rough treatment.

Nash pushed his spectacles up his nose, peered close for a few seconds, then straightened. "All right, now," he said. "All of y'all get on out and leave us be."

Jesse said, "Joe and Willie can stay," and the two of them sat back down while the others shuffled out into the kitchen to drink and smoke until they could come back and resume the watch.

Nash eyed Jesse. "Guess you want a shot," he said.

"Hell, yes, I want a shot!" Jesse said. Joe and Willie laughed.

The doctor fished in his bag for a brass syringe and a vial. As Joe watched and Willie listened, he opened the bottle and used the syringe to draw off half the liquid, then jabbed it into Jesse's thigh without bothering to disinfect the spot. He hesitated before putting the solution back in the bag, as if thinking about helping himself.

Within a few seconds, Jesse's eyes went dim again and a lazy smile curved his lips. "That's better," he said. "And you can leave the rest." He closed his eyes and dropped into a black well.

"All right, I'm ready in here!" Nash called out.

Martha brought the shining implements on a dish towel that looked none too clean. Nash nodded for her to lay it out at the foot of the bed. Martha stared in dismay at Jesse's exposed wound before backing away.

"Now what?" Joe asked.

"Now I'm going to go in and see if I can get the damn slug out," the doctor groused as he selected a scalpel. "Ain't that what I'm here for?"

"What if you can't?" Joe asked him.

"Then I can't," he said. He wiggled the blade in Joe's direction. "You want to give it a try?"

"Just don't make him worse," Joe told him.

The doctor gave him a cold glance. "Or what?"

Joe smiled without humor. "Or I'll throw you down the fucking steps, *doctor.*"

"Another hard case," Nash said, and bent to his work.

Willie was just as glad he couldn't see what was going on. He heard Joe grunt in revulsion, the sound of a knife insulting flesh and the suck and slurp of visceral fluids. Nash's huffs of exertion weren't a good sign; the man was working too hard. Presently, he felt someone's gaze resting on his face as Joe, unable to watch anymore, turned away. After several more minutes of this butchery, the doctor let out a blunt curse.

"It's too deep," he muttered. "Can't get at it without cutting him to pieces. He wouldn't last the afternoon. Ain't worth it."

"So?" Joe said.

"So now I'll patch him up. S'all I can do." Nash dug out a needle and suture and went to sewing Jesse's gut. Joe watched for a few seconds, then looked away again. He'd seen Christmas turkeys get better treatment. The sound of their voices brought Martha into the doorway. She crossed her thin arms, insulted by the messes men made.

"What's going to happen now?" Willie said.

"He'll either live with that bullet in him or he won't," Nash said. He finished in silence, taking minimum care in fashioning the bandage as Martha looked on with disapproval. As soon as he left, she'd do it right. The doctor tossed his implements back into his bag and snapped it closed.

Glancing between Joe and Willie, he said, "All right, then. Who's paying?"

Joe wanted to say, *paying for what?* Instead, he said, "How much?"

"Three dollars."

Joe went into his pocket, took three bills, and held them up. "You sure you can't do anything else for him?"

Nash didn't bother to answer. He snatched the money, grabbed his bag, and stalked out of the room as if he had another appointment, which if he did would be with a needle or pipe. Joe got up to catch him just as he reached the kitchen door. One gambler he knew slightly and another of Jesse's whores were at the table drinking coffee laced with whiskey and studiously ignoring the two men.

Before Joe could say anything, Nash jerked his head toward the bedroom and said, "That boy's bound to die. There's infection setting in. It's just a matter of time 'fore it kills him."

"And you can't stop it?"

"No, it's too far gone," Nash said. "Go ahead, carry him somewhere else if you want. I say he's finished."

"How long?"

"He might last a week. Not much more, though."

Joe grabbed him by the arm. "Don't tell anybody about this," he said. "You understand? Nobody."

"Who the hell am I gonna tell?" the doctor said. "Who the hell cares?" With a rude shrug, he walked out, closing the door behind him.

When Joe stepped back into the bedroom, he found that Willie now had his guitar in his lap and was strumming soft chords on the twelve strings. Jesse had dropped off again.

"You flush these days, Joe?" the blind man said.

Joe stopped, then shook his head, bemused. Willie had heard him fan his roll and could likely tell him how much was there. The blind man went back to his guitar. Joe sat down to listen, and after hearing a few bars, picked up a pattern that sounded sort of familiar. He thought Willie was about to play "The St. James Infirmary" or maybe "The Streets of Laredo," tunes everyone knew.

It wasn't either one. With a small smile, Willie half sang a line. "Little Jesse was a gambler, night and day . . ." Hearing the words, the man on the bed stirred and opened his eyes. Willie played the chords over another time and sang, "Yes, he used crooked cards and dice."

Jesse's pained face broke open as Willie went to humming a melody without lyrics. At the sound of the guitar, the couple who had been at the kitchen table got up and stepped into the doorway to listen. Willie had a sweet voice, especially when he sang a lament in a minor key, the kind of dirge played for the dead.

Over the next hour, Jesse went in and out of his stupor three times. The last time, he came up and gazed around blearily to see Willie in the corner with a woman and a man and some character he didn't know. Joe slouched in the chair next to the head of the bed.

Jesse listened to Willie playing and singing little snatches of lyrics for a few moments, then looked down at the bandage that swathed his midsection. He tamped it gently with the fingers of his right hand. "Sonofabitch didn't fix me, did he?"

Joe shook his head. "He said it would have killed you, Jesse."

"Well, I'm going to die anyway, ain't I?" His voice was bitter.

Willie was busy with his guitar, and the others in the room weren't paying attention. Joe leaned close to Jesse's sickly face.

"Why the hell did that copper shoot you?" he whispered. "What'd you do?"

"Didn't do nothin'." Jesse sounded sulky as he gazed past Joe to something on the wall. "I never had no business with him at all."

"You didn't get on his wife, did you?"

That brought a short, pained laugh. "If he got one . . . you know . . . she'd be a damn cow."

"He ever roust you?"

Jesse said, "Not that I recall." He heaved another breath. "I just seen him around . . . he's a drunk . . . never harmed nobody . . . not that I know . . ."

"What happened, then?"

"I was . . . at the crap game," Jesse stuttered, pulling a breath between every few words. "You know we got us . . . a regular game. Every Saturday night . . . over on Fort Street. Took my money . . . and left out." He made himself smile. "Gonna go see a woman I know . . . in a house downtown. I was on Court-land . . . corner at Edgewood and he . . . he come up behind me."

"Logue."

"That's right. Logue." He stared, drifting off again.

Joe prompted him. "Jesse?"

Jesse blinked like a lizard. "Then he say, 'Hey, nigger! Your name Jesse Williams?' Then he said . . . somethin' I didn't catch . . . and he . . . he snapped his pistol."

"That's all?"

"He jes . . . walked away. Let me there to die." His eyes found Joe's. "And that's just what I'm 'bout to do, ain't it?" The question came off on a failing breath.

He was struggling with his answers, so Joe let him rest as he pondered. There was something wrong about it. Whether Jesse was lying or evading or suffering the effects of the wound, there were pieces missing from his story.

Before Joe could question him any further, Little Jesse raised his head an inch or so. "Listen to me," he said, gritting his teeth. "I didn't no way have this comin'. You understand?" He caught a hard breath. "You know . . . I done plenty wrong in my life. I likely should have been . . . been dead long time ago. But I . . . I for damn sure don't want to go like this." He raised up a little more, straining. "That fucker shot me . . . for *nothin'*." His voice broke and he sank back on the pillow. His eyes got wet. A mo-ment passed and he said, "You got to help me, Joe."

Joe said, "Do what?"

"Don't wan' die . . . for nothin'." The words went into a slur.

"Jesse?"

"You got to . . . to help me . . ."

Joe started to protest, then stopped. Jesse had gone out again. For a second, Joe wondered if he had just passed over. Then he heard him sigh, long and low. It wasn't done yet.

Joe looked in Willie's direction and saw the blind man tilting his head their way, listening to every word.

Rather than drive back to his house, the Captain asked Lieutenant Collins to drop him off at police headquarters. The lieutenant was dismayed, thinking Jackson was now going to order him to work through the Sunday afternoon. But when they pulled up to the building on the west end of Decatur Street, the Captain told him to take care of one piece of business before he went home. Once he had related the details, he got out of the car and, with a wave that was almost sprightly for that dour man, sent him on his way.

Collins watched the Captain amble across the sidewalk, up the steps, and through the doors, thinking it was odd that he seemed so unconcerned about all the trouble over the theft of the jewelry from the Payne mansion. But of course, the man had a reputation for closing his cases, one way or another.

To please Jesse, Willie spent time toying with more words to the song he had begun. To the first couplet, he had added,

> *A sinful guy, black-hearted, he had no soul*
> *Yes, his heart was hard and cold like ice*

Jesse was delighted, even as his mind wandered away and back again. His spirits lifted some, and so Willie switched to playing songs at his request. The blind man was a walking music book, with what seemed an endless store of vaudeville tunes, hillbilly cants, blues laments, rags, spirituals, and popular songs of the day swimming around in his head. Not one of the people drifting in and out of the room could stump him. With his keening voice and the brassy sweep of the Stella's twelve strings, he filled the next two hours, aided by the glass of whiskey that was topped for him regularly and the appreciative murmurs from those gathered at Jesse's bedside.

At one point in the middle of the afternoon, Joe happened to overhear a couple of rounders whispering about a jewel heist but couldn't catch any of the specifics over all the chatter, and then was distracted by Jesse muttering something he couldn't understand any better.

Not too long after that, Robert Clark appeared in the bedroom doorway. He didn't come inside once he saw the crowd that had gathered, instead lingering only to stare at Jesse with guilt-stricken eyes.

Joe was surprised to see him and when their gazes met, Robert looked startled and faded back. By the time Joe got up and worked his way through the crowd to the kitchen, he was gone. Joe stood on the landing, looking up and down a deserted alley.

Back inside, he puzzled over the hurried flight of the one other person who had been on the scene the night before. Willie said it was Robert who had found Little Jesse. Apparently, the man didn't want to talk about it.

Jesse weakened as afternoon crept toward evening. Just after the sun went down, Martha walked in with a bowl of hot chicken broth and told them all it was time to leave. Joe and Willie remained behind.

Martha stepped up to the bed. "You best let him be," she told them in a voice that was sweet and gentle for such a hard-looking woman. "Leave him to me."

The two men put on their coats and walked out and down the stairs to amble up the alley and onto a Decatur Street that was quiet in the Sunday evening rain.

Joe raised a hand in farewell. Willie called him back. "You
know I heard what he said up there." Though he had been drinking the better part of the afternoon, his voice was deliberate.

Joe said, "What's that?"

"I said, I heard what Jesse said. About not wanting to die for
nothing."

Joe shrugged, not surprised that the blind man had caught a
whisper from across a room or that he could recall it hours later.

"So what are you going to do about it?" Willie said.

"About what?"

Willie's dark brow stitched. "About finding out why some
damned cracker cop walked up and shot my friend Jesse down."

Joe laughed shortly. "What makes you think I can do anything about it?"

"You was a policeman," Willie said. "And a detective. Ain't
that right?"

"I was a cop for a year," Joe said, sounding impatient. "And
I worked as a Pinkerton for six months. That don't make me a
police officer, Willie. Or a detective."

"You're about as smart as anybody I know," Willie said
earnestly. Joe rolled his eyes at this flattery, but the blind man was
serious. "There's somethin' wrong about it, Joe. You know it's
true."

"I asked him," Joe said. "He won't say."

"It don't make sense."

Joe shifted on his feet. "Maybe it was just one of those
things, Willie," he said. "Some cop who don't care for black
folk. Jesse said he was a drunk. Some people are like that. Could
be Jesse just got in the man's way at the wrong time. Or maybe
he fucked with him somehow. Sassed him or whatever. You
know how he is."

Willie had his head cocked in that peculiar way he did when
he was listening to every nuance in a voice. Now he shook his
head stubbornly. "Then why doesn't he say so?"

"Ask him," Joe said.

Willie pursed his lips and huffed with petulance.

Joe said, "I don't need to get messed up in this, Willie. I've got my own troubles."

"That boy's on his deathbed," Willie said. "You know you can't deny him. So I'd say you *are* messed up in it."

When Joe didn't respond, he adjusted his guitar across his back, turned around, and strolled away, following the path he held inside his head.

Joe walked up Courtland Street, passing the very spot where Jesse had fallen and thinking about what Willie had said. Though his short stints as a copper and a detective barely counted, he knew that if he didn't poke around, it was unlikely they'd ever know if a policeman named Logue really had shot Little Jesse Williams in the dead of night.

It was also true what he had told Willie: He had problems of his own, problems that got worse the moment he rounded the corner onto Houston Street and saw the APD sedan at the curb in front of the Hampton, the engine idling. He stifled the urge to turn around and go back the way he'd come, even though he knew it would make him look guilty of something.

It was too late, anyway; the car door had swung open and a man in a gray overcoat and black Bond Street hat put a foot onto the running board, then stepped to the sidewalk. The officer had seen him coming in the outside mirror, and now went into a pocket to produce a badge in a black leather wallet, which he held in clear view. Joe put on his best innocent face and approached at a stroll.

The cop was around Joe's age, of medium height and solid, with a common American face—the type who would be hard to pick out in a crowd. His eyes were a clear blue as he studied Joe up and down, taking his measure. He wasn't one of those angry sorts, just a fellow who enjoyed his work.

"Mr. Rose," he said as Joe drew close. "Lieutenant Collins."
He put away the badge.

"Yes, Lieutenant," Joe said.

"When did you get to town, sir?"

"Couple days ago."

Collins was watching him with what seemed a vague interest.
"I'm here to deliver a message from Captain Jackson," he said.
"He wants you in his office tomorrow morning. Ten o'clock.
No later." He gave Joe a look. "You be there, all right? Because
I don't want to have to come find you." He reached for the
chrome handle and opened the door.

Joe wanted to ask how the Captain happened to know that
he was in town, then thought better of it and said, "So what's this
about?"

Collins's eyes lightened as if Joe had said something humor-
ous. "Tomorrow morning at ten," he repeated. He slid into the
seat and slammed the door.

Joe watched the car pull away from the curb and chug down
the hill toward Courtland Street, the taillights glowing red in the
dark of the falling night. He cursed under his breath, then turned
and pushed through the doors into the hotel.

Upstairs, he was relieved to find Adeline long gone, with only
a faint strand of her perfume left around the bed. A smart girl,
she knew better than to press a good thing. Joe had treated her
right, taking her to the speak and buying her all the gin rickeys
she could handle, then giving her pleasure in the bed when she
woke up in the morning.

He had an eye for women who could have a good time and
let it go at that. Though every now and then he slipped, and one
of them got it in her foolish head that he was marrying material.
It was preposterous; but some females flat lost their minds once
they imagined themselves in love. Unable or unwilling to grasp
the fact that all Joe wanted was some decent company and a good
fuck, the woman went on a campaign that included hints of an

arrangement and plans to introduce him to the family. Soon the dizzy bride-to-be would go about fashioning an idyll, only to find that he could disappear like Houdini, and he hadn't wandered across the street for a packet of cigarettes, either.

It was a risk he took because he adored women and couldn't get enough of their mysterious, entrancing, enticing selves. So he loved them and left them, and sports from New York to Miami delighted in recounting tales of his escapes. The only one he couldn't shed was the most troublesome of the lot, and one of the few who never breathed the word *marry*.

No matter; it wasn't any woman who had him thinking about pulling one of his evaporating tricks and catching a night train for Mobile, New Orleans, or another of his winter haunts. Captain Grayton Jackson was after him, and that was no joke.

The last thing anyone on the wrong side of the law in the city of Atlanta wanted was to tangle with the Captain. The man could make any rounder's life a misery. Just thinking about it sent him after his bottle. He poured himself a drink and carried it to the window to look down on Houston Street, trying to imagine what Jackson wanted with him.

He hadn't done anything so far, except to happen onto the shooting of Little Jesse Williams. That couldn't be it; the Captain wouldn't care if every black man in Atlanta was gunned down in the street. Even if it happened the way Jesse claimed, it wouldn't signify much. Policemen shot Negro criminals all the time.

The Captain was well into his cups by the middle of the evening, and he stalked around the living room and kitchen of the house on Plum Street, his mouth loose as he described the crime that had been committed the night before and threw out hints of how it was going to end up making him a hero.

His wife, May Ida, found herself intrigued, though not by her husband's role in the story, real or imagined. Rather, she was dazzled that some bandit had found his way into the Payne mansion, of all places, and during their Christmas gala, of all times, making off with a cache of jewelry. It was some brazen caper, and the Captain described a mayor and chief of police floundering about in helpless fits.

"And who do they call?" he inquired of no one in particular—certainly not her. He jabbed a thumb at his chest. "They call *me*, that's who." He all but smacked his lips. "The same sons of bitches that were gonna put me on the street, walking a beat. Now look at what we got here!" He came up with a surly grin of triumph.

May Ida knew better than to comment. He gave not a whit what she thought about this subject or any other. So she let him rail on with his odd mutterings, no more interested in him than he was in her, and returned to her own thoughts with his drunken gripes playing like bad music in the background. It was a typical night at 446 Plum Street.

Skulking back to his rooming house in the evening darkness, Robert Clark had a powerful sense of dread, a swirl of hoodoo that had been hanging at his shoulder like a black cloud ever since he had run off into the darkness, leaving Little Jesse Williams bleeding on that cold corner. Now he couldn't shake the feeling that someone or something was creeping his bed and following in his path and that eyes were on him everywhere he went.

It was his own damned fault. Instead of buying a bottle, going home, and keeping his mouth shut after he'd left Jesse, he had wandered around to the crap game in the empty Raspberry Alley storefront. Even then, he could have enjoyed a last drink and left out. He didn't, though; and that was one dumb-assed mistake.

He didn't know that he had repeated what he'd seen until it was too late. He had finished his own pint, took a couple drinks from the bottle that was going around, and came abruptly out of a fog to realize that he had done just that.

As the blur cleared, he saw that the game had stopped and the boys were all staring back at him in the light of the fire they had built in a can on the concrete floor. When one of them asked for details, Robert mumbled something and made a clumsy exit—another mistake. He should have stayed and explained that what he was saying was actually secondhand, that it was some other fellow who had heard the cop and then the gunshot and had peeked around the corner of the building to see Little Jesse Williams fall. Though he could barely remember who had been in the game, he had no doubt that among their number was at least one rat who would hurry right out on the street to try to trade what he'd heard for something.

After that, Robert went to his room and fell into bed, wishing he could crawl under it. Unable to sleep the rest of that night and into the day, he hurried down to Schoen Alley to ask Jesse what he should do. Somewhere in this addled mind was the notion that he could erase what he had heard and seen, or maybe play it backward like one of the funny bits in the moving pictures, so they could forget the whole thing. But Jesse was in too sorry a state. He couldn't talk if he wanted to. There were at least a dozen people crowded about his rooms.

Then Robert saw Joe Rose, the white man or Indian or whatever he was, looking at him with those shining black eyes, like he could see inside his head. Right away, he was sure Rose knew, and back out the door he went, and down the stairs and around to Hilliard Street before Rose could catch and corner him.

Now he walked along, glancing over his shoulder every few steps. He figured the best he could do was leave it be. Keep his mouth shut and wait for things to calm down. Maybe those crapshooters would think him nothing but a drunken fool and would forget what he'd said. Or they might figure that he'd just been bragging on something someone else had seen. Maybe he'd be fortunate that way. Though he'd never been lucky before.

# FIVE

Little Jesse had spent tortured hours with his fever spiking and falling and his guts twisting like someone had parked broken glass in there. When the morphine ran out around midnight, he woke to moans and groans, then realized they were coming from his own throat. He thrashed about, his sweat soaking the sheets. Shapes moved in and out of his field of vision, and he felt a woman's hands on his face, soothing his burning brow. Other kind fingers changed the dressing on his wound. One of the women, trying to joke him out of his pain, slipped her hand under the sheets and between his legs, whispering that everything seemed quite all right down there. Jesse smiled, even though he couldn't feel a thing.

When he cried for more dope, someone said, *There ain't no more, Jesse,* and he yelled a curse, swearing some goddamn fuck of a low-down rounder had found it and stole it away. He kicked off the covers and had to be held down. He wept for mercy. There were more whispers and someone left in a hurry, slamming the door. An hour passed by, then another. A shade flitted through the doorway, and a few seconds later, the point of a needle glistened over his bare thigh.

The relief came on him like a warm dawn, a shot of amber

light that went down to his last toe. His eyes drooped, his flesh melted from his bones, and he sighed long and low. Through the dirty window, he saw the first red rays of sun coming over the buildings. The rain had gone and he would wake to the new day.

When he got to Atlanta, Joe liked to eat breakfast at Lulu's, the tiny diner diagonally across Houston Street from the Hampton. The weekday cook, an ex-convict named Sweet Spencer, had a way with a plate of sugared ham and eggs, and his cathead biscuits were the best in downtown. He'd learned his skills in the joint.

Joe considered other choices for his morning meal, then decided to make his visit to Lulu's and get it over with. The last thing he wanted was Sweet getting a notion that he was avoiding him, though it was exactly what he wanted to do. Sweet was one of those types who could rattle a man's bones with one look, and Joe didn't need him for an enemy.

Before he got around to that business, he decided to take a walk on Peachtree Street. It was his first Monday morning in the city in six months, and he wanted to amble around a bit. He had visited Central Avenue his first day in. Now he would survey the other side of Atlanta.

Bundling up for the cool morning, he went out the door. Joe's favored winter wear was a gray wool coat that had been taken off a pile of uniform items stripped from the German dead. After his discharge, he paid a Philadelphia tailor to remove the epaulets and then dye the coat a darker gray. It fit him well and was warm enough for any weather. He liked especially the four secret pockets: one under each arm, meant to hold a pistol but useful for stashing burglary tools and stolen goods like watches and jewelry, and two smaller pokes tucked along the seams in the lining, one on either side. He had been told that the Germans used these cavities to hide tiny weapons, razor blades and such, and even poison capsules. All four pockets were difficult to detect, their edges cut to appear as seams. Joe had gone through more than one frisking holding gems that were never found.

He crossed over Ivy Street and reached Peachtree to find that the Atlanta beehive was buzzing ever more frantically every time he came back. Even at this early hour, the sidewalks were getting jammed as workers rushed along to the downtown offices, huffing little clouds, and the main and crossing streets were packed with automobiles, trucks, bicycles, a few motorcycles, and fewer horse-drawn hacks.

Joe noticed right away that two new electric stoplights had been installed on the main thoroughfare, so there were now a half dozen of the signals in as many blocks. One by one, the crow's nests were being replaced. Not that the lights eased the congestion.

The city was dirtier, too. The pall of soot that had hung in the air since he first passed through seven years before seemed to grow thicker every time he returned, advanced by the unending string of coal- and wood-burning locomotives passing through the railroad yards not five blocks away, the belching from the stacks of the factories and the chimneys of the homes clustered around the downtown blocks, and the growing multitude of automobiles and trucks. Indeed, with all that, it was nigh onto impossible for anyone who lived or worked there to stay clean. A white sheet hung out to dry in the morning would be gray by afternoon. Just about every other person passing on the street exhibited at least a mild cough.

Then there was the smell, a fetid combination of engine exhaust, horse manure, rusting pipes, woodsmoke, and damp rot, along with contributions from the nearby Atlanta Livestock Center, famed for its stench. He never quite understood how the citizens tolerated the stifling heat of summer, and always made a point to be elsewhere during the hot months.

When he reached Harris Street, he crossed over and came

back down the other side, where the sidewalks were even busier. Atlanta just kept growing, out and up, and it had been going on that way for a long time.

As he ambled among the heat and close odors of human crowding, he remembered being cornered in a speakeasy one winter evening some years back and treated to a lecture on the history of the city by a drunken professor. The scholar, deep in his cups and provoked by one of those innocuous barroom questions that don't require an answer, lurched to his feet and into a spiel that began with a claim that Atlanta was founded as a backwoods depot called Terminus, which was still marked by the zero milepost that stood on Alabama Street.

Later, the name of this way station was changed to Marthasville, after the then-governor's daughter. When it was selected for a north–south rail line because of the gentle slope of the surrounding land, Miss Martha lost her place in history in favor of *Atlanta,* a name some engineer threw out on a whim. More rail lines followed, so that by the onset of the Civil War, the town had gained strategic value. Indeed, the drunken professor avowed, Jefferson Davis had sealed the fate of the Confederacy when, facing an advancing Union army, he stupidly refused to order the destruction of the rail lines over some petty squabble with local politicians.

At this point, another sot rose to dispute the notion that Jeff Davis *ever* did anything stupid, and demanded the lecturer step outside to answer for so dishonoring the Confederacy. Joe settled this by treating the rebel diehard to a few hard slaps that put him in his place. The professor was entertaining, and he wanted to hear the rest of the story.

The rest of the story was that the Confederate officers and brave troops who tried to save the city were no match for Sherman's overwhelming force, and Atlanta was pounded almost into oblivion by shelling and burned into ashes by set fires. The general recognized that his victory would have been more arduous save for those rail lines, and left them intact to use for his march to the sea.

After swigging from his glass, the professor launched into act two, relating how the hearty citizens rebuilt their city, literally from the ground up. The rail lines multiplied once more, and soon a thousand freight and passenger cars were rolling in and out of Atlanta's yards every day. The population grew at an astounding pace. By the turn of the century, the city held almost one hundred thousand citizens. Ten years later, it was half again that number. When the 1920 census appeared, the scholar opined, it would show that the population would pass two hundred thousand with no slowing in sight. This, less than sixty years after being a city of ashes. Shortly after delivering this last proclamation, he wound down to a string of disjointed mumbles and then dropped his head onto his folded arms and into a peaceful doze.

Joe wasn't surprised at the business about how the city had flourished, more so in the last five years. The boll weevil had devastated cotton crops across Georgia, and farm families by the thousands had packed up and left the land. Atlanta offered work, in the rail yards and the mills and in private homes. From what Joe could tell, at least half of the new arrivals were black. They laid track and ran looms and dug ditches and raised the children of white families. Musicians like Willie McTell followed this wave of migration, their guitars strapped to their backs.

It was no easy ride for the migrants who huddled in sections like Cabbagetown for the whites and Mechanicsville for the colored. Poor and dirty and dangerous, they were also the sort of neighborhoods Joe sought out. He was comfortable among working people and the floating population of working folks, gamblers, petty thieves, confidence men, and whores. Meanwhile, he stayed in cheap downtown hotels like the Hampton and the Atlanta just up the street, places where everyone minded their business and a fellow could stay out of sight and out of trouble.

Not this time, though; his second night in town, he had stumbled upon a shooting followed by something even more ominous, an invitation—that was a joke, it was an *order*—to visit the Captain.

First, though, came breakfast. Joe arrived back on Houston Street and stepped inside Lulu's door. Once he had called out his order to the fellow behind the counter, he took a corner table. While he waited, he perked an ear for any snippets of gossip about crimes around the city, always a subject of interest. Two office clerks in white shirts and ties were talking at the next table over, and Joe caught the words *jewels* and *mansion*. Under the guise of picking up the newspaper that someone had left on the next table, he shifted around to a chair that was closer to the pair.

Over the next few minutes, he gleaned pieces that assembled into a story, and was stunned to learn what he had missed the day before, that someone had gotten into the Payne mansion on Elizabeth Street during a Christmas charity event and made off with a catch of jewelry. The clerks snickered giddily over the crime and batted it around some more without adding any details.

Joe shared in the frivolity right up until the moment it dawned on him that this was the reason for the summons to police headquarters. The Captain wanted to grill him about the burglary, and might even suspect that Joe had a hand in it. His gut sank at the thought of what he was facing, though not enough to ruin his appetite, and when his breakfast arrived, he plowed in.

As he ate, he looked over the front page of the newspaper. There were articles about trouble in Germany, rioting in the streets as part of a rebellion against the leaders who had lost the last war. Meanwhile, civil war was brewing in Cuba. Another item described a shipment of thirty thousand bottles of Scotch that had been intercepted in Maine, with an estimated value of four million dollars. Joe grinned over that, then laughed when he read in a local story about a still that had been found in the basement of a house just a few blocks north of where he sat. He recognized the character who had been arrested as a loudmouth who was known to sample too much of his own product. This time the fight was with a police officer, and as a result the fool's source of income had been smashed to pieces.

He flipped through some more pages, dawdling. He wasn't looking forward to his visit with Captain Jackson. Though if he didn't show up, Collins or some other cop would come looking for him, and the slight would put the Captain in an even worse humor. With a reluctant glance at the clock on the wall, he put the paper aside and left his twenty-five cents, with a nickel tip for the girl.

Stepping onto the sidewalk, he strolled around the side of the building and in through the kitchen door. The Negro cook, dark and burly, with a round shaved head and shoulders like a steer, peered from his station at the stove. His broad face sported a half-dozen scars, souvenirs of battles in the hellhole where he had spent three of his years.

"Mr. Joe," Sweet Spencer said. "I heard you was in town."

"Came in Friday," Joe said.

"What's the word on Williams?" Sweet's voice was cool.

"You heard about that?"

The Negro shoveled scrambled eggs and a thick slice of ham onto a plate and put it in the window. "Yeah, I heard 'bout that sonofabitch," he grunted. "He got shot. Now, there's a damn surprise." Sweet had no time for slicks like Jesse.

"Any talk going around?"

"No," Sweet said. "And if they is, I don't want to hear it." He made up another plate and set it in the window for the waitress. His eyes slid to Joe. "What do you care?"

"He's a friend. I've known him a while."

"I guess that's your problem, then," the cook said. Though he radiated danger from every pore, he wouldn't dare use such a caustic tone with another white man. Joe was different that way.

Sweet's eyes flicked. "I also heard some jewels got stole out in Inman Park Saturday night." He kept his eyes on the stove. "That what the Captain be wantin' to talk to you about?" he inquired casually.

Joe was not surprised that Sweet knew about it; that kind of word would travel. "That's right," he said glumly. "I'm going down to see him now." He nodded a good-bye and the Negro turned back to his work.

Joe had just reached the door when Sweet said, "She was out there."

Joe stopped, puzzled. "Who was out where?"

"Pearl was at that house. The Payne place. Where them things got snatched. She was there."

Joe took a startled step back. "Jesus Christ, Sweet!" He lowered his voice. "It was *her*?"

Sweet shook his head. "No, it wasn't her. She got hired on as a maid for that Christmas party they was havin'. She does that kind of work sometimes. You know that."

Joe let the jibe go by. "She was . . ." He stopped, baffled by this news. "Well, that ain't good."

"No," Sweet said shortly. "It ain't."

Joe looked at him. "Is there something else?"

"That ain't enough?"

Joe could see from Sweet's deadpan expression that he wasn't going to get any more out of him. "I better get on," he said.

"Mr. Joe?" The Negro's eyes were like pieces of flint. "That, there, is all the more reason you want to stay away from her," he said in a rumble of a voice. "Even if she comes knockin'. That would be my advice. You hear what I'm saying?"

"I hear you, Sweet."

Sweet came up with a dim smile. "Stop by any time," he said.

Joe took the prison glint that had rested in the dark gaze out the door with him. It gave him something else to think about on his way to Decatur Street.

As usual on a Monday, the weekend's gossip made the rounds as the first order of business. The whispered word about the theft at the Payne mansion spent Sunday traveling from one maid to the next, and from that maid to the lady of the house, and then along church pews from Druid Hills to Buttermilk Bottom. By the time evening rolled around, it had spread to every corner of the city.

Still, the news needed a busy workday to soak in. With the arrival of the morning's first rush of clerks, secretaries, and shop-keepers, the talk set offices and shops along Peachtree Street to humming. The chatter was rife with amazement that such a grand address could be so easily breached. Privately, there were snickers aplenty at the humiliation of the proud, tightfisted Paynes. In all but the most patrician quarters, whoever had pulled the daring job was a hero.

City Hall was buzzing, too. Mayor Sampson's first call that morning had been to Chief Troutman at police headquarters, and the chief had in turn summoned Captain Jackson. Within minutes, the chief, the Captain, and Lieutenant Collins were in a car and on their way to City Hall.

Once they had been ushered into the mayor's office, Captain Jackson went about putting on a performance. He was careful not to belittle the new chief, allowing the mayor to draw his own conclusions about the man's competence. Instead, he snapped through his strategy to find the guilty party and reclaim the miss-ing jewels, one that had in fact already begun with his visit to the Payne mansion the day before. He would accomplish this by working with informants, one of whom would give him informa-tion he could use to effect an arrest.

It was a strange and stilted delivery, punctuated by smiles that would have been coy on a more relaxed man. Jackson reminded the mayor of nothing so much as a ventriloquist's dummy, the thick body stiff and glazed eyes hardly blinking as he snapped answers out of a rigid face. At the same time, his delivery was so squarely to the point that by the time Chief Troutman realized he'd been upstaged, it was too late.

The Captain finished with a flourish. Mayor Sampson gave a quick nod and turned to his chief of police.

"Make sure Captain Jackson has everything he needs to get this matter settled," he said.

Chief Troutman, blanching, opened his mouth. Jackson got there first. "I've got everything I need, Mr. Mayor," he said.

Lieutenant Collins would later recall that the silence in the car during the ride back to Decatur Street was so thick he almost choked on it.

The newspapers had done their civic duty by keeping a lid on the story, only to find themselves running after it. Having missed the opportunity for articles in the morning papers, editors at both of the dailies came rushing out of their offices yelling for their ace reporters to get moving.

These reporters, having just rolled in from breakfast on full stomachs, had no intention of incurring the wrath of Grayton Jackson, and turned immediately to their cubs, directing them to run to police headquarters, interview the Captain, and come back with the details, including quotes from that officer's mouth.

All in earshot knew what this meant, and as the cubs headed out, the two newsrooms fell silent, as if witnessing the last walks of condemned men.

When the reporters showed up at 179 Decatur Street, they were told to wait in the second-floor hallway, and spent the next hour either sitting at opposite ends of the bench or pacing and eyeing each other like cats in an alley. Every time the door at the end of the hall opened, they came around, then let out a shared sigh of relief that it wasn't the Captain.

He surprised them by stalking from behind, shaking his square head in vague disgust that the cowards at the papers had sent these two lambs to the slaughter. Before either one of them could utter a word, he said, "We're investigating a possible burglary at a home in the Inman Park neighborhood. The details are not clear at this time. When there's something to report, we'll send it over. That's all."

The braver of the two stuttered, "Is the Payne fam—"

"I said, that's *all!*" the Captain barked, and the reporters nearly jumped out of their drawers, then tripped over each other as they went scurrying like frantic mice along the hall and down the staircase. One side of the Captain's mouth twisted into a smile at the echo of their harried steps.

Joe was in no mood for what was coming this morning, and made the six-block walk downtown a slow one. He arrived at police headquarters with only a minute or two to spare.

He knew why Captain Jackson had summoned him. The Inman Park burglary was his kind of heist. He had, in fact, pulled other jobs in other homes of wealthy Atlantans. The Captain knew he was guilty but could never catch him cold, and that made this little encounter a dicey proposition. Jackson had a reputation for walking over due process when it suited him. Joe would be a fly on the edge of the Captain's web; one little misstep and he'd be all the way in.

Inside the lobby he approached the desk, stated his business to the sergeant, and then made a point of asking after Detective Albert Nichols. He wanted someone friendly to know that he was in the building.

A few minutes later, a uniformed officer appeared to escort him upstairs. He was delivered to a room on the second floor that contained a half-dozen chairs, lined up against the wall. Joe knew that once the door closed, the Captain could do anything he wanted, including forgo the niceties of due process, pin a charge on him, and come up with whatever he needed to make it stick. He could arrest him for the burglary and then find a witness and cajole or beat testimony out of him that Joe had shown him the jewels from that job before he had fenced them.

So he was relieved when Captain Jackson walked in with Lieutenant Collins on his heels. The junior officer dragged one chair from the wall for the Captain, another one for himself, and jerked his head for Joe to take a third one. The Captain settled, put his hands flat on his thighs, and waited for Joe to sit, his eyes as blank as a storefront mannequin's. Anything could be going on behind them, or nothing at all.

Joe was not physically afraid of Jackson, and he could hold any stare, but a challenge would only make things worse, so he shifted his gaze between the two policemen, as if politely waiting for one or the other to speak up. Collins took out a notepad and pencil, all patience.

"Mr. Rose," the Captain said, breaking the silence. "When exactly did you arrive in Atlanta, sir?" His north Georgia twang held a spiky edge, belying tension below the surface.

"I came in on the train on Friday afternoon," Joe said. "So that would be three days."

"Train from where?"

"Louisville."

The Captain turned his head slightly, and Collins dutifully wrote on his pad.

"We're going to check. See if anything's gone missing up there."

Joe brought out a puzzled expression. The Captain's blank eyes settled, and Joe was faintly aware of Collins smiling. He wasn't fooling either one of them, and told himself he'd have to do better with his facades.

"We had a burglary at a house in Inman Park on Saturday night," the Captain went on in his flat and mechanical voice.

Joe raised one eyebrow, waiting.

"Not just any house," the Captain went on. "The Payne mansion. I'm sure you know the place. It happened during the Christmas party they hold every year. It's a charity event, and they only invite the most important people in the city. The mayor was there, the Candlers, the Woodruffs, that sort. People with influence."

Joe tried to look appropriately impressed. The Captain's jaw clenched into a square.

"Well, some fucker got in and made off with a stash of jewelry while this affair was going on," he said. "I mean got inside, snatched jewels that belonged to Mrs. Payne, and got back out. It was a goddamn embarrassment for Mayor Sampson. So he's unhappy. Chief Troutman's unhappy. And that means I'm unhappy."

Joe said, "Is anybody else unhappy?" and immediately regretted it.

The Captain's bottle-green eyes flared. "Listen, wise fellow," he snarled. "You're going to be more than unhappy if you don't watch your fucking mouth. You think this is a joke? I said, do you think this is a joke?"

Joe shook his head. "Not now, I don't." Out of the corner of his eye, he noticed Collins smiling again, as if he *did* think it was a joke.

"You came into town Friday," Jackson said, jabbing a finger. "And within about twenty-four hours, we have a major theft of jewels. And we ain't had a major theft of jewels in over a year. That's interesting timing, I'd say."

Joe looked at him, looked at Collins, then looked at the Captain again.

"But I don't think you did it," Jackson said, and sat back a little. "Because I don't think you could show up in town and plan and pull off a crime like that in one day. I don't think you're that smart. You might think you are, but I don't."

Joe settled his face into a polite *then what am I doing here?* expression.

"But listen to this," the Captain said, drawing it out. "You know who was there when it happened? Tell him, Lieutenant."

"Pearl Spencer," Collins said quietly. "She was working as a maid."

Joe realized he was tugging at his ear, his one nervous habit. The Captain noticed and came up with a smug look.

"Don't you think that's funny? That she was there when the theft happened?"

Joe said, "Well . . ."

"Because she's a pretty fair thief herself. Among other things." He let that hang for a few seconds, noting Joe's discomfort. "You know her pretty well, ain't that right?"

"I know her, yeah," Joe said.

"Uh-huh. Have you seen her since you got to town?"

"I haven't," Joe said.

"Been in touch while you been away?"

"Not at all."

The Captain shifted in his chair. For a moment, he seemed distracted, as if some other matter had crossed his mind. Joe and Collins waited.

"So what about this burglary?" Jackson said, breaking the silence.

"I just heard about it this morning," Joe said.

"And what did you hear?"

"I mean I heard some fellows talking about it, that's all."

The Captain regarded him blankly. "Where did you eat your breakfast today?" Now his voice was idle, as if he was satisfying a curiosity.

Joe thought about lying, decided it wasn't worth it. "At Lulu's. It's across from—"

"I know where the hell it is," Jackson interrupted him. "Don't treat me like I'm a goddamn fool." He settled. "Was Sweet Spencer working?"

Joe said, "He was, yes, sir."

"You talk to him?"

"Just for a minute."

Something like a smile crinkled the corners of the policeman's mouth. "What's he have to say about you and his little sister?"

Joe stopped short. Despite the danger, he was getting tired of the Captain's coy questions and his own hedging. He met Jackson's gaze and said, "He doesn't like it much."

"I'll bet that's true," the Captain said. "I'll bet he thinks the two of you are in cahoots, and I don't mean on a mattress, either. And him right out of the joint. I'll bet he don't want you anywhere near her."

"Well, I haven't seen her," Joe said.

"But you will," the Captain replied without inflection, a simple statement of fact. His eyes shifted, and for the first time, Joe got a sense of a different game going on, one he couldn't quite fathom. Jackson was watching him closely, as if looking for a clue of something. Another moment passed, and he sat back and shrugged. "It would be a hell of a thing if she was involved," he said. "She gets sent up for a job like that and you won't see her for a long, long time. She'd be an old woman. If she doesn't die inside." He let that hang for a few seconds, then turned his gaze elsewhere. Collins closed his notepad.

"Go ahead, take him out of here," Jackson ordered. He crossed his arms and gazed pensively at the wall.

Joe got to his feet and followed Collins. He stopped at the door and said, "Excuse me, Captain."

The Captain turned stiffly in his chair, frowning. His conversations were usually one way.

Joe said, "A Negro named Jesse Williams was shot downtown on Saturday night."

The Captain treated him to a cool gaze. "So?"

"I was wondering if there's anything on it," Joe said.

"What's the name?"

"Jesse Williams. He goes by Little Jesse."

"Yeah, I know that one." The policeman's eyes were empty.
"He dead?"

"Not yet. He's in bad shape, though. He could go any time."

"He identify his assailant?"

Joe hesitated for a quick beat. "No."

"Well, there's your answer." Jackson shrugged his square
shoulders. "We have about a dozen niggers shot up every weekend." His gaze settled on Joe's face, though it seemed unfocused,
like he was looking through him. "Why are you asking about this
one?"

"I know the man," Joe said. "And I was there on the street
just after it happened. So . . ." He didn't know what else to say.
It wasn't much of an explanation.

"Was there an officer to the scene?"

"Not that I know about," Joe said, feeling himself wilt under
the cops' stares. "We were worried about getting Mr. Williams
some help."

"Then there wasn't any damn report," the Captain said irritably. "And I don't have to tell you that any shooting is police
business. Don't matter if the victim is white, colored, or . . ."
Here he produced a faint and cold smile. ". . . something else."
He unfolded his thick arms and rose to his feet. "If I was you, I'd
be worrying about my own self, instead of some damn rounder
getting shot on Courtland Street. Anyway, it ain't none of your
affair, so you want to stay clear of it." His lips twisted coldly.
"Or somebody might shoot *you*."

With that, he made a slow, thumping exit. In his wake,

Collins escorted Joe out the door, along the hall, down the two flights of steps, and out the front doors, all without speaking a single word. Joe spent the time thinking about what the Captain had said, fixing on the cop's mention of Courtland Street. He hadn't said anything about where it had happened. He wondered if the lieutenant had noticed that, too.

Joe strolled through Five Points and had just rounded the corner onto Ivy Street when he sensed someone coming up behind him. For a second, he wondered if the Captain had decided to close the case the easy way. Then he turned around and saw who it was.

The thin man in a long topcoat and fedora took his elbow and steered him off the sidewalk and along Harris Row, one of the dozens of narrow alleys that webbed the downtown Atlanta streets. The man was below medium height, wiry, his cheeks splattered with smallpox scars, his eyes an even blue, his hair and mustache showing a reddish tint.

They stopped in a vacant doorway, and the man produced a pack of Chesterfields. Joe accepted a cigarette and the light that went with it. For a few silent moments, the two of them leaned there, out of sight of the street, puffing the rough tobacco.

Joe had known Albert Nichols since the time they worked for the same Pinkerton office in Baltimore. Albert's history was not unlike his own: a rough childhood, some minor crimes, then police work, as he wandered from one side of the law to the other. They had pulled each other out of various scrapes by offering useful alibis. They stayed in touch after Albert left Baltimore for Atlanta, where he became a cop; a firmly honest cop, in fact, which put him in the minority. He was one of the few policemen Joe could trust.

Albert now regarded him through a spiral of smoke with a familiar laconic smile. "You rob those rich people or was it your sweetheart this time?" he inquired.

"It's pleasant seeing you again, too," Joe replied.

Albert laughed, then coughed. He was never in the best of health. "You hear what's been going on around here?"

"Some," Joe said.

"Well, you missed a lot of excitement." The detective chortled. "They were running dirty cops out the door by the dozens. Even got the chief. It was a goddamn rout."

"I see you still have a job."

"There was never nothing that bunch had that I wanted," Albert said. "Anyway, keeping track of dirty money is bad for my nerves. So I stayed clean."

"And how the hell did Jackson hang on?"

Albert laughed again, coughed again. "The word was that he was next. Him and a couple others. Then comes this incident in Inman Park. Soon as I heard about it, I thought of you. Ain't no surprise he pulled you in." He puffed meditatively. "It's a hell of a thing, all right. And I guarantee someone's going to take a fall for it."

"As long as it ain't me," Joe said.

"Well, it might be." Albert's tone was sharp. "There's going to be an arrest, one way or another. You can count on that." He looked off down that alley at the pedestrians passing by, all hunched against the chill. "Can you imagine someone pulling a snatch like that?" he said in a tone of wonder. "With all those hoity-toits in the house?"

"Hell of a time to go in," Joe said.

"Unless you already happened to *be* in." Albert treated Joe to a wry look. He paused for a moment. "I heard she was there when it happened."

"She was," Joe said. "But she's not that stupid."

"Then what was she doing there?"

"Working. As a maid."

"And that's all?"

"As far as I know."

Albert said, "Well, looks bad, and that's enough to put her on a spot. And you, too." Albert took a last drag and flicked the butt away. "The Captain told the chief he'd deliver. So he's got to clear it in a hurry. He might go ahead and just grab somebody he's been wanting to get rid of. Maybe some fool who played him. Or screwed his wife."

Now it was Joe's turn to cough. When he caught his breath, he said, "Can we change the subject?" Albert smiled and shrugged. "You hear about Little Jesse Williams?"

"The gambler?"

"And pimp. Yeah, him."

"What about him?"

"He got shot. Saturday night on Courtland Street. You didn't hear about it?"

"I haven't heard anything."

Though there was no one else in the alley, Joe dropped his voice. "The way he tells it, a cop did it."

"Yeah?" Albert said, raising a thin eyebrow. "He say which cop?"

"A patrolman named Logue."

"Logue?" The detective came up with an incredulous look. "I know him. He's an old street bull. And a drunk. I mean, hopeless. He keeps getting busted down, so he still walks a beat. He ain't the murderer type, that's for sure. He probably couldn't hit the side of a house."

"Little Jesse says he walked up and shot him, just like that."

"Then it was probably some kind of spat."

"That's not what Jesse says."

"And you believe him?"

"I don't know," Joe said. "Have you seen him around?"

"Who, Logue? Not lately, I ain't. We travel in different circles."

"I need to find him."

Albert gave him a long look. "What for?"

"Because . . ." Joe shrugged. "Because I've known Jesse for a while. He's all right."

Albert laughed and shook his head. "He's a pimp and a card-cheat sonofabitch, Joe. He ain't no goddamn good and never was."

Joe looked down at the bricks frowning. "Yeah, well . . ."

Albert was waiting for more, but he really didn't feel like explaining.

A few seconds went by. Sounding amused again, the detective said, "So your friend was working at that party."

"Seems so."

Albert straightened from his slouch and buttoned his coat. "Probably be good for everybody to get that business settled real fast." He held a hand over his hacking mouth. Then he said, "You need to ask her if she saw or heard anything. If you happen to run into her, I mean."

He strolled away, leaving his friend leaning in the doorway.

"I still need to talk to Logue," Joe called out softly.

The detective raised an acknowledging hand and cut around the corner onto Ivy Street.

Joe lingered in the alley, deciding what to do. He knew that if Pearl didn't come around, he'd have to track her down. Not yet, though; not with what Sweet and the Captain and Albert Nichols had said knocking around in his brain. Finding her could wait a little while longer.

Instead, he walked out of the alley and ambled south to the Ivy Street overpass, stopping in the middle to gaze down at the tangle of tracks leading in and out of Union Depot. Something in his purview was moving at all times, a constant shifting and snaking pattern, as cars by the hundreds rolled in and out. After what he'd gone through that morning, he wondered if he'd be better off riding away in one.

The long train came huffing from beneath him and into the

shadow of the station and brought thoughts of the one part of the Captain's story that always made him feel better.

Though it was true that Grayton Jackson had always appeared to the denizens of Atlanta like a chunk of granite, in truth his bulwark had a gaping chink that came in his five-foot-three-inch pleasingly plump cupcake of a wife, May Ida.

Had Joe not learned firsthand that her tale was genuine, he would have taken it for one of the kind of crazy fiction created and then embellished for the delight of men who drank in speakeasies and had nothing better to do with their time.

Growing up in a little town just east of Atlanta, May Ida had been somewhat chubby—*Junoesque* in the parlance of the day—and much sassy. Upon meeting her, a stranger's gaze would be drawn immediately to her eyes, bosom, and bottom, all of which were prominently rotund. She was pretty in an old-fashioned way, the nubile farm girl of the jokes when she left herself plain, a Kewpie doll when she put a little powder and paint on her face.

Emerging from the innocent haze of her childhood, she developed an alarming fascination with her body and the pleasure it could generate. By the age of sixteen, she seemed to be constantly in heat. May Ida loved the boys, and then the men, and they loved her right back, on what was a daily basis, or so said the hometown wags.

No one could say precisely when, where, and to whom she had surrendered her innocence. Once she had, though, she was a filly bolting from the gate, and a marvel when it came to finding locations for interludes: closets, attics, root cellars, toolsheds, barn lofts. She was democratic with her favors, too. Around the village of Scottsdale, they'd tell you she had initiated more boys than the Scouts. She even batted her eyes and twitched her plump tail at some of the young Negroes, all of whom immediately ran the other way. Once she was introduced to French pleasure, she acted as if she had invented it, and went about showing off her new skills with abandon.

She didn't slow down once she left school. None of the local fellows would court such a coquette, and whatever job she found was nothing more than a portal into more amorous adventures. Her family didn't know what to do with her. They couldn't afford the kind of sanitarium that might offer a cure for her affliction.

It was then that an unlikely salvation appeared, in the person of Grayton Jackson.

The Captain, who was then a sergeant, hailed from the village of Marietta, and so had no knowledge of May Ida's lurid past. He was a man without social skills whose only intimacies had been the occasional cold caresses of Atlanta whores. A fellow police officer who knew both his situation and the plight of May Ida's family stepped forward, and Sergeant Jackson was encouraged to ask for her plump hand.

The marriage was seen as a way to kill two birds with one stone, providing him with domestic comforts and at the same time corralling a young woman's bawdy behavior. The idea was that if anyone could put a harness on May Ida, it would be a severe, no-nonsense sort like Grayton Jackson. For him, it was a way to get a spouse without the discomfort of courting, a ritual at which he would have been hopelessly inept.

It was unclear how May Ida had been talked into this farce. From one side of the city to the other, there was much laughter when the two exchanged their vows. A justice of the peace conducted the ceremony, and the couple moved into a small house on Plum Street, around the corner from the Luckie Street School.

Despite the hopes of the concerned parties, the plan failed. May Ida soon realized that monogamy was not to her liking, even less so when it involved a frigid and dour mate like Grayton Jackson. For some weeks after her wedding, she fidgeted about in an overheated flush, all but bursting from her clothes. It was her good fortune that the Captain couldn't tolerate children and had no thoughts of hitching her to that harness. In truth, he was married to his job. Most days, he was up and gone before dawn and didn't come home until late.

With so much free time and unfulfilled ardor, May Ida went back to entertaining men, though she now had to be more creative about it, lest her husband find out. No more bricklayers who could work like plow horses, dull but steady, lasting for hours. She could now engage only sly and nimble men, the kind who could thrill her in the time it took to hard-boil an egg and then get away clean.

The Captain became her unwitting accomplice. He was always grousing over the breakfast or dinner table about this rounder or that one, calling them by their full names or monikers and describing their wiles in much detail. As she sat listening to him relate the antics of these felons, May Ida felt flashes of heat in her lap. The Captain did nothing to quench the fire; he was mostly a feeble man in that respect, the complete opposite of the virile front he presented around police headquarters.

In any case, May Ida knew what she wanted, and went about sending her Negro maid to the rough sections of the city to find the sharps and invite them around. The backyard of the house was shielded by a fence that was a riot of morning glories and honeysuckle vines and let out into a narrow alley from West Pine Street, so her paramours could come and go as if invisible, which was one of their talents, anyway. Once the sun was up and the flowers had opened, it was safe.

The whispers started right away, and soon crazy stories about May Ida abounded. The rounders chuckled over retellings of her fountains of protest as she parroted lines from dime novels of the romantic sort and from the cards that appeared between scenes in the moving pictures.

"Oh, sir, I won't do any such thing!" she'd cry. "How dare you! You are so impudent! I should have you thrashed!" All the while the lover of the moment would be removing various articles of clothing to expose her pink, moist, trembling flesh.

"Oh, stop!" she would wail, as some rake descended on her like a fly diving into a honeypot. "Don't you dare! Wait until my husband learns what you did!"

In fact, her husband never learned what she did. If it seemed odd that a police officer of the Captain's expertise could not discern his own wife's deceits, it was also true that for all his cruel proficiencies, Grayton Jackson was a fool. He was so arrogant that he never bothered to learn about his betrothed's history before the nuptials, and it never occurred to him that his wife would dare open her rosy thighs for any man she could entice, no matter how rabid her appetites. And he was *busy,* his attention diverted by the mechanics of collecting graft, the abuse of hapless "suspects," and finding new ways to lay his lips ever more gently upon the buttocks of his superiors.

Having suffered a drought, May Ida was eager to get caught up. The path from the back door through the morning glories and into the alleyway was worn bare by leather soles. Never the prude, she cast her eye on more than a few of her female friends and, in one case, had cast more than an eye on one of the young colored maids.

It didn't take long for Joe Rose to hear the rumors about May Ida, and it was just a matter of time before she heard about him, a rounder who flew south like a snowbird in the wintertime and was reputed to have a wicked way with women. She sent the maid with an invitation.

Though Joe recognized a risky proposition, his curiosity got the best of him. He had heard the stories and had to see if any of it was true.

But he was smarter than the others and refused to go to her house. It was too risky. Instead, he invited her to meet him at the Dixie Hotel. So if there was trouble, she would be the one ex-

plaining what she was doing in a man's room in the middle of a
January afternoon. Not that Joe would just stroll away whistling.
Even if he did escape, he'd never be able to show his face in At-
lanta again.

So when the appointed day came, he paid a bellboy to bring
her inside through the back entrance and upstairs by way of the
freight elevator. She tapped on the door, and he let her in. She
stood primly before him, her hands clutching her purse. After a
few nervous moments, she let him lift the veil that was attached
to the brim of her hat and shielded her identity from prying eyes,
revealing a plump and pretty face. Her startling blue eyes blinked
and skittered, as if she was unsure about what she was doing
there.

Joe wasted no time reminding her. Within a few short minutes, he had her out of her clothes and in the bed, the comedy ac-
companied by her chorus of *here now!*s and *you stop that!*s
Meanwhile, she didn't raise a finger to slow his advances.

Once he got her going, she was like a freight train rolling
downhill. Liberated from any worries of her husband bursting in,
she gave herself up to a rollicking good time, throwing herself
about like a circus performer, contorting this way and that. The
shrieks and moans that erupted from her throat were so ungodly
loud that Joe had to push a pillow to her mouth before they got
complaints. The sheets were soon soaked with sweat and various
other fluids. It was a rodeo ride, for sure, and he uttered a silent
prayer of thanks that he wasn't called upon to satisfy her every
day.

Or, he decided, ever again. Once the heat of the battle had
subsided, he realized that May Ida was crazy, though in a hap-
pily delirious way. Her blue-eyed gaze was a step shy of de-
ranged, and he figured it was only a matter of time before she
crossed the line and did something so outrageous that the Captain would finally get wise. Then there would be the worst kind

of hell to pay, and God help the poor fellow who had the bad luck to be the one caught between those dumpling thighs. It wasn't going to be Joe Rose. From that day on, he avoided her. When her maid came around with another invitation, he gave the girl some money to say he couldn't be found. Just to be sure, he made a point of moving from the Dixie Hotel to the Hampton.

Since that incident, he had nurtured a fantasy of meeting the Captain one day and saying, "Oh, by the way, half the criminals in Atlanta have fucked your wife, and we all agree that she's a peach." Then he thought about whether he'd like to be buried in Oakland Cemetery or some other resting place.

This made him all the more nervous being in the caustic Captain's eye. And yet there he was, and there he would remain, until the man got what he wanted. He shook his head over ending up so innocently in this corner, and walked off the bridge as the trains huffed in and out beneath his feet.

It was a bright day, the temperature already in the high thirties, certainly not cold enough to keep the likes of Willie McTell indoors. Not to mention that feeling the warm sun on his face would dispel some of the gloom that he had carried away from Little Jesse's rooms.

Street by street, Willie heard pockets of noise, caught their echoes, and sensed the way the air moved around in different places. Once he had settled in Atlanta the previous spring, it had taken him no time at all to map the city by way of sound. It was something no sighted person could ever understand. His blindness had so heightened his other faculties that people marveled at the tricks he could perform. Telling a one-dollar bill from a five simply by touching it, or picking out conversations across a street full of rattling automobiles. He could identify people by their smells and the way their clothes rustled on their bodies. It was this other sense, really a combination of his hearing, smell, and touch, that guided him through the city as if he was on a private rail. He didn't need any help at all, though he sometimes lost his talent when a nice-sounding woman offered to guide him.

He was coming up on Houston Street, on his way to catch the lunch crowd on Auburn Avenue, when he heard Joe Rose call his name. Footsteps brought Joe to his side. He lifted his head and frowned a little. "A Chesterfield?"

Joe grinned and shook his head. "Damn Willie. You ought to be in a carnival with that."

"I've been in a carnival," Willie said shortly. "More than one." They walked on a little ways. "Where you been this morning?"

"I paid a visit to the Captain," Joe said quietly.

The blind man cocked his head. "About that Inman Park business?"

"That's right," Joe said. The word was on the street, and it didn't surprise him that the blind man's ears had swept it up.

"He thinks you done it?" Willie said.

"He thinks I might know who did."

"You talking a—"

"Yeah. Her." His mouth twisted in a dim smile. "She was working there when it happened."

"Working there?"

"As a maid for that party."

Willie mulled this news for a few seconds. "What are you gonna do about it?"

"Don't know what I can do."

As they made their way down the block, Joe was too distracted to notice the looks the odd couple received from both the white and colored pedestrians. They stopped at the corner of Pryor Place to wait for a creaking hack to roll by.

Joe said, "I asked him about Little Jesse."

Willie said, "And he don't know a damn thing. Ain't that

right? Don't care, either. Just another nigger shot down on a Saturday night."

"That's pretty much it," Joe said.

The hack passed and they started across the street.

Joe said, "All that time you've been over there, has he said anything else about what happened?"

Willie thought about it and said, "A couple times, I did hear him kind of mumbling some things I didn't understand."

"Like what?"

"It was the same thing a couple times over. The way it sounded, I first thought maybe he was praying." Joe looked at Willie for a moment, and both men laughed. "I know," Willie said. "But that's how it sounded."

"You catch any of it?"

"A little bit. First he said, 'I done it. Yeah, I done it.' Then he said, 'Don't got nothin'. Nothin'.' Like that."

"That's all?"

"S'all I heard." They reached the other side of the street, and Willie raised his foot and stepped onto the curb without a hitch. He tilted his head in Joe's direction. "What are you going to do now?"

"About what?"

"About Little Jesse."

"I don't know," Joe said. "First I need to find that cop. Logue. See what he has to say." He paused. "And Robert Clark, too. You know he came by Little Jesse's? He ran off before I could talk to him."

"Ran off? You mean like he was scared?" Willie said.

"Yeah, like that."

"Well, he was shit scared Saturday night, all right."

"You know where he stays?"

"I don't," Willie said. "He's just one of them that's around a lot."

"Not now, he ain't, and I need to find him," Joe said. "You let me know if Jesse says anything else."

"I will." Willie frowned and shook his head mournfully. "But I don't know if he's gonna last much longer. That doctor didn't do him no good at all. He's gettin' worse all the time."

"Then he needs to speak the hell up," Joe griped. "You can tell him that."

"All right, Joe."

An automobile pulled to a stop at the curb and sat, idling. Joe glanced over and said, "Quarter says you can't name it."

"Four-cylinder Sears," Willie said absently. Joe went digging for the coin. "I don't need the twenty-five cents, thank you."

They lingered there for a moment. Jesse would be heading east on Auburn Avenue, Joe south to the Hampton.

"I'll be back over there a little later on," Willie said. "I want to be around while he's still alive."

"You really don't think he can last?" Joe said. "He's always been a tough one."

"He ain't that tough," Willie said. He hitched his guitar, offered Joe his hand, and continued along the sidewalk, swerving nimbly around the pedestrian traffic as if guided by perfect eyesight.

# SIX

The Buick sedan passed through the little community called Buckhead, heading due south. The car moved slowly, bouncing through the ruts in the hard red clay as the rear end, laden with the several hundred pounds of recording gear that was crammed in the trunk, scraped over exposed rocks.

The driver of the sedan, Jacob Stein—Jake to his friends—was relieved to see the signs announcing it was only another three miles to Atlanta. It had been a long drive, a good part of it on rural southern roads. The newly minted graduate of Fordham had heard the stories, knew the territory below the Pennsylvania state line could be hostile for some types, and he wondered if the city they were approaching, by far the largest in the South, would prove any less so. It was, after all, the locale of the infamous Leo Frank case, which had transpired only eight years before. He had read in the New York papers how that tragedy had drawn Jewish communities together at the same time it enhanced the power of the Ku Klux Klan. As if to punctuate this recollection, a half mile farther on, he peered to his right to see a building marked with a proud banner identifying the headquarters of that same organization.

Jake glanced over at the man who was snoozing in the passenger seat. "Mr. Purcell?"

George Purcell, twenty-five years Jake's senior, opened his eyes from his drowse, blinking in the late morning sun.

Jake said, "We're almost to Atlanta."

Purcell sat up, stretched his thin arms forward, and yawned. He looked around at the landscape passing the windows. They were now on an unevenly paved, two-lane road that ran by little clusters of homes, the occasional store, patches of farm fields, and small stands of trees that had recently been woods. Purcell noted the street sign at the next intersection.

"So this is the famous Peachtree Road." He treated the younger man to a quiet smile. "Have you seen any peach trees?"

"No, sir," Jake said, then realized he wouldn't recognize one if he had.

"That's because the name of the street doesn't have anything to do with peaches," the older man said.

"No?"

"No. Before there was any Atlanta, there was just a little crossroads next to a huge pitch tree."

"*Pitch* tree?"

"A pine tree. Somehow it got turned into a *peach* tree."

Jake raised his eyebrows with appropriate interest.

"That's one story. Another one says the Cherokee did name it for a peach tree."

George Purcell was a font of such arcane knowledge. He had kept Jake entertained with all sorts of trivia over the week it had taken them to drive down from New York. Where and when he had collected all the curious lore was a mystery, since the man worked day and night either making sound recordings or arranging to do so. When he wasn't out on the road, he was ensconced in a studio or office somewhere. Jake sometimes wondered if Mr. Purcell fabricated his stories just to pass the time. What would Jake, a New Yorker all his life, know from peach or pitch trees?

It was no less a puzzle how this learned man came to be traveling the lost back roads of the South seeking out only what common folk sang and played, which in this part of the world meant either hillbilly music or blues. Jake admired him for giving up a comfortable home and academic career to travel these dusty and sometimes dangerous byways in search of what his peers viewed as marginal music. And he was glad for the opportunity to share the adventure, though the driving was brutal and some of the locales they visited gave him nightmares.

None of it seemed to worry his employer. Indeed, Mr. Purcell never failed to proclaim himself a New Yorker, and had no fear of charging into the places he clearly wasn't welcome in order to collect more music. He wanted to be first, and so he took the risks. No matter where they went, the musicians warmed to his passion.

Despite the doubters, Purcell was proving that there was a market for unschooled music. When common folk came home from work, they didn't want to hear the *good* music that the Carnegies and Rockefellers and Fricks with their grand opera houses and symphony halls wanted to shove down their throats. They wanted to hear the ballads and dance to tunes their families had been nursing for generations, songs that rang with a fervor that echoed the joys and agonies of their hard lives. Purcell had discovered that even a poor man or woman would spend a precious quarter for a record to play over and over and hear an echo of the ages. And there were millions of people like that with millions of quarters in their pockets.

Jake, who had stumbled into the job right out of college, first thought it a lark, then became a believer, taking pride in the knowledge that they were doing important work. He hoped the word had gotten out in advance and that Atlanta would be a boon for recording and a safe place to land for a little while.

Looking ahead, he saw houses spotting the sides of the road, mostly frame structures, along with some sturdy brick homes on little plots of land.

"Where are we going first?" he asked.

"This will carry us right downtown," Mr. Purcell said. He went into his pocket for a piece of paper and read over it. "We're looking for the Dixie Hotel. Keep on until we get to Walton Street, then take a right turn."

Jake was wondering what kind of city Atlanta could be. He could see the shapes of tall buildings, now within walking distance, even as they drove past plots of thickly wooded land and rolling fields where cows grazed. At the next intersection, he saw chickens pecking on the ground while a pig dozed in a patch of dirt.

Another half mile and they came upon the train station at Brookwood, beyond which was a vast web of rails, roundhouses, and thousands of freight and passenger cars, sitting still or moving in slow motion. Mr. Purcell had described Atlanta as a colossal railroad hub and here was the proof. It stretched as far as Jake could see, acre upon acre, all the way to downtown. The smoke from the trains, along with what belched from the factory stacks that poked up like ghostly fingers in the distance, had shrouded the panorama in a tepid brown cloud for which the weak winter sun was no match, so that the most distant corners of the yards looked like they were submerged in dank water.

The city arrived abruptly. At the next corner was a Gothic mansion, then a cluster of two- and three-story office buildings, followed by a stretch of large mansions. The cityscape increased steadily from this point, and within ten minutes they were driving into the heart of the downtown area, with towers that reached as high as ten and twelve floors and the usual palette of stores and eateries. The streets were jammed with automobiles, trucks, horse-drawn hacks, and the occasional carriage, so that they crept rather than motored along. Jake rolled down the window and took a whiff of the air. It certainly smelled like a city.

As they made their way down Peachtree Street, he let out a deep sigh of relief. The hotel couldn't be far. It had been a long grind, and he ached right down to his bones.

That relief would have to wait; Mr. Purcell wasn't quite ready to stop. "Let's drive around a bit," he suggested, pointing to their left. With a grunt of frustration, Jake Stein turned the car east on Auburn Avenue. When they came to a stop three blocks down, a blind Negro crossed before them, dressed in a natty gray suit with a twelve-string guitar strapped across his back.

"I'd say we've come to the right place," Mr. Purcell said.

Grayton Jackson stood gazing out his office window at the downtown streets and mulling the jagged and treacherous path that had brought him there.

Over the past decade, corruption had flooded the city like a dirty tide, and few fingers had been lifted to halt it. Atlanta had been a wide-open town, the kind of place where crooks, yeggs, and confidence men could practice their illicit trades with only token interference from the law. The well-oiled machine created by a boss named Floyd Woodward had run most of the criminal enterprise, with bootlegging, narcotics, counterfeiting, scams, gambling, and prostitution fueling the engine. Even after Woodward fled the city to escape a trumped-up murder charge, the business was too robust and lined too many pockets to fold.

Once large chunks of the police department had been bought off, the graft and various other abuses became facts of life and hard habits to break. Critics brave enough to speak up pointed out that many of those who had sworn to protect and serve had come to protect criminals in order to serve their own greed.

As he rose through the ranks, Sergeant, then Lieutenant, then Captain Jackson had taken his share from the illicit trough, though never allowing it to get in the way of his prosecution of felonies. Capital crimes were viciously enforced when the victim was white. Petty thieves and swindlers were dispatched with a brisk and brutal efficiency. Beyond that, the water got muddy, because the Captain believed that most human vices did little harm and were, in fact, an asset to law enforcement, if properly controlled. A man with a brain full of opium smoke or veins swimming with morphine was not apt to commit an act of violence. A drink and the affections of a female to calm a bully's rough urges made the city a safer place for everyone. Whose business was it if some fool wanted to risk an addiction or a venereal disease? And who could deny that when such trade was outlawed, the crooks fed off it?

So it had happened in Atlanta as the police department and Woodward's crime machine joined hands. The marriage might have gone on for a long time, except for some hogs who couldn't get enough, bringing an outraged citizenry down on their heads.

When the Captain saw how strongly mayoral candidate John Sampson's promise to clean up the department was resonating, he imagined his career going up in smoke. As one of former chief Pell's men, and in fact his most able enforcer, his head would be on the block.

The brass couldn't believe the party was over. The Captain, reading the signs, knew better, and in the months leading up to the election, deftly stepped away from the carnage, so neither Chief Walters nor Chief of Detectives Pell collected him on their way down.

As it turned out, his bad disposition was his good fortune. While it had always galled him that he was never allowed near the top of the pyramid of graft, he realized that the disdain of those who dangled gold braid could be his salvation. All he had to do was to keep his head down and avoid being tarred with the new mayor's brush of reform.

When the dust settled and he found himself still standing, his imagination got the better of him. He even allowed himself to dream about the chief's job; or, if not that, chief of detectives'.

There was a certain sense to it. Who better to step into one of those fourth-floor offices than a man who had a long record of results?

Rather than leave it to chance, he went about showing himself in the best light. He made sure he was on the scene of major arrests, and personally chopped a whiskey still to pieces for the benefit of a newspaper photographer. He planted a rumor that he was a candidate for one of the open posts, and in the overheated weeks leading up to the election, the rumor grew into a forecast, then an accepted fact. The only question seemed to be which office Grayton Jackson would assume.

While he was plotting, Mayor Sampson was acting, disbanding the corrupt police commission for his own police board and moving control of the department off Decatur Street and into his City Hall office. Ignoring the courting by Jackson and other pretenders, he installed as chief a man named Clifton Troutman, a nothing who had gone through the ranks from patrolman to a desk job. So in one quick stroke, a glorified clerk became chief of police for the city of Atlanta. The chief of detectives post was left open, with an announcement that the search for a candidate would continue. In that one stroke, Grayton Jackson's glorious hopes tumbled as if shot from the sky and he fell into a black and furious pit.

The day the word came down from above about the new chief of police, the Captain heard a ruckus in the hall and stepped outside to see Troutman surrounded by a bevy of backslapping well-wishers, their faces pink with feigned admiration.

Then one of their number saw Captain Jackson looking their way with a glare that traveled over the fifty feet of air like an electric arc. One by one, the heads came around and the gay chatter died. Eyes shifted and throats were cleared. The Captain kept his face stony, showing nothing in his terrible moment of humiliation. He let it stretch to a torturous length, then swiveled on his heel and disappeared back into the detectives' section, leaving an echoing silence. Not a word was spoken until he was gone, and then the voices were muted.

The Captain stalked past the desks and into his office with his jaw clenched so tightly his teeth were ground together and his temples ached. He closed the door behind him so no one heard the dark growl that rose from his gut.

In his sick fury, it dawned on him how ably he had been used. After all he'd done, the mayor and his men thought him nothing but a thug. They held him in such low regard that even though he knew where bodies were buried he rated not even a nod of recognition. Indeed, over the next few days, hints were passed his way that he was damned lucky to have a job at all.

If the mayor and his new chief were expecting him to resign in defeat and skulk away, they were mistaken. With a mammoth effort of will, he swallowed his bile and went back to work as if nothing had happened. He kept his face blank as thoughts of revenge raged. At the same time, he knew Sampson and Troutman wanted to force him out the door and overheard whispers that the first day of the New Year would be his last day as an Atlanta police officer.

Then a burglar invaded the Payne mansion, and in a matter of hours, everything was turned around. The mayor and the chief were suddenly in a terrible spot and didn't know what to do. All their talk of law and order, and they couldn't manage to guard the richest people in Atlanta against a common thief. With no chief of detectives upon whom to foist the mess, they called on the Captain, who did know what to do. Once again, Grayton Jackson's head was filled with rosy scenarios of the mayor anointing him to the head spot in the detective squad; or better yet, to relieve the incompetent dunce Troutman and make him chief.

Whichever it was, he wasn't about to leave it to chance. This time, it would be his game to win or lose. He understood that it was all hanging by a thread from the Inman Park burglary, and he was doing everything he could to make sure it came out his way.

There was still plenty of risk, with enemies like Troutman on one side and the likes of Pearl Spencer and Joe Rose on the other. So he could still fail miserably, and in his darkest moments, the idea of putting a bullet from his police revolver in his own temple did not seem out of the question.

As he gazed down from his window, his mind circling in a slow ellipse, it took a few moments for him to realize that the figure crossing the scope of his vision was none other than that same son of a bitch Joe Rose. Seeing which way that Indian thief was headed, the Captain muttered a small curse. Thoughts of Rose's insolent face brought along an image of Pearl Spencer's, and he turned from the window in order to escape them both.

Joe showed up at Jesse's at five o'clock, just as daylight was failing and high streaks of cloud were moving through the gray sky on gusty winds that dropped the temperature on the streets. There was no black wreath on the door in Schoen Alley, nor any of the amulets of the kind that traced back to Africa, which told Joe that Jesse was still hanging on. He climbed the creaking wooden stairs and stepped inside to find a different set of callers in attendance, including a couple of rounders he knew vaguely and two women he didn't recognize at all.

Willie was there, drowsing with his cheek resting on an arm that was draped over the big body of his guitar. Jesse was asleep, his face even more gaunt and ghostly. His cheekbones were jutting and his eye sockets had deepened. He was already beginning to look like a corpse.

When Joe sat down, Willie raised his head and stretched.

"How's he doing?" Joe said in a muted voice.

"He's out a good bit," Willie said. "When he's awake he eats some soup and drinks a little water, that's all."

"How's he fixed for medicine?"

"He got enough to hold him through the day, but he's gonna need some more. I believe it's the only thing keepin' him alive."

He tilted his head toward Joe. "You think you can help out with that?"

"One of those fellows in the kitchen can," Joe said. "I'll talk to them."

They sat in silence for a few moments before Willie flexed his hands and began lightly strumming the strings of his guitar. At the sound of the first few trembling bars, Little Jesse opened his eyes and stared at Willie as if he couldn't quite place him, then looked over at Joe with the same blank expression. He licked his dry lips and Joe picked up the glass of water from the night table to give him a drink.

Jesse closed his eyes in thanks, then cleared his throat and said, "How's that comin', Willie?"

"I'm workin' it," Willie said.

Little Jesse rolled his head in Joe's direction. His gaze was milky, and Joe wondered if Jesse recognized him. "Willie's writin' a song for me," he said.

"I heard," Joe said.

"He needs to get his black ass movin' on it," Jesse said tartly.

Willie smiled, shook his head, and strummed some more chords. Clearing his throat lightly, he started to sing.

*Little Jesse was a gambler, day and night,*
*Well, he used crooked cards and dice.*
*A sinful guy, black-hearted, he had no soul*
*Yes, his heart was hard and cold like ice*

*Jesse was a wild reckless gambler, he won a gang of change*
*Many gambler's heart he let in pain*

He stopped.

"Well?" Jesse waited, then said, "That ain't all, is it?"

Willie hesitated for a few seconds. "I'm messin' with this next here little bit . . ."

*When he began to spend and lose his money,*
*he began to be blue and all alone*
*Boys, his heart had almost turned to stone*

"Yeah," Jesse croaked. "That's right. Go ahead on."

"That's all I got," Willie said. When Jesse grimaced sourly, he said, "You want it done right, don't you?"

"I want it done *now,* son!"

"Why, you goin' somewhere?" Willie shot back.

Little Jesse started to say something, then coughed before he could get it out. Joe knew how much he loved the dozens. Any other time, he'd snap back with something sharp, and it would just go from there until he and Willie would be dogging each other down, laughing like a couple of schoolboys, along with everyone else in the room.

*Hey, Willie, I know you blind, boy. So you couldn't see that damn woman you was with last night was so ugly . . . she was so ugly that the ugly stick done run away!*

Little Jesse, frail and tottering, his flesh sagging from his bones and his face drawn, couldn't summon any of that now.

Willie went back to fingering the strings and murmuring bits of lyric. Joe took his mind off Jesse for a few minutes to listen, captivated by the way Willie worked, drawing pieces together, trying it this way and that, until he found something that sounded just right. Given enough time, the blind man would build a song from spare parts.

Joe eavesdropped until the repetition got to him. He returned his attention to the man on the bed. Jesse had sunk down onto the pillows and closed his eyes.

"Jesse?" He kept his voice low, just above a whisper.

"Hmm?" Little Jesse sounded like he was answering from far away.

"I asked around a little bit about what happened to you."

"Asked who?"

"Actually, I asked the Captain."

Jesse's eyes opened again. "What the fuck?"

"I got pulled in about a burglary. After he was done with me, I asked about you."

Jesse swallowed, looking scared. "What the hell'd you do that for?" he hissed. "You say about Logue?"

"No, I wasn't about to do that."

Jesse stared, then relaxed again. "Well, that's good." He took a moment's pause. "So he say anything about me?"

"What do you think?" Joe said. "He didn't know a damn thing about it."

"Is that all?"

"That's all. Nobody else is talking, either."

"Somebody will." Jesse nodded shallowly. "You just need to keep on it."

Joe shifted in his chair. "You need to tell me about Saturday."

" 'Bout what, now?"

"Saturday."

"I done told you already." Jesse raised his head a little and his hand waved toward the bedside table. Again, Joe picked up the glass of water and held it to his lips. Jesse drank gratefully and settled back. "That cop walked up and shot me down."

Joe said, "I mean before that. During the day. And on Friday. Anything that wasn't usual business?"

Jesse's jaw tightened in a spasm that came and went. "I didn't do nothin' to that damned copper," he insisted stubbornly. "Not then, not ever. Didn't hardly even fuckin' *know* him."

"So he shot you for target practice?"

"Maybe so," Jesse grunted. "Maybe that's just what he did. Wouldn't be the first time somethin' like that happened."

"Could he have been doing a job for somebody else?"

Jesse didn't say anything for a few seconds, and Joe couldn't tell if he was catching a breath or hedging. Then he said, "Why? Who else you think wants me dead?"

Joe had to smile at that. "I don't know. You got any enemies? You cross anyone lately?"

Jesse's eyes burned with an odd light and his brow creased as if he was struggling with a thought. He opened his mouth to respond, then closed it and gave a slight shake of his head. Joe got an odd sense that he was lying, or at least holding back, and was about to push him some more when Willie spoke up.

"Jesse, what was the name of that Alabama woman you was so sweet on a while back? You remember?" The blind man couldn't see the annoyed look Joe gave him.

"Al'bama?" Jesse was quiet for a moment, thinking. "Oh . . . that was . . . the Cherokee gal. Lorena." His gaze wandered dreamily. "I always wondered what happened with her." His gaze moved to the window. "I cared for that woman, I sure did," he said. "But she just woke up one morning, packed her bag, and left out. Up and gone out the door. And I never saw her no more after that." He looked over at Willie. "Why you want to know 'bout her? You thinking of lookin' her up?" His smile was weary.

"I just need a woman in this here song." Willie strummed two chords. "And she needs to be some kind of heartbreaker."

"Well, she was that, all right," Little Jesse said with a sigh. "She done broke my heart, but good." He turned his head and treated Joe to a piercing look. "They'll do that, won't they?"

"What's that, Jesse?"

Jesse's eyes glinted almost accusingly. "You know what I'm talking about. You ought to. They'll break your damn heart, for sure."

Joe frowned irritably. He didn't need Little Jesse falling into a glum spiral over a lost love. So he sat forward and said, "We were—"

"I know, I know." Now Jesse sounded petulant. "There ain't nothin' more I can tell you about it, Joe. Wish I could, but I can't."

Joe didn't fail to notice the difference between *I can't tell you* and *I don't know.* He also saw the stubborn set of Jesse's chin, and changed tack. "Who else have you had trouble with lately?"

Jesse shook his head and produced another pained smile. His breathing got shallow. "Only people mad at me was . . . the usual dumb niggers who lost all their money and . . . then say I cheated 'em. Them, and a . . . a few womens here and there. That's all. I ain't had no problem with no police . . . not for a good long time."

Joe thought for a moment. "What about Robert Clark?"

"What about him?"

"You know where I can find him?"

Little Jesse's brow knit. "Why?"

"He was there. He might have seen or heard something."

"Don't think so. It was all done when he come up. Anyway, Robert's a goddamn fool."

Joe sat back, vexed by the false echoes in Little Jesse's tone. It could have been anything, though; the man was dying and knew it. He might even be feeling some late remorse for those he had wronged. Or maybe it was simply a lifelong habit of evasion, what a rounder did to survive the streets. Anything that came out of Little Jesse Williams's mouth was suspect. What he couldn't figure was why Jesse would beg for his help, then hold out on him. Especially now.

It didn't appear that he would get an answer this afternoon. Jesse had sunk down into his pillow, his face turning another shade grayer. Some moments of silence went by with Joe listening to Jesse's short breathing.

Then Willie spoke up, breaking the still silence. "Okay, y'all, listen here . . ."

He began playing the minor-key dirge. The two girls came in from the kitchen and the two rounders stood in the doorway to listen. The blind man sang the first lines.

*Little Jesse was a gambler, night and day*
*Well, he used crooked cards and dice*

*A sinful guy, good-hearted, but had no soul*
*Heart was hard and cold like ice*

*Jesse was a wild reckless gambler, he won a gang of change*
*Many gambler's heart he let in pain*

*When he began to spend and lose his money,*
*he began to be blue and all alone*
*But boys, his heart had even turned to stone*

Willie hesitated, then spoke the rest of it.

*What broke Jesse's heart, why he was blue and all alone*
*Sweet Lorena packed up and gone . . .*

At that, Jesse opened his eyes again and smiled, his face soften-
ing with a sweet sadness. "You gonna make me famous, Willie?"

"I don't know, Jesse," Willie said.

Jesse brooded, then went about summoning the energy to
push himself up a few inches. "I wanna tell y'all something," he
said, his voice taking on a bit of timbre. As he looked around, a
sly gleam appeared in his eyes, a hint of the Little Jesse they all
knew.

"If I got to go . . . y'all need to know how . . . how I want it
to be when my time comes." His mouth stretched in a thin smile.
"I want every goddamn . . . gambler in Atlanta come out. Every
one of them motherfuckin' fools say I been . . . takin' they money
all these years. All of my womens, too. I means the ones on the
street, and . . . whichever ones you can find out of the Hampton . . . and the Atlanta." He paused, gasped, and coughed. When

he recovered, his lips made a wicked arc. "See if y'all can get Judge Harris, too. He done sent me up about thirteen, fourteen times. He and the solicitor. They wasn't unkind." His grin and eyes darkened. "I want a police escort for my wagon. Hell, I give 'em enough business."

Everyone laughed. Jesse took a moment, then forged on, sucking breath between each few words. "I mean it, now. I want y'all . . . good and drunk. Y'hear? And no goddamn . . . weepin' and moanin' over poor Jesse. You can get me a . . . a preacher. Got to have music. 'Cept no women out of no amen corner . . . singin' about glory. Everybody be dancin', too." He faded a little more. "You play your guitar, Willie . . . and sing that song. You sing it over my grave."

Willie said, "I hear you, Jesse."

"I want all of that!" Jesse said, raising his voice one more time. "Every one of them people! Ya'll make sure!" His eyes slid toward Joe. "And one more thing. The Captain oughta be there. See if he got anything to say about me then."

"I wouldn't count on him," Joe said dryly. "I don't think he's much for Negro funerals."

"Well, he oughta . . . be at this one," he gasped. The effort was too much, and he seemed to fold inward, as if his bones had betrayed him. "Damn, I'm tired." He cast one dark eye on Joe. "I ain't dead yet, am I? Sure feels like it."

"Not yet, Jesse," Joe said. "You still got a ways to go."

Jesse closed the eye. Some seconds passed and he fell into an exhausted slumber. Willie went back to strumming his guitar.

*When he began to spend and lose his money,*
*he began to be blue and all alone*
*But boys, his heart had even turned to stone*

*What broke Jesse's heart, why he was blue and all alone*
*Sweet Lorena had packed up and gone . . .*

He stopped and cocked his head, as if listening to something beyond the walls of the room and his face toward Jesse, as if he could see him.

*Po-lice walked up and shot my friend Jesse down . . .*
*Boys, I got to die today.*

Willie stopped playing, his face now somber. The show was over and the four who had come to the doorway went back to the kitchen and the bottle.

Willie said, "You hear what he asked for, Joe. We need to get it for him."

Joe laughed softly. "That'll be some job."

"Don't matter," Willie said. "We at least need to let everybody know. And I mean right away. So they can come see him before he goes and be 'round when he die. Just like he said." He stopped and his voice fell off. "He ain't got much time. Tomorrow, the next day. Maybe. And he'll be gone."

Joe stared at the blind man. "That's not what the doctor said."

"I don't care what the damn doctor say," Willie whispered urgently. "Death's already been creeping this room."

Joe didn't doubt him at all. "All right, Willie," he said.

The blind man turned his head in the direction of the bed once more. "Poor Jesse," he said. "Whatever he did, never should have come to this." He mused darkly for a few seconds, then started up the moody pattern again.

Joe said, "You know what you're going to call it?"

"What, the song?" Willie's mouth dipped into a melancholy smile. "Yeah, I do. I believe I'll call it 'The Dying Crapshooter's Blues.'"

Joe stayed until the early evening, when Martha came in to tend to Jesse through the night. She went into the bedroom to find him sleeping peacefully, and set to washing the glasses from the day's drinking.

Willie had spent the hours working on Jesse's song until the bells struck seven, and he put on his coat, hoisted his guitar, and left out for a job he had playing at the 81 Theatre.

Joe went to use the bathroom. When he came out, he stepped into the kitchen and whispered in the ear of one of the rounders. The fellow promised to come through with some morphine to help Little Jesse through the rest of the night.

Joe slipped back into the bedroom to get his coat and saw that Martha had turned the lights way down low and had a candle burning atop the dresser. Jesse was on his back, as still as stone, as though he was already laid out and waiting for the hearse to arrive.

Joe descended the steps into the alley. He was in a mind to go back to his room and lock the door. Instead, he made his grudging way out onto Decatur Street to cover the blocks between Butler and Hill streets.

As he moved from storefront to doorway to facade to theater, he encountered a selection of characters he knew at least slightly, most of them Negroes, a half-dozen whites, and one or two in between. He stopped, spoke a few words with each, asking that the news be spread that Little Jesse wanted everybody to start gathering around. He also took the opportunity to ask if anyone had heard any talk about what had happened to put Jesse on his deathbed and to inquire into the whereabouts of Robert Clark.

He got the reaction he expected: sincere nods of pity over little Jesse's plight, smiles of expectation of the wake, then narrowed eyes on stony faces, heads shaking side to side, and glances averted, as if something interesting had occurred across the street once the subject of the shooting came up. No one knew anything about that or about where Robert Clark might be found.

Joe walked on, snickering over the way some of the rounders' faces had lit up with greed over Jesse's demise. One of them would have to pick up his action once he was gone.

It took him a half hour to arrive at the corner where Bell Street turned into Hill. From there on, the blocks were colonized by little shacks, clapboard hovels, a rooming house or two, vacant storefronts, the odd corner grocers. Mondays were generally slow, and Joe came upon only two crap games in progress. He passed the word at the first and was greeted by silence and much shifting of dark eyes. He got the same treatment at the second and was walking back toward town when he heard a voice call his name.

He stopped and turned around to see a small-time crook who went by the moniker Mouse hurrying along in his wake. Mouse caught up, stole a rodent's furtive glance around, then said, "Robert Clark."

"What about him?" Joe said.

"He come by the game Sa'day night," Mouse said. "I mean Sunday mornin'."

"What game was that?"

"That one down Raspberry Alley. Used to be Harper's Barbershop, but it shut down. In there."

Joe feigned disinterest. "So he came by."

"We had a bottle and he had him some drinks," Mouse said.

"And?" Joe's voice was impatient.

"And he start talkin' about how he seen Little Jesse get shot," Mouse said quickly, and stole another sneaky glance over his shoulder. "He say he heard this here cop talkin' befo' it happened, too."

"Yeah? Did he happen to mention what the cop said?"

Mouse smiled. His teeth were brown and rotting. "Whatchu think that be worth?"

Joe went into his pocket and held up an eagle quarter.

Mouse snatched the coin. "Robert say that cop tell Jesse he done crossed the wrong man. Like that. That's what Robert say."

"That's all?"

Mouse cocked his head knowingly. "Soon as it come out his damn mouth, I could tell he wished he didn't say it. He looked scared, and he just run on out of there. I ain't seen him since."

"Does he have a job?"

"Sometimes he do and sometimes he don't," the black man said craftily. "I don't know that he got anything right now."

"You know where he stays?"

"I don't," Mouse said. "But I sure will tell you if I find out, Mr. Joe. You know I will." With that, he scrabbled away.

It was late when Joe got back downtown. The streets were cold with swirling winds, his feet were tired from the walking, and he was ready to end his day.

Before he did that, he decided to make one more stop at a speakeasy in Kenny's Alley called Big Bill's. The joint was frequented by all sorts of low-rent criminals and marked a sort of gateway to the scarlet trade on Central Avenue, which was just out the back door. The man who ran it was one of those rare southern-bred men who not only abided Negroes but enjoyed their company, as long as they had some class to them. So it was always possible that Joe could pick up information he couldn't find anywhere else. Maybe some helpful soul would sit down next to him and explain in detail why a cop named Logue had shot Little Jesse Williams on Saturday, and he could then lay the whole mess aside.

He wished it could be that easy, because it was starting to turn into a tangle, with Jesse's evasions, Robert Clark's shifty behavior, and the complete lack of any other talk from the street, which was strange. Behind it all was the question of why Logue would want to shoot Little Jesse, a no-account rounder who really didn't bother anyone much. It didn't make sense.

Like all those who hustled for a living, Joe hated being worked, and that was exactly how it felt. It wasn't only Little Jesse's shooting, either; he was slowly being sucked into the burglary in Inman Park by the very woman he had come there to see. If it wasn't for her, he wouldn't be there and in the middle of the mess.

He had stepped off the train from Louisville ready to relax after being sated with the easy theft of a diamond necklace and the attentions of a red-haired woman named Annabelle. They'd known each other in years past, when she went by another name. Though now a respectable married woman, she was still happy to see him. One afternoon, he left her dozing in her four-poster bed and wandered downstairs, out into the garden, and through the ivy to the mansion next door, where he slipped by the house staff to help himself to the best piece he saw. He was back in Annabelle's bedroom in minutes, and the next morning, he boarded a train to Atlanta. If he had known what would be waiting for him, he would have stayed where he was.

Someone moved by him to sit at the end of the bar, a young fellow in a poor suit and old overcoat, his face pinched with melancholy and eyes distressed.

Joe knew the look. "What's her name?" he asked.

The young fellow squinted at him. "What's that?"

"The woman," Joe said. "What's her name?"

"It's . . . Betty."

Joe gave an absent nod. "I've come across a few of those," he said. "Still know one or two." He got up from his stool. "Well, don't kill yourself over her, friend."

The young man gazed back at Joe with helpless, liquid eyes, and for a moment Joe wondered if he was going to burst into tears. Then Bill the bartender served up a shot of whiskey and a glass of beer, and he went about dissolving his sorrows that way. Bill left the young heartbreak and stepped over to Joe with a wry smile.

"A double shot will do," Joe said.

Bill poured the whiskey into a glass that looked none too clean. Joe drank anyway, then whispered something under his breath. The bartender leaned closer.

Of course Bill knew Logue. The cop spent time in all the downtown speaks, cadging free drinks when he didn't have the money to pay. He made the Central Avenue rounds, too. The bartender repeated the story of the night the cop got so falling-down drunk that some of the street rats stripped off his uniform and left him snoring on the floor. His fellow officers came to roust him the next morning. They got the uniform and the weapon back and told everyone to keep quiet about it, but it got around anyway. Nobody could take Logue seriously, but he didn't cause anyone trouble, either. He was just a harmless old shaking wreck of a drunkard who happened to wear a badge.

Not quite harmless, Joe mused, then asked if Logue had been in that evening. Bill said he hadn't seen him in a week, and that he had no idea about later on. Then he rolled his greasy eyes around the room before dropping his voice to ask Joe for the lowdown on the Inman Park caper.

"I know as much about it as you do," Joe said in an offhand way.

Bill raised bushy eyebrows. "That's not what I heard," he muttered. "I heard you was in a spot."

"What else did you hear?" Joe asked.

The bartender shrugged his rounded shoulders and what was left of his neck disappeared into folds of flesh. "Just that the Captain's gonna take somebody down for it. He's got to, is what people are saying."

Joe decided he'd heard enough. He finished his drink, thanked Bill, dropped some coins on the bar, and went out the door.

Walking back to the Hampton, he figured he'd find Logue in the morning, maybe catch him in the midst of a hangover, and get him to spill something. He had done all he could for one day. He wasn't a magician and couldn't reach into a hat and pull out the reason why Little Jesse was shot, any more than he could make the Payne mansion jewels appear from thin air with a snap of his fingers. It was all too much, and he was ready for his room, a last drink, and his bed.

As he turned the corner onto Houston Street, he mused briefly on the sad young fellow at Big Bill's, his broken heart on display like a sign carved out in deep indigo. Joe wondered which one of the half-dozen Bettys he knew around town had done the poor boy wrong. They were all able; what woman wasn't? Jesse was right about that.

He pushed through the hotel doors and crossed directly to the front desk to get his key. Handing it over, the clerk raised his eyebrows and pointed with his chin to the far side of the lobby. Joe's first thought was *cops,* and he took his sweet time turning around.

She was standing against the opposite wall, in a shadow where the lamplight didn't quite reach. Keeping a nonchalant gait, he crossed the tiny lobby, unable to quell the thumping in his chest at the very sight of her.

"What are you doing here?" he said.

Pearl's smile was white and wicked on her dark face. "I'm getting in out of the cold," she said.

J. R. Logue thought he had a bottle stashed somewhere in his Cain Street room, but when he went looking, he couldn't find it. He figured he must have finished it off and then forgot to go get another to replace it. He did that sometimes.

He stumbled to the door, opened it, and poked his head into the hall. It was quiet, no one talking, and no Victrolas playing. It was too late to go knocking at the other rooms, and Mrs. Cotter had told him never to bother her at night unless the house was burning down. She couldn't abide the behavior that went with his drinking, and he felt like she was always on the verge of putting him out of the house.

Twenty-four hours earlier, he could have climbed the steep blocks to Peachtree Street to buy a bottle, but the fellow with the still had gotten arrested after starting an altercation that brought a patrolman to his door. There had been witnesses all over the street, and so there was nothing the cop could do but bust it up.

Knowing he wouldn't last the night without a drink, Logue pulled on his high-topped shoes and headed out, trekking down Bartow to Marietta Street like a lumbering bear. He glanced up at the street sign on the corner where it changed to Decatur with a little flutter of anticipation, tasting the raw smoke of bad whiskey and the sweet burn coursing through his veins. Though it was cold out, the alcohol that had long ago saturated his very bones kept him warm.

He stopped at the next corner and looked up to see the sign for Courtland Street. Sudden images rose before his eyes, pictures playing in slow motion and filtered in blue shadow. The colored boy was ahead of him, and he heard himself call out a name. Williams? Was that it? The fellow turned around with that look in his eye, like he knew what was coming. That he had done wrong, and was about to pay. Logue's service revolver had jumped into his hand, and a shot cracked, echoed, and died. He watched Williams crumple to the sidewalk, then put his pistol back in its holster and walked away, feeling the street tilt a little bit. The thought went around in his muddled brain: *I just shot a man.*

Even now, he saw those dark accusing eyes and it made him think of hell. *I just shot a man.* He wondered if Williams would be waiting for him when his time came.

He was startled by the sudden wail of a siren and glanced around to see a police wagon pulling out of the lot three blocks down. It gave him a moment's pause, as he realized he had no business wandering around those dark and lonely streets at that hour. What if someone knew what had happened? What if there had been eyes watching from a shadow? And what if the word was around about what he had done? Lord help him if any of these roughhouse, backstreet niggers had gotten wind of it. White man or not, policeman or not, they could cut him into so many pieces that his own mama wouldn't be able to figure out what went where.

He knew it would be wise for him to turn around and head back home, but he needed his pint, needed the smoky liquor soothing his nerves and blanking his thoughts. At least he had the wits to stay off the main drag, and instead looped a block north on Courtland to come around on Gilmer Street to Maddox, which was actually a crooked alley. There were a couple addresses he knew down this way, places that were good for a bottle at any hour of the night.

It was still and quiet and he stepped uneasily, searching the shadows. He leaned on a telephone post and went digging for the flask he always carried, only to find it empty. Of course it was, or what would he be doing there? He shook it to make sure. It was a special piece, polished brass with a dent where a bullet aimed at his broad ass had been deflected. That fellow who tried to gun him down, or at least give him something to explain, a piece of white trash named . . . named . . . what was his name? Who could remember? He was dead now. And Williams was dead, too. Or maybe not . . .

Now it came back, nagging him. He had fired, watched the man fall, then walked away without checking to make sure the job was done. It was driving him crazy that he hadn't remembered to do that. In a lucid moment Sunday afternoon, he had used Mrs. Cotter's telephone to call down to the precinct and check for a report of a Negro shot on Courtland Street. The desk sergeant said there was nothing of the kind.

He made calls to Grady Hospital and some of the colored funeral homes. No one had any information about such a subject.

He considered that the people he spoke to were lying to him, which was what they did by habit when they dealt with a white policeman.

If Williams wasn't dead, it would mean all kinds of trouble, and it wasn't even his fault! What had he been doing there in the first place? His brain was muddled about that.

He put the flask away and had just started off again when he heard voices, and turned around to see three colored boys amble by the mouth of the alley behind him, staggering into one other as they engaged in a bleary argument. He thought to chase after them and brace them good, see if they'd give up any talk about the Williams fellow. Maybe that was a way for him to—

"Logue!"

He jumped and came back around. A man had come up on him from the other end of the crooked alley without a sound to stand not ten paces away. Though Logue didn't quite recognize him, he straightened, hearing rough authority in the voice.

"Yes, sir?" His voice was shaky.

"You're a drunk, Logue," the man said.

The cop didn't know if he was expected to agree, argue, or stay silent. He was still mulling his choices when a revolver came up. "And you're a terrible damn shot."

The pistol coughed loudly in that narrow space, and Logue staggered, his hands flapping at the hole in the middle of his chest. He tipped over, the back of his head slamming onto dirty bricks, and found himself looking up into a cold face. The world shifted at a rough angle. Grunting in pain, he tried to get to his feet.

"You start something, you finish it," the fellow muttered, and then without a second's pause, shot him in the precise center of his forehead. There was a splatter of blood and matter and a little puff of hot smoke where the bullet exited from the back of his skull. The man put the pistol back in his pocket, straightened, and walked away, heading off through the cold shadows toward the lights of Bell Street.

# SEVEN

Two brothers who worked as porters on the Georgia Southern were walking to the station in the chilly six o'clock darkness when the older of the pair happened to glance into the narrow gap at Maddox Street to see the body lying sprawled on the cold bricks. He touched his brother's arm. They stopped, stared, and then edged into the alleyway.

The heavyset white man was dead as could be, with one black hole high on his chest and another almost between his eyes. Dried blood had webbed a pattern on his face and down his shirt. He wore no overcoat and his trouser pockets had been turned inside out.

The brothers gaped for another few seconds, wordless in the wake of whatever violence had befallen the poor soul, then hurried off to call the police station and report what they had found. Anonymously, of course.

Even before the break of day, there was a cheerful clamor on the first floor of the Dixie Hotel that rippled from the lobby into the parlor. As soon as the dining room doors opened, almost every seat was taken, so that the regular guests stood grumbling in a line at the door. Some of them gave up and walked out into the brisk morning. Those who didn't care what they ate crossed the street to the Checker Diner. Others took the desk clerk's advice and headed four blocks west to Lulu's on Houston Street, with Beck's Café on James as a second choice.

Out in the lobby, the crowd of four dozen men and twenty-odd women swirled about like eddies in a rolling stream, raising a giddy row. In turn, a guitar or banjo would appear from a case or come unslung from a shoulder and a ripple of steel strings would rise up, followed by a voice that rasped, crooned, or warbled. Meanwhile, the parlor piano, an old upright that was slightly out of tune, got worried to death as one player after another sat down to try out a tune. Strange, plaintive harmonies rose from tables in the dining room. The competing sounds echoed about the ground floor in the manner of a jungle flush with exotic birds. Though a less charitable soul might have described it as more akin to a barnyard. Meanwhile, the regular guests hurried in and out, looking askance, as if they thought an invasion was in progress.

The news had spread faster than anyone might have guessed, with telephone calls and telegrams flying like startled quail to all parts of Georgia and into South Carolina, Tennessee, and east Alabama. In the twenty-four hours before George Purcell and Jake Stein finally stepped to the front desk in the lobby of the Dixie Hotel, certain men and women in far-flung hollows and pastures laid their work aside or whoa'd their mules. Others toiling away in small towns were taken with sudden bouts of dyspepsia and fever and had to leave their jobs immediately. Still others, laboring in dirty mills, simply vanished when no one was looking.

Late in the evening, through the night, and into dawn, trains pulled into Terminal Station, their cars disgorging an extra number of passengers in their fines carrying stringed instruments. Others, less well dressed, rode the blinds. The railroad bulls threw up their hands as men and even a few women scrambled from beneath the freight cars and hightailed it across the yard, their guitars and banjos banging off their sides as they headed for the safety of Broad Street. More rode on jitneys that rolled in from remote country crossroads and in flivvers that rattled down from mountains to the north of the city.

However they had arrived, all headed for the Dixie, crowding the lobby with bodies, chatter, and music. It grew so chaotic that the desk clerk, a red-haired, pimple-faced young fellow named Sidney Petty, woke the hotel manager, Mr. Morgan, who got dressed and came down from his suite on the second floor to survey the rowdy scene. He made a quick decision to let the crowd stay. While the music was raucous to the ear, the players weren't causing any trouble; indeed, though excited, they were to a woman or man humble and polite, unlike some guests he could name. Not to mention that they were purchasing so many breakfasts that the Negro cook had to send a boy racing with his wagon to the market on Butler Street for more eggs and ham.

Lieutenant Collins had just settled down at his desk with his first cup of coffee when his telephone set jangled. He picked up the receiver, listened to the muttered message, then replaced it in the cradle.

"Sonofabitch," he whispered, and then called out the news. The other cops gave him a brief, startled look that was followed by a flurry of motion and noise as they rose from their desks and hurried for their coats and hats.

Collins took Detective Sergeant Nichols aside. "I'm putting you in charge," he said. Nichols looked momentarily surprised, then headed out with the others.

Collins crossed to stand by one of the tall back windows that looked down on the tracks of the Georgia Railroad Yard. Without knowing the details, he was not much surprised to learn that patrolman J. R. Logue had been found dead in an alley just a few blocks away.

It made a sad kind of sense. Logue had a problem with drink, to put it kindly, which was the reason he was still walking a beat while in his forties. It was a standing joke around headquarters that he had been busted down so many times he had stopped bouncing. Such a hopeless sot had no business wearing a uniform. Yet there he was, an Atlanta police officer. Or had been until last night.

Logue had been assigned to a beat in the rough colored streets that ran from the rail yards north to Ellis Street between Courtland and Fort. These blocks, still swathed in a morning gray that Collins could see from the window, contained dozens of Atlanta's meanest speakeasies, pool halls, and storefront gambling parlors. Part of a beat cop's job was to collect the weekly "business fee" from these low-down joints, then move on to the next one. Logue couldn't handle the duty because once he made a stop, he tended to stay and spend whatever he collected, lose it at cards or dice, or have it picked from his pocket.

Collins tried to remember if Logue was the one who had once gotten so drunk in one of these dives that he had been stripped of his uniform and his revolver and left snoring in his union suit on the sawdust floor. The story had gone around for years.

The lieutenant could not fathom how the man had managed to stay on the police force all this time, even one as incompetent and corrupt as Atlanta's. Logue was no good to anyone, a bumbling liability who could not be trusted with even the simplest graft. And yet no matter how many reprimands were tucked in his file or how many clownish scrapes entangled him, he had never been put out. Someone had been protecting him, and Collins assumed it was Captain Jackson. Even a drunken fool like Logue could serve as a loyal soldier for a man like the Captain, asking only to retire with a pension large enough for him to drink himself to death.

If that was the case, the lieutenant reflected, the plan hadn't worked out. J. R. Logue had retired, but there would be no pension. He wouldn't need it.

Collins was about to turn away from the window when he saw a police sedan pull in off the street and come to a stop directly below. The passenger door opened and the Captain unfolded from the street. Collins recognized the driver, a thick-bodied corporal named Baker, known as a physical brute, the kind that struck mortal fear in the hearts of suspects. He was an odd choice for a driver, but then the Captain would have his reasons.

The lieutenant grabbed his coat and left the detectives' section on his way to the Maddox Street scene of the homicide of patrolman J. R. Logue, using the back stairs in order to avoid his superior officer.

The two fellows from the record company had taken one room and one suite on the top floor of the hotel, the room for sleeping, the suite for auditions and recordings. They had hopes for a steady crowd; neither expected a mob, though it was a cheerful mob all the same. The only trouble came from some guests who were incensed at having their morning routines disrupted. Every few minutes, a sales agent would step to the desk and ask what all the damned hicks were doing there, and in a voice loud enough for anyone to hear, had anyone been listening. Sidney Petty would explain about the recording, and Mr. Morgan would chime in to suggest the fellow think of it as a circus passing through. Even more impressive, the Dixie Hotel was going on the map as the place where records that would be heard from coast to coast had been made. This bit of news seemed to placate most of them. The few who continued to complain were just the crabby sort.

Standing by the front desk, Mr. Morgan watched and listened for a little while longer. It was an orderly enough assembly and a true boon in the slow days before Christmas. At least none of the country folk had shown up with a chicken or a pig in tow, though some of the clothes they wore made them look like they had come directly from a vaudeville show. He told Sidney to keep an eye out for trouble, then went back upstairs to his rooms.

As dawn broke into day, the news about what was going on at the hotel made its way to the offices of the city's two dailies, and an early arriving editor sent a reporter to see about the commotion. What the scribbler found was a milling, noisy crowd and much music. He made his way up to the fourth floor to speak to a distracted Mr. Purcell about the goings-on in the lobby, and then, miffed that the record man didn't drop what he was doing to answer his questions, returned to the newsroom to explain that there was nothing worth filing, just a swarm of hillbillies plucking banjos, all intent on their raw and boisterous music, and not a buffoon or funny drunkard among them.

Anyway, something more promising in the way of headlines was brewing in an alley off the colored end of Decatur Street, and the reporter was sent off to see about that.

Meanwhile, the hotel doors swung open as more musicians trickled in. A few of the later arrivals looked around and grumbled that more days should have been scheduled. Those were few and far between; most of them were pleased just to be there. A handful of performers of the music hall variety arrived with scores in hand, gaped at the unwashed assembly, and walked right back out.

The list of performers was tended by Jake Stein, who every fifteen minutes or so would escort the next half-dozen hopefuls up to the fourth floor. The candidates would wait in the hallway to be called into the suite and invited to perform two songs for Mr. Purcell and his assistant.

After the second song ended, a few terrible seconds would pass as the two men in the chairs consulted in whispers. Then Jake would either issue an invitation to come back in the afternoon or offer a polite dismissal in the form of a suggestion that they try again the next time the company was in town. He would also mention that he'd heard that the Victor people might be making a visit soon. . . .

Those who were asked to come back would descend to the lobby on a cloud, delighted at the prospect of cutting a record, though unaware that they were a small part of history. Meanwhile, those who had been rejected would skulk down the stairs and out the back door. A few might gather themselves and return in coming years, all the more determined. Most of them would never be heard from again, though over the years they would rhapsodize about that time they had auditioned for Mr. George Purcell.

The lobby stayed busy until nine o'clock, when the din settled a bit as the first wave of commotion broke and receded.

Some minutes went by, and a sudden *chang* like a passel of brash bells rang out over the roil of voices and instruments. There was a second of startled silence, and then heads turned, voices faded, and fingers went still. At the front desk, Sidney noticed the sharp change in the room and stood up on his tiptoes, but he was still too short to see what was going on.

A twelve-string guitar echoed, now sounding like fingers slamming down on the keys of a harpsichord. A clear and high tenor voice with just a bit of a smoky edge and a familiar gospel tinge pierced the air over the assembled heads.

*Feel like a broke-down engine*
*Ain't got no drivin' wheel,*
*Feel like a broke-down engine*
*Ain't got no drivin' wheel,*
*Y'all been down and lonesome,*
*You know how a good man feel.*

With the first boom of his Stella's strings, Willie sensed the pause, then the stares turning his way as the chatter ebbed. No one yelled for him to stop, so he launched into the song and another wave of murmurs crossed the room.

Some of the bodies parted as people shuffled to get a closer look, and Sidney was finally able to see the young man in a three-piece suit playing the big guitar. A young blind man. A young *colored* blind man. The clerk stared for a second, then whispered to the bellboy to go fetch Mr. Morgan again.

Five minutes and two songs later, Mr. Morgan came down the stairs, frowning grumpily at being disturbed. He could hear the brassy voice and guitar as he skirted the edge of the crowd to the desk. He bent his head and Sidney told him about the Negro in the corner, how everyone else had gone quiet when he started playing. Mr. Morgan nodded, his eyes flicking. He knew that colored singers were allowed on the porches of hotels during tobacco season, but it was as far as they got, and it was down in the country, where it didn't matter.

He walked to the staircase and mounted a half-dozen steps so he could see over the crowd. A circle had opened around a young, well-dressed Negro with a big-boxed guitar. The manager, who knew more than a little about good music, perked an ear, momentarily entranced despite himself. This was no street-corner moaner; the man's voice had depth and timbre, and he picked his guitar with his fingers, so that it sounded like a piano. The song ended to applause and a swell of chatter. There were calls for more, and the Negro started another song, this one in a minor key.

> *Big star fallin', mama, t'aint long fore day*
> *Big star fallin', mama, t'aint long fore day*

Mr. Morgan stood there listening for another half minute. As good as the fellow sounded, he couldn't let this go on. He descended the steps and worked his way back to the front desk to whisper instructions to the clerk.

Someone came knocking early on Joe's door, a hard thump that brought him out of his sleep in a sharp jerk. Blinking, he imagined Adeline out there or, worse, Sweet with one of his big kitchen knives in hand.

He turned his head, saw only the impression of Pearl's body, and caught the scent she'd left on the sheets, a mixture of magnolia perfume and an earthier musk. A bleary glance around the room told him that she had dressed and gone, all without a sound.

"Who is it?" he called.

"Message!" a voice called out. A folded sheet of paper appeared under the door. Then quiet footsteps receded down the hall.

Joe sat up and swung his legs off the bed, gazing blankly at the paper as the night before came back to him.

Pearl, working her lush magic, had cadged her way into his room, then used her other charms to work her way into the bed. He knew he needed to ask her about the Payne mansion, but before he could speak the first word, she had dropped onto the mattress and stretched her long, sinewy, heavy-breasted body, stunning him as if he'd been poleaxed. He hadn't seen her in almost six months and, as always, it was like he was meeting her for the first time, being dazed by her beauty and overcome by her carnal heat all over again. So he surrendered all over again.

As he tumbled with her, he said, "Sweet's going to kill me."

To which she replied, "Then I better make this worth it."

Joe had laughed, because she could do it. Then he groaned a little. There was nothing funny about what her brother would do if he found out he'd let her in. He had as much as made a promise to stay away from her and the Inman Park burglary was all the more reason to keep it. He just couldn't do it.

Sitting on the bed, he revisited the blissful moments just before they settled down to sleep. He had been too drowsy and too drunk on her to make his brain work enough to ask her about Saturday night. The one time he started to, she put her lips to his ear and said, "Don't worry, it's going to be all right," as if she'd read his mind. That was the last thing he remembered before he drifted into the sweet cocoon of her body curling around him.

That tender memory went away, and his smile with it. He had told himself they'd talk about it in the morning, only to find she had slipped away before he could get to it. Frowning at the paper on the floor, he came back to the hard present, wondering if now might be a good time to pack his suitcase, go by Schoen Alley to offer a last farewell to Little Jesse, and catch the next thing smoking out of Union Depot.

That wouldn't work and he knew it. One taste of Pearl was never enough, and the thought of being without her again made his chest ache. And she wasn't the only thing holding him; he was obliged to Jesse, too.

For the hundredth time, he wished he'd kept his mouth shut about his brief stint as a Philadelphia police officer and his shorter career working for the Pinkertons in Baltimore. He didn't remember when he had first announced these facts, though he assumed he had done it to impress some woman. He just had to show off that one time (or was it more?) and found himself with a reputation. So instead of looking forward to a day seeing friends, scouting income sources, and then getting back to Pearl, he had work to do.

At the washbasin, he splashed some water on his face to wake up and clear his head. He turned around and bent to pick up the slip of paper from the floor and unfold it. On a sheet of hotel stationery, someone had scrawled the words:

*Maddox Street, off Pratt*

He studied the message for a few seconds, then tossed the paper on the bed, among the mussed sheets.

Sweet had been up drinking coffee as he got ready to head off to work when he heard the key rattle in the lock. He stood in the kitchen doorway, his thick arms crossed, as Pearl stepped inside, looking sleepy and happy. She stopped, then rolled her eyes when she saw the reproach in her brother's gaze.

Sweet opened his mouth, closed it. There was nothing to say and they both knew it. She had run to Joe Rose and Joe had let her stay, in spite of Sweet's hard warnings. What could he do with them?

Pearl started for her bedroom, leaving him fuming in the doorway. Halfway down the short hall, she turned and came back, stood before him, and stretched on her toes to kiss his dark, rough cheek. She could feel him wilt a little as he let out a sigh from deep in his chest. He raised a hand to hold her chin in his palm.

"Little sister . . ." He started but couldn't finish.

Pearl gave him a sad smile of her own and backed away.

While she was changing clothes, she heard the front door open and close as he went out into the cold darkness.

She had misjudged the time, hoping to creep back in while he was still asleep. It was later than she thought, though, and he had been waiting for her. She could tell by the look on his face what kind of look she was wearing on hers, and how much it vexed him. He knew where she had been, who she had been with, and what she had been doing. Though it saddened her to hurt him so, she was relieved to see nothing more in his angry stare over chasing after Joe Rose.

For all their quarrels, Pearl loved her brother desperately. He had been her protector in their dead father's place. He had done his best to keep her on the straight and narrow, and had gone to prison for killing a man who had tried to get rough with her. Now he believed she was betraying him by dallying with a rounder like Joe.

She knew Sweet blamed himself for starting her down the wrong path with his own evil ways. The difference was that he had changed. Prison had taught him a number of hard lessons, the most important being that he didn't ever want to go back. He had left his criminal days behind for the straight life, taking a regular job and steering clear of his old cronies. Then he dragged home a series of hardworking, churchgoing *Negro* men, hoping one would catch her fancy. None of them took; she was too far gone on the likes of Joe Rose. Sweet fumed, sure that part of the reason she took to Joe was to confound him and the decent people around the Fourth Ward neighborhood.

Dropping her clothes into the wicker laundry basket, she pulled on a white cotton shift that was worn soft by use and crawled under the blanket. If she had known she was going to get caught like that, she'd have stayed at the hotel. She lay there longing for Joe, feeling the heat tingle down to her last nerve.

She dozed, swirling down into darkness, then came awake, pitched out of a nightmare that featured Captain Jackson standing before her like an evil god, his green eyes glittering as he got ready to devour her, one way or another. Even in the chilly bedroom, the sheets and pillow were damp with her sweat.

She got up and stumbled to the bathroom, then padded out to the kitchen to make coffee and fix something to eat. All the while, the Captain's grim, cold, accusing sneer hovered before her eyes and didn't disappear until she managed to conjure Joe's face again.

Joe came out onto the sidewalk, glanced over Lulu's facade, and walked on. Sweet Spencer was the last man on earth he wanted to see this morning.

Sweet didn't understand about Pearl and him at all. The thought of them together got his blood up, because Joe was a criminal and a bad influence, because mixing was dangerous even if he was an Indian, and because he had a reputation for doing women wrong. While Joe didn't mistreat Pearl, he didn't court her, either, and Sweet took that as some sort of an affront to the family pride.

Though Joe wasn't a coward, Sweet scared him the same way fathers and brothers had made him quail when he was chasing skirts as a kid up north. In those days, if a young villain laid with the daughter or sister of an immigrant family, the men would demand their own justice. The choices were marry, run, or die. It was primitive, tribal, and mired in blood, and no one argued the point.

Joe with Pearl wasn't quite the same, of course; she was a grown woman. And Sweet couldn't afford to commit violence on Joe or any other man or he'd risk going back to prison. Still, Joe knew better than to push him. He couldn't just show up at the café as if nothing had happened, either. If Sweet didn't already know about Pearl's visit, one look at Joe's face would fix that. It was a small relief that he didn't have the time to stop for breakfast. Or so he told himself.

Instead, he bought a biscuit with ham and a carton of coffee from the wagon that was parked at the corner of Broad Street. Leaning next to the window of the Oppenheim Cigar store, he watched the pedestrian traffic while he ate his breakfast. It was a sweet idle; the young women looked pretty bundled in their winter coats, though too many of them were too thin. It was the style of the day, and he didn't care much for it.

He finished his biscuit and coffee, dropped the trash into a can, then headed south on Peachtree Street. A half block on, he dug in his pocket for the note and stared at the four words. He couldn't tell if the hand that had scrawled them was masculine or feminine, done in poor penmanship or by someone in a rush. He had stopped to ask at the front desk, only to find that the clerk wasn't the one who delivered it. Joe knew that anyone familiar with the Hampton could enter undetected.

Walking along in the brisk morning, he passed a number of men hurrying by with stringed instruments in hand, and he remembered what Willie had said about some people from the Columbia record company setting up at the Dixie.

When he got to the corner of Decatur Street, he noticed the unusual flurry of activity farther down the block, with cops in blue uniforms, milling from police headquarters to the east end of the avenue. He corralled a Negro newspaper boy to ask about the fuss.

The kid was excited. "They found a cop down Maddox Street!" he crowed. "He been shot. I mean dead!"

*Maddox Street, off Pratt.* Joe muttered a short curse under his breath, thanked the kid, and started off again, taking a roundabout path to the corner of Moore and Decatur. He lingered there, watching the cops who were grouped around the mouth of the alley on the opposite side of the street. An ambulance from Grady Hospital had been parked at an angle to the curb, and a crowd of pedestrians, mostly colored, a number of them familiar, stood apart in little circles, pointing and whispering.

Joe spotted Albert Nichols and ambled across the street, just another curious spectator. After a minute, the detective noticed and walked over just as casually to greet him.

"What are you doing here?" he asked in a low voice.

"I got your note," Joe said.

Albert frowned. "My what?"

"It wasn't from you?"

"What are you talking about?"

"Never mind," Joe said. "Is it Logue?"

Albert nodded.

"What happened?"

"Shot twice," Albert said. "Once in the chest, once in the forehead. A small-caliber pistol at close range. He was robbed, but I think that came after. Somebody found him like that." He grimaced. "Fucking animals."

The circle of uniforms shifted and Joe caught sight of the victim, lying on his back on the alley bricks, his thick arms splayed out. Logue was dressed in his street clothes and wore no overcoat.

"Any suspects?" Joe said.

"What do you think?" Albert said, and eyed Joe narrowly. "Did you get to talk to him?"

"I didn't," Joe said. "I only had last night to track him down and he wasn't around."

"Looks like he was on his way to getting a bullet between the eyes." Albert's voice was flat. They watched the activity around the body for a silent half minute.

Joe said, "He's dead because of Jesse Williams, Al."

"You know what I can't stand?" the detective said abruptly. "I can't stand these fellows who spend a few months walking a beat and then think they're detectives."

Joe laughed shortly as Albert pulled his packet of Chesterfields from a pocket. He offered one to Joe, who refused. The detective lit his cigarette, coughed, and blew a thin cloud. "You want to play cop?" he said. "How about that theft out in Inman Park? Why don't you play cop with that one?"

Joe waited a moment before saying, "She came around the hotel last night."

The detective turned to look at him. "And?"

"And we didn't talk about it."

Albert came up with a lazy smile. "Too busy with other matters?" He puffed on his cigarette, and the smile evaporated. "You know you're out of your damn mind, messing with her right now."

Joe gave a bleak nod.

"Did she snatch those jewels?"

"I don't know." The detective treated him to a hard stare. "I don't."

"She was there and you didn't think to ask her?"

Joe avoided his friend's eyes.

"Uh-huh," Nichols said. "Well, you might want to do it. Because if it was her, it's going to bite you, too. The Captain'll see to it. That's why he brought you in yesterday."

"Yeah, that's what I figured," Joe said. "But she didn't take those goods, Al. She knows better."

"Because you taught her?"

"I explained some things."

Albert nodded slowly. "Well, maybe she just happened to be working there. It still don't look good."

Joe said, "I know."

"So?"

"So I'll talk to her."

The detective regarded him for another second, then turned his attention back to the busy scene around the body. A photographer was bending down, snapping pictures on a box camera, the flash powder popping white in the gray morning.

"What about him?" Joe said. "You know his story?"

The detective coughed into his hand, then said, "There ain't much. He was from somewhere around Smyrna. Worked as a sheriff's deputy up there for a couple years, but they couldn't put up with his drinking and ran him off."

"And he came to Atlanta?"

"That's right." Albert paused. "What I heard was that was the Captain's doing. He got him hired."

Joe was surprised. "When was that?"

"Ten or eleven years ago. He never did much of a job, but he never made any trouble, either. Never bothered anybody. He took care of the bag down here. Or he was supposed to. He couldn't ever get it right, with the drinking and all. He's just one of Jackson's boys, just waiting to get his twenty in."

"You know where he stayed?" Joe said.

Albert tapped some ash away. "He kept a room in a house on Cain Street. At the corner of Walton."

"Anything else?" Joe said.

Albert shook his head.

"It ain't much."

"That's all I have, and it's all you're gonna get," the detective said snappishly. He waved his free hand in abrupt anger. "This is police business, goddamnit!"

Joe said, "He shot Williams, Al. And now he's dead."

Nichols wasn't having any of it. "Don't you have other things to worry about?" he said. "Like what your friend Pearl Spencer was doing in that mansion right about the time a bunch of jewelry went missing." He flicked what was left of his cigarette into the gutter and made his way back into the alley to join the crowd of cops that had circled the body of Officer Logue again.

Joe got the message and turned to leave. As he walked off, he happened to glance across the street to see Lieutenant Collins slouching against the fender of an APD sedan, smoking a cigarette of his own and gazing calmly back at him. He stopped at the next corner and looked back. Collins had moved away from the automobile, crossed the street, and was stepping up to tap Albert Nichols on the shoulder.

Joe kept going, cutting between the closed-down 91 Theatre and Ike Clein's billiard hall and into Schoen Alley. He climbed the stairs and knocked, and the thin whore Martha let him in without a word of greeting.

A different pair of rounders sat at the table, drinking short glasses of whiskey and playing penny-ante poker with a dirty deck of cards. Martha looked morose and weary as she sipped from a cracked coffee cup. Her mourning had started early. There was no sign of any of those characters who had sworn to Joe that they'd come join the vigil, but then they were a late-rising crowd.

He stepped into the bedroom and found Little Jesse looking worse for the wear, his face gaunt and bone jutting, his eyes with a dead cast. Still, Jesse managed to rouse himself a little when Joe appeared, enough to ask about all the commotion out on the street. A couple fellows had been in and out jabbering about a dead cop.

Joe glanced toward the doorway to make sure no one was listening, then whispered that what he'd heard was true and that the dead cop was Logue.

Jesse was as astounded as a man in his condition could be, raising his head to croak, "Jesus! They know who done it?"

"They don't," Joe said. "Why? Do you?"

Jesse grimaced as he let himself down again. "How would I know that?" He wouldn't meet Joe's eyes. "Damn. Shot dead. That's a hell of a thing, ain't it?"

Joe agreed that it was. "So now what am I going to do?"

Jesse eyed him. "Whatchu mean?"

"The man you say shot you is dead."

"I ain't just *sayin'* it. He sho'nuf *done* it."

"Right," Joe said. "And what I'm telling you is with him gone, I've got next to nothing. Robert Clark, maybe. But that's all." He paused. "Unless there's something you haven't told me."

Little Jesse gazed at him, and Joe could see something going on in those dark eyes. Another second passed, and the gaze shifted away.

"You need to keep looking," he said. "Maybe you can find out who it was shot that damn cop."

"It ain't that simple, Jesse." Joe took a moment to settle his annoyance, then said, "Do you know something or don't you? Because I don't see where I can go from here."

"You gonna let them get away with it?" Jesse treated Joe to a resentful glance. "Yeah, who cares if some cracker cop shoots another nigger? Is that what you mean to say?"

The talk outside the door ceased. Joe felt his skin prickle and his face get warm.

Jesse came up off his pillow, his gray face flushing with sudden emotion as he jabbed with a shaking finger. "You know that cop's dead because of what he done to me, goddamnit! Now I'm layin' here fixin' to die and you say you can't do nothin' to make it right?"

Joe said, "All right. Calm down." He could sense the silence and feel the stares from the doorway. "I'll see what I can do."

"Well, I appreciate it, Joe." Wearied by the outburst, he closed his eyes. "Willie comin' 'round?" he asked momentarily.

"I'm sure he'll be by later on," Joe said.

Jesse's mouth curled into a slight smile. "I hope so. He needs to get on up here and finish my song. So I can hear it 'fore I go."

Joe heard movement and looked up to see Martha standing in the doorway, watching Jesse as if already pining his passing. Joe never got over his amazement at the kind of devotion the man in the bed inspired from his floozies.

He got up from his chair, leaving it to her.

The news about Logue had greeted Captain Jackson the minute he walked through the front doors. He listened in silence, then asked for Lieutenant Collins and was told he had gone to the crime scene. He sent a man to fetch him and when the lieutenant appeared a half hour later, the Captain waved him into his glass-walled office and asked for a report. Collins delivered the details of the crime, no frills, the way his superior liked it. Patrolman Logue was a victim of a homicide; as yet, there were no suspects and no apparent motive, other than a possible robbery.

After Collins finished, Captain Jackson didn't say a word, keeping the blank and brooding look on his face, as if he hadn't been listening. Collins had seen it before and knew to allow time for the information to sink into the Captain's brain and digest.

The second hand on the clock finished its circuit. In an absent tone, the Captain said, "Any evidence at the scene?"

"No, sir, it's clean."

"What about witnesses?"

"No, sir, not yet," Collins said. "I think it's unlikely. The shooting occurred in the dead of night. And the body wasn't discovered until early this morning."

"Who's down there now?"

"Sergeant Nichols is in charge," Collins said. "He's got—"

"Nichols?" Jackson seemed to come awake with a frown. "Who assigned him?"

"I did, sir. He's our best—"

"He's to be pulled off that duty," the Captain cut in curtly. He snatched up his fountain pen. "Take care of it. Get him off and you take the lead. We don't need it hanging around, so wrap it up."

He didn't wait for a response as he bent his head over some papers.

Detective Collins stepped out of the office with the clear understanding that while Captain Jackson didn't care much who had murdered Logue or why, he did care who was managing the investigation. The Captain didn't like Detective Sergeant Albert Nichols because Nichols was an honest cop. There was that, and his friendship with Joe Rose, a sly customer whom the Captain also despised.

As for Officer Logue, he was no loss, a hopeless drunk and sorry excuse for a police officer who would not be missed. The murder represented a problem solved.

Lieutenant Collins considered that Grayton Jackson was the coldest fish he had ever encountered, one who didn't care for much beyond his own weird and narrow purview.

Collins mulled this as he stepped into the corridor, on his way out to relieve Nichols. Glancing back through the open office door, he caught sight of the Captain hunched over his desk, his jaw set in a steely clench as he gazed at a point in space. The rectangle of a face was cracked by a strange grin that reminded

Collins of one of the ghastly comedy masks that was often carved on the facades of the theaters, paired with a tragic twin. The Captain's face displayed that same cruel humor, and Collins was glad to have an excuse to escape it.

Joe was thinking about Pearl as he walked across town, recalling Albert Nichols's testy suggestion that he talk to her about the Inman Park caper. He should have done it when he had her in his room, but Pearl, as always as slippery as a fish, had bewitched and hypnotized him and then escaped before he could get around to it.

Now, instead of heeding Albert's advice, he was ambling merrily along on his way to do exactly what the detective had warned him not to do. He was heading in the wrong direction to study the wrong crime, doing Little Jesse Williams's bidding instead of Albert Nichols's. Though even Albert would have to admit that it wasn't so simple to separate the two. The same night, within hours of each other, in fact, and Joe Rose was caught up in both. What were the odds?

Joe couldn't believe it was coincidence that the policeman who shot Little Jesse had himself been murdered not two nights later, though he also knew it wasn't a matter of revenge. The idea that some miscreant would try to even the score by killing a cop was ridiculous. Logue might have been a useless drunk, but he still wore a badge, and there was no quicker route to the gallows in the yard at Fulton Tower than to gun down an officer of the law. Jesse Williams did not have the kind of friends who would go that far. Not even his women would kill to avenge him.

The only thing that did make sense was that Logue had been murdered to keep him from talking about Little Jesse or from making another foolish try on his life. So had there been bad blood between Jesse and the drunken police officer? And if that was the case, why wouldn't Jesse say? Why beg Joe to puzzle it out and then hold back information? What secret was he willing to carry to hell or whatever his next stop would be?

The questions kept mounting, and Joe realized that Jesse had hooked him into his grim little drama, but good. That was one thing; God only knew what would happen if he left Pearl to the Captain. The two of them had him coming and going.

He was running out of time, too. He didn't know how long Jesse would last. The cops might already be well on their way to burying any evidence that might remain, right along with Officer J. R. Logue's body. If he got too close and made the wrong person nervous, he could find himself charged with a crime. The burglary in Inman Park would do nicely.

He was in such an intense brood over all this that he got turned around and had to spend some time wandering the streets just west of downtown until he found the house where the late officer J. R. Logue had kept a room.

Albert Nichols was not surprised when Lieutenant Collins stepped up, looking sheepish, to inform him that he was being pulled off Officer Logue's homicide. No more than he was when he arrived back at the detectives' section to find a stack of file folders on his desk with a note on top directing him to review the contents of all of them for any leads that might have been overlooked.

It was a detective's nightmare, a tedious scouring of other cops' work for gaps or mistakes on cases that went back years, drudgery that would produce no results. Normally, the task would have been handed to the greenest rookie, if assigned at all. The detective was being punished for sticking his nose where it didn't belong. There wouldn't be any chasing down leads on the shootings of Officer Logue and Little Jesse Williams. He was off that investigation, effective immediately; and as if to punctuate the message, whoever had carried the stack from the basement hadn't bothered to dust it off.

He stole an idle glance around the room to see the detectives at the other desks conscientiously avoiding his gaze. It was like he had a mark painted on his forehead.

Captain Jackson's office door was closed, and Albert figured that was a message meant for him, too. He was being pushed out into the cold. Not that he'd ever been welcome inside. The Captain didn't like or trust him, a backhanded compliment. It said something if you could count a tyrant like Grayton Jackson as your enemy.

The detective stared numbly at the stack of musty folders for a few moments, then got up and wandered out into the hall. Gazing out the window at the trains rolling through Union Depot, he pondered this unpleasant turn of events, for which he could thank his old friend Joe Rose.

Joe located the house by asking a dirty-faced kid who should have been in school if he knew where a copper named Logue lived.

"You mean that whiskey head?" the kid said with a smirk, and pointed down the way.

The house was white clapboard, in good shape, standing solid on the corner of Cain and Walton streets, in the neighborhood to the west and below Peachtree Street. As Joe came up on it, he saw a neat ROOM FOR RENT sign attached to one of the porch columns. He made a quick survey of the intersection, then stepped onto the porch and went inside. The door on his right bore a number 1 and a little brass plate inscribed with the word MANAGER.

Joe knocked and waited. A woman of middle years opened the door. A bit on the fleshy side and handsome in the face, she sported wire-rimmed glasses and hair that was hennaed a dark red.

"Good morning," Joe said. "I'd like to see one of your rooms."

Her gaze was cool and curious as she looked him up and down. "How long were you wanting to rent?"

"I don't want to rent," Joe said. "I just want to see inside one of them. Officer Logue's."

The landlady's brow stitched. "What the hell are you talking about?" she said, her voice coming down a notch from polite to something closer to Joe's native tongue.

"He's dead," Joe told her quickly. "They found his body this morning."

The woman put her hands to the sides of her face. "Good lord!" she said. "The poor man! What happened?"

Her tidy apartment consisted of three rooms and a bath. She led him through the living room and into the small kitchen, where she waved for him to take a seat at the table. She poured him a cup of coffee from the pot percolating on the stove then topped her own. Though Joe wasn't in the mood to sit, he knew he'd never get what he wanted if he didn't accept the courtesy.

"You going to tell me your name, friend?" she asked as she sat down.

"It's Joe," he said. "What's yours?"

"Beverly Cotter. Mrs. Though the 'mister' is long gone. Thank god." She regarded him more closely. "Joe Rose?" Surprised, he nodded. "I believe you used to be friendly with one of my girls. I never forget a face."

Joe had already figured her for a madam. She had that look about her: kindly, but with iron in her backbone. A woman engaged in the commerce of sin who would go to church every Sunday morning. It was good news. She spoke his language and would know how to keep her mouth shut. At the same time, he could only trust her so far.

"So what happened to him?" she asked him.

"He was shot to death sometime last night," Joe said.

"Where?"

"In an alley off Decatur Street."

"Do they know who did it?"

"No. That's why I'm here."

She regarded him for another somber moment. "What's your interest?" she said.

Rather than try to explain, he went into his pocket, produced a dollar bill, and laid it on the table. "I need whatever you can tell me about him," he said. "And then I need to see his room."

"I don't want any trouble."

Joe went into the pocket for another bill, and put it down alongside the first. When the landlady didn't move, he shrugged and moved to take the money back. Mrs. Cotter snatched the bills before they disappeared, then tucked them away beneath the lapel of her housedress. "I really don't know all that much about him," she said.

He had expected the dodge. "Then tell me what you do know," he said.

She thought for a moment. "He was a bachelor. He came from Smyrna. I believe he worked for the sheriff up there before he came to Atlanta. He stayed here for almost six years. He didn't cause me any problems. He went to work in the morning and didn't come back until late. I know he liked to drink. When he didn't stay out in some speak, he drank in his room."

"He have any friends?"

Mrs. Cotter smiled sadly. "Just whatever bottle he was holding."

"Women?"

When she hesitated, Joe went into his pocket and put another dollar on the table. "What's her name?"

The landlady smiled tightly as she curled her painted fingernails around the bill. "Daisy," she said. "She used to work for me when I ran the house down on the Avenue."

"That was before you went away?"

Mrs. Cotter's face got hard. "Before I got set up and sent down the river. Got on the wrong side of the wrong cop. Floyd was gone, and so I didn't have a chance. I should have had my hand slapped, but I did three years." She took a moment to calm herself. "Anyway, I knew Logue when that was his beat and I introduced the two of them. She's still down there. She's clean and lively. I never minded sending a fellow her way." She stopped to sip her coffee. "In the last year or so, I got the idea that John was sweet on her. You know, the way some fellows are with a sporting woman. Like that."

"John?"

"John Robert. He just went by J. R."

"What about family?"

"I asked him about that when he first came here, and all he would say was something about *my baby.* I tried to talk to him and he just got this look on his face. So I left it alone. I pretty much left him alone." She heaved a sigh. "And now he's dead. Well, my lord."

"All right, then," Joe said. "He goes to work and pretty much stays drunk and once a week or so, he goes to see Daisy the working girl. Do I have that right?" Beverly nodded. "No other visitors?"

He saw something pass across the landlady's eyes. "Well . . . ," she said, "someone came around just the first of last week. Monday or Tuesday. It was in the early evening. The sun hadn't been down too long. I heard voices up in his room."

"Who was it?"

"I don't know. I didn't see."

"Did you hear anything they said?"

"It wasn't that loud."

"Then what?"

"Then I heard someone on the stairs. The front door opened and banged shut. That was all. Whoever it was, was gone."

Joe kept his gaze fixed on her face. He wanted to let her know that he was wise to the fact that she had seen or heard something. No matter what she said. She had probably eavesdropped on the argument and then poked her nose through the curtains to see Logue's visitor making his exit. Still, something told him not to push it.

"Did you ask Logue about it?"

"The next day, I did. He said it was nothing."

"What do you think?"

"I don't think anything," Mrs. Cotter said.

Now Joe saw a glint in her eyes that told him she'd gone as far as she was going to go. She was letting him poke around in Logue's quarters, which meant she was playing some kind of angle of her own.

He sat back and took one more sip of his coffee to please her, then said, "I'd like to see the room now."

The landlady treated him to a sidelong glance. "You going to tell me what you're after?"

"You don't need to know that part."

"You're right, I don't," the landlady said, and stood up. "I'll get the key."

They climbed the stairs without speaking. Mrs. Cotter led him down the hall, stopped at the last door on the right, and unlocked it for him.

"I'll be fine from here," he said.

She watched him for a tense second, probably wondering if she was making a mistake. Then she said, "You hurry, hear?" and went back down the stairs, leaving him alone.

Joe pushed the door open and stood at the threshold for a moment before he went in, perking an ear for any boarders who might be listening from behind their doors. He had an extra sense about silence that he had picked up from years of creeping about houses. This one did feel just a little too still for his comfort, but he couldn't worry about that now.

He closed the door gently and found himself a cramped

space, twelve feet by fourteen, so compact that he figured he would be able to case it in a matter of minutes. An iron-framed bed took up most of the far wall. A chest of drawers with a wash-basin and mirror on top was at the foot of the bed with a ladder-back chair alongside it. One dirt-streaked window looked to the north of the city. The only adornment on the dingy plaster was a Coca-Cola calendar. Joe noticed that Saturday the fifteenth was circled in pencil.

It was a forlorn place, a lonely man's cell, the kind of quarters that always made him dispirited, and he didn't want to hang around any longer than was necessary.

Though he had forgotten most of what he had learned as a detective, he was still a pretty fair thief, and could work a room for worthwhile goods in quick order, covering all the hiding places that made people feel clever until they realized that some-one like Joe had found them.

J. R. Logue didn't have much of anything in the way of pos-sessions. There was nothing under the bed. On top of the dresser he found an ornate plate holding some loose change and a pair of cuff links. He went into the dresser drawers, poked around, and came up empty in the bottom three. The only thing out of place in the top drawer was a single photograph.

The frame was cheap, the photograph a little blurred, and the little girl posed clumsily and too far away. Yet she was a sweet-looking child with white blond hair, chubby cheeks, her whole face lit up with a smile. For all that, she looked lonely; or maybe it was that the photograph was the only personal item that J. R. Logue seemed to have kept. Joe wondered if she had been the cop's own child, a niece, or just someone he knew. She could be lost, all grown up, alive or dead.

Joe stared at her blurred face for another few seconds, then turned the frame over to check the back and found nothing hid-den there.

He returned it to where he found it, closed the drawer, and

opened the narrow closet. Three police uniforms were hanging in a row, along with some civilian shirts and trousers and a gray suit that had seen some wear. A pair of dress shoes and a pair of house slippers were arranged on the floor.

Joe closed the door, then opened it again. Pushing the hangers aside one by one, he went through the pockets of the uniforms and found them empty except for some random bits of paper, packs of safety matches, and other scraps. He moved to the suit, and went over it until he came upon something solid in one of the inside pockets. Poking with his fingers, he drew out a blue booklet with ATLANTA NATIONAL BANK embossed on the cover.

Turning to catch the window light, he flipped the pages, noting the puny sums that had been added and debited, right up to the last entry. A deposit of two hundred dollars stood out in bold relief. The lone three-figure sum was dated Friday the fourteenth. Officer Logue had made a deposit equal to a month's salary the day before he shot Little Jesse.

Joe was puzzling over this when he heard the sudden crunch of automobile tires rolling to the curb in front of the house, followed by two slams, and a few seconds later, the squeaking of the hinges on the downstairs door. A rapping hand vibrated through the house.

"Police!" a muffled voice called.

Joe didn't know if he had been tailed or if the cops were trailing behind on their own, and he wasn't about to wait around to find out. He had a minute, two at most, to get out of there.

He glanced at the window. It would be a twenty-foot drop to the ground, and even if he could take the leap, the open sash would give him away. His only choice was to get into the hallway, run to the bathroom, and hope the cops didn't check it.

He could hear it now: "What's this criminal doing in your toilet, ma'am?"

He slipped out the door, closed it gently behind him, and

padded along the hall with a silent, splayfooted thief's gait. As he crossed the landing top of the stairwell, he turned his head slightly to catch a glimpse of a tall figure standing at Mrs. Cotter's door.

Just as he reached the other side he heard the footsteps start up the stairs. As the landlady led the cop to the second floor, she did Joe and herself a favor by climbing at a slow pace and talking loudly. He reached the bathroom in four strides, only to find the door locked. No one called out when he twisted the knob; it was likely one of those houses where each tenant kept a key.

The landlady and the policeman were halfway to the landing. He had another few seconds before they'd spot him, and he was trying to figure a way to become invisible when the door of the room on his left jerked open a few inches. A young woman with a round, freckled Irish face and red marcelled hair gazed at him, her green eyes wide and startled. Joe shot a fast glance down the hall and saw the toe of the copper's shoe on the landing. He pushed past the woman and closed the door behind him, hoping to God she wouldn't let out a scream.

She didn't; instead, she stood back with her hands clasping nervously against her bosom.

"All I want is a way out," he said, holding up a palm to calm her. "That's all. But there's a copper out in the hall, if you want to call him. I won't make a fuss."

She shook her head slightly, looking scared, though not anywhere near hysterical, and Joe noticed the tiny glimmer in her eyes. She caught her breath, then gestured with a short nod of her head toward her window. Joe stepped over to see a sloped roof that covered a side porch. He slid the lock and threw up the sash. Cool air wafted inside.

The girl said, "What are you doing here?"

Before he could respond, they heard a man's voice in the hallway, followed by something back from Mrs. Cotter. If the cop knew his business, he'd be knocking on the young lady's door. Joe had to go. As he ducked out, he mouthed, *What's your name?*

"It's Molly," she whispered.

With a quick smile of thanks, he climbed the rest of the way out the window, then scrabbled to the edge of the roof, dropped on his gut, and went over the side. Once he had shinnied down the corner post to the wooden railing, he hopped to the bare ground. He cut around the back of the house and walked through the tiny yard and into the alley that led out to Cain Street. A thick oak tree gave him cover to spy on the police sedan that was parked at the curb in front of the house and the uniformed cop who was standing on the porch, looking bored.

As he stepped out from behind the tree, he caught a flash of color at a window, and looked up to see Molly standing there, peering his way. He waved at her and hurried off.

He began the climb up Cain Street toward Peachtree, feeling the tension going out of his bones. If the cops had caught him in the house, they would have taken him in for sure. If it wasn't for the red-haired Molly, he might well be on his way to jail.

As to Mrs. Cotter, there was no reason for the landlady to speak up on his behalf. Not for the three dollars he'd paid her, and not if she wanted to keep her tidy little situation. She'd done what she could.

At least he had gotten some information for his trouble. He now knew that Logue had lived a sorry drunken bachelor's sorry life. He had quaffed his whiskey and visited a Central Avenue whore named Daisy once a week. Other than that, he had stumbled fecklessly about the Atlanta streets he was hired to police and got drunk in the speaks instead of collecting from them. He had no business being an officer of the law, and yet he'd been kept on through a dozen besotted years. Somewhere in his sad drama was a child. This was the man who had set out to murder Little Jesse Williams.

Joe understood all too well that a policeman shooting a black man on a rough nighttime street was not so uncommon. When it happened, the officer simply offered a timeworn explanation.

*Why, that crazy nigger drew down on me . . .* or *I ordered him to stop, but he ran so I fired . . .*

It could have been that easy for Officer J. R. Logue, just one of those things that happened in a place where a low-down Negro's life didn't count for much.

Joe stopped on the corner of Spring Street to watch the bustling traffic for a few moments. He wished it was as simple as that.

Now there was another twist to the story. Joe dug Logue's bankbook out of his coat pocket and opened it. He stared at the page where the last deposit was noted as if trying to decipher some message there. Then he put it away. When the traffic passed and he started walking again, the muddy stream in which he'd been wading suddenly cleared a bit.

Logue had been paid to kill Jesse Williams. That was the reason for the visitor coming to the house and for the two-hundred-dollar deposit. When Logue failed that like he failed everything else, he had to be eliminated before he could open his loose drunkard's mouth or, worse, create more of a mess trying to finish the job.

Joe slowed his steps as his thoughts jumped ahead. What if getting rid of Logue was part of the plan from the beginning? He was a worthless drunk with no family or friends, and he wouldn't be missed, except by Daisy the prostitute and the little girl in the photograph. Maybe.

Huffing up the steep incline, Joe felt like he had just peeled back the skin on something, and realized that he wouldn't be able to walk away. The hook was set, but good. He'd gone too far and would need to finish this; or at the least, get something he could give to Albert Nichols. That would mean trying to pry loose whatever Jesse was holding. It would mean tracking down the invisible Robert Clark and the sporting girl named Daisy who worked in a house on Central Avenue. It would mean paying a visit to Molly to see if she could tell him what the landlady wouldn't.

Finally, he'd have to do it all in a hurry and without raising sand. All he needed was for the Captain to find out what he was up to, and if he knew Willie McTell at all, the word was already on the street.

*Joe Rose is bound to find out what happened to Little Jesse, y'all.*

That's right, Joe Rose, the *detective.*

By the time he reached the crest of the slope and turned south on Peachtree Street, he was so overheated by the climb and his agitation at being suckered in by a sharp like Jesse Williams that he took off his overcoat and slung it over his shoulder.

He had gone a block south and just crossed over Ellis Street when a police sedan pulled to the curb a few paces ahead of him. He slowed his steps and peered inside to see Lieutenant Collins slouched in the passenger seat and the uniformed cop from Mrs. Cotter's porch at the wheel. Keeping his expression blank, he sidled to the car just as Collins rolled the window down.

"Good morning, Mr. Rose," the lieutenant said. He took a moment to study Joe's face. "You look like you're about to pass out, sir." He smiled his boyish smile, though now Joe caught the sharp glint behind it. He wondered if they had been on his tail or had just been driving along Peachtree and spotted him. For all he knew, they'd been dogging his tracks since he walked away from Maddox Street.

As if to echo that thought, Collins said, "Didn't I see you at the crime scene this morning? Talking to Detective Nichols?"

"Yeah, that was me."

"You know him from Baltimore, is that correct?"

Joe nodded, pondering where Collins had picked up the information.

The cop's brow stitched. "What business did you have down there?"

"I was passing by," Joe explained lamely.

"On your way to Schoen Alley?"

Joe said, "That's right." And where had the lieutenant gotten *that*?

"You walked a little too far."

"Well, I saw the crowd . . ." He shrugged.

The detective cocked his head, waiting for something, and Joe realized he wasn't going to get out from under that gimlet stare. While he didn't exactly trust Collins, he figured at this point he had more to gain than lose by speaking up.

"That shooting that happened on Courtland Street," he said in a voice too low for the patrolman to hear. "The one I asked the Captain about yesterday."

Collins didn't respond for a few seconds. Then he opened his door, put a foot on the running board, and stepped out to his full height, his hands jammed in his coat pockets.

"You talking about the Negro?" he said. "What's his name? Williams?"

"That's right."

"What about it?"

"The way he tells it, it was Officer Logue who shot him that night."

Collins stared hard at him, though he didn't look at all surprised. Joe wasn't sure he'd even heard. The lieutenant turned and bent down to address his driver.

"Go down and park around the corner on Houston," he said. "I want to stop for lunch at Lulu's. I'll be there in a few minutes." He closed the door and stepped up onto the sidewalk. They watched as the driver put the sedan in gear and pulled into traffic.

"Nice day like this, I feel like walking," Collins commented, and started off. Joe pulled on his coat and trailed along. They strolled halfway down the next block before the detective spoke up. "So Mr. Williams says Logue shot him."

"That's what he said."

"And you believe him?"

Joe hesitated for a second, then said, "The man's dying. He might already be dead. He's got no reason to lie."

Collins's eyes flicked his way. "There's always a reason to lie, Mr. Rose."

Joe didn't know what to say to that, and kept quiet.

"He mention anything else?"

"Nothing that makes any sense," Joe said. "He's been delirious about half the time."

"Morphine?"

"Quite a bit of it."

Collins said, "So you just didn't happen to be down on Maddox Street today."

"No. I heard what happened."

"And that's why you tossed Logue's room just now."

Joe didn't ask if Mrs. Cotter had given him up, if he had left a trail, or if Collins had just surmised. It didn't matter. "That's right."

The detective eyed him. "You know what I could do to you for pulling a trick like that?"

"Yeah, I know," Joe said dolefully.

"You want to guess what Captain Jackson would do if he knew?" Collins added.

Joe shook his head.

"The last time I looked, you were not a policeman," the lieutenant went on, his voice edgy with irritation. "So you got no business nosing around a crime happened down off Decatur Street. Especially a serious crime like the shooting of an officer of the law. That ain't smart at all."

Joe was aware of this, too, and nodded.

Collins switched to a more conciliatory tone. "If I was walking around in your shoes, I'd be more concerned with this other problem," he said. "I mean that burglary out in Inman Park. Because that's going to be trouble for someone if that doesn't get fixed in a hurry. I believe the Captain's about ready to pick a likely suspect and make a case, and that will be the end of it. Somebody's going to do a stretch of hard time."

"Well, that ain't going to get the goods back," Joe said, suddenly irked. It was the second time this day he'd been lectured on the same subject. What was it to him? He didn't steal the goddamn things.

Collins gave him a cool look. "You hear what I just said? It's going to be a whole lot easier on everyone if we settle this." He took a few steps to regain his calm, then stopped, reached into the pocket of his overcoat, and produced a pack of Pall Malls. He snapped a cigarette into his mouth and dug around some more until he found a match, which he sparked off his thumbnail. He didn't offer the pack to Joe, in case there were any illusions about the two of them being on equal footing.

"Well?" The cop tilted his head in the general direction of Walton Street. "Did you find anything down there?"

Joe said, "Down . . . ? Oh. There wasn't much time. You came along right behind me. So no, I didn't."

Collins gazed at him with a faint shadow of amusement passing over his face. "How did you get out?" he said.

"Window."

The detective didn't ask which window. Gazing at the burning ember of his cigarette, he said, "Why do you care who shot Mr. Williams anyway?" He smiled. "He kin to you?"

Joe smiled at this stab at humor. He didn't have an answer Collins would understand. Then he thought, *what the hell.* He was already in too far.

"He's dying," he said. "He asked me to see if I could find out what happened. Why it happened, I mean. Why Logue shot him."

"He asked you because you were a policeman once?"

Joe nodded. "Partly, yeah."

"But not a detective."

"I worked for Pinkerton."

Collins's eyebrows arched in derision, and Joe shrugged. They started walking again. The lieutenant pursed his lips thoughtfully and said, "You have some interesting friendships, sir. Mr. Williams has got a sheet of arrests from here to the sidewalk. He's run games and women. Not exactly what we consider a law-abiding citizen. Whatever he told you, he's likely lying. Or he knows more than he's telling."

"Maybe so," Joe said.

Collins dragged on his cigarette and blew the smoke from the side of his mouth. "There were no other witnesses to the crime?"

"Which crime?"

"Mr. Williams's shooting. Isn't that what we're talking about?"

Joe thought about it and said, "No, just after it was over. This blind Negro singer came along."

Collins smiled. "That's not much of a witness."

Joe said, "You'd be surprised."

"He's the only one?"

"I didn't see anyone else."

The detective caught the dodge, but didn't press it. Gazing off down the street, he said, "If you have any information that relates to Officer Logue's murder, you'd be wise to share it. And I don't mean with your friend Albert Nichols. With me." He took hold of Joe's coat sleeve, halting him in his tracks. "And just so you understand," he said. "I don't tell Captain Jackson everything I hear."

Joe kept the vacant look on his face, in spite of this odd twist. "I don't have anything right now," he said.

"But if you do?"

"Then I'll tell you," Joe said. "Only I don't want—"

"No one will know where I got it," Collins said quickly. He eyed Joe. "You sure there isn't something you want to talk about now?"

Joe thought the bankbook in his pocket felt like a brick. "No, not now," he said.

They walked on until they reached the intersection of Houston Street. Collins paused for a few seconds to eye Joe speculatively, then said, "Be careful, Mr. Rose. Watch where you go and what you do."

The way the words were spoken, Joe understood that the lieutenant also knew some things that he wasn't sharing, and it gave him pause. Collins smiled his easy smile, then turned away and crossed the street without looking back.

# EIGHT

It was midafternoon when Sweet shuffled into the house, sagging from eight hours on his feet. He took off his coat, hung it on the peg, and stepped into the kitchen, where he found Pearl sitting at the table, wrapped in a silk kimono and drinking coffee. A book lay open and facedown next to her elbow. Sweet guessed it wasn't a Bible.

In a brooding silence, he took the bottle of whiskey down from the cupboard and he poured himself a small glass, a rare event. Time was, liquor made him do crazy things. Now it just eased his mind a little. He sat down at the table, his clothes reeking of fried food, and took a tentative sip.

"You workin' tonight?" he asked.

"Ain't had any calls," Pearl said.

"Maybe you oughta call them."

"I've got something else to do," she said, and absently started pushing her fingers into her dark curls.

Sweet's broad face creased with displeasure as he eyed his sister's languid pose. She looked like a hussy. He said, "You know they's lots of honest work out there."

"I'm sure that's right."

Another few seconds, then Sweet said, "People are talkin'."

"Talking about what?"

"About how you was at the scene of a crime, that's what."

"Some folks don't know when to shut their damn mouths is all."

"They's gonna be trouble," Sweet said.

"What trouble?" Pearl said, giving it right back.

"What was you doin' out there? Of all the places you coulda been."

Pearl's brow stitched. "You know something, say so."

Sweet said, "I know you got yourself in a corner, and ain't no Joe Rose gonna be able to help you out of it, either." He wrapped a thick hand around his glass like he meant to crush it. "You can't be bringin' this kind of shit down on our house, Pearl. I mean it. You can't."

For a moment, their gazes crossed like swords. Then Pearl's softened with affection and she smiled impishly.

Sweet, frowning, said, "What?"

"Sarah Everett brought an apple pie over," Pearl said. "Smells good. I'm pretty sure it ain't for me."

Sweet tried not to smile. Pearl unfolded from the chair and went to the cupboard to cut him a slice of Sarah Everett's pie, gently kissing his forehead as she passed by.

May Ida Jackson stood gazing out the kitchen window of her frame house on Plum Street, watching the bare trees and the blue cloudless sky and thinking about a boy she had known a long time ago. He'd been sweet and kind and though she could still picture his face, she couldn't recall his name at all.

She remained lost in her reverie until the running water sloshed over the edge of the sink to splatter the linoleum and her house slippers.

She murmured, "Oh, my!" at the wet mess she had made, and fumbled to pull the stopper and turn off the faucet. She studied the small puddle at her feet as if she had never seen such a thing before. In fact, it had happened a dozen times.

She stepped out of the slippers and went off to fetch a towel from the bathroom, which she dropped on the kitchen floor. Momentarily, her gaze wandered back to the window, and she noticed something about the shape of one of the trees . . . it was like a hand reaching to heaven . . . she floated away on that image, another wisp on the breeze. A sedan crossed her line of vision, the dark shape moving slowly along the street. When she blinked again, it was gone.

May Ida sometimes missed parts of days as she wandered in and out of her little fogs. She would somehow waft from a period of crystal clarity into a haze and not realize it until she reappeared and found herself doing something: standing before a mirror, tending to her flowers in the garden, handling dry goods in a store. She wouldn't remember how she had gotten there, only something had guided her unerringly along. It had been that way for as long as she could remember, going back to the dreamy mist of her childhood.

Sometimes it was a light absence, as if she had stepped aside for a quick moment. Other times she was sure she had disappeared for what must have been days, only to find a single minute had slipped away and that her husband—the *Captain*—was staring at her with that face of his as he waited for her to respond to whatever he had said. Of course, she had missed it entirely, inflaming him all the more. Then he would give her his disgusted look.

At first, she tried to recover, only to find that he had already lost patience and his lip was curled in disdain. He wasn't really interested in anything she had to say, anyway. Nothing she did had ever pleased him. She was just something that was there, another piece of furniture. Realizing this made her own bile rise. If he, with his icy arrogance, knew how many men she'd entertained, and how many more she would have in the days and weeks and months to come, it would drive him berserk. It made her feel like an actress in a play, and delighted her.

She held the secret of the May Ida who lived inside and carried on like a harlot when a mood came upon her, putting out a scent that drew gentlemen like bees to honey. May Ida understood in a vague way that she was supposed to feel shame over behaving like a bitch in heat. In truth, she was fascinated by the carnal stranger who inhabited so much of her waking life. The woman had power.

She also knew that if she had been born male, her conduct would be applauded with admiring winks and lewd snickers. A woman acting that way was worse than a whore, because at least the strumpets got paid for their favors. She accepted these facts without bitterness; it was the way of a world run by men.

She sometimes imagined that the minister at their Baptist church tailored his fire-belching sermons around her wickedness. She could have been the star in the lurid tales of sin that he spun with such relish. But he was just another fool talking about what he didn't know. Still, she didn't dislike him. He seemed kind enough when he wasn't in his pulpit.

Though she had moments when she sensed something dark and frightening lurking under her skin, those were few and far between and over as abruptly as they began. The terror of her nightmares was always washed away by the morning's light.

As a young girl, she had been taken to doctors intent on finding out what was *wrong* with her. Her behavior baffled them, which baffled her. She didn't understand. She was a cheerful person who greeted her days with a smile. She was never cruel or spiteful. She was clean and did not drink whiskey or take potions or powders to relieve her miseries.

Still, they said she was ill and that the cure for what ailed her was a marriage to Grayton Jackson. She was agreeable; she had always imagined that one day she would be a happy bride. That dream died quickly, just as soon as it became clear that instead of a loving husband she was betrothed to a harsh, bitter, cold-blooded crab of a man. So she reopened the doors she had closed, reluctantly at first, then with her old abandon.

She had long wished that there might be one fellow who could satisfy her completely, but as yet she hadn't met him, and so she went about her delightful adventures. And the Captain never knew; or maybe knew and didn't care.

For all her regular vacancies of mind and her crazy compulsions, May Ida was not stupid. She had periods of clarity so sharp and brilliant that she surprised herself, her vigilance honed by escaping detection by her police officer husband.

Over the past two weeks she had begun sensing something different from his usual grim and caustic self. His tone had changed. When he was at home, he talked to himself more than usual, even laughing, as if listening to some private joke. While he wasn't any kinder to her, he did seem to notice her now and then, if only as an audience.

Then it began to dawn on her what had him so absorbed, and she wondered if she could steal it and then deflate or even destroy him, in retribution for his absent cruelties. If she couldn't do him in with a gun, knife, or vial of poison, perhaps she could inflict pain that was all the more excruciating for him and that much sweeter for her.

It seemed a delicious prospect, and she stood at the sink, rolling it around in her mind and musing on the various angles, until she heard the colored girl knock at the door and went to let her in.

By one o'clock, all the hopefuls had been in and out, and they had enough to fill the disks they had brought along. Mr. Purcell planned to stop for lunch, then begin recording. Of the two dozen acts waiting in the lobby, half of them might pass muster with New York. Of those, two or three had a chance of turning a dollar, and one might become a known name.

Mr. Purcell was going over his notes from the morning when Jake walked into the room to tell him that there was a Negro out on the sidewalk who had been waiting with the others since breakfast.

The older man stepped to the window and looked out on Walton Street to see a well-dressed man holding a large guitar.

"He's the only one?" He had been wondering why he hadn't seen a single Negro face all day.

"I think everybody figured we only wanted the hillbilly music," Jake explained.

Purcell grunted with annoyance. It was true that he had forgotten to specify. He didn't think he needed to in a city like Atlanta.

"Isn't he the same one we saw on the street?"

"That's him," Jake said.

"Did you hear him play?"

"I did. And I think he might be the best of the lot."

"Really?" Mr. Purcell said. The younger man nodded quickly. "Well, what's he doing out there?"

"They put him out of the lobby."

"Who did?"

"The desk clerk. He says the manager told him to. So he chased him outside."

"Well, go down and bring him up."

"I can't. They don't allow Negroes in the rooms unless they're working."

Mr. Purcell looked at him, his face pinching in distaste. "Don't allow . . ."

He understood this sort of thing perfectly, because his family's original name was not Purcell at all, but Perzel. He, like his young assistant, was a Jew, and was well aware of the Frank case, which had ended with the lynching of an innocent man. He knew

passions still ran high in these parts. The Klan held meetings outside the city at Stone Mountain, burning crosses by the dozens as
they swore their hatred for Negroes, Jews, Catholics, Arabs, Ital-
ians, Greeks, and whoever else offended them.

The whole matter exasperated him. It was the third decade of
the twentieth century, after all. "Go find Mr. Morgan, please,"
he said. "I want to talk to him."

Jake was back with the manager at his side.

"There's a fellow outside on the sidewalk who came to audition for us," Purcell said. "He waited all morning in the lobby.
Before we could get to him, your desk clerk put him out. Now
the clerk says we can't have him up here."

"Because he's colored," Jake Stein put in.

The hotel manager smiled for a quick instant, looking from
one to the other, as if his guests were making some kind of an
odd joke. They were Yankees; it might be their idea of humor.
The smile went away when he realized they weren't doing anything of the kind.

His voice caught a little when he said, "It's hotel policy not
to permit Negroes to the upper floors of the hotel, unless they're
in service."

"I heard that," Mr. Purcell said. "I'd like you to make an
exception."

"I'm afraid that wouldn't be possible," Mr. Morgan said,
blanching. "If the other guests noticed . . . or someone from . . .
uh . . ." He swallowed nervously. "I'm sorry, I'm not per—"

"We've taken a room and one of your suites, and in the winter," Purcell said brusquely. "And I believe every table in your
restaurant has been filled since it opened this morning."

"Yes, that's true, and we certainly appreciate all the business,
of course . . ." The manager's Adam's apple bobbed. "It's just
not . . . not possible for me to allow that. The fact is I could lose
my job."

Mr. Purcell eyed Mr. Morgan wisely. "Are you a member of the Ku Klux Klan, sir?"

The manager's back straightened and his face flushed with color. "No, sir, I am not." After another moment's hesitation, he said, "But of course the owners are."

Mr. Purcell stared through his spectacles for a long moment. Then he said, "Thank you for your time." He closed the door.

"I'll be in the office if you need anything further," Mr. Morgan called from the hall, his voice faint.

Purcell turned to his assistant. "What's the colored fellow's name?"

"It's Willie. Mc-something. McTell, I think."

"He's that good?"

The younger man was emphatic. "He is, yes, sir."

"Then let's bring him up here." He winked, as furtive as a spy. "One way or another."

With a wide grin, Jake went for their coats.

But when they got outside, the blind singer was gone. The desk clerk's face reddened as he explained that he had apparently given up and left. Asked where he might have gone, Sidney said there was no telling.

Mr. Purcell's face flushed and he raised his voice as he opined that *no telling* wasn't much help.

"I can tell you that them colored musicians is likely to stay over that way," Sidney said, pointing in a general easterly direction. "You got Decatur Street and you got Auburn Avenue and they got all kind of colored places. He could be anywhere down around there."

Purcell looked at Jake, sighed, and turned away.

At that moment, six blocks distant, Willie was climbing the steps to Jesse's rooms, feeling the weight of disappointment lingering in his gut.

When the young man from Columbia came downstairs, and

Willie asked that his name be added to the list, he caught the stutter of hesitation, a signal of surprise that was easily read. He was the only colored person in the lobby who wasn't carrying a tray or a mop. The young fellow wrote down his name, as polite as could be, then introduced himself as Jake Stein, and said it would be an hour or more before they could get to him.

Willie would have waited all day for his chance, but once the crowd in the lobby had thinned, the desk clerk wasted no time in telling him to move outdoors. He explained that he was on the list. The clerk insisted that he leave, though he could tell by his tone that he didn't feel good about it. Several of the other musicians grumbled about the treatment, and yet no one called him back.

Willie had been asked to make records before, but they only wanted coon songs, and he wasn't willing. He wanted to select from his own song bag, the kind of material he'd picked up out on the road: blues, ragtime numbers, even some of the tunes that were popular during the war, all of them done up his own way, along with some songs he'd written on his own. He believed his were a match for any white man's and better than most. No one he'd ever heard had anything like his booming twelve-string and sweet, churchified tenor. So he deserved a chance to record on the Columbia label, and was willing to stand out in the cold for as long as it took to do it. If nothing else, he might catch one of the record people stepping out for lunch.

He had been on the sidewalk a cold hour and had two dollars in nickels and dimes dropped into the box of the Stella when a kid came along with a message from one of the women tending to Little Jesse. Jesse was going down fast, the boy whispered, and he'd been asking for Willie and Joe Rose.

Realizing he was giving up his chance, Willie dug into his pocket and gave the kid a dime to carry the message on to Joe Rose at the Hampton Hotel. Then he started south on Walton Street.

———

When he stepped into Little Jesse's bedroom, he understood that his troubles were nothing. He could smell that whatever had infected Jesse down in his gut was emitting an odor so sour and heavy that it stung his nose. The air in the room was close, as more people had gathered around with the word that the end might be near.

There was a rustle of motion and a murmur of voices as they made way for Willie and his guitar.

Jesse's breath was low as the blind man settled into the chair in the near corner. "Hey, Willie . . ." He barely opened his eyes. "You got my song done yet?"

"Almost." Willie sat down, cradled the box on his lap, and brushed his fingers across the twelve-string. "Don't worry. I'm getting right up on it."

The faintest ghost of a smile curled Jesse's lips. "I believe I can wait a little bit longer," he said.

Joe Rose was not at his hotel, so the kid left the message with the man at the desk.

After Joe watched Lieutenant Collins cross to Houston Street and step into Lulu's, where the driver was waiting, he turned around and went the way he came at a quick pace, cutting down James Street to West Cain. If he'd had any doubts about being in the middle of something, the lieutenant had settled them during their five-minute stroll along Peachtree Street.

When he reached the corner, he scratched some gravel off the ground and tossed a tiny bit at the second-story window, the oldest trick around. A few seconds passed, the curtains parted, and he was looking up at a freckled Irish face. He saw Molly's sudden smile, even in that dim light. With a quick glance up and down the street, he hurried onto the porch, stepped inside, and climbed the stairs, making barely a sound. She was waiting on the landing. She went ahead of him down the hall and into her room.

"Why didn't you come in the way you left?" she said as she closed the door behind him. He noticed the brogue in her voice.

Joe smiled and shrugged, and spent a moment doffing his cap, straightening his coat, and giving his host a closer look. Her deep green eyes were merry over freckled cheeks. He thought she looked like nothing so much as one of the paintings of lasses that appeared on calendars. She was short, not fat but sturdy, more like a shop girl than some hoity miss who would put on airs; the type who wouldn't dream of opening the door for a stranger ducking the cops, in other words. All in all, she presented a kind picture, and yet there was something just a little cunning and watchful in her expression.

"Is your last name Malone?" he asked her. "Or Maguire?"

She shook her head slightly. "It's O'Connell."

"Joe Rose," he said. He went into one of his inside coat pockets and drew out a gold cross on a gold chain. "This is for you," he said. "To thank you for your kindness."

"You didn't need to do that," she said. "This wouldn't by chance be a hot item, would it?"

"No, it's not." This was a lie; it was one of those stolen trinkets he kept on hand for just such instances.

Molly accepted the charm with a smile that told him she wasn't fooled. Laying it aside, she said, "You didn't come back just to give me a gift, did you?"

"No," Joe said. "I want to talk to you about Officer Logue."

"Ah, I thought you might." She gave a sad shake of her head. "Mrs. Cotter told me what happened. My sweet Jesus." She sighed, then gestured to one of the chairs arranged on either side of the small table in the corner. "Would you like to take off your coat?"

He removed the coat, draped it over the back of the chair, and sat down, thinking how easily she was treating a stranger walking into her room and her life. He was in for another surprise.

"Is it too early in the day for me to offer you a drink of Irish whiskey?" she said. "It's the real thing. I'll tell you, I could do with it."

No man in his right mind would turn down such a treat, any time of the day. Not that Molly waited for an answer before stepping to her closet to open the door and retrieve a squat bottle and two short glasses. She stood at the table and poured, and Joe caught the scent of peat and smoky oak. Compared to the rotgut passing as liquor in Atlanta these days, it smelled like perfume, and in the light through her curtains, gave off a deep amber glow.

Once Molly was settled in the opposite chair, they tapped glasses in a small toast. Joe passed his whiskey under his nose and sighed with pleasure.

Molly took a sip and gazed idly into her glass, her face falling into a mask of distress. "I couldn't believe it. He was a nice fellow, mostly. He was always kind to me." Her brogue was getting deeper by the word.

Joe said, "How well did you know him?"

Molly tipped her glass this way and that. "When I first moved here in September, he came knocking on my door. He was very friendly. Drunk, of course. I didn't often see him sober. Now and then he'd come around to talk."

"Talk about what?"

"Some about his life. Where he grew up and like that. A bit about his police work and that sort of thing. Nothing very interesting." Her eyes shifted slyly. "He did let me know that anything I wanted, he could provide. Jewelry, dresses, whiskey, anything like that. All I had to do was ask."

Joe wasn't surprised. That sort of merchandise was an extra benefit to a street cop's low-paying job.

"I didn't take him up on it," Molly went on in a cool voice. "Because I knew I'd end up paying for them, one way or another. Isn't that how it works?"

Joe mused for a moment, thinking this young lady was not such an innocent, and most likely had a story of her own.

"Other than that, he was nice as could be," she said. "Sometimes he got sad when he was drinking. Lonely-like. You know how some people get that way."

Joe said, "Did you notice anything different about him lately?"

She said, "I think something was bothering him the last couple weeks. He didn't talk as much when I saw him in the hall. Just hello, and that was all. Then that last time I saw him was when he came to tell me about leaving."

Joe was surprised. "He said he was leaving? When did he tell you that?"

"It was maybe two weeks ago. He came knocking and said he had some news. He told me he was moving out. Said it would be soon, but he hadn't told Mrs. Cotter. And he didn't want me to say anything to her."

"Did he say where he was going?"

"No. He acted all mysterious about that. Just *away*. That's all he'd say."

"That's all?"

She pursed her lips thoughtfully. "Well, he did talk about having it his way. 'Now I'm going to have things my way,' or something like that. Does that help at all?"

"It might." Joe drank off some more of his whiskey, putting this last bit of news next to what he already had. He thought of something else.

"I found a picture in his room. A little blond girl."

Molly's eyes got tragic. "I know about that. He showed me."

"Who is she?"

"His daughter," Molly told him. "He talked about her sometimes. Said he was going to get her back. He'd call her 'my baby.' Like that." She sighed. "I don't know where she is or anything else about her. And now he's gone. So sad."

Joe mulled this new information. Between Mrs. Cotter and Molly, this man he'd never known was beginning to take on the trappings of a life. "Did he ever talk about a woman named Daisy?"

Molly frowned. "Maybe so. I really don't remember."

"Anything else come to mind?" he asked her.

"No, that's all," she said. "I try to not get too much in other people's business, if you know what I mean." She paused for a few somber seconds then regarded him curiously. "Why are you doing this? What's he to you?"

Joe shifted in his chair. "Two nights before he was killed, he shot a fellow on Courtland Street. A Negro named Jesse Williams."

"A criminal?"

"It wasn't an arrest, if that's what you mean. He just shot the man."

Molly came up with a troubled frown. "That doesn't sound like something he would do."

"Well, he did it. But I don't think it was his idea. I think someone put him up to it. I think he was paid to do it. Maybe the person who was in his room, arguing with him, what was it, last week?"

Molly nodded quickly. "I heard the voices when I came out of my bath. Mr. Logue and another man. I heard the door open and then footsteps on the stairs. A little bit later, I saw John in the hall. He didn't look so well, and I asked him if he was all right. He got real quiet for a little while, and then he started talking about how a person sometimes had to do things he didn't want to. He said something else about it not being fair, but that he was in a corner. I asked him if that was what all that commotion was about and he said, 'Never mind about that.' Then he said he was doing me a favor not telling me."

"That's all?"

"Until I heard what happened, yes." She took another small sip from her glass. "If you don't mind me asking, this Negro fellow, was he a friend of yours?"

Joe said, "See, I started this and . . . it's . . ." He stopped, began again. "Actually, he was a pimp and a rounder. He cheated at cards and he ran women. That sort. But with all that, he wasn't a bad fellow. He was just a sport, making his way. He never hurt anyone that I know of."

"But someone wanted him dead?"

Joe nodded. "And I think it was whoever was arguing with Mr. Logue that night."

"Oh, my . . ." Her gaze flitted for a moment. "Maybe I shouldn't have told you about that. I don't even know who you are."

"You know me well enough to let me in your room," Joe said.

Molly smiled shyly. "You don't scare me, that's all."

Joe sipped the rest of his whiskey, savoring it. When she didn't move to refill his glass, he rose to his feet and pulled on his coat, musing on his own strange behavior. Molly was pretty and full-bodied, the kind of woman he liked, and yet he was making no move to get her from upright to horizontal. His life was already too complicated.

She stood up, too, studying him gravely. "You have such worries on your mind. Is it all because of the Negro?"

"No, that's not all of it." He sat down again and heard himself saying, "There was a burglary at a mansion in Inman Park on Saturday night. And the police have been leaning on me to find the person who did it."

"Why you?"

"I happen to know people in that line of work," he said carefully.

"Because you're one of them?" It wasn't really a question.

"Well, I have been," he admitted.

Molly watched him steadily. "Is there by chance a woman mixed up in it?" she said. Joe raised an eyebrow. "You have that look about you."

He laughed shortly. She didn't miss anything. "It happens there is," he said.

She nodded with sympathy. "Well, I'm sorry for your troubles."

He mused for a moment on the strange turn in the exchange, and then got to his feet, saying, "If you think of anything else about Mr. Logue, I keep a room at the Hampton on Houston Street. You can send a message there."

Now she eyed him with sprightly humor. "So, you're quite the gentleman, aren't you?"

"Excuse me?"

"You didn't try anything fresh with me," she said. "What kind of sporting man are you?"

Joe felt his face getting red. "What do you know about sports?"

"Oh, Mrs. Cotter tells me stories." She lowered her voice. "Do you know she used to be a madam in one of those houses? I'm learning all sorts of things."

Again, he caught a hint of something devious and thought to pry a bit more. Instead, he simply thanked her for her time and went for the door before he did something stupid.

She called his name and he stopped. "You can come back and visit again, if you like," she said.

He couldn't read her expression. Though guileless, something odd was traversing her eyes and he got a sudden sense that she was hiding in that room. Perhaps she was on the run from a bad man or some unnamed crime. She could be escaping the troubles across the water in Ireland. He'd come across a few fellows like that in his travels, never a woman, but who knew? She was another puzzle, the next chapter in the mystery of the female gender, one he'd never solve.

He slipped out the door, along the hall, and down the stairs, all without making a sound. As soon as he found himself on the street, he looked back and saw her silhouette in the window and raised a hand to wave. She didn't move, and he realized that she couldn't see him for the sun in her eyes.

One of the fellows who had been lounging around the kitchen came in to whisper in Willie's ear. The blind man asked the sport to repeat it. He spent a few moments watching Little Jesse, who had dropped into another tortured sleep. He got up to speak briefly to Martha, then pulled on his overcoat, slung the Stella over his shoulder, and headed outdoors.

He found the two men standing on the Decatur Street corner, Jake Stein and an older fellow who introduced himself as George Purcell, both of them with nervous Yankee accents. Each man took his hand and shook it, something a white man rarely did with a Negro, and Willie felt a spike of worry that someone might have seen.

Mr. Purcell was in charge, and he didn't waste any time stating their business. Willie was stunned with pleasure and agreeable, though it wouldn't be a simple matter. It would have to be handled cleverly. He told the pair that he would make his own way to the Dixie, describing the service entrance around back, accessible from Fairlie Street, and explaining exactly what had to be done. Murmuring agreement, Purcell and his young assistant shook his hand a second time, and went on ahead.

Twenty minutes later, Mr. Purcell approached the front desk of the hotel and engaged Sidney the clerk and the house detective, who happened to be loitering nearby, in a frank discussion that was entirely fabricated, some nonsense about the annoyance of stragglers not showing up on time and still wanting to audition.

The detective, bored to his socks, made a big deal of describing all the various ways to keep that sort from causing trouble. Mr. Morgan had passed the word about the guests' unhappiness over the Negro singer, and they were eager to be of service.

Meanwhile, Jake Stein was paying one of the colored bell-boys fifty cents to clear a path and escort Willie through the alley entrance of the building and into the freight elevator. In another few minutes, the door had closed on the fourth-floor suite with the blind man safely inside.

Once Mr. Purcell finished his little charade and made his way upstairs, they went right to work. There would be no need for an audition; anyway, there wasn't time. Willie asked if the first song could be for practice, and Mr. Purcell agreed, then turned and winked at Jake, signaling the younger man to go ahead and turn the machine on, anyway. If he thought the singer wouldn't catch this, he was mistaken. Willie could hear the flutter of a butterfly's wings at twenty paces. To him, the switch being flipped sounded like a firecracker going off.

It was over in less than a half hour, and Mr. Purcell knew he had something. Giddy with excitement, he went about hustling the singer out of the hotel the same way he had come in. Though this time, it didn't go quite as smoothly. As they hurried along the hallway, they failed to notice a guest who had opened his door and saw the young Negro carrying a guitar and plainly not hired help, in the company of two white men.

Every city had a tenderloin, and Central Avenue was Atlanta's. Crossing over Hunter Street in a bleached afternoon sun, Joe failed to see much evidence of the crackdown he'd been hearing about during his travels. Maybe the police had other things to do that afternoon. It was a weekday, and that accounted for some of the calm. Friday and Saturday were the nights that raised the hackles, with the rowdy noise, drunkenness, and fighting, all amid a cascade of illicit commerce.

Now it was generally quiet. Joe had always thought it interesting that all the day-to-day iniquity along the avenue went on within sight of the second-floor windows of Girls High School, and no one seemed to mind. He couldn't imagine what those innocent young ladies thought when they gazed and beheld the scarlet trade in full flush.

He had spent enough time on those blocks to know the house Mrs. Cotter had mentioned. It was on the east side of the street, just north of Mitchell. He found the address, knocked on the door, and was ushered in by a squat fellow who looked like he might have been a prizefighter at one time, his face a map of battered geography. Joe asked for Daisy and was told she was busy with a customer. He was invited to have a seat and wait. He said he'd rather come back in a little while.

He wandered down the avenue to Fair Street, then turned around and came up the other side, paying little attention to his surroundings as his thoughts drifted to another drunken cop, this one a Philadelphia detective named Glass, who regularly opined his long-held belief that if a coincidence occurred, it was rare. When two things happened in conjunction, he asserted, it was no accident. The detective liked to talk especially about the coincidence of a man being out of town when his hag of a wife met with a fatal accident.

"You know how many times that's happened and the party was innocent?" he inquired. "Once in a blue fucking moon. In other words, right there next to never."

Joe had taken that lesson with him, one of a few he learned while policing that he could still use. And so he couldn't ignore the idea nibbling at the corners of his thoughts that the Payne mansion burglary and the shooting of Little Jesse were somehow tied together. Glass might have puzzled it out, but he was long dead, the bottle taking him as everyone assumed it would. Maybe his old friend Albert Nichols or his new pal Lieutenant Collins would step forward, but he wouldn't hold his breath for either one.

When he arrived back at the house, the bouncer told him Daisy was free now.

"Upstairs, second door on the left," the pug said. "It's two dollars. You got fifteen minutes."

Joe smiled, thinking of this boxcar of a man acting as the madam of the house. He felt the fellow's eyes on him as he made his way up the stairs to knock on Daisy's door.

"Come on in," a woman's voice called.

He stepped in to find her standing by a window that was filmed with brown soot, cast in profile and smoking a cigarette as she gazed out at the afternoon. She didn't turn to him right away, and he took the moment to study her. She was short and thin and not bad-looking, with regular features except for a nose that was a little large for her face. Her hair was curly and bleached blond. She wore a kimono with a faded peacock design.

When Joe didn't speak up, she turned to look at him.

"Afternoon," she said. "What's your pleasure?" From her tone, his pleasure was the last thing she cared about.

"I need a few minutes of your time," Joe said. He laid his two dollar bills on the dresser to his right.

She gazed at him coolly, then glanced at the money, her mouth pinching in disgust. "You one of them wants to talk?" she said. "Ask me why I do? What led me to my life of sin? How I'm getting along spreading my legs or going down on my knees for a dozen men a day? Or what it's like to put a—"

"That's not what I'm here for," Joe cut in. He gave her a curious glance. "You get a lot of that, do you?"

"Enough," Daisy said.

"Well, I paid," Joe said.

"All right, so talk," she said. "Or I'll tell you a hot story and you can jack yourself. Do whatever you came to do."

"I came to ask you about J. R. Logue."

She stopped, her face fell, and her mouth quivered a little. "I figured somebody'd be around about that," she said flatly. "You ain't a cop." Joe shook his head. "Pinkerton?"

"Just someone with a few questions. And I pa—"

"—paid. I heard you. Okay, ask." She stubbed her cigarette out and immediately lit another one from the pack on the table, the flare of the match illuminating the lines on her face.

Joe leaned against the wall next to the door, put his hands in the pockets of his overcoat. "How long did you know him?" he said.

"Six or seven years. Maybe longer."

"He come by every week?"

"Every week. Same day, same time. Saturday at six o'clock. Before it got busy." She smiled without a trace of humor. "While I was still . . . fresh."

That gave Joe a moment's pause. "Was he here last Saturday?"

"He was."

"Anything different?"

She considered, and he could tell she was weighing her words. "Well, he didn't look no different. He was wearing that brown suit of his. Same one he always wore. I think it was the only one he owned."

Joe pictured the cop lying dead in the alley. "No, he had another one, too."

She peered at him. "What?"

"Nothing. What else?"

She watched Joe through the curl of cigarette smoke, as if trying to decide something. Then she said, "Yeah, there was. He couldn't do nothing. I tried to help, but it wasn't no good. He got like that sometimes, because of the way he drank and all. I could always take care of him, though. Make him feel good. Not this time. It just didn't work, and he told me to stop." She shrugged. "Then he said *he* wanted to talk."

"About what?"

She returned her gaze to the window. "About . . . about how things were about to change," she said.

"Change how?"

The dim smile reappeared. "He asked me if I was ready to get out of here."

"Out of the house?"

"The house. The city. The life. He wanted me to go away with him."

"And do what?"

"Be with him, what do you think?" She frowned vaguely. "Men asked me that before. More than a few. I never bought it. Some of them was kids who had it with me their first time and thought they was in love. Or some fool looking for some free tail and making a promise, thinking I'd be too much of a dunce to figure it out." She paused as the smoke from her cigarette twisted upward. "Johnny actually meant it."

*Johnny.* It was strange to hear his name spoken that way, stranger still to hear the faint hint of affection when she spoke it.

She turned her head and gave Joe a hard look. "First, I told him he was a goddamn fool. He wants to marry a whore? And I'm going to be a wife to some cop? A drunk cop?" She stopped. "I didn't say that part. But I was thinking it."

Joe said, "Maybe he would have given up the bottle for you."

"You know, that's what he said." She sighed. "He swore he was going to change that, too. He said, 'I promise you.' Said once he took care of one thing, he'd be ready if I was." She sagged a little, and with a glance at the clock, said, "Your time's about up."

"Did he say what thing?"

She gave him a blank look.

"He was going to take care of something. Did he tell you what it was?"

"No. And I didn't ask."

"All right, what then?"

"He told me he was going to come back after I was done on Monday and take me out somewhere. Maybe for a meal and a show. And then we'd talk some more. Make a plan. I told him he was crazy, but he said to just make sure I didn't work late on Monday night. Well, I stopped around eight o'clock, but he didn't show up, and so I figured he had just been lying. Or maybe that he got drunk again and forgot. The next day, I heard he was dead." She tamped her cigarette out. "And now I told you everything."

Joe doubted it, and let her know by the look he gave her.

She frowned in return. "Well, what?"

"Aren't you leaving something out?"

For a second, he thought she was going to yell for the roughneck to come toss him outdoors.

"If you don't help me, he's nothing but a drunk cop who ended up dead," Joe said. "And that's all." He paused to let it sink in. "He cared for you, Daisy."

She said, "I know he did," her voice down low.

"So?"

She kept an unfocused gaze on the floor. "He was going to have the money and he was going to have someone beholden to him. 'He's gonna owe me,' is what he said. I asked him who he was talking about, but he wouldn't say." She shook her head slightly. "He said he didn't want me to know." She stayed quiet for a few seconds. "Now that really is all," she said, and nodded toward the door.

Joe stepped away, then stopped and said, "I think he meant what he said."

"About what?" Daisy said, sounding weary to the bone.

"Taking you away from here."

"Yeah? How do you know that?"

"He talked about leaving," Joe said. "He told someone who told me." He paused for a moment. "He said he wanted to take the little girl, too."

Daisy turned to stare at him.

"You and her, together," Joe said.

Daisy's chin set as she bit down hard on whatever was coming up from inside. Her voice trembled when she said, "I don't want to hear no more about it," and waved him out of the room with a rough hand.

The Captain called Albert Nichols into his office. Lieutenant Collins was standing by and the two junior officers exchanged a nod.

Captain Jackson sat back in his chair, folded his arms across his broad chest, and glared at Nichols. "You're friends with that fucking Indian, Joe Rose," he said by way of greeting.

"I know him," Albert said. "But I'm not sure he's an In—"

"And that ain't all, is it?" the Captain interrupted. "You worked with him somewhere, too." He shot a glance toward Collins. When the lieutenant didn't volunteer the information, he brought his attention back to Sergeant Nichols. "Where was it? Up north somewhere?"

"Baltimore," the detective said.

"Uh-huh. He the one who told you about this pimp got shot?"

"Which one is that?"

"Don't play me for a goddamn fool, Nichols! He's got you sticking your nose into business that don't concern you or him. He's about this far from going down the shit hole, and you'll go right along with him if you ain't careful." The Captain stopped to catch his breath. "You're an Atlanta police detective. So you don't talk to him or any other civilian about any no-account niggers getting shot. Or anything else related to this department. Understand?"

Albert said, "Yes, sir."

"You want to talk to him, talk to him about coming up with something we can use on that crime in Inman Park. Since that colored gal he chases after was there when it happened."

"I did mention that to him."

Captain Jackson stopped, his lips pursing. "Did you?"

"Yes, sir. And he said he'd try to come up with something just as fast as he could."

The Captain produced a cold smirk. "He's screwing with you, Nichols. You just don't know it." He glared for another second, then flapped a hand in the air, a cutting gesture of dismissal.

As the detective walked out, he stole a look at Lieutenant Collins and saw him gazing at the Captain instead of at him with an expression that was sharp with disdain.

Coward that he was about facing Sweet, Joe took the long way around to Fairlie Street and then across to North Pryor, coming up to the back entrance to the Hampton, just in case the black man was standing outside Lulu's having a smoke. Even though it was likely that Sweet was long gone, having put in his usual breakfast and lunch shifts. Or maybe he wasn't even working that day. Still, Joe pictured him lingering in hopes of catching the man who had gone against his wishes and right back to corrupting his little sister. That Pearl had come to Joe's room wouldn't signify any more than her age. Sweet apparently imagined her a helpless lamb, under a spell with no will of her own. When in fact Pearl Spencer had will by the bucketful. The songs the bluesmen sang about hardheaded women could have been written about her.

Once inside the lobby, he peered out the wide front window. Sweet was nowhere in sight, which made him feel even more like a fool. Sweet surely had noticed that Joe hadn't been in for breakfast in two days and would know why. Joe shook his head at this folly and headed for the staircase. It was only a matter of time before he would have to tangle with Sweet. It could wait just a little bit longer.

When he stepped into his room, he was once again greeted by the sight of Pearl stretched on his bed, naked except for the gold bracelet around her wrist. She was lying perfectly still, on her side and propped on one elbow. The afternoon light through the window created the aura of an old painting, the colors fading to sepia. He took a moment to settle himself, then tried to be severe with her. "How did you get in?"

She smiled and dipped her forehead. "I've got my ways."

"Did anyone see you?"

"What do you think?"

He understood. She had slipped in through the back, just as he had, then climbed the stairs and picked the lock, all without being spotted. Or maybe she had put on like she was one of the maids cleaning rooms. She had done that before, too. It was some feat for a woman who tended to stand out in any crowd, but she had been taught well and had the benefit of lots of practice.

"So, Joe, what are you doing way over there?" she asked him, her voice as languid as slow water.

Despite the display, Joe was incensed. She was crazy coming there in the daytime, with Lieutenant Collins and who knew who else watching him.

He looked away and said, "Cover up, Pearl."

"*Cover up?*" Her mouth tilted as if he had made a joke.

"I mean it."

"I can't hear you," she said. "You'll have to move a little closer." When he didn't budge, she came back with a cool smile. "Oh, I'm sorry. Am I acting like a hussy?" She pulled the sheet over her legs, hips, and torso, and Joe felt a pang watching her disappear by inches under the cotton spread. He crossed to sit at the foot of the bed, folding his arms as a message to her.

Pearl, watching his face, said, "Why you treating me so mean?"

"We need to talk."

"Oh?" Her eyebrows arched. "Then it's a good thing I'm here."

He let out a short laugh. "Sorry. What was I thinking?"

Their eyes met. He looked away first.

"What's wrong?" she said. "You been talking to Sweet?"

"Not if I can help it. I've got other trouble. And it has to do with you."

"What trouble is that?" she asked, though of course she already knew.

"Captain Jackson pulled me in yesterday," Joe said. "He thinks you had something to do with those jewels that went missing from the Payne mansion."

She shifted against the headboard. "He questioned me about that."

"Questioned you when?"

"Sunday morning. They brought all of us that was working Saturday night back to the house. I told him I didn't take nothing. And I didn't say your name, either. He did that."

"Because he thinks you pulled that job, and that I'm mixed up in it. He's got a man watching me."

Perturbed, she looked away. "I don't give a goddamn what he thinks. He ain't nothing to me."

"He knows we work together, Pearl. And the rest of it, too."

"Then why don't he come arrest us?"

"He doesn't have a case. He thinks I can work you to get them."

She caught his eye. "You know you can work me anytime you want, Mr. Joe."

He stared at her, wondering why she couldn't grasp the fix they were in. "This is no joke."

She sat up from her slouch, smiling her serpent smile as she spread her arms wide. The sheet slipped away. "Do I look like I'm joking?" she said.

"All right, that's enough!"

It came out sharper than he'd intended, and she gaped at him for a second, then sank down again, looking wounded. She reached for the sheet and pulled it up, again refusing to meet his gaze, instead turning toward the window and lifting her chin righteously.

"I'm sorry," he said.

"Why don't you just walk away?" she said in a voice that was cool with accusation. "Go on and leave, and you won't have to deal with none of this. You come and go whenever you please, anyway."

"I can't," he said. "Not now."

Her eyes flashed at him. "Can't why? What's stopping you?"

"Because of this other thing."

"What other thing?"

"You hear about Jesse Williams?"

"Yeah, I heard." From the look on her face, she shared Sweet's opinion of the man in question. "He got shot."

"That's right."

"He ain't dead yet?"

"I don't know. He's dying for sure, though. He could be gone, for all I know."

"Too bad for him." Her face was still tight with anger. "What's that to you? Or me?"

"He asked me to find out why that cop shot him down on Courtland Street. And I said I would."

Her gaze narrowed in distaste. "Why? You ain't got nothing better to do?"

Joe was tired of trying to explain it. "It's his deathbed wish." He produced a thin smile. "You know. I just don't want a ghost walking around my bed at night."

Pearl's eyebrows hiked and she snickered. "Good lord, listen to you! You sound like some kind of damn Geechee nigger. *Haints* and all. That's your reason?"

"At first I just did it to humor him and be done with it. I thought it would be nothing. Just some spat between the two of them. Well, it ain't. I think there's more to it."

"How's that?"

"For one thing, the same cop he said shot him was murdered last night."

Pearl stared at him. "What cop?"

"His name was Logue," Joe said. "He walked a beat downtown. He was a good-for-nothing drunk. Jesse says he was the one shot him Saturday night. Two nights later, Logue turned up dead in an alley down off Decatur Street with one bullet in his chest and one in his head."

Pearl stirred, coming up with a fretful frown. "Now you're talkin' about a dead cop? You know you don't want to be messing with that."

"I didn't kill him," Joe said.

She turned her face away again and pulled the sheets a little tighter around her middle. She stayed quiet for a long moment. When she spoke again, her voice was dreamy.

"You know, we could both just leave," she said. "Get up, get on a train, and get out of here. We wouldn't have to mess with none of this." She turned back to look at him. "No, I guess not," she said, and settled back against the headboard to tell him what had happened on Saturday night at the Payne mansion.

The way she described it, the young girl named Sally Frost came into the kitchen of the mansion and handed her a note. Sally explained that she was on her way to work and just a little ways down the sidewalk from the front gate, a man had stepped out of the shadows to hand her the slip of paper with instructions to turn it over to Pearl. He had given her a new quarter for her trouble.

"The note said, 'Pearl, Go to the basement and unlock the door. Important.' And it was signed with a *J*."

"Like Joe."

"Like Joe," Pearl said. "I thought maybe you had found out from Sweet or somebody where I was working and came to see me." Her black eyes danced. "Like maybe you couldn't wait."

"Except it wasn't me."

"I guess not."

"Do you have it?"

"Have what?"

"The note."

"No, I threw it away. Didn't want to get caught with it."

"All right, so what did you do?"

"I made sure no one was watching and went down and un-locked the door. Big ol' heavy lock and a big ol' heavy door. I opened it and called your name. But there was nobody there. I waited a minute. I knew they'd be looking for me, so I closed the door and went back up."

"You didn't lock it?"

"No, just in case it was you, and you needed to get in," she said. "Then I went back upstairs. I asked Sally if she saw where the fellow who gave her the note went. She said he just walked away. I asked her what did he look like, and she said she didn't really notice."

"Or maybe she didn't want to say."

"Maybe. Anyway, what she said was he had a coat and hat on, so she couldn't see him too good." She shrugged. "I thought maybe it was you."

He took a few moments to mull the scene she'd described. "Does this look like a setup to you?" he said.

"A setup?" Pearl gave him a curious glance. "Why?" she said.

"You got enemies?"

"A few," Joe said. "But none of them knew when I'd get into town."

"Yeah, you're late this time," she said.

"I got held up in Louisville," he explained.

Pearl studied her fingernails. "What was her name?"

Joe prudently ignored the question and made himself appear distracted. Pearl shifted her position, inclining a little way to lay her head on her folded arm.

"What's the worse he could do to us?" she said absently.

Joe said, "Who, the Captain? For a start, he could bust through that door with a skeleton key, drag us out, and put us both in jail just for being here. They got a name for you and me being together. You know that. And it's a crime."

She raised her head. "Here I thought you was one of them *Injuns*," she said lightly. "Now you're tellin' me you're a white man?"

"I don't know what I am," he said. "And it doesn't matter. If he needs to, he'll find a charge and lock us up. You and me both."

"He ain't done it, though."

"Because he needs us on the street. For now."

"Then I guess what you need to do is get gone. I mean today. Go on back to Louisville or Mobile or wherever the hell you came from."

"It sounds like you're trying to get rid of me."

"I'm trying to keep you out of trouble, is all. Ain't that what you want?"

Joe shook his head. "It's too late."

She stared hard at him. "Yeah? Why's that?"

He sat down on the end of the bed. "I came into town, minding my own damn business, and within forty-eight hours, I'm in the middle of two crimes."

"So you had some bad luck."

"That's not it. What do you think the chances are they're not connected? It's like somebody wanted me here on purpose."

Pearl's gaze seemed to go past him. In a vague voice, she said, "Who would do that? And why?"

"I don't know and I don't know," Joe said. He fretted for a moment, then with a sigh, settled on the end of the bed once more. "What I do know is that somebody's out to fuck me, but good."

Pearl's gaze came back as if she was breaking out of a day-dream. Her mouth curved with a sweet sadness as she raised her hand and said, "Well, that would be me, Joe."

Joe, watching her face, saw a familiar light in her eyes, along with a heat that infused her dark flesh. As always, it made everything else go away. With the time it took his heart to beat, there was no dying crapshooter, no missing jewels, no cops or brothers on his trail. There was no somber reminder that the law said they didn't belong together. It was just the two of them in that dingy room on a late December afternoon, with the weak winter light coming in through the dirty window.

Carefully, Joe unlaced and kicked away his shoes, then crawled up the bed, pulling the sheet down as he made his way toward her.

When they were finished, she lay with her eyes closed, smiling sleepily, at peace as he gazed out the window. The late afternoon sun was painting the sides of the buildings that face south and west in shades of red. Soon it would sink below the rooftops, and the streetlamps would come on.

He could almost imagine them hiding away in that room, lost in the shadows for hours or days or weeks. Lazing in the bed with her was so serene that Joe wondered why he kept on leaving Atlanta—and her. It was true that this was his habit to escape after he got his way with a woman. The chase enthralled him, but once he had nabbed his prey he was ready to move on. Sometimes seeing their tears or hearing their pleas or threats stung him. Stung him but didn't stop him. Except when it came to Pearl. It got harder to leave her each time.

He turned to look at her and found that she had dozed off,

her breath low and her chest rising and falling gently. He mused on running away the way she had described it. What she didn't mention was how far they would have to run to get away from everything that would haunt them.

It didn't matter, because he wasn't going anywhere. There would be no dreamy interlude for the two of them. What seemed a pathetic little bit of violence on an Atlanta street and the snatching of a rich woman's trinkets had melded and blossomed into something larger and darker that wasn't going to just blow away on a wisp of winter wind.

He was musing on this when he heard footsteps and then a soft knock on the door. Startled, he sat up and swung his legs off the bed. At the squeak of the springs, Pearl opened her eyes. He put a finger to his lips, then pulled on his trousers and his undershirt.

Pearl looked around, as if searching for a place to hide. *Now,* he thought, *she gets it.*

Joe went to the door. "Who's there?" he said.

"Mr. Rose? Got a message for you."

He let out a breath of relief and opened the door a crack to see the desk clerk standing there. "Colored boy came by and said they want you on Schoen Alley."

"All right," Joe said.

"I had it since a couple hours now," the clerk said. "I didn't know you was up here or I would have brought it before." He was trying to peer past Joe and into the room. "Didn't see you come in, is what."

Joe, blocking his view, didn't bother to explain, instead going into his pocket for a quarter, which he tossed in the air. The clerk caught it, winked a thank-you, and sauntered away.

Joe closed the door and locked it again. The message likely meant that Little Jesse was getting near the end, if he wasn't there already. So he might well have carried any secrets he was holding to his grave.

He looked over at Pearl and saw her gazing back at him. "I need to go," he said.

She kept her troubled eyes on him for a long time. Then she said, "I don't want you to."

He saw her down the back stairs and out into falling evening. She had asked if she could wait in the room until he got back, but it was too dicey. The Hampton was a white hotel, just like the Atlanta across the street and the Oliver a few doors down. The colored establishments were located in another part of town; and though it was true that both white and Negro sporting women used rooms in all three, the law said Pearl could go to jail if she was caught doing anything but changing sheets at any of them. Or Sweet might decide to come looking for her, with his first stop the sign that read HAMPTON HOTEL.

They didn't speak at all as they walked through the evening fog down Houston and then one block over to wait for the Auburn Avenue streetcar. When it drew near, Pearl turned to Joe as if she wanted to say something.

He said, "What's wrong?"

She began, "It's just . . ."

"What?"

Before she could say it, the car rolled up, and with a small, sad smile, she stepped on.

Joe stood on the corner watching the lights fade away, then started walking south in the direction of Decatur Street.

Willie had passed the afternoon hours sitting in the corner chair, reworking the lyrics a line at a time as Jesse slipped in and out of consciousness, digging what seemed a deeper hole each time he went down.

The giddy excitement of recording in the room at the Dixie had faded. It had all gone so fast. They came to collect him, rushed him into the room, turned on the machine, and rushed him back out. Tomorrow, they would pack up and leave for New York, and then who knew what would happen to the records once they got home.

There was nothing he could do, and yet he was feeling blue down to his soul. He knew that had more to do with being there at Jesse's bedside as he slipped away. It was melancholy business.

With an absent ear, he'd caught the creaking of the back door, the shuffling of shoe leather, the low voices lapping like water as visitors arrived and stepped inside. He understood. The word had gone out; they knew what was coming and were gathering around.

He overheard whispers from the other room. They weren't talking about how long Little Jesse could last anymore, only when he would go and what would happen then. There were some sobs from the women, too; and a couple times Jesse came out of his stupor to croak, "I told y'all, *stop* that!"

Once he whispered wearily, "You tell them, Willie," and Willie called out, "Folks, y'all don't be standing 'round cryin' like that."

Jesse smiled with a hint of the old wickedness, and the thought crossed Willie's mind that if he had his way, everyone would be doing the Charleston right there in the room.

He chuckled softly at the image. Without opening his eyes, Jesse said, "What's funny?" It sounded like he didn't care much anymore.

The only time he showed any signs of life was late in the afternoon when he came up long enough to add to his last request. His eyes lit up the way they used to when he won a stack of money at dice or laid his eyes on a good-looking woman, and he began spewing more demands that were hysterical and heartbreaking all at the same time.

"I want *all* them crook motherfuckers off the street!" When he tried to yell, his voice cracked. "I said every one of those no-good goddamn rounders better show up. Y'hear me? They sho' enough was easy to find when I had somethin' they wanted. I done took their money and their women, and they goin' to want to be here when it come my time to go!"

There were snickers from the men in the bedroom doorway, and laughs erupted from the kitchen, where all the drinking was going on.

When Willie explained that the word had gone out to a good number of the downtown women, Jesse got loud again. "Get *all* them whores in here, goddamnit! There's some up at the Hampton, a few more out of the Dixie, and I want 'em *all*. You hear what I say, Willie?"

"I hear you, Jesse."

"'Cause I think maybe I got to die today."

"You lasted this long," Willie said.

Jesse's face scrunched into a perturbed look, as if Willie was feebleminded, and got back to the business at hand.

"Lookie here, now," he muttered, sounding like he had a mouthful of gravel. "You think I don't know what the hell's going on? It's my damn body." His wide gaze found Willie and behind the unutterable sadness was a wild joy, as if this was all a joke. The blind man could hear it echoing in his voice when he said, "You make sure you finish the song. And you sing it over my grave. You promise me that."

Willie said, "I promise, Jesse."

"And don't make it so damn sad, either."

"I'll do it right," Willie said.

Jesse sagged into the mattress, gasping and sweating. "Can you play me what you got?"

Willie said, "All right," though he never liked singing a song until he was done with it. This was different, and he knew where he was going, anyway, building it around the chord pattern of minor to fifth and back, over and over. There were only a few lines he wasn't sure of. That didn't seem to matter now.

He sang what he had. Once he reached the line *Police walked up and shot my friend Jesse down* . . . he hesitated for a second, completing the next phrase in his head. Then, in a somber tone, he said:

*Boys, I got to die today*

Jesse laughed breathlessly. Willie sang,

*He had a gang of crapshooters and gamblers at his bedside*
*Here are the words he had to say:*
*I guess you ought to know exactly how I want to go . . .*

"Hey, Jesse . . ."
Willie stopped. Jesse cocked his head. "Joe."
Standing in the doorway, Joe said, "How you doing?"
"I'm still here, ain't I?"
Joe looked over at Willie, who shook his head. Joe turned back to Jesse, bending down closer and smelling something that made his eyes water.
"It's time for us to talk," he said, putting an edge on the words.
"I know," Jesse grunted. "I got some things to tell you. Only not now. I got to hear my song first. After that."
Joe started to argue, only to catch a hard eye from the man on the bed. Jesse shifted his gaze and said, "Go on ahead, Willie."
Willie said, "Maybe you ought to talk to Joe now. I'll play it later."
"Ain't no *later*," Jesse said. Though weak, his voice had an edge of strain. "Joe ain't goin' nowhere. So go on ahead."
Joe sat back and Willie started playing again, picking up from where he left off, turning the dirge into a jaunty, bouncing vamp with a thumping bass string.

*Eight crapshooters for pallbearers*
*Let 'em be veiled down in black*
*I want nine men going to the graveyard, buddy*
*And eight men comin' back*

Joe felt Jesse's eyes on him and tried to read the faraway smile. If there was a message, he didn't get it. Men and women were now crowding the doorway to listen.

*I want a gang of gamblers gathered round my coffin side*
*A crooked card printed on my hearse*
*Don't say them crapshooters are liable to grieve over me*
*My life's been a doggone curse*

Some of the rounders snickered and a couple of the whores called out affirmations, like they were in church.

*Send poker players to the graveyard*
*Dig my grave with the ace of spades*
*I want twelve policemen in my funeral march*
*The Captain playin' blackjack and leadin' the parade*

The tempo increased just a bit and Willie sang,

*He wanted twenty-two women out of the Hampton Hotel*
*Twenty-six off of South Bell*
*Twenty-nine women out of north Atlanta*
*Know that Jesse didn't pass out so swell*

Now there were little hoots of laughter from the men and chuckles from the women.

*Now his head was achin', heart was thumpin'*
*Little Jesse went down, bouncin' and jumpin'*

*Folks, don't be standin' around ol' Jesse cryin'*
*He want everybody do the Charleston whilst he dyin'*
*One foot up and a toenail dragging*
*Throw my friend Jesse in the hoodoo wagon . . .*

Willie slowed again, returned to the original funereal pace.

*Come here, mama, with that can of booze*
*Dying Crapshooter's Blues, I mean,*
*The Dying Crapshooter's Blues . . .*

Willie plucked the last notes and looked over to see the odd, faraway ghost of a smile on Little Jesse's face. He gasped, "You hear that, Joe?"

"I heard, Jesse."

"People gonna remember me, ain't that right?"

"Nobody's gonna forget you," Joe said. "You don't have to worry about that."

"I'll make sure," Willie said.

"You do that. Please . . ." His smile faded as a gray cloud moved up his chest to invade his face. His lips moved and he tried to whisper something to Joe, who bent his head to listen.

"What is it, Jesse?" Joe said.

Little Jesse tried to mouth something, but instead of words, an eerie breath came up from his chest, one with a weight that seemed to charge the air over the bed; then, nothing more.

Willie said, "Oh, Lord . . ."

Time slowed and hung like a shroud. No one spoke or moved. Jesse opened his eyes, then closed them again, and let out one long, deep, shuddering sigh that was nothing if not full of the relief that comes at the end of a wearisome road. In the next second, his body stiffened, then relaxed and settled in the mattress.

Joe, feeling his voice catch, said, "Well, goddamn."

"He gone?" Willie said. It wasn't really a question and no one answered.

Gradually, a ripple went out from the room. The whispers grew louder and there were a few sobs. Joe heard Martha begin to weep, keening as she pushed through the crowd to kneel at the bedside and take hold of Little Jesse's cooling hand.

Hearing some of the other women moaning with grief, Willie called out, "Hey, now! Y'all heard what he said. He didn't want none of that. Somebody get a bottle goin' 'round." After a pause, he said, "Go on, Jesse." He tilted his head in Joe's direction. "You'd best cover him up," he said, and Joe pulled the sheet up over Little Jesse's dead face.

In the commotion that followed, no one noticed the small-boned Negro who slipped out the door. He hurried through the alleys until he could cut across Decatur and come around the side entrance of police headquarters, where he delivered the message that Little Jesse Williams was dead, receiving a quarter for the tip.

The drinking started up in earnest and went on until someone called out that the hoodoo wagon was turning into the alley. Presently, heavy footsteps came clumping up the stairs. Two men from the funeral home, dressed like twins in black suits and somber derby hats, walked in carrying a folded stretcher. With the help of Joe and another man, they went about the clumsy business of getting Little Jesse's cadaver onto the stretcher, out of the apartment, and down the steps to the alley. Everyone who was inside came outdoors, and more people from the Decatur Street speaks, pool halls, and gambling rooms showed up. Martha stood on the rickety landing at the top of the wooden stairs, watching it all with tired and damp eyes, her thin arms crossed against the cold wind.

Down below, a bottle was going around, and in spite of the somber presence of the black carriage and the two dark-clad valets, a general mood of hilarity animated the alley as they settled Little Jesse for his ride to the funeral parlor. The two men climbed up, one snapped the reins, and the wagon clattered off, negotiating the narrow byway, then turning east on Decatur Street. The word went out about the wake as the party moved back upstairs.

Joe went inside to talk to Willie, and found the blind man in the corner chair of Jesse's room picking his Stella and looking tired and somber. He stopped playing and raised his head when Joe walked in. No one else wanted to be in haunted space, so it was just the two of them. For his part, Willie didn't at all seem worried about any juju that might be lingering.

Joe listened to the hypnotic minor-key drone and said, "Sounds sweet."

"I'm bound to play it over his grave," Willie said.

The crowd of Jesse's friends and rivals and not a few strangers started filling the rooms and getting louder by the minute. The revelry would last through the end of the day and through the night, replete with drinking, fighting, and fucking, all in Little Jesse's memory. Joe accepted a quick glass of whiskey out of respect for the deceased and made his exit. On his way out, he shook Willie's hand, and promised that he'd come by and see him later at the 81.

Joe wandered the dark downtown streets, walking aimlessly, feeling the hollow weight of having witnessed a man's death, then pondering the fact that the person who could have told him exactly what happened on Courtland Street on Saturday night was gone. It had been some scene in that room, bleak with grief at a man's passing and yet with a certain wild edge, ending with the song Willie had written, as if the blind man had distilled Jesse's life to its essence in those last moments.

Except for one small part. What was it that Little Jesse wanted to tell him? Was he finally going to offer Joe the other pieces of the puzzle? Why had he waited so long, indeed until it was too late?

These thoughts went around as Joe hunched his shoulders against the night's chill, wondering why Little Jesse hadn't spoken up sooner. Instead, he had hedged his wager, playing another in an endless chain of angles, waiting for the right moment to show his hand. But his time ran out and the infection or whatever it was killing him had moved too fast. The gambler had bet and lost, and his last deal had gone sour. As much as Joe mourned his passing, he couldn't shake his anger at him for being such a fool and holding out like that.

He came around the corner at Cone and Walton and passed by the facade of the Dixie Hotel. The lobby was lit up, a glow of cheery yellow against the dark of the night.

Joe knew that if he wanted to drop the whole mess, this was his chance. Few would know and fewer would blame him. He could take Pearl's brokenhearted advice and leave, and that would be the end of it.

Before the thought had crossed his mind, he knew he wasn't going to do any such thing. He was in, and he wasn't going to get out by walking away. Pearl, the Captain, Lieutenant Collins, and the deceased J. R. Logue had all done their little bits to hold him fast.

Shuffling through the cast of characters, he thought of Robert Clark, who had witnessed the first act in the drama. Joe knew he'd have to find him, starting with Bell Street, where he'd last been spotted. If nothing else, he'd know he'd turned over every stone.

Before he went chasing that goose, he stopped at Beck's Café for a solitary dinner. Though he didn't have much of an appetite, he hadn't eaten since the morning, and figured it could only make him feel better. The place was known for chicken and biscuits, and that's what he ordered, along with a dish of greens and a cola to drink.

The after-work crowd had come and gone, and it was quiet, an ordinary night, missing only one pimp and crapshooter. Six blocks away, the wake for Little Jesse would be getting rowdy. None of the customers in the diner or the pedestrians on the street would know one way or another. The December night went on as usual, just a little more foot traffic on the sidewalks, as Christmas shoppers hurried from store to store.

As he waited, he glanced around to see a young fellow sitting at the other end of the counter. Joe studied him with an idle interest, noting the way he kept shifting about, like he couldn't get comfortable on his stool. Though it was plenty warm inside the diner, he kept his heavy coat on, and Joe saw the bulge in one of the pockets. The fellow was toting a pistol and couldn't quite get right with the feel of it, like he was not used to the encumbrance. One of Joe's few cop nerves told him there was something going on there, perhaps some mayhem in the making. He would not be surprised to pick up tomorrow morning's paper and read of a crime that had involved a troubled young man and a pistol. He had seen it too often: a kid with no sense, a gun that was made for killing, the wrong words spoken in the wrong tone of voice, and then blood on the floor.

The girl stepped up with his plate, breaking into his thoughts. The chicken smelled wonderful and he didn't realize how hungry he was until he started eating. After a few minutes went by, the fellow in the overcoat put down his coffee with a clatter, tossed some change on the counter, and made a busy exit. Joe finished his dinner, drank a cup of coffee, and went out onto the streets of Atlanta in search of Robert Clark.

The light of day was long gone, and Robert was ready for the end of his labors. He tossed the last bag on the wagon and sent it off toward Track Three. It would arrive in Pittsburgh sometime the next afternoon.

Like any number of common laborers, Robert worked off

the books and was paid in cash at the end of every shift. He was one among a population of drunks, tramps, and other dregs who couldn't or wouldn't hold a regular job. The railroad porters in their uniforms looked down their noses on this crew, though they understood that if it wasn't for fellows like Robert, they'd be the ones loading the baggage cars. So these two-dollar-a-day rascals were tolerated as long as they got the bags into the cars and didn't steal.

It was a good situation for someone who didn't want to be found. At least half the men working the cars used monikers. They were invisible to the outside world and mostly to each other, as they toiled away the hours in the belowground shadows of Union Depot.

Robert was tired and glad of it. Maybe he'd be able to sleep. What he'd heard and seen on the Courtland Street corner hung on him like a cheap suit of clothes, and no amount of homemade whiskey had been able to shake it loose.

Except for the one visit, he had steered clear of Schoen Alley, though he knew he owed a visit to the man's deathbed. He couldn't go back and risk running into Joe Rose again. The way that Indian stared at him . . .

After his visit to the crap game on Saturday night, Robert hadn't spoken another word about what he'd seen. He kept his mouth shut and ears open, so he overheard the talk about Jesse dying. One of the men mentioned that Willie McTell had worked up a song about him, telling of a gambler in the last minutes of his life demanding liquor and whores. Robert wished he could go by and see Jesse, pay his respects, give up what he knew—give it *back* if he could—but he couldn't take the risk.

Now it was too late. One of the porters had come to work with the news that Little Jesse had died and the wake had already begun. They talked about going to join the party, as it would likely still be going on in the morning. As bad as he felt hearing the news, Robert couldn't deny a certain relief. Maybe it would all fade away now, and he'd be left alone.

Or maybe he'd find Joe Rose, tell him everything, and let him do what he wanted with it. Maybe he could still do some good for poor Jesse's soul.

All this ran through his mind as he walked along the gravel pathway that adjoined the eastbound tracks. There was a stone staircase at the end of Moore Street, and once he got to the top, his first stop would be Bell Street and a bottle. Then he would go to his room and sit on his bed and drink to the memory of Little Jesse Williams.

He reached the stone steps and heard the whisper of traffic up on the street. The railing was cold in his bare hand as he pulled himself up. It had been a long day. He figured he had hoisted a good ton or more of white folks' bags. Back in the country, it would have been a ton of cotton. Those days were over, though. The cotton was all gone.

He was three steps up when he became aware that someone had started down from the top. Robert glanced up, then dropped his eyes again. All he could make out was a shape. He took another two steps.

"Hold it, now." The voice was soft, though with an edge behind it that gave Robert pause. His stomach began to churn with a primitive fear, and he took a desperate glance back the way he had come. The pathway was deserted the entire distance to the terminal. They were alone out there. The only things moving were the engines in the yard, blowing gray smoke and making that grinding railroad racket.

Robert couldn't see the face above him because of the backlight of the streetlamp, and it began to dawn on his slow mind what was happening. Now he turned and took a step back, downward, as if he had just thought of something he had forgotten.

"I said hold it right there." The voice wasn't mean or loud, just insistent.

Robert bowed his head, as if meekly complying. Then, in a sudden motion, he leaped back to the gravel at the bottom. His feet kicked up clouds of black railroad dust as he started to run, and he thought he was away clean, until the concussion and searing heat hit his back, like he'd been slammed with a hot hammer. He tried to keep going, but his legs gave way in a stumble, and he found himself tasting dark dust. Digging his fingers into the sharp gravel, he struggled to his feet and started on again. The depot lights were coming closer.

The second bullet found a spot just between his shoulder blades, and Robert was on the ground again, his chin splitting open almost to the bone, though he could barely feel it. He was aware only of footsteps shuffling close. He knew what was coming and wanted to say that he wouldn't talk, would never talk, and his mind even streaked to the two dollars pay in his pocket, thinking he could somehow ransom his life, but nothing emerged from his throat except weak breath.

Faintly, he heard the metallic cock of the hammer. The next second brought an explosion of black light.

The steps receded to the bottom of the stone stairs and then up to Moore Street and away into the December night.

The revelry was still going when the pawnbroker turned off the lights of his shop downstairs, locked the doors, and went to catch the streetcar that would take him to his home in West End. Later, not long before dawn, the police would come around to break it up, and two drunks would get hauled off to Fulton Tower because they couldn't keep their mouths shut. As soon as the coppers left, the carousing started up again.

There was a show at the 81 Theatre that night, and Joe found a place in the back where he could watch and listen. His search of the Negro speaks and gambling rooms at the end of the street had been a waste of time. Robert hadn't been seen in days.

Among the colored members of the theater audience were a dozen pale faces that stood out starkly. All but two were at ease, regulars like Joe who cared more about the entertainment than the color line. Then he saw one couple who clearly didn't belong. Likely they had wandered in while the lights were down and when they came up again, found themselves bobbing on a sea of African faces. Getting out would have caused more commotion, and so they stayed put, watching the show on the stage with glazed eyes.

When Joe came in, frustrated by the time he had wasted trying to find Robert Clark, there was a comic onstage telling a salty joke about a country boy who had an unnatural love for a watermelon. Many of the people laughed, others eyed the comic speculatively, as his delivery seemed a throwback to minstrel days, pooching up his thick lips and rolling his big eyes. Joe peered at the lonely white couple and noticed that they seemed giddy over this segment, as if they had found themselves on more familiar territory. The man chuckled after the other laughter had died, and cool, dark eyes slid his way. Joe was sure that if the poor fellow could have made himself disappear in a puff of smoke, he would have done just that, and left his wife to fend for herself.

The comic made way for a line of tap dancers, pretty girls in skimpy outfits. While they drummed the boards, Joe went back outside and along the brick walkway between the theater and the next building over. Though the night was chilly, a half-dozen girls waited with eager eyes by the stage door in hopes of meeting one of the performers. A short and thick-bodied Negro stood guard, chatting easily with the giddy young ladies. He winked and held the door open. Joe slipped a half-dollar into his palm as he passed inside.

He found Willie standing in the backstage shadows, his head bent over his guitar.

He cocked his head at Joe's approach. "I didn't know if you were going to make it or not."

"It's been a hell of a day," Joe said. "Thought I'd give myself a little entertainment. I could use it. You feel like playing tonight?"

"I got to," Willie said. "My name's on the card." He was quiet for a long moment while the gay music and rattling taps echoed from the stage.

He said, "Jesse's gone, Joe."

Joe said, "I know, Willie. He was in bad shape, though. It was his time."

"Never told you nothin', did he?"

"Another minute, and I think he would have," Joe said.

Willie sighed. "Well, Little Jesse was a gambler, all right."

A young fellow in a shirt and tie, carrying a clipboard, hurried by, calling, "Two minutes, Willie!"

The blind man nodded, then cocked his head toward Joe. "You hear about Robert Clark?"

Something about Willie's tone made Joe's gut sink. "What?"

"He's dead," Willie said. "Shot."

Joe stared at him. "Where?"

"In the yard outside the depot. He was shot three or four times."

"When?"

"'Round about six thirty this evening, is what I heard. He was working down the Union Depot. He finished and left out. Someone found him in along the tracks about an hour later."

"Do they know who did it?"

"Don't think so."

Joe remembered the look on Robert's face as he came up on the scene that night. Now he was dead, too. And there went the last witness.

"I got to get ready right about now," Willie said and moved into the wings.

Joe couldn't think anymore, so he followed along. The dancers tapped their way to a rattling crescendo that was followed by a loud surge of claps and whistles. The troupe came bouncing off. Normally, Joe would have been delighted to observe such a lovely procession. This time, it barely registered.

The host on the stage made the introduction, and modest applause swelled again as Blind Willie McTell walked out onto the stage, leaving Joe in the darkness.

# NINE

The sun broke through and by nine o'clock had burned off the last of the morning mist. The temperature rose a few degrees and then fell again as a cold front moved in from the northwest.

The snap in the air seemed to cheer the pedestrians who were milling along the downtown sidewalks. The Christmas decorations that adorned the storefronts and lampposts glittered in gay shades of red, green, silver, and gold. Shoppers, mostly women from the tonier neighborhoods north and east of the city, hurried into the stores, picking over the bountiful displays and crowding around the radio sets that were on sale for the first time this season, listening to the music and perhaps the word that Atlanta's one annual day of snow might be on the way.

Joe woke up with his arms wrapped around something soft and warm, only to find that it was his pillow. He pushed it away and rolled over to gaze drowsily at the ceiling.

The career of the previous day and night came back to him in a shuffling of cards. It had begun with the discovery of the killing of one stranger and ended with another, with a friend dying between the other two. It was a grim trio of events for one sweep of the clock. Someone had stayed busy cleaning up a mess. Whoever had paid Logue to shoot Jesse had gotten rid of him and then the only witness. And if Little Jesse had hung on, Joe had no doubt that someone would have come for him, too.

He pushed himself up against the headboard and turned to gaze out at the morning as his brain came unstuck. He thought about who could maneuver such a bloodbath and the only name that came to mind was Grayton Jackson, though he couldn't see any reason why the Captain would want a common criminal like Jesse Williams dead. There were dozens like him and worse working the Atlanta streets. Jackson had bigger problems than him.

One in particular was the burglary at the Payne mansion, a crime that had the mayor, the chief of police, and some rich citizens very upset. The Captain clearly suspected Pearl, and the way she kept edging around the coincidence of being at the mansion when the jewels went missing had Joe vexed, too. Was it really true that she just happened to be there? He knew how his old friend Detective Glass would answer the question.

But Pearl was too clever to pull such a brazen theft. Any decent thief would know that a home was best breached when the occupants were off the premises, at work, during church, or away on a vacation. Making a snatch like that during an event like the Christmas party, with so many people milling around who might spot an intruder, had been either a foolish blunder that had come out lucky or done for show. If that was the case, then dragging Pearl and Joe into it as a diversion would not be such a dumb move. In Joe's criminal gut, it felt right.

He closed his eyes and flipped through the mug book that he kept in his head, trying to pick out any characters who could pull that slick of a job. There were only a few with the wits, and he hadn't seen any of them around. And yet it looked likely that someone had plotted the theft and the subterfuge that went with it.

He was back from the bathroom and had just finished dressing when there was a tap on his door. He opened it to find Albert Nichols standing there. He stepped back, inviting the detective inside.

"I could use a cup of coffee," Albert said, smiling lightly. "What say we go across the street?"

"That's not a good idea," Joe said.

Albert snickered. "Are you still hiding from him? Isn't that a lot of damn work? Why don't you marry the girl and get it over with?"

Joe didn't think that was funny at all.

The detective took a moment to cough into his hand. "Or don't you want to be seen with me?"

"You don't need to be seen with *me,*" Joe said.

Albert frowned with impatience. "You want to talk or don't you?" he said. "Hell, you're talking to everyone else." With that, he took a step back and strolled off down the hall.

The detective was sitting over a steaming cup, watching the bustle on Houston Street and noting the characters strolling in and out the doors of the Hampton, when Joe walked in and crossed to the counter. Momentarily, he stepped up to the table with a coffee cup of his own in hand.

"I thought you might have changed your mind," Albert said. His eyes shifted toward the kitchen window. "He in there?"

Joe shrugged. "I didn't look."

"Well, sit down, then." Albert smiled, noting that Joe did so to give himself a clear view of the kitchen and a clear path to the front door.

Albert sipped his coffee and put his cup down. "I heard Williams died."

Joe sighed. "Yeah, I was there."

"How was it?"

"He went easy."

"Did you get anything else from him."

"No," Joe said. "I didn't."

"And that Negro who was shot down on the tracks. Your witness. Clark. Anybody else I don't know about?"

"This ain't my fault, Al."

The detective's mouth settled into a hard line. "I got called off into the Captain's office yesterday," he said. "Just long enough for him to tell me to stay the hell away from you and this shit you're stirring up. So you better make this little visit worth my while." He treated Joe to a pointed stare.

"All right, then." Joe dropped his voice and said, "Logue was paid to kill Jesse Williams."

"That's not what I want—"

"Wait a minute," Joe interrupted. "This isn't what you think."

Albert shifted in his chair. "Go ahead, then," he said.

"He deposited two hundred dollars in the bank last Friday," Joe said. "So either the chief is handing out Christmas gifts this year or someone else gave him the money. The next night, he set out to kill Jesse Williams. Two nights after that, he was shot down. And now Williams is gone and so is the one witness to what happened down there on Courtland Street."

Albert eyed him. "How do you know about the money?" When Joe didn't answer him, he said, "You didn't happen to break into his room, did you?"

Joe said, "I didn't break in anywhere."

Albert laughed and shook his head. "You're such a swell fellow. I can see why the ladies are so sweet on you."

Joe went through the rest of it, using his fingers to count down what he had, and arriving at the conclusion that it was all tied together somehow.

Albert mulled for a few seconds, then said, "You know your deceased friend Mr. Williams had a long sheet of arrests. He was trouble for years."

"Nothing serious, though. Nothing to kill him over."

"Not that we know of," Albert admitted.

"He was just another rounder, Al."

"It doesn't matter what he was," the detective retorted. "It's over. There's no place to go with it. You've got two dead Negroes, and we've got a dead cop. I'd call that a dead end."

"Maybe for you," Joe said. "I'm still stuck in the middle of it."

"Then you better get some help."

"I was hoping the police department might lend me a hand."

"We don't work for you," Albert said, sounding gruff. "Stop stealing and pay some taxes and we'll see about it then."

Joe grinned as he sipped his coffee. "I can't wait that long," he said, then shrugged. "This is your case, too, Al."

The detective's expression darkened. "No, it's not," he said. "Not anymore. They took me off it and put me on a desk. I'm sitting on my ass going through old files."

Joe said, "Damn . . ."

"Yeah. That's what I get for talking to you. They think you've got something and you're not sharing. And somehow it's my fault."

"I know." Joe looked around for a furtive second. "Collins braced me."

"When?"

"Yesterday. Right up on Peachtree. It was after he saw me talking to you at the scene down there."

"Goddamn," the detective said. "He must have tailed you. What did you tell him?"

"What I told you. That Logue shot Little Jesse."

Albert frowned irately. "What did you do that for?"

Joe hesitated. "I thought it would be okay."

"Well, it wasn't. Did he ask you about the burglary, too?"

"Yeah, but I didn't give him anything. I don't have anything."

Albert stopped to treat Joe to a searching look. "You don't, huh? Why do I find that hard to believe?"

Joe held out for a few seconds, then related the story Pearl had told about Saturday night, adding his own conclusion that the crime was committed in a way that would entangle the two of them.

Al didn't see it. "That's crazy," he said. "There's too many things could go wrong. Who would go to that kind of trouble?"

"No one I can think of," Joe said.

"More likely you just walked into something. Who knew you were in town?"

Joe thought about it and said, "Well, I went to Decatur Street on Friday. Saturday night I was in that speak on Lime Row. The Ace Club. And then I was out there on the street after Jesse got shot. I've been down on Central Avenue, too."

"In other words, maybe half the criminals in Atlanta saw you at one time or another."

"I guess so." Put that way, maybe it really was just a dose of bad luck.

"What about Pearl?" the detective inquired.

"What about her?"

Al smiled dimly. "Maybe she's the one out to get you."

Joe said, "Why would she?"

"You'd know better than me," the detective murmured. "You cross her?"

"No more than the usual."

Albert laughed shortly. "What else have you got?"

"That's all," Joe said. "Really."

"Then you better get some more," the detective said. "The Captain's about to start climbing up your back. I mean it. His ass is in a grinder. If he doesn't break this burglary, he'll be lucky to get a job cleaning up after the horses. This was a man who thought he was next in line for chief of detectives."

Joe smiled and said, "That job's still open, ain't it? Maybe they'll give it to you."

Albert's dark eyes flashed. "Listen, goddamn it, this ain't a joke! It's one thing to have crime down Central Avenue. It's something else when it's at the Payne mansion during their fucking Christmas party! This is serious. You follow me, pal?"

His voice had gone up, and a couple heads at other tables turned their way. Joe gaped, startled at the performance.

Albert coughed into his napkin, his face turning crimson as sweat popped on his brow. When he could talk again, he said, "Are you getting all this? Because I don't want you to be the next carcass they pick up off the street." He stared at Joe for another moment, then pushed his chair back and stood up. "We're finished here," he said.

As he started around the table, Joe grabbed his sleeve and whispered, "I don't know how, but that sonofabitch has got both hands on this."

The detective didn't say a word in response. He donned his hat, walked to the door, and stepped out onto the street, leaving his cold cup of coffee.


The telephone call from City Hall came in around midmorning, and one of the clerks carried the message upstairs to Lieutenant Collins, along with copies of the last night's arrest reports. The lieutenant wasn't at his desk and the other detectives were out, so the clerk peeked into the dark office and was surprised to find Captain Jackson staring pensively down at the floor, one side of his face illuminated by the winter light through the window.

"What?" the Captain said without looking up.

"The arrest reports, sir. And there's a message for you from the mayor's office."

Jackson cocked his head in the clerk's direction and held out his hand to snap the paper away, hardly breathing as he read through it. Then he reached out with his other hand for the stack of index cards, blue for the incidents involving white victims, yellow for the colored. "Anything else?" he said.

"No, sir," the clerk said and backed away. At the door, he stole a glance back and saw the Captain holding one of the yellow cards before his eyes, staring at it with this mouth twisted into an odd, crooked smile.

Ten minutes later, Captain Jackson was stalking up and down along the side of the building, blowing little puffs of steamy breath, when Corporal Baker drove up in an APD sedan. The Captain climbed in with a grunt. Baker took one glance at his face and spent the drive staring straight ahead and not uttering a word. Not that he talked much anyway.

Meanwhile, Captain Jackson's mind was raging as in a fever. In the first moments after he received the message, he had entertained the giddy notion that this was what he'd been waiting for, that he was being summoned so that the mayor could offer him the chief of detectives job.

That thought came and went, blown away by a cold wind that told him the real reason for the summons was for a dressing-down over the Inman Park business. They might even pull him off the case. Four days had gone by, and he had produced nothing. Even if he pinned the charge on one of the sneak thieves who swarmed the dark sections of the city like so many rats, he wouldn't have Mrs. Payne's jewels in hand, and they'd know it was a frame job. He had hoped that his threats might work, that even a smart fellow like Joe Rose would do the smart thing and come up with something. In fact, Rose and his black gal Pearl Spencer had called his bluff. For all he knew, Rose hadn't done a damned thing about the burglary.

A low, strangled sound came from his throat, as if he couldn't catch his breath. Corporal Baker glanced over at him with dull eyes, then returned his attention to the busy morning traffic.

The Captain had made a point of using Baker, partly because the corporal was too stupid to be devious, partly to let Lieutenant Collins know he was no longer trusted. Not him, and not Sergeant Nichols, either. The both of them with their righteous noses in the air. Aside from the random piece of fruit from one of the stands, or a cup of coffee from Beck's or from Lulu's Diner on Houston Street, neither one ever took a thing, including any of the ready cash.

Now one of his spies had passed the word that Nichols had been spotted earlier that morning in Lulu's, the same place where Sweet Spencer worked, talking to Rose like they were a couple old pals. And after he'd told the sergeant to stay away from that character. For all he knew, Collins had joined the party, too, and they were plotting his destruction. If that was the case, the Captain swore he'd take all three of them down with him.

Mayor Sampson was slouched behind his desk, drumming his fingers, his ruddy face pinched in displeasure. Chief of Police Troutman stood at his left, as rigid as a toy soldier. A blank-faced assistant in a suit waited on the other side of the desk. His name was Mr. Gilbert and his most—his only—striking feature was hair slicked down and so shiny with oil that it fairly gleamed under the lights. Mayor Sampson murmured to him at intervals, and Gilbert's birdlike eyes followed the mayor's every word and move. There were already jokes going around about "Sampson's shadow."

They all looked around as the door opened and Captain Jackson was ushered in. The Captain forced his legs into a brisk stride, and his earnest expression showed no trace of concern, though anyone watching closely enough would have noticed the strained flicking of his eyes. He glanced at the three men, trying to read their expressions. Seeing nothing to encourage him, he readied himself for a duel.

"Mr. Mayor," he said crisply. He did not look at Troutman, instead offering a quick nod as he grunted, "Chief."

Troutman glared at the discourtesy and started to say something. Before he could, the mayor spoke up. "Thank you for coming by on short notice." He stared hard at the Captain. "I'll get right to it. You led us to believe you could close this theft at the Payne mansion, find whoever committed the crime, and return the stolen goods, all in quick order. Isn't that what you told Chief Troutman?"

The Captain now felt the chief's cold eyes on him and knew the man was enjoying this. He said, "I did, Mr. Mayor, yes, sir, and I'm—"

"Do you have any suspects in custody?"

"We're very—"

"And what about the stolen items?"

The mayor's had gone shrill. The Captain licked his lips, found them dry. He could feel his face getting hotter. "We'll be closing the case soon."

"*Soon?*" the mayor barked. "*Soon* isn't good enough, damn it!"

Chief Troutman straightened his shoulders imperiously. "Are you playing some sort of game, Jackson?"

The Captain looked over at him, thinking, *What I'd do if the mayor of the city wasn't sitting here* . . . He cleared his throat. "What do you mean, sir?"

The chief's knowing gaze slinked toward the mayor. "Well, if someone wanted to make Mayor Sampson look bad, stalling the investigation of a crime like this one would be one way to do it." He pulled his eyes off the man at the desk to glare at the Captain. "Do you agree, Captain Jackson?"

The Captain felt his scalp prickle with sweat and his stomach heaved as the six other eyes in the room fixed on him. That would do it. Run away before he vomited on the mayor's carpet and he'd be finished for sure. They'd be hooting over the story for years. It took an effort of will to stanch the disaster that was brewing in his gut and cool his brow. He drew a breath and steadied himself, feeling some of his equilibrium return. He glimpsed an opening. Another breath, and he was back. Now it was his turn.

"I don't know, sir," he addressed the chief smoothly. "I haven't been thinking about how someone could do harm to the mayor. But if you say so."

Chief Troutman's face went pink at the sly retort and in the corner of his eye, the Captain thought he saw the mayor smiling slightly.

"I *do* say so!" Troutman snapped back. "And we can't have it! I have other officers I can put on this if you're not capable. We've lost a lot of time, but if you want out, I'll take care of it. Right this minute!"

The Captain refused to rise to the chief's bait. "That won't be necessary at all," he said evenly. He looked at the mayor, cutting Troutman out of his line of vision. "I promised you results, and I'll deliver."

Mayor Sampson nodded and sat forward in his chair. "I hope you do," he said. "We can't afford to have it hanging over our heads any longer. I've got important people calling every day, wanting to know what we're doing to guard their welfare. I want this put away in the next forty-eight hours. You understand?"

The Captain said, "Yes, sir."

"No longer. Or there will be consequences."

"Yes, sir."

"Chief?" the mayor said. "Are we clear on this?"

Troutman's face went a shade darker at finding himself a target of the diatribe. "Yes, Mr. Mayor," he said, sounding like he was gagging.

The Captain all but clicked his heels, turned smartly, and walked out, holding his face and posture rigid.

Jake finished packing the trunk. He wasn't looking forward to the drive, but Mr. Purcell was anxious to leave. It didn't matter to him that they had been up until two o'clock the night before. He could sleep in the car. Jake was the one who would take the beating.

Right now, the weather was clear all the way up the eastern seaboard, and Purcell made the prediction that they'd be in New York no later than Sunday. Jake rolled his eyes in dismay. That translated into three spine-breaking days behind the wheel for him.

Once they had everything loaded, they climbed in and left Atlanta the same way they had arrived, moving quickly from the city to town and then farmland. Mr. Purcell fell oddly quiet for the first hours, and Jake figured he was still fretting over the business just before they left with the Negro singer.

Mr. Morgan had come steaming to their door at the crack of dawn. The man was furious. A guest had complained that he had seen the two of them walking down the hall with a Negro carrying a big guitar. The man had griped loudly to the desk clerk about *allowing coloreds in the hotel,* and other guests had overheard. The house detective was sent to search, but could locate neither the two New Yorkers nor any Negro with a guitar. He went into the back of the house and grilled the colored help. They were silent to a man.

Mr. Morgan wanted answers.

"We brought him in," Mr. Purcell told him directly. "We were able to come through your back entrance and get him upstairs without anyone seeing. We had no help. The fellow didn't know where he was. He is blind, you know. It was completely our doing. Is that clear enough?"

"We can't have it!" the manager said, his face flushing. "I'm sorry, but you'll have to vacate."

"We were checking out anyway," Mr. Purcell said, and closed the door.

This was true, though they might have stayed another day to try to round up and record more Negro singers. New York wanted the disks yesterday, in a rush to duplicate the masters and get the thousands of vinyl copies in the stores and catalogs. There was money to be made.

It was a clear sign that the recorded music business was on the verge of something. No longer were phonograph records only for the well-to-do. Poor families, black and white, could afford a small Edison player. Mr. Purcell knew that he and Jake would be back to the city, time and again, and so would Vocalion, Okeh, and every other label with the budget to send an engineer and rent a room. Atlanta was going to be a busy place for the record companies for years to come.

Lieutenant Collins looked up from his desk as Captain Jackson came stalking into the detectives' section like a careening truck, growling under his breath. The other detectives had seen this before and knew to keep their heads down and eyes averted. Collins didn't have the luxury. The Captain glared at him as if he'd done something wrong, which brought a moment of panic that went away when he realized it was just more of the man's ongoing rage.

Jackson made a sweeping gesture with his hand, and Collins got up to follow him into his office. Once inside, the senior officer jerked a thumb over his shoulder. Collins closed the door and waited.

Captain Jackson stood staring down at his tidy, severe desk without moving or speaking, his face a chunk of bloodless stone. For almost a minute, there was no sound except the traffic outside on Decatur Street and the ticking of the clock on the wall.

The lieutenant pictured the other detectives on the other side of the wall with their ears poised, waiting for the explosion. Though Collins was used to the Captain's catalog of bad moods, this one was dragging on too long. He reached behind him for the door-knob with the intention of slipping out unnoticed.

"Wait a minute!" the Captain said. Collins stopped. "Run down that fucking Joe Rose and arrest him."

"On what charge, sir?"

"I don't give a goddamn!" the Captain barked. "Suspicion of something. Pick him up, bring him in, and put him in a cell." He banged furious knuckles on his desk. "Then find that nigger gal of his. You know the one I'm talking about?"

"Yes, sir, but she—"

"Pearl Spencer. The one with the smart mouth. Let's see how smart she is when she's locked up in the Tower. Pick her up and bring her in. Go find her brother, too."

Lieutenant Collins was genuinely surprised. "What did he do?"

The Captain glared. "You hear what I just said?"

"Yes, sir."

"He works at Lulu's on Houston. You know that place, don't you?" He treated the junior officer to a sidelong glance.

"Yes, sir, I do."

"And if he ain't there, they got a house on Lyon Street." The Captain stopped, and a certain wild light came into his eyes. "Make sure they put him and Rose in a cell together."

Collins blinked. "Rose is white, sir."

"I don't give a shit if he's blue!" the Captain yelled. "Take them down to the colored section and toss them both in the worst cell they got. You understand that?"

Collins nodded. "Yes, sir."

Jackson glowered for a few seconds. "Where's Nichols?"

"He comes in at noon."

"As soon as he gets here, stick him on that desk." He treated his subordinate to a narrow-eyed stare. "He's not to move. You understand?"

"Yes, sir. I'll take care of it." The lieutenant reached for the doorknob again.

"That ain't all," Jackson said. Collins stayed where he was, wondering frankly what he had ever done to end up assigned to this madman.

"I want every officer we can spare out on the street. Send half of them down Decatur and the other half on Central Avenue. They're to round up every goddamn criminal they can lay hands on. Tell them they can crack as many heads as they want. I want it all shut down. No more liquor, no more numbers, no more whores."

Collins did his best to hide his astonishment. "Are you talking about a sweep?"

"I'm talking about law enforcement!" the Captain thundered. "You know what that is? Does anyone in this building know what the hell that is?"

Collins kept his mouth shut. This was crazy.

"I want both them damn streets as clean as church on Sunday morning!" the Captain raged on. "I don't want a drop of whiskey or one damn betting slip or a piece of pussy for sale anywhere downtown. Is that clear enough?"

Collins nodded, though he knew it was an impossible task, and was sure the Captain didn't have the authority to order it. The mayor and the chief of police had announced a plan to clean up the two scarlet thoroughfares, designed to show both of them in the best light. Now Captain Jackson was staging his own assault without even consulting them. They'd be furious. The bedlam it would cause, on the street and in the official corridors, would be a huge waste of time and effort that would produce neither the items stolen from the Payne mansion nor the thief who had stolen them. If that was his intention.

The lieutenant also understood that this was not the time to raise these points. Captain Jackson was in full rant, pointing a wild finger out his window and the streets beyond.

"I'm finished fucking with these people!" he snarled. "Someone's going to give up those jewels and the party that stole them by sunup on Friday! Is that clear to you?"

Collins gave a quick nod and made a quicker exit, out into a room that was dead with silence. The other detectives sat staring at him. He spent a few seconds considering resigning on the spot, then gestured for them to gather around.

Pearl was heading back into town to see Joe, intending to fill in what she hadn't told him in the room. Not everything; she didn't owe him that. She just didn't want him caught in the middle. That went for Sweet, too, though he wasn't a part of anything, except for being her brother. That was trouble enough as far as he was concerned.

Halfway up the Houston Street incline, she spotted the blue Atlanta police wagon and realized she was too late. She ducked into the space between Kelly's Grocery and the bicycle shop. Peeking out, she saw Joe come around the corner from Peachtree, and felt her heart jump into her throat. She wanted to call out to warn him, even though it was too late for that, too.

She watched him stop and saw his body tense with an urge to bolt. Then he relaxed and started walking again. A police detective intersected his path, and two uniformed cops appeared from behind to slap cuffs on his wrists and walk him to the wagon. She got a second shock when the rear doors swung open and she saw Sweet sitting inside. Her gut twisted and she leaned against the bricks for support. A few seconds later, the nausea was swept away by a spike of fear. She slipped away from the street through the alley, then turned east for home. If she hurried, she might beat them there and have time to grab some things to take with her.

———

When Joe rounded the corner at Houston Street, he saw the police wagon parked in front of Lulu's and knew it was there for him. Then he caught a glimpse in the open back doors and was astonished to see Sweet Spencer sitting inside, his hands in cuffs that were shackled to the floor. Sweet, staring morosely out the open doors, lifted his chin as his eyes flashed a message that told Joe if he wanted to run, now was the time.

Joe knew that would be foolish. An officer was already moving from the passenger side of the wagon and he sensed someone else coming from behind. A quick look told him that two cops had been posted by Lulu's and were now moving at an angle to block him from escaping back the way he came. Not that he intended to run. They'd get him, now or later. If he bolted, he'd have to keep going, and stay away for a long time.

Lieutenant Collins was leaning against the hotel's facade, right next to the double doors. He dropped his cigarette, straightened, and stepped to the middle of the sidewalk. His boyish face wasn't so placid and in fact was drawn with a certain tension.

Joe knew it was real trouble when the detective went through the formality of producing his badge again.

"Mr. Rose," Collins said. "You're being taken into custody, on suspicion of burglary." He bit off the words as if it was Joe's fault he had to perform this ridiculous duty.

Joe knew there was no point in arguing. The arrest had to be the Captain's doing, and nothing he said would change anything. Collins jerked his head, and Joe started across the street with a patrolman on either side of him. One of them snapped handcuffs on him. He didn't have to be told to step up into the wagon. They didn't shackle him to the floor, a deliberate nod to his pale skin, and an acknowledgment that Sweet unbound might be a dangerous character.

Joe slid along the bench until he was across from the Negro.

Sweet stared into his eyes. "You're fucking up my life, Mr. Joe," he said softly. "I knew you was going to, soon as you showed up in the kitchen. I knew it."

"I didn't do any crime, Sweet."

"You laid down with my little sister. How about that for a start?"

Joe said, "She's twenty-three years old. And they ain't taking me to jail for that."

"You know they gonna get her, too?" Sweet said. "They gonna stick her in the women's wing. Least I hope that's where she's goin'."

"They haven't got anything," Joe insisted. "They're fishing."

Sweet gave him a hard stare. "She was workin' at that house that got robbed. Don't matter if they fishin' or not. They got her right there."

"You know if they had any proof, we wouldn't be sitting here."

Sweet grunted and looked away, his brow folding stubbornly. "You need to give them whatever the hell it is they want. Both of y'all."

Joe said. "I don't—"

"Y'all better get me out of this shit!" Joe was surprised when Sweet's gritty black eyes came around all fretful and his voice broke a little. "You listen to me," he said. "I can't go back in. If I do, I know I'm gonna kill the first man crosses me. You understand? I don't care if it's the damn warden or some poor nigger sissy, someone gonna die. And then they'll hang me. I'll end up a dead man. All 'cause you can't keep your damn hands off Pearl. And because you didn't have nothin' better to do than mess with a fool like Jesse Williams."

Joe gave him a curious look. "You think this has something to do with him?"

Sweet ignored the question. "What the hell's wrong with you, anyway?"

Joe kept his mouth shut, puzzling over Sweet's mention of Jesse. The Negro glared at him for another few seconds before his gaze wandered off again. The cops closed the back doors of the wagon and the clack of the steel lock echoed off the sheet metal roof and sides. The engine coughed, the gearbox rattled, and they rolled out into the street.

"You hear what I'm saying?" Sweet said after they had gone another block. "I can't live inside no more." He jerked the chain, and the metal floor of the chassis buckled a little where the eye was connected. "So you better get me out of this, Mr. Joe. You get me out of this here shit, or I swear to God, I'll make you wish you had."

When Chief Troutman heard about the orders that had gone out from Captain Jackson's office, his first urge was to race down the one flight of steps and into the detectives' section and fire him on the spot. He could make it even more of a spectacle by bringing the biggest patrolmen he could find to escort the Captain out the door. Clearly, the man had lost his mind. He had nothing even close to the authority to mount such a stunt, never mind that his actions were blatantly disloyal. Troutman had all the reason he needed to put him out and was ready to do it.

His first day on the job as chief, he had quietly assigned certain trusted officers to keep an eye on the Captain, along with a few others from the prior chief's den of thieves who had somehow managed to hang on. He would have been happy to get rid of Jackson, except that the man was a crack hand at wrapping cases when no one else could. Every organization needed such a soldier. So when the mayor woke him up on Sunday morning with the mortifying news of the theft at the Payne mansion, he was only too glad to have a Grayton Jackson in his arsenal.

Even at that early hour, the hunger in Jackson's voice had seeped through the cool front, as he no doubt imagined the door to a glorious future opening before him. What he didn't know was that the chief and Mayor Sampson had long ago decided that he would get nowhere near a title within the department. The idea was preposterous; he was a step above a thug and already had too much of a reputation around the city.

And wasn't this day the proof? By the time the man had arrived back at police headquarters from the mayor's office, he had hatched a plan to roust every criminal in the city. As if that would produce the Payne mansion jewels. While that tempest was still brewing, word arrived that he had also ordered the arrest of a sneak thief named Joe Rose, along with a Negro brother and sister named Spencer, all on a vague suspicion that they were involved. It was floundering of the worst kind and proved that the Captain didn't have the first idea how to close the case, no matter what he had claimed. It was just more bluster.

The chief, who had spent most of his police career in administrative services, hated disorder, especially the kind represented by a lunatic like Grayton Jackson. The catchphrase "loose cannon" had come into vogue recently, and the chief couldn't think of a better description of the Captain, or a better image than a piece of loaded artillery careening wildly about the pitching deck of a ship, threatening to go off and blow a hole that would sink the vessel. And this was the fellow who had somehow convinced himself that he was chief of detectives material!

Instead of following his first instinct, the chief fell back on his habitual control. He was nothing if not a calculating man, and he wasn't about to give Jackson the advantage of being turned into a hero who had tried to make a difference, only to be stymied by a timid functionary. Mayor Sampson would have his hide if that's the way it played out.

Better to sit back and wait. The Captain's lunatic behavior would cause an uproar that would resound all the way to City Hall, maybe enough to wreck the man's career. Publicly, the chief would express his dismay over the reckless action; meanwhile, he had already passed word down the line that the officers on the street were to keep up with their duties but under no circumstances instigate the sort of rout Captain Jackson had decreed. Just the defiance of his orders might drive the Captain to do something crazy enough to finish it. If the burglary in Inman Park went unsolved, they'd all just have to live with that.

Having settled on this waiting game, the chief swiveled in his chair to gaze out the window. To the south, Fulton Tower stood stark against the gray midday clouds. He spent a few idle moments musing further on Captain Grayton Jackson and wondering if the whispers he had once heard about the man's wife could possibly be true. He doubted it, but one never knew about these things. He'd make a point of finding out. If nothing else worked, maybe he could use her to drive the Captain out of the Atlanta Police Department for good.

Fulton Tower served as the jail for both the city of Atlanta and Fulton County. Located at the corner of Hunter and Whitehall streets, it was a three-story brick complex of two wings with a sixty-foot spire up the middle, hence the name. The top floor was taken up by administrative offices, interrogation rooms, the infirmary, and the chapel. The wings of the ground floor were set aside for white prisoners and the basement for colored, each with a section reserved for women. There was an exercise yard that had also been the location of the gallows up until local politicians decided that hangings did not suit a modern city like Atlanta, and tore the structure down. Nonetheless, a visitor gazing at the skyline of the city would note that the highest profiles were the dirty smokestacks of the downtown factories and mills and the ominous profile of the Tower.

Joe and Sweet were delivered to the front desk, then taken into processing rooms, where they were stripped, sprayed down with cold water, then powdered for lice. Their street clothes were replaced by striped one-piece prison overalls that smelled like they hadn't been washed in years. Together, they were escorted to the worst cell in the foulest corner of the colored section, a concrete box with a hole in the floor and nothing else, not even a bare pallet. The walls, plaster over brick, were damp and the smell was nauseating even in the chill. Joe couldn't imagine how unbearable it would be in summertime.

A general racket of shouts, cries, and crazy whimpers echoed along the corridor, and Joe and Sweet weren't locked in for ten minutes when they heard the sounds of some poor prisoner taking a fearsome beating. Everybody got quiet, listening as the noise went from bellows of agony to pained shrieks and then into girlish whimpers as the bulls worked the fellow over. Finally, the cell door clanged shut and heavy steps clumped away. From the silence, the victim might have been dead in there.

Sweet turned to give Joe a cold look that said, *look what you got me into.* It was true; Sweet hadn't done a thing, except to have a little sister who had a yen for bad companions. Tangling with one such character had cost him a three-year stretch in Milledgeville. Now another one had him locked in a filthy and putrid cell that he might never leave.

There was nothing Joe could say, even if Sweet would listen, which wasn't likely. The black man turned his back and stared through the bars at nothing. Joe got the message and crouched on the floor to wait for the next chapter in this nightmare, and to fret over what might have happened to Pearl.

Pearl had just stepped onto the porch of the house on Lyon Street when a detective and a cop in uniform appeared on either side of the porch. The patrolman whistled and a police sedan came around the corner from Fort Street.

They acted bored as they got her settled in back and carried her across town. She was taken into the section of the Tower reserved for colored women and placed in a cell with a hard case of questionable gender.

"What'd y'all bring Miss Dolly today?" her cellmate grunted.

Miss Dolly, almost six feet tall and two hundred pounds if she weighed an ounce, was done up flapper-style and sported a mouthful of badly made false teeth. She looked Pearl up and down, grinning like she had been presented with a meal on a platter, and Pearl got ready to fight.

One of the two matrons who had brought her in told Pearl not to worry about Miss Dolly, because she might be getting transferred to another section soon. When Pearl asked what section that would be, the matrons exchanged a glance. The talker of the two said that since they weren't about to allow her in the white section, there was only one other place for her to go.

"But don't you worry, honey," the matron said as they walked off. "They pro'bly go ahead and put you in with the *white* boys."

The Captain fumed around his office in a rage of indecision for another hour before coming to his senses and realizing that sending flying squads to Decatur Street and Central Avenue could be a stupendous blunder. He was sure Chief Troutman was looking for an excuse to fire him and that would do it.

The Captain still held the trump card: He was the only one who had any hope of closing the burglary case. So he caught himself in time to rescind the orders. Except for one sporting house on Central Avenue, neither thoroughfare was open for business anyway. He sent word for the cops to stand down, then mulled at his desk until he came up with another ploy.

He used his telephone to make a quiet call to the mayor's office and was passed through a series of functionaries, only to be told that the mayor wasn't available, which didn't surprise him at all. Still, he managed to get the mayor's assistant on the line, and Mr. Gilbert agreed to come to police headquarters to meet with him and the chief.

Not ten minutes after he laid the telephone in its cradle, a call came from upstairs. Chief Troutman wanted to see him at two thirty. The Captain sat back, imagining how Troutman must be fuming at being outmaneuvered again. He was delighted by the progress of his scheme, and called out to Lieutenant Collins to inquire after Rose and Sylvester and Pearl Spencer.

"They've got Mr. Rose and Sylvester in the hole at the Tower," Collins replied as he stepped into the doorway. "Miss Spencer is on the women's side."

"Good enough."

"How long do you want to hold them?"

"Long as it takes," the Captain said decisively. "They need to know I mean business. One of them'll crack. You wait and see." He arranged some papers on his desk, then told the junior officer about the meeting in the chief's office. The lieutenant recognized the shifty ploy and also what a dangerous game Jackson was playing.

"Come back at two fifteen and we'll go up together," the Captain said.

Collins understood. When it came time to face the chief and the mayor's man, Jackson wanted a cohort, a witness, and maybe a scapegoat.

Captain Jackson did not fail to notice the flicker of cool contempt in Collins's expression as he excused himself, and he didn't like it. He felt his sharp distrust of the lieutenant return even stronger. The man was not a team player and a little too smart for his own good. In other words, he did not treat every word that dripped from the Captain's mouth as gospel and did not go along with the action on the street. Lately, he seemed to be running his own detective agency, maybe in cahoots with Sergeant Nichols. The Captain swore that if somehow he did end up in the chief of detectives' chair, those two and a few others he didn't like would be gone.

The police car came roaring up from behind, the siren sending up a wail like a suffering cat. Jake saw the car in the mirror and pulled over to let it go by. Instead of passing, it slowed and pulled off thirty feet back. Two uniformed officers stepped out, taking their time, and started a slow stroll up to the sedan.

Mr. Purcell looked out the back window and said, "Now, what the hell is this?"

One of the cops stepped to the driver's-side window, the other to the passenger side. Jake was about to ask the officer what was wrong when Mr. Purcell put a hand on his arm to silence him.

The policeman bending down to Jake's side took a long moment to gaze at the both of them. Then he said, "Y'all like to step out for a moment?" He straightened and moved back a few feet.

The two men opened their doors and got out to find the two policemen staring at them flatly, thumbs hooked over their gun belts. The one who had done the talking wore sergeant's stripes. His partner wore no insignias on his sleeves, a rookie. Both of them were too heavy for their frames and their faces were pale and doughy. They looked enough alike to be brothers, and maybe they were.

The sergeant shifted his gaze from Mr. Purcell and Jake and peered into the backseat. "What do we got here?" he asked.

"We're employed by the Columbia Record Company," Purcell said. "Those are master recordings we made in Atlanta, and we're taking them back to New York."

"New York," the sergeant mused. "Is that right?" He rolled his head from Jake to Mr. Purcell and back again. "You're the ones, then."

"Beg your pardon?"

The officer ignored the question. "Let's have a look in the trunk."

Purcell nodded slightly, and Jake stepped around with the keys. The second officer stood back a few feet more, eyeing him as if he was prey, fixing on his features. Jake was thinking, *He knows I'm a Jew,* and kept his own face impassive. He opened the trunk to reveal the recording machine and the cutter. The two cops studied the tangle of boxes, dials, and wires as if it had come from outer space.

"What's all that?"

"It's a recording machine."

"All right, then." The senior officer addressed Mr. Purcell. "We got a call about y'all. Seems there was a complaint swore out in Atlanta. Says you had a nigra in your hotel room. That's against state law and city ordinance."

"Then why weren't we charged at the time?" Mr. Purcell asked politely.

"I don't know nothin' about that," the cop said.

Mr. Purcell said, "Are you about to arrest us now?" It sounded like a challenge. It was meant that way. He had decided that if they wanted a fight, they could have it.

The sergeant seemed to grasp this in some dim way, and hesitated, unsure of what to do. "What you got here was obtained illegally," he said.

It was a ridiculous argument, and Purcell would have smiled had he not been so annoyed.

"So we got to confiscate it," the sergeant finished.

"Confiscate what?"

"Whatever it was you did with the colored man you had in your room."

Mr. Purcell gazed at the sergeant without speaking for such a long time that the junior officer felt compelled to hitch his gun belt and speak up. "You hear what he said, mister?"

"I heard him." Without shifting his stare or changing his tone, Mr. Purcell said, "Jake, get the list."

Jake turned to stare at the older man as if he couldn't believe what he was hearing.

"Get the list," Purcell repeated.

Jake went into the backseat and rooted around until he found the binder that held the tally of the recordings, the names of the performers with corresponding numbers. He crawled out and handed it to Mr. Purcell, who ran a finger down the top page.

"Thirty-two A, B, and C," he said quietly. "Get those disks for the officers, please."

Biting down on his anger, Jake went into the backseat once more, this time pawing through one of the boxes of masters until he located the correct ones. He lifted them from the box as if they were made of fine china and handed them out.

"Here we are," Mr. Purcell said. He took the disks in their paper sleeves from Jake and held them out before him. The sergeant drew back, at a momentary loss as to what to do, as if he had expected the two Yankees to make some sort of pathetic plea. He hefted the three disks for a few seconds, then handed them to his partner.

Mr. Purcell's eyes rested on the boxes briefly as they were passed. "Can we go?" he inquired.

"Yeah, I s'pose y'all can go," the sergeant said. "Just don't come down here tryin' no more of this kind of shit, y'understand?"

Mr. Purcell didn't answer. Instead, he said, "Officer? I want to tell you that what you've got there might be worth a large amount of money someday."

The sergeant frowned. "What now?"

"I'm telling you that someone would be wise to hold on to those," Mr. Purcell said.

He saw the glimmer of stupid greed in the policeman's eyes. He left it there, motioning Jake back into the car. The younger man, seething over the surrender, refused to look at him. Instead, he glared at the mirror and watched the two cops move back to their car, heads together as they conferred over what they now possessed.

They got in their car and waited until Jake turned the key, stepped on the starter pedal, and pulled out onto the two-lane, then followed, dropping off once they reached the county line.

—————

As they stood waiting outside Chief Troutman's office, Lieutenant Collins noticed that Captain Jackson had spent some time
in the men's room. His suit was precise, with not a stitch out of
line, and his hair had been combed into a severe helmet. When
the door opened, he marched into the chief's office like he was on
honor guard. Despite the gravity of the business at hand, Troutman had to turn his head for a moment to hide his amusement
at this preening display. It was all the more evidence that the Captain was losing his wits.

For his part, Captain Jackson was delighted to note that his
preparation had been worthwhile. As promised, Mr. Gilbert
from the mayor's office was present, and no doubt ready to report back. There was no way Chief Troutman could bury him;
and if the chief had agreed to the meeting in the hope that Jackson would make a fool of himself, he had miscalculated.

Still, it was his office, and the other three men had to wait
until he crossed his arms and raised his thin eyebrows expec-
tantly for Captain Jackson to begin.

"I want to report progress on the Inman Park burglary," he
announced without preamble. "I have three people in custody in
the Tower, and at least one of them was at the Payne home Saturday night." He leaned in the direction of the mayor's assistant
with a cloying little smile and said, "So you can tell the mayor
we're in sight of closing the case."

The chief stood by, itching to ask Jackson why he had waited
so long to bring in these *suspects*, then thought better of it. Any
opening would lead to more of the show, and he saw how Mr.
Gilbert was now regarding the Captain with some interest,
though he couldn't tell if the mayor's man was impressed or
amused by the dramatics.

Quickly, the chief said, "Very well, then," and stood up to
end the session. It wasn't just that Jackson gave him the willies.
He wanted him out of the office before he could completely win
over Gilbert, who of course had the mayor's ear.

The Captain understood this. His face flushed with the pride of victory and he all but bowed as he made his exit. Lieutenant Collins, who had spent the tortured minutes wanting to blurt out that it was all a sham, and that in fact the Captain had nothing except three bodies in jail, followed along behind.

# TEN

Less than an hour after Pearl had been locked in the cell with Miss Dolly, the two matrons returned. Keys jangled and the door swung open.

"Out," said the talker of the two, and that was all. There was no doubt who the order was meant for; Miss Dolly didn't glance up from the yellowed pages of her romance magazine.

The matrons were regarding her with a cold apathy that frightened her, and she had to bite down on her fear. The cell door slammed shut, and they started down the corridor. When she glanced to her left and caught the quiet one treating her to a dirty stare, her stomach twisted.

They ushered her up the stone staircase to the ground floor, then turned into the north wing. She was sure of it now: They were going to put her in with the men and let those animals have at her. She clenched her jaw and braced herself, swearing she would not go through what they were planning. She'd fight, so they'd have to beat her unconscious or kill her.

They passed along the corridor between the cells, and when the men noticed her passing, a frenzy went down the line like a kerosene fire. They shrieked inhuman sounds and reached from between the bars with filthy, grabbing paws, the faces red and contorted and the yellowed teeth bared. The matrons slapped the hands back as if they were swatting flies. The swell of howls echoed crazily off the stone walls.

All the while, Pearl refused to turn her head, keeping her chin up and eyes straight ahead, inflaming the prisoners all the more. Some of them were actually shaking the bars like apes in a zoo. A few grabbed their crotches and started pulling just at the sight of her.

Though the ordeal lasted no more than a half minute, it felt like it took ten times that long to reach the squared space at the end of the corridor. On either side of this box was a cell with a solid wood door with a tiny slot of a window instead of bars, special rooms for some special kinds of confinement. The silent matron unlocked the door on the right, and her partner waved Pearl inside.

Now she wondered if they were going to install her there to let the men line up and take turns. Imagining this horror, she felt like sobbing for mercy. The door closed with a thump and the lock clacked behind her.

She waited until the matrons had moved off before settling herself enough to take a look around. The cell was ten feet wide and twelve deep, with mortared stone walls. There was an uncovered pallet on the floor and a privy hole in the corner. A window six inches high and a foot wide was cut into the back wall. The door was two-inch-thick oak with iron fittings. Through the heavy wood and stone muffled sound, she could still hear the men's shouts from outside, though over the next minutes the chaos subsided. The other prisoners had either been put down or placated with a promise.

She walked the perimeter of the cell one time, encountering the usual small armies of roaches and other vermin swarming over the walls. She stepped to the window and peered out. The sun was a dim yellow circle above the brown cloud that rose from the rail yards, making the city look like an old faded photograph.

She turned away, in her misery thinking about Joe and wondering if he was going to come and save her. Not that she deserved it.

Joe and Sweet sat in the cell for the rest of the afternoon with no cigarettes, food, or water. The hole in the floor that served as a toilet was stopped up. With the sun gone, the only light came from a bare bulb outside.

A few minutes before six o'clock, a jailer appeared to unlock the cell.

"Let's go, Rose," he said.

"Go where?"

"Captain wants to see you."

"What about him?" Joe said, gesturing to Sweet.

"He ain't none of your business," the jailer said. "Now let's go."

They took him two floors up to the end of a hallway and into a windowless interrogation room with a heavy door, the kind that would mute shouts, cries, and moans. Inside, the Captain and a thick-bodied young man wearing corporal's stripes on the sleeves of his uniform were waiting. A table had been pushed against the side wall, and two of the three wooden chairs had been shoved into the corner. The third one remained in the center of the floor.

The Captain was leaning against the back wall, his arms folded across his chest. The corporal, a little shorter than his superior but as thick as a barrel across the middle, slouched in the corner on Joe's right, an immobile lump, though Joe had no doubt the man could snap out of his crouch and be on him. He had seen the type before, a hard case with the kind of dead eyes that revealed nothing save a talent for delivering serious pain or worse. Gun bulls who had been on the job too long had that same look, a general statement that they would crush a man or an insect with an equal amount of efficiency of emotion. All of them had wretched histories that they paid back every waking day.

Captain Jackson nodded curtly to the chair. Joe sat down. The Captain stared at him for almost a half minute, the gaze fixed somewhere past him. Joe waited. Finally, without moving a muscle except for those around his mouth, Jackson said, "Your gal steal those jewels?"

"What gal is that?" Joe inquired. In the heartbeat's pause that ensued, he realized he had made a mistake. The next thing he knew, he was sideways, the left side of his head had collided with the floor, and stars were exploding behind his eyes.

The corporal had apparently been instructed to listen for just such a gambit, and had come out of the corner in one large stride to smack Joe with a hand as broad and thick as a beefsteak, knocking him out of the chair. Instinctively, he curled into a ball. When his vision cleared, he saw that the corporal had retreated into the corner, slumping and yawning as if nothing had happened.

Captain Jackson was regarding him with a flat expression. "Get up," he said. "We're going to try it again."

Joe rose to one knee, his ears still buzzing. After a few seconds, he righted the chair and pushed himself into it, blinking to clear his head.

"She got those jewels?" the Captain said in exactly the same tone of voice.

"If she does, she didn't tell me so," Joe said.

"What did she tell you?" the Captain said. "You didn't spend all your time in that room at the Hampton fucking, did you?"

Joe wasn't surprised that they'd been watching. It made him wonder why they hadn't come after the two of them sooner.

"She's got a story about what happened that night," he said.

"She does, does she?" the Captain said. "And you believe it?" He stopped and his thin lips barely curled. "She's a fine-looking piece for a colored gal. And I'd guess that once she spreads them legs, you'd believe just about anything she says. Wouldn't you?" He studied Joe for a grudging moment. "All right, let's hear this *story* of hers."

Joe said, "She got hired on to work at the Christmas party."

"I know that part."

"One of the other girls passed her a note. She thought it was from me."

"Was it?"

"No, it wasn't."

"Then where'd it come from?"

"Some fellow handed it to the other girl outside. It was dark and she couldn't make out his features."

"What did this note say?"

"For her to go down to the basement and unlock the outside door."

"And that's what she did."

"She thought it was from me." Joe felt his face reddening. "So . . . yes, she . . . she did it."

The Captain said, "So she gets this note and goes downstairs, thinking you wanted to get in and rob the home. Is that what you're saying?"

"Except for the last part," Joe lied.

The Captain cocked his head. "What about the last part?"

"She thought it was me, but she figured I just wanted let in to see . . . to meet her."

Jackson shifted his weight from one leg to the other, his first sign of life, and came up with a smile that was cold and jagged. He said, "You telling me that she thought it an invitation to go down to the basement to meet you for a quick fuck? Do I have that right?"

"She didn't know I was in town, so it—"

"I didn't ask if she knew you were in town," the Captain snapped. "What I did ask was did she think the note was an invitation to go down to the basement to meet you for a fuck."

Joe said, "I guess that could be true." As he hoped, the Captain was too caught up in the *fuck* part to catch his falsehood.

"All right, then," Jackson said. "She goes downstairs with her drawers all wet, 'cause she thinks she's about to get some Indian dick, and unlocks the door, expecting you to be standing there with a hard-on."

"We call it a totem pole," Joe said.

He had the sense not to crack a smile and wait to see if the Captain or the corporal did. It would have been a long wait; both policemen held their dead stares. He might as well have delivered the quip to two blocks of Georgia pine.

"See, I don't know . . . I'm not sure if I'm Indian or not," he offered lamely.

"Expecting you to be standing there with a hard-on," the Captain repeated, as if he hadn't heard a word.

Joe nodded, in one crazy corner of his brain thinking, *Yes, pretty much like your wife did that day,* knowing that if he was insane enough to actually make such a crack, he'd never get out of there alive.

"But you claim you weren't around," the Captain continued.

"That's right. Nowhere near."

"Where were you at the time?"

"I was at the Ace Club in Lime Row. With a young lady."

The Captain's eyebrows hiked. "Is that so? Is this young lady around to provide you with an alibi?"

Joe said, "I don't know where she is."

"Uh-huh." The Captain stared. "So after Miss Spencer sees you ain't there, she goes back in, but instead of locking the door, she leaves it the way it is. Why would she do that?" He seemed to be thinking out loud, and turned to the corporal, as if the dullard might illuminate him on this point. When the patrolman didn't offer any comment, he said, "That was how the perpetrator got in, then. We checked. The butler recognized every person that came through the front door, and they all had invites. So it sounds to me like Miss Pearl Spencer's an accomplice."

Now he unfolded, bending down, laying his hands on his knees, and getting on eye level with Joe, fixing him with a cold, green gaze. Unconsciously, Joe drew away.

"You know I can keep her locked up as long as I want," the Captain said, his eyes brightening. "And I think I'll do that. I'm going to hold her until you come up with something I can use. You can do that, seeing as you're a goddamn *detective* now." His snicker sounded like an icicle breaking. "And if you don't deliver, and I mean quick, I'll just hand her over to our male inmates for the evening. If I still don't get results, then I'll introduce her to Corporal Baker here." He tilted his head in the corporal's direction. "He needs some amusement. And that brother of hers? We'll put a charge on him. Aiding and abetting, maybe. He'll go to Milledgeville and this time he won't come back. You won't see either one of them for a long time, and when you do, I can guarantee you won't like it. You know what ten years of hard time can do to a man? Or a woman?" He stared at Joe another few seconds, then straightened. "You've got twenty-four hours to come up with something." He started to move toward the door.

"Why me?" Joe demanded, and then flinched, expecting the corporal to be on him.

The Captain stopped and his cold smile came back. "Why you?" he said. "Because you deserve it, that's why. You're a no-good thief. You've been getting away with stealing from decent folks in this city for too long. Because you keep going into places you don't belong. Because you went and stuck your nose in police business over some goddamn pimp. Because you put your goddamn *totem pole* up a woman who's guilty as hell. Because I told you what I wanted, and you still came here empty-handed. Because you don't cooperate. That's why you."

He straightened to his full height and took a moment to tug at the lapels of his jacket as if he was adjusting a suit of armor.

"Now I'm going to cut you loose," he said. "And the next time I see you, you better have something. You can run, but you'll be leaving Miss Spencer and her brother to me. And your friend Sergeant Nichols. Him, too. You understand?"

With that, he turned away and marched out. As soon as the door slapped closed behind him, Corporal Baker took two strides and swung his other hand, this time catching Joe on the left side of the head and knocking him out of the chair again. A reward for his insolence toward the Captain, he had seen this one coming and still couldn't avoid it. As he lay there with his head vibrating, the cop walked out the door, leaving him to get up on his own power.

The two turnkeys who had brought him there were waiting outside to grab his arms and escort him downstairs. As they passed through the first-floor lobby on the way to the back door, he saw Albert lurking a few steps down one of the corridors. Apparently, the detective had gotten word that he was there and had shown up to make sure he wasn't murdered in his cell. Joe felt a thump in his chest at this unexpected kindness and made a move to call out, but Albert gave a sharp warning shake of his head and quickly turned away.

After they finished with Rose, the Captain told Corporal Baker to go fetch the car, bring it around back, and wait. Baker did not ask how long he would be waiting, or where they would be going. Baker never asked about anything. It was one of the things the Captain liked about him.

Once the corporal went away, Jackson descended the back stairs to the basement and negotiated several corridors to reach the guard's desk. The officer on duty turned over the keys without hesitation and directed the Captain to the cell at the end of the row.

Pearl heard the footsteps approaching. The bolt slid back and the door swung open, creaking with rust.

"Good evening, Miss Spencer." The Captain stood staring at her for a long moment. "I just had a nice talk with that friend of yours, Mr. Rose," he said, and then stepped into the cell and closed the door behind him.

The Buick rattled over another mile of dirt road and then it was asphalt again. The night was falling and the headlamps picked up a signpost announcing another sixty miles to Charlotte.

Jake Stein hadn't said a word since they drove away from the policemen, fuming in silence over the way Mr. Purcell had surrendered the best of what they had recorded, and to a couple bumpkins who were assuredly Klansmen. He responded to the older man's attempts at conversation with monosyllables, and made a point of ignoring his lectures on the amusing trivia they passed along the way.

Finally, exasperated, Purcell ordered him to pull over, and Jake steered the sedan onto the berm, then sat flexing his fingers on the steering wheel. The professor stayed silent for so long that he started getting antsy. He gave up, and looked over to see those gray eyes regarding him kindly.

"I had to do it," Purcell said. "Otherwise, they might have taken everything. And then they'd be waiting for us when we come back. And we will. We'll do even better. No rushing."

"But we lost those disks."

"They'll turn up someday." He smiled wistfully. "You might be an old man and I'll probably be gone. But they'll surface. You wait and see. And then you can come to my memorial service and tell me I was right."

Jake was amused. "Come to your service?"

"You'll be welcome," George Purcell said. "Now can we please go home?"

Joe, woozy from the beating, stumbled his way across the aqueduct from Whitehall onto Peachtree Street until he found himself lost among the throngs of workers starting for home and Christmas shoppers heading for the stores. It was like he had entered another world. A light rain had begun to fall, and the faces of the pedestrians he passed were all turned down, whether in day's-end weariness or the distraction of recounting the gift lists in their heads. No one noticed him and his bruises. No one knew that he had taken a beating. No one knew or cared about Pearl or Sweet still sitting in their cells in Fulton Tower.

When he arrived back at the Hampton, he was surprised to find Willie pacing up and down, his guitar strapped across his back. Random raindrops were dotting the sidewalk.

"What are you doing here?" Joe said.

"I come by to let you know about Jesse's funeral, and the man at the desk told me the police pulled you in," Willie said. His face was knit with concern, and for the second time in the past half hour, Joe felt a rush of gratitude at a kindness.

"What happened to you?" the blind man said, and without waiting for an answer, raised a hand and ran the tips of his fingers deftly over one side of Joe's face, then switched hands and felt the other side.

"Who did that?" Willie said.

"One of the Captain's boys laid me out good."

"What for?"

"It's this burglary business," he said glumly. "They want me to give them something. Or someone." His legs were feeling shaky, and he waved for Willie to follow him inside. No one at the Hampton would say anything about it, due to Joe's standing as a regular and Willie's blindness. Still, they moved to the far corner of the lobby, where they were mostly out of sight, and sat down in the worn chairs.

Momentarily, Joe felt a little better as the buzzing in his ears subsided. "What about Jesse's funeral?" he asked.

"They burying him tomorrow," Willie said. "Procession starts at Eaton's on Nelson Street."

"What time?"

"Ten o'clock. You gonna be there?"

"If I ain't back in jail." Joe closed his eyes. "Or worse."

Willie was quiet for a minute. Then, thinking to change the subject, he smiled slightly and said, "You know I cut some records for the Columbia people, Mr. Joe."

Joe opened his eyes. "You did?"

"They come by yesterday, in the afternoon." Willie was smiling. "Took me 'round to the Dixie and I sang six songs for them. I didn't say nothing when I got back because Jesse was doing so poorly. And he was gone, and . . ."

Joe said, "Well, good for you, Willie. Did you use that one you wrote for him?"

"Naw, I didn't want to. I'll cut it someday, though."

" 'The Dying Crapshooter's Blues,' is that right?"

"That's it, all right."

"So Little Jesse'll go down in history."

"Well, I don't know," the blind man murmured modestly. It was a pleasant interlude and they got quiet again, listening to the rain pocking on the window.

After some minutes went by, Willie said, "You figured out why he got shot like that?"

Joe paused before he spoke. He really didn't want Willie dragged into the mess along with him. On the other hand, he was the one who had started it.

"I was starting to get somewhere, but then I got knocked off it. Jesse died, and then they found Robert. I still might have been able to keep going. Except this burglary in Inman Park got in the way."

"That's funny, ain't it?"

"What is?"

"The way you couldn't get to one because of the other."

Joe stared at him for a moment, then looked away. The raindrops danced on the dark window ledge behind them.

Presently, Willie tilted his head in Joe's direction and said, "You think they're mixed up some way? I mean what happened to Jesse and this here burglary business that's got the Captain so riled."

Joe treated him to a narrow-eyed look. "Why you ask that?"

Willie shrugged. "They happened right on top of each other, ain't that so? And somehow you got stuck on one and then the other."

Joe mused for a moment on how sharp Willie could be. Sometimes he saw things more clearly than a sighted person.

"Maybe they are," he said. "I think Jesse knew why he got shot, but he was waiting to tell me why. Then just when he was ready to do it, he died." He paused for a few seconds, brooding. "What I know is that the cop who shot him was in cahoots with the Captain at the same time the Captain was on the hook over that burglary." He drew a circle in the air for his own benefit. "So you get to the end of one, and you're at the beginning of the other. And I keep going around and around in there."

"What are you going to do about it?" Willie said.

Joe shifted in his chair. "I have to get Pearl and Sweet out of the Tower. To do that, I have to find who the hell snatched those goddamn jewels. I just hope to God whoever it was ain't left town, because I only have about twenty-four hours, and then it's over."

"What about Little Jesse?" Willie said.

"I can't do anything for him now. He should have talked

while he had the time. The only thing left is to put him in the ground. We'll probably never find out what happened." He shook his head glumly and said, "I wasn't the person for that job, Willie."

"But you're all we got, Joe." The blind man stood up, hoisting his guitar. "You want me to come by and fetch you on my way to the funeral?"

"Yeah, that'd be fine," Joe said, now sounding like the weight of the world had landed on him.

Willie came up with a bemused look. "You know what your problem is?" he stated wisely. "You spend way too much time with black folks."

Joe laughed, allowing that the blind man had a point. "Ain't nothing I can do about that, either," he said.

Waving a hand in farewell, Willie walked off across the lobby and out the door with his usual perfect sense of direction. Joe sat for another few minutes, then pushed himself out of the chair and headed for the staircase.

As he passed the front desk, the night clerk looked up. "Got something for you," he said, and handed over an envelope, expensive-looking, cream white.

Joe thought, *Now what?* and thought about giving it right back. Every message that had come his way lately had led to bad news and he wasn't in the mood for more. Not this night. He tucked the envelope in a coat pocket and continued on.

When he got to his room, he hung his coat and hat on the back of the door, then took two aspirin and washed them down with a palmful of tepid water from the pitcher. He sat down on the bed and took off his shoes. A few minutes went by as he stared dully at the worn carpet and felt the throbbing in his head recede.

The envelope hovered at the edge of his vision as it peeked from his coat pocket. He didn't need another problem or another anything to frazzle his brain this evening. At the same time, if he didn't look, it would just drive him crazy. And who knew? Maybe the solution to all his problems was in there, printed out in neat letters. So with a resigned sigh, he got up and went about extracting the envelope and tearing it open to read the inscribed note.

*Mr. Rose, Please contact me on a matter of immediate urgency.*

*Mrs. May Ida Jackson. 5-6799.*

Joe slapped a hand on his forehead in exasperation. Of all the times for the crazy woman to decide she wanted his company! As if he didn't have enough trouble. He threw the note aside and went to the dresser to get his bottle and a glass, then carried the drink to the bed and stretched out, his head propped on the pillow.

The whiskey relaxed him and he found himself laughing quietly. Poor little addle-brained, ravenous May Ida, popping up like that. She could not have picked a worse time, the very moment he happened to be locked in a grim battle with her husband. As he sipped his drink, he picked up the note and read it again, his thoughts rounding a corner.

The timing was simply too odd, and settling on the words *immediate urgency* didn't sound like her at all. The notion crossed his mind that she could be up to something other than an afternoon's dalliance. He wondered if she knew something or was mounting some crazy and devious plot of her own. One side of his mind told him to go downstairs and call her, while the other told him she was the last person in the world he needed to be talking to now.

He went around with it a few more times and then gave up. It was too much at the end of such a wearying day and the whiskey was knocking him out. He laid back and let the note drop from his fingers as he drowsed off. Time passed, and the characters in the story promenaded by in a dream parade, starting with Pearl, and followed by Little Jesse, Willie, Sweet, Albert

Nichols, the Captain, Lieutenant Collins, Officer Logue, Daisy, Molly O'Connell, Mrs. Cotter, Robert Clark, a different Pearl, and finally May Ida. It ended with her.

He came awake and sat up, his head clearing. There was no way he could ignore May Ida. He had to find out why she had chosen this moment to send a message. If she was setting a trap or just looking for a lover boy, he'd sense that easily enough and make a quick escape. He'd only done it about a hundred times before.

Downstairs, he crossed the lobby and stepped into the telephone booth. He lifted the earphone, turned the crank, and waited. When the operator came on the line, he read off the number. A few seconds later, he heard a low muttering buzz.

On the third ring, the connection was made. "Good evening. Jackson residence." The voice was breathy and florid.

"This is Joe Rose speaking."

"Why, Mr. Rose!" May Ida twittered. "What a pleasant surprise."

"It's pleasant to talk to you again, too," Joe said, thinking how foolish he must sound. "I got your note."

"Oh, yes! My note. I was wondering if perhaps we could meet." Now she was twittering like a canary.

It was all too familiar, and Joe figured he'd made a mistake calling her. She had nothing he wanted, and with his luck of late, if he did see her, she'd crack right before his eyes and bring the rest of Captain Jackson's wrath down on his head.

He cleared his throat. "Well, that sounds swell," he said. "But I don't know when I could make an appointment. Right now I'm in—"

"You can stop that!" The sweet twitter turned brittle, and Joe stood there, his mouth dropping, startled at the sudden change of tone. "Now you listen to me." She was biting off her words. "I've got something you need, and it might not be what you think. It will be worth your while to meet me."

Joe thought for a second. "All right," Joe said. "When?"

May Ida's sweet side resurfaced as quickly as it had departed. "I think tomorrow would be fine. I'm going to do some Christmas shopping. I'll be at the back entrance of the Rich's Store at exactly noon."

"All right," he said.

"I'll hope you'll be there," she went on. "So we can talk."

"What do—"

"I look forward to seeing you." The line went dead. Joe stared at the telephone, then stepped out of the booth. He climbed the stairs back to his room and went to work on the drink he hadn't finished.

Earlier that evening, May Ida had been sitting on the couch, her mind miles away as she fell under the spell of the sweet croon of Mr. Russ Colombo, when she was snapped out of her swoon at the sound of the key in the lock. The rosy mist evaporated as she blinked in confusion and then sighed with dismay to find herself in that little room in that little house in that dull corner of the city. She laid the afghan aside as the door swung open and Grayton came stalking in. A glance at the clock on the mantel told her he was even later than his usual late self. She reached over to lift the arm on the Victrola (her husband didn't care for music at all) and stood up to welcome him home.

He barely greeted her and as usual displayed no affection. In fact, he never came home hungry for her. She considered this a blessing.

For the first few months after their marriage, he had done his duty and went about mounting her, though so clumsily it almost brought her to laughter. That a grown man could be so inept! He reminded her of one of the country boys she used to lure into haylofts back in Scottsdale—worse, even. He didn't seem to get the idea, other than as a way to relieve an urge.

In any case, he soon tired of that and let her know that from then on he wanted French by shoving her to her knees and unbuttoning his trousers. She complied dutifully, though without any pleasure. After a few dozen times, even that failed to move him and he stopped demanding anything, other than that she keep the house clean and cook the meals.

He did not touch or kiss her and did not look at her ripe figure when she undressed. He had not tried to love her in any manner for almost two years. She didn't know if someone else was servicing his needs and didn't care. They'd been sleeping in separate beds since their first night together because he couldn't stand another body that close to him.

It was just as well he didn't try to take her or she might have some explaining to do. If the Captain paid any attention at all, he would by now have caught the scent left over from an afternoon's interlude. A prudent woman who was deceiving her husband would bathe and employ a douche the moment her paramour left the house. May Ida never bothered. That a police officer of his stature couldn't put such a simple two and two together amused, saddened, or angered her, depending on her mood at the moment. As time went by, the only thing she felt for him was a grim revulsion.

On this night, like every other one, all he wanted was his supper and his bottles, and she stepped into the kitchen to warm a plate of pork chops, parsleyed potatoes, and lima beans. He took off his coat and loosened his tie, picked up the evening newspaper, and carried it to the kitchen table, where he made a noisy show of sitting down and fussing like an impatient diner in a restaurant where the service was slow. She went to the ice locker to fetch him a bottle of beer without being told. She hoped he was thirsty.

"There you are, dear," she murmured, and placed the bottle at his elbow. She wanted him good and drunk, and the strong home brew would be a start. He'd get to the hard liquor soon enough.

The Captain snatched up the bottle and drank it halfway empty in one long swallow. Banging it down on the table, he wiped his mouth and belched loudly. Then he snapped open the newspaper. May Ida went about playing a private joke as she prepared his meal, bending down to present her round bottom, then bending forward so he could view her bosomy cleavage. As usual, he took no notice.

By the time he had reached the fold, the first bottle was empty and she was there with a fresh one. She returned to her stove, casting the occasional glance over her shoulder to check on his progress. Had he looked up, he would have seen eyes that gleamed with venom that would have startled him. Though he was far too oblivious for that.

He read down the rest of the front page, making angry little sounds, as if every word inflamed him. She knew that what he took from his reading was that the whole world was a mess peopled by fools—not counting himself, of course. He punctuated his point by rustling noisily through the remainder of the pages.

It got quiet, except for the ticking of the clock on the wall over the sink. A silent minute passed, and May Ida turned her head to see him staring dazedly at the newspaper, his face blank and bloodless, wearing a kind of ghastly smile as he held the edges of the page crumpled in his fingers. She had seen that look a lot lately. It was her first sign that told her that something strange was going on.

Quietly, so as not to break his mood, she put his dinner before him, along with a third bottle of beer. She didn't know where it came from, only that once a week a fresh case turned up on the back porch. She set his place the way he liked it, then took the opposite chair, put on her best innocent face, and said, "How was your day today?"

He came out of his funk to glare at her as if she was to blame for the woes that had befallen him. She was used to that, too.

He went about attacking his dinner with a wolfish vengeance, plainly not tasting what he was eating. Halfway through, he stopped and sat sulking for a few dark seconds, staring at nothing, his mouth an inverted U. He picked up the bottle to swill some more beer, took up his fork, put it down again, and pushed his plate aside. The remainder in the bottle was gone in one long draft.

May Ida's face remained blank as she picked up the plate and carried it to the sink. Always the dutiful wife, she went under the sideboard for the fifth of whiskey that was stashed there.

The Captain kept the good stuff, real Canadian that he had taken from a runner caught coming through the city on his way to Florida. There were four cases stacked in the basement. He had laughed darkly about the incident, opining that the runner had probably ended up dead for losing the load. Too bad; the fool should have gone around.

She now poured a tumblerful, knowing he would switch from the beer without a pause, and that's when his tongue would get really loose.

She knew he held her in such little regard that he didn't care what he said in front of her. She didn't care to hear it much, either. He was mostly just crabbing about police department politics. But over the past several weeks, she had begun to discern something in his blather that took on a certain life and shape that even her addled mind couldn't ignore. She listened more closely, picked up more pieces to add to the ones she'd already collected. A delicious thrill traveled from her brain and spread to her chest, stomach, and loins that he couldn't detect this trickery. It was better than slipping around with paramours, and when she realized that what she had learned could ruin him, she decided to do just that. He'd never know what hit him.

Most nights, she would have a glass or two of whiskey to ease her loneliness, dull her anger, and help her sleep. The Captain didn't notice that she hadn't taken an evening drink in two weeks. She made sure his glass was always full and hers was always empty, so that her mind was as clear as the winter's first ice.

It worked. He held so much anger beneath his hard crust that once the liquor cracked it, all sorts of secrets seeped out. This was how she learned about a number of the ne'er-do-wells she later arranged to meet. She also picked up all sorts of luscious gossip. Such as the high-ranking and pious city official who regularly had light-skinned Negro girls released from jail to do domestic chores at his home, though not one of them ever spent a minute cleaning house. Or the cabal of upper-level officers who—until Mayor Sampson got elected—made a nice living diverting stolen goods from the property room to family, friends, mistresses, and fences. Or one of the former mayor's closest advisers who was having illicit trysts with the sixteen-year-old (and presumably virginal) daughter of the president of the city's largest bank, livening their interludes with an opium pipe. Or the well-regarded Baptist minister who was reputed to enjoy giving long baths to boys still in knee pants. And so on.

If May Ida had managed to keep track of these scandals, she might have made herself rich as a blackmailer. But she was forever getting things mixed up and just forgetting. This time, she was determined to fix her skittish mind on something and keep it there.

The Captain picked up the whiskey glass for a fast swig. He brooded for a moment, his mouth drooping into a jagged gash. Another long sip of liquor and he growled something, the kind of gruff mutter that told May Ida that his ire was bubbling like a pot coming to boil. She produced her best face of simpleminded interest.

Among the staccato fragments he spewed out over the next minutes were the usual "sons of bitches," "fucks," and "bastards." She waited, making sympathetic sounds, and gradually he began mouthing complete thoughts, speaking as if she—or some other invisible party—had been engaged all along in the dialogue that was going on inside his head.

"—should have seen the look on that fuck Troutman's face when the mayor lit into him," he said.

"You saw the mayor?" She knew he was vain when it came to important people.

"Was in his *office*." He smiled—to himself, of course. "Thought they had me, but I won that round." Then he laughed shortly. "They think I'm some kind of goddamn fool. They don't know what I know."

May Ida widened her already wide eyes, appropriately impressed.

"And I *know*," he pronounced with an ominous note in his voice.

May Ida saw the hard light flashing in his eyes. He was looking at her as if he had just noticed her sitting there and didn't like it.

"Something wrong?" she asked.

"Something wrong . . . yeah, I'd say there's something *wrong* . . ." He produced a cruel smile. "It's gonna get fixed, though. Everything's going to get fixed. Every damn thing." He drank some more. "I had to lay down with some filthy goddamn dogs." He stared at her, his green eyes swimming out of focus. Abruptly, he said, "But I know who has the goods."

"The . . . what goods?"

"The *goods*!" He glowered at her like she was an imbecile. Then his gaze shifted again. "She thinks she's going to get away with it," he growled in slow syllables. "But she ain't gonna get away with *nothin'*."

"Who are you—"

"You wanna play games with *me*?" He glared at her suddenly, his eyes wild and his face going red. "You think you can cross Grayton Jackson?"

May Ida felt her heart jump into her throat. A terrifying moment went by before she saw that his fury wasn't directed at her at all, but some other invisible presence that was bedeviling him.

"She's gonna . . . they're *all* gonna end up the same way if they cross me!" he snarled roughly. "Six feet in the ground. The pimp got his, all right, and that bitch'll be next. And that fucking *Rose,* too."

May Ida froze at the mention of the name, and held her gaze steady, lest he read something in her eyes. The clock on the wall ticked away. She stole a peek and saw that the Captain had fallen into a deeper funk. It lasted nearly a minute, and when his face arranged itself into a familiar self-pitying frown, she breathed again. She knew what was coming.

It began with his eyes blinking as if he was holding back tears. "This here's a decent city to live," he said. "And you know why? Because of men like me. And what thanks do we get for it?" He flapped a loose hand in the air. "None! Not a fucking word! And what happens when it's time to fill a job? They don't even look at me." He emptied his glass, and when he set it down, it tumbled onto its side. "Goddamn them . . ."

May Ida quickly righted it and poured another two inches for him. He picked up the glass, drank off the whiskey, and then seemed to choke on it. His craggy jaw trembled, and for a bizarre moment, May Ida thought he was actually going to start weeping. Then he caught himself and flopped an arm on the table, grasping for the glass. With a gentle motion, she pushed it a few inches forward until he found it. He held it tight, steadying his shaking hand.

"Well, not anymore," he muttered. "It's my turn to be on top, goddamn it." He looked blearily past May Ida, as if addressing a roomful of people. "You understand what I'm saying? I got both of 'em dancing to my tune. Troutman . . . the mayor . . ." He brought the glass to his lips, then put it down again without drinking. "This time, it's going to come out my way! And we'll see who the hell gets the last laugh." His voice went up again. "I said, it's gonna come out my way, or else! Some more people got to die, then some more people got to die. I ain't goin' out this way . . . I ain't . . ." He was sputtering as he wound down. "Nobody's gonna . . . I took care of it, all right . . . I fixed that business. It's my turn, goddamnit. My turn. It's . . ."

By now, he was too drunk to make his mouth work. He lifted the heavy glass to his lips, and when he found it empty, threw it across the room, missing May Ida's head by inches. The glass bounced off the wall, cracking the plaster, and rolled across the floorboards. The Captain stared down at it with dull eyes. Abruptly, his gaze shifted to his wife, and he glared, his eyes piercing, as if he could see through her. She entertained another rush of fear that he knew what she was up to and with evil purpose was just waiting for the right moment to turn the tables.

Still, she didn't flinch and the moment passed. Let him try, she thought. She still had him. He had blurted dark secrets and now he'd have to kill her to keep her from using it and save himself. Of course, he had no idea. The thought of the danger she was in brought another tingle that was almost sexual in its intensity. The Captain didn't notice.

Meeting his hard gaze with her own, she said, "What is it? Is there something wrong?" All the while keeping so much honey in her voice she hoped he'd gag on it.

With one last mad glance, he rose unsteadily from his chair and lurched out of the kitchen. A few seconds later, she heard bedsprings squeak as his weight came down on them.

She waited to make sure he was out. Except for the occasional snore or rattling breath, the house fell quiet.

She went to the desk in the front hall and got out a sheaf of notes and envelopes and a fountain pen. She spent ten minutes writing down everything she could remember. Even with her florid hand, it fit a single page. Every word counted, though.

When she finished, she laid the page aside and got up to walk into the back hallway. The bedroom door was open and she looked in to see his figure sprawled on his bed. In his sweat-stained union suit, wrapped halfway in a blanket, he looked flabby and vulnerable.

She stood there for a few moments, thinking about how easy it would be to take a knife from the kitchen drawer, slip to his bedside, and plunge it precisely into his throat. A twinge of pleasure at the thought came and went. She knew it would be so much sweeter to do it this other way. She would draw out the betrayal, and tell his secrets to a man who had cuckolded him. Drop by drop, she'd draw off his power and cause his ruin. They'd see if he ignored her then.

She backed out of the doorway and went to the telephone stand in the foyer to ring the operator and asked to be connected to one of the city's messenger services. Then she sat down at the rolltop desk to compose a note. When she finished, she folded it into an envelope, then went into the kitchen to pour a victory glass of good whiskey for herself. Sometime later, she heard the squeak of a bicycle outside the house.

# ELEVEN

Joe was up before the first light of day, coming awake with a jolt, as if startled by a sharp noise. His chest hammered and stomach churned in a burst of panic as he conjured Pearl locked in a Fulton Tower cell. He remembered the beating from the pain in his head and neck, and groaned when he rolled out of bed to make his way down the hallway to the bathroom.

When he got back to his room, he swallowed three aspirin, got dressed, and hurried out onto the dark and quiet streets, stopping in the lobby only long enough to snatch a few pages of hotel stationery.

He retraced his path from the evening before, back over the aqueduct to the Tower. Inside, he found an officer dozing at the front desk. Before the guard could gather himself, Joe started waving the pages of stationery in the air and chattered busily, as if he was on some pressing errand. He went through the doors before the officer could come to his senses.

The hard-faced matron who was at the desk on the colored women's side gave Joe a surly once-over as she stepped up. She didn't appear at all surprised to see him there.

"What'll it take to get into the cells?" he asked her directly. She had that look about her.

"What do you got?" she said.

Joe made a half turn away from her probing stare, slipped a hand inside his coat, and produced a gold pocket watch. He held it up by its chain.

The matron shifted her thick shoulders grudgingly. "Let's have a look," she said.

Joe handed it over. The woman cradled it in her palm, opened the lid, put it to her ear, then dangled it before her eyes. She gave him a cold glance. "You want somethin' else?" she said.

Joe turned around and hurried through the archway. The cell block was dark except for the one bare bulb at the far end. He peered into each of the cells as he passed by. All the women were asleep except for one, who sat on her pallet staring at nothing. She didn't even blink when he went by. He peeked through the bars until he saw Pearl lying on a pallet, with her arm flung over her eyes. When he whispered her name she turned over, then got to her feet. Some lump of humanity snored away on the other pallet.

Even in that dim light, Pearl looked poorly. Her dark flesh had a gray tinge, her curls had fallen into a twisted mess, and her eyes were wild, like a crazy woman's. But she was alive, and exhibited no signs of a beating.

The first words out of her mouth were, "Who told you I was back down here?"

Joe was confused. "Down where?" Joe said. "What are you talking about?"

"They had me up in the men's," she said.

"Jesus, Pearl!"

"Nothin' happened," she said, sounding sharp. "How did you get in?"

He tried for a small joke. "I've got my ways."

She didn't smile; rather, she looked fretful. "You didn't come to try and get me out, did you?"

"I can't. There's no—"

"Because he said he'd let me go."

"Who said?"

"The Captain, who do you think?" She took a quick glance down the row.

"When was that?"

"Don't let them catch you here!"

"I just wanted to see if you were all right."

"I am," she hissed. "Now, leave. Go. Please."

"Wait a second, when—"

"You hear me?" Her voice went up a notch. From down the row of cells, one of the other women yelled, "Shut up, bitch!"

Joe backed away from the cell. With a last glance at her face framed between the bars he made a quick exit. A woman—the one who had yelled at Pearl—was at the bars of her cell. When she saw Joe, her eyes went wide and she produced a toothless smile.

"You come to fix somethin'?" she called to him. "I got somethin' you can fix right here!" In the next few seconds there were sounds from the other cells as her sisters caught on to a man in their midst.

The matron, hearing a disruption, started in his direction. Joe trotted past her, up the stairs, and across the lobby. Now awake, the desk guard yelled at him, but he kept going, hitting the Whitehall Street sidewalk just as the first light of dawn was washing the tops of the buildings. He took off at a fast lope and didn't slow down until he got to the other side of the aqueduct.

Weaving through the army of early morning workers, he realized that he had just done a stupid thing. He could have been nabbed, arrested, and tossed back in a cell, wrecking what little of a plan he had. But he couldn't stand the thought of Pearl locked up, alone and helpless, so off he went.

Though the way she had acted in the Tower threw some doubt on the helpless part. She said that Captain Jackson promised to let her go. Joe wondered when exactly the Captain had told her that. They hadn't gotten around to that part.

By the time he turned the corner onto Houston Street, his stomach was growling, so he crossed over to Lulu's and ordered breakfast and coffee. For once, he wouldn't have to worry about Sweet.

There was only one other customer in the place. The manager, a chubby fellow named Heeney, was in back, cursing over the hot oven. He saw Joe through the kitchen window and called him over to ask about Sweet. Joe made up a story, explaining that the arrest was a mistake and that Sweet would likely be back within the next twenty-four hours. Heeney said he hoped so; he couldn't hold the job open. He'd have to put a sign in the window. The customers had already started complaining about the food, and he was losing business.

As soon as his breakfast arrived, Joe understood. Though it wasn't bad, it wasn't Sweet's. It would be worth getting him out of jail for that reason alone.

He ate only half of what was on his plate, finished his coffee, waved to the harried owner, and stepped outside. Across the street, he walked into the lobby, headed for the telephone booth, and asked the operator to ring the detectives' section at police headquarters. When Al Nichols came on the line, he sounded tense, edging on dismissive, and Joe figured he was performing for someone. Joe told him about Pearl and Sweet still sitting in cells at the Tower.

Al huffed with exasperation. "I can't do anything about that," he said curtly.

Joe started to push it, then changed his mind. He had displayed enough stupidity for one morning.

"I'm going to have something for you later," he said, making sure the detective heard the insistence in his voice.

Al got it; there was a pause on the other end. "What kind of something?" he said, his tone warming a few degrees.

"We'll talk later," Joe said, and put the earphone back on the hook.

He stepped out and looked at the clock on the wall above the desk. It was still early, only a little after eight o'clock. He dragged himself upstairs to wait for Willie and the melancholy business of escorting Little Jesse Williams to his final rest.

When Captain Jackson's wife woke him to announce that Corporal Baker was waiting outside in the car, her voice sounded like a saw ripping through metal. He roused himself in minute stages, each motion sending a shock wave across his temples. Stumbling against the walls, he made his unsteady way to the bathroom, where he promptly disgorged the sour contents of his stomach. He pawed blindly in the medicine cabinet over the sink, grunting with relief when he clutched the small brown bottle of paregoric. With a savage twist of the cork, he tossed half the liquid down his throat, then closed his eyes and waited, understanding in that moment why people were lured by the instant comfort of a needle. As it was, it took a few minutes for the first numbing wave to reach his stomach. From there, the potion went coursing through his veins to his aching head.

It felt like a rheostat had been drawn back, gradually shutting off a harsh current. He sagged on his bones as the pain ebbed. Momentarily, he was able to steady himself enough and wash his face, and swill mouthfuls of water to clean his mouth.

He pulled on the old gray trousers that were hanging on the back of the door and crept to the kitchen on legs that were still rubbery. May Ida was fussing at the stove, and the smell of the eggs and bacon in the frying pan turned his stomach all over again. He sat down, mumbling that he wanted only some coffee and toast.

She put a steaming cup in front of him and he sat for a while, trying to piece together the previous night. Though it was mostly a blur, he had a sudden and sharp memory of the way May Ida's eyes had glittered as she listened to him. It was like a mask had fallen away, revealing something dark and wicked underneath. He stared into his coffee, trying to remember if that had been real or just part of a nightmare. Was that vulture the same plump woman who was now humming vacantly as she spread butter on a thick slice of bread that she had toasted by hand to light-brown perfection? It didn't seem possible, though he sometimes wondered if his wife was truly crazy. It could be; she often acted like she was off in another world. Though he didn't pay that much attention.

He took his first tiny sip of coffee. As he watched her putter about, what she'd said in the bedroom came back to him.

"Did you say Baker was outside?"

May Ida stepped to the table with his slice of toast. "Yes, he's in the car," she murmured, and put the plate at his elbow.

"Well, my lord!" The Captain pushed the chair back and lurched to his feet with an angry glance, which she returned with a stare so chilly that it gave him a small start. She took it with her as she retreated from the table.

"Don't let the man sit out there in the cold," he said, losing some of the snap in his voice.

When she didn't make a move, he went to the front door, opened it, and waved the corporal inside.

Baker lumbered up the walkway and followed the Captain into the kitchen, where he sat in vacant silence, keeping his coat and hat on like he was some peasant waiting for a train. The Captain finished his coffee and only half the slice of toast before heading to the bedroom to dress, leaving May Ida alone with the corporal. She gave Baker one brittle glance, then ignored him completely. She was relieved when her husband stepped into the kitchen doorway and waved the corporal to his feet. He did not say good-bye.

By the time they turned the corner onto Hunnicutt Street, the Captain had erased May Ida and everything except the important matters at hand from his thoughts.

Once he emerged from his hangover, he began to feel in his

bones that this was the day. It had been a long time coming, and on a risky path. As they rode into the city, he could picture how the last act would play out. Everything was in place. By sundown, all accounts would be settled, and in his favor. Just to be sure that nothing slowed him, he was carrying the rest of the paregoric in his coat pocket.

When they arrived at headquarters, he gave Baker his instructions and sent him on his way. Upstairs, he walked into the detectives' section to see Lieutenant Collins and Sergeant Nichols at their desks, along with a few of the other men. The lieutenant was in the process of organizing the prior night's arrest reports. Nichols didn't look up from the hopeless stack of files.

When Collins rose to follow his superior officer, the Captain waved him off. The reports would wait, and there was nothing he needed to know, anyway. He closed his office door behind him and crossed to his desk. Snatching up his telephone, he went about his first order of business, and called the administration desk at Fulton Tower with instructions regarding the prisoner Pearl Spencer.

The procession for Little Jesse's last ride began outside the Eaton Funeral Parlor on Nelson Street. It would take a route along Trinity then west over the bridge behind Terminal Station to West Side Cemetery, a walk of a little more than a mile.

It was cold enough for humans and horses to puff little clouds into the morning air. The congregation was all Negro, except for Joe and two other white men, rounders who knew Jesse and were too low-down to have to worry about color. As soon as the hearse started to roll, a woman with a good voice began a hymn. Much of the crowd joined in. This was against Jesse's wishes, but he couldn't exactly object, so once it started, it just went on. Willie walked with Joe, his guitar slung in front, his face etched in sadness.

Most of those in attendance knew Joe and nodded their greetings. Then they stared at the bruises. No one asked where they'd come from.

It took a half hour for the parade to wind through the lower streets and arrive at the entrance to the cemetery. Normally, it would have been an easy fifteen-minute walk. However, a number of those in the procession were still feeling the effects of drinking through the night and couldn't stay in a straight line.

Joe knew he shouldn't be taking the time, not with what he had hanging over him. But he'd never hear the end of it if he missed Jesse's funeral. And the truth was he didn't know where he'd go and what he'd be doing anyway. He'd been a step behind all the way and he wasn't going to catch up in the last twelve hours.

As they ambled along, he told Willie what had transpired that morning. The blind man was irked at Joe bluffing his way into the Tower.

"You're lucky you got out with your damn ass in one piece," he said.

"Or anything else," Joe quipped. "They got some hungry women in there."

Willie snickered over that, then asked if Joe had figured anything more than he did the night before. Joe shrugged off the question; the less Willie knew, the better. All he would say was, "The Captain told me I have until tonight, and then it's all over. If I don't come up with anything, I'm done. I'll be back in jail. I can run, but he'd still have Pearl, and Sweet will get sent down to Milledgeville. That's the deal."

Willie frowned and shook his head. They dropped the subject and walked on. Presently the stones of the cemetery appeared out of the mist, and the line snaked through the open gate and along the path to circle the fresh grave. The preacher who had been brought along respected Jesse's wishes and stayed to the back, rocking on his heels and keeping his prayers to a whisper. So the late Mr. Williams did not quite escape blessings.

One by one, men and women stepped forward to speak a few words about the man in the pine box. Some of the testimonials were heartfelt, some were comic, others were delivered by people who seemed not to have known Jesse very well, and one or two others sounded baffled by the whole business, as if they had been swept along by the wake and didn't know where they were or what they were doing there.

Joe and Willie stood back, listening to these bleary eulogies. The sun had broken through the clouds and dappled the brown grass and gray and white stones with patches of pale light.

"You gonna say something?" Willie murmured in Joe's ear.

"Just as well if I don't," Joe said. "But it's about time you stepped up there."

"I suppose that's right," the blind man said, and started through the crowd. Everyone made way.

Joe watched as Willie shared a joke with Jesse, plowing toward the grave as if he had no sense of space and might fall in. Murmurs of concern rose up and a couple people stepped forward to catch him. Of course, Willie had located the edge of the grave exactly and stopped with his toes hanging over it.

The crowd fell silent. With the slow wind at his back, Willie strummed the first minor chord and sang "The Dying Crapshooter's Blues," just as he'd promised.

For all the friends, enemies, and strangers Joe had seen laid to rest, it still affected him in a grim way. At the same time, a fair share of the Negroes at the graveside chose instead to celebrate the passing over into a better land, and to a glory that was beyond this vale of woe.

Still, he couldn't imagine Little Jesse in an afterlife being anything other than the same rounder he had been on the streets of Atlanta. Something about him in a gown of white sateen with little wings attached and a halo over his nappy head didn't fit. Joe closed his eyes for a moment and smiled at the image.

As he mused about Jesse, he was aware of Willie's sweet tenor with the textured guitar beneath it and the lyric retelling of his final moments.

> *What broke Jesse's heart,*
> *Why he was blue and all alone*
> *Sweet Lorena had packed up and gone . . .*

Something caught, like a windblown rag on a bare branch. Joe recalled sitting at Jesse's bedside and seeing the look on his face as he mourned a lost love, mourned his own fading life, mourned the life he was leaving behind. He had looked Joe right in the eye. *You know how a woman can break your heart, Joe.* Joe supposed he did know, though maybe not the way Jesse had meant it. One woman had wounded him almost thirty years ago, and it was true that he had never really gotten over it.

Jesse would claim that any female was capable of inflicting such heartache. Was that what he meant with that piercing stare? Joe would never know; it was another question unanswered.

Willie finished his song. It was followed by a murmur of low voices as the crowd broke apart. Some of them would make their way back to Jesse's rooms for one more round of drinking and carousing. Soon, tomorrow probably, the landlord would come around to sell off or give away whatever was left. Other than that, Little Jesse Williams wouldn't even leave a shadow.

They ran into Martha as they made their way out of the cemetery. She looked particularly bereaved, her back bent under the weight of her grief, and Joe felt sorry for her. Of all the women, she was the one who seemed to have loved Jesse truly, and so would most mourn his passing. She would never betray him, not like Lorena in the song, or any other—

"Mr. Joe," she greeted him as they came up alongside her. "Willie."

"I'm sorry for your loss," Willie said.

"I'm sorry, too," Martha said faintly. "Don't know what I'm gon' do now."

They walked on in silence and didn't stop or speak until they got to the street and had to wait for the now-empty hearse wagon to pass by.

Martha sighed and said, "I jes' keep thinking that if he'd have gone to jail like he was s'posed to, ain't none of this would have happened. He'd be locked up, but at least he'd be alive."

Joe didn't know what she was talking about. "Jail for what?"

"For running that game."

"When was this?"

"About . . . a month ago? Somethin' like that."

"But he's been running games for years. Everybody does it."

"All I know is they came and busted it up," she said. "And then they took him in. I went to see him in his cell. He thought he was a goner. Said they told him they was gonna th'ow away the damn key. But then later on that same day, they drop the charges and let him go free. They'd'a kept him, he'd be alive right now."

"You remember who arrested him?"

"No, I don't know nothing else about it," Martha said.

Joe was curious. It was the first time he'd heard this, and it didn't make sense. Why break up a game in the first place? There were dozens of them running every night, all over the city. At the worst, some cops looking for cash so they could buy lunch or a bottle of beer might come by, get their money, and go. All the big games paid regular graft to the beat patrolmen.

The wagon passed, its wheels creaking. Instead of stepping into the street, Martha stood looking back toward the grave site.

"Don't none of it matter no more, does it?" she said. "He's gone."

She didn't seem inclined for company, so Joe and Willie left her standing there as they started the trek back into the city.

They came to let Pearl out at 11:40. The matrons, the same two who had brought her in, walked her to the desk to collect a paper sack of the clothes she had been wearing when she came in, and made her change right there in front of them, watching with their porcine eyes. She noticed that her jewelry, two rings and a silver bracelet, had disappeared, and knew better than to say anything about it.

All the way to the door, she was sure she would hear a shout and feel rough hands that would drag her back inside to spend now and forever in that place. Then she was standing on Hunter Street, and her feet were carrying her back downtown, and she got lost in the morning crowd, her shoulders hunched and head bent to the sidewalk.

She had been unable to eat what little of the awful food they gave her, especially after the Captain's visit, and her stomach was wrenching. Still, she was desperate to find Joe. After his stunt at the Tower early that morning, she was afraid he would try something else just as reckless and drag them all into deeper trouble.

So she headed for the Hampton. As she made her way along, a momentary reverie overtook her, and she imagined him next to her, his head on the pillow, his face soft and pale with sleep. It was dark and quiet, with only the sound of raindrops tapping the windowpanes, and it seemed that time had stopped.

Someone passing by jostled her and she snapped out of it. She was coming up Peachtree Street and crossing Poplar when she was startled to see a familiar gray coat as the man from her daydream appeared, cutting at an angle through the busy traffic to her side of the street. She felt a rush of relief and thought to call out, then caught herself. What if someone was watching? Better to follow him and wait for the right moment.

A half block on, he turned into James Street, a short and narrow thoroughfare. He was halfway to the next corner and she was just about to call his name when she saw a white woman with wide hips and jutting bosom step out the back door of Rich's Department Store. The woman barely glanced at Joe, but then moved casually in his direction. Pearl read instantly from their postures that they were meeting, though neither one spoke a word or made a gesture of greeting.

She watched Joe stroll past the woman, who waited until he had gone on another twenty paces before following behind. She felt her gut churn. Joe Rose, her *hero,* was meeting a woman, a fancy white woman, while she was supposed to be locked up in the Tower.

She seethed, imagining how the tryst would unfold. He would lead the woman in a loop around the block and through the side streets to the back door of the Hampton. She would find her way upstairs and into the same bed in which Pearl had laid not thirty-six hours before. The thought of it made her want to kill the both of them.

The moment passed and she got hold of herself. She couldn't afford to cause a scene. And as she calmed down, she noticed that there was something not quite right about this little interlude, and in a sudden moment it came to her who the woman was and why she was meeting Joe in that place. She went through it in quick jumps, frightened about what it meant and yet spellbound by the intricate drama—a spider's web. She knew what he was doing, and knew she would have to let it happen. There was no other choice. Sadly, he was doing it for her.

All the same, she couldn't stifle the sick pain in her chest. No matter what his intentions, there was no doubt in her mind what would happen once he got the woman to his room, and it was her fault that it was unfolding this way. With a last glance at their retreating figures, she turned around and started for home.

———

Joe turned the corner onto North Forsyth Street and saw May Ida appear from the back entrance of Rich's Department Store, so close to the stroke of twelve he could have set his watch by it. A few seconds later, the noon bell at North Avenue Baptist tolled.

She was wearing a cloche hat that fit tight over her curls, with a brim down low in front. The wide collar of her twill overcoat was turned up, so only someone peering close would recognize her. At the same time, Joe noticed at a glance that her chubby cheeks were pink and her blue eyes were all aglitter with excitement.

For a brief second, his neck prickled with a sense that some-one was watching him, and he stole a glimpse over his shoulder, ready to scrap the plan and scurry away. He saw no one suspicious; still, he wasn't about to take any chances and ambled by May Ida as if they were strangers.

He felt rather than saw her fall into step a dozen paces be-hind him. Though she was making all the right moves, he didn't relax until they wound their way around the block, cut across to Ivy Street, and slipped into the alley and through the back door of the Hampton. She followed him up the staircase, keeping one set between them.

Joe entertained a brief flush of shame as he made his way along the hall, thinking the only good thing about Pearl being locked up was that she couldn't catch him at this subterfuge. When he got to his room, he left the door open the barest crack, and a half minute later, May Ida slipped inside and closed it be-hind her.

She turned down the collar of her coat and gave him a smile that was full of affection. She was happy to see him again. Though they'd only met the one time, her memories of him were vivid and very fond. He was different from the others. Being there thrilled her all the more because the rendezvous was transpiring almost under her husband's nose, and because she was playing such a dangerous game.

For his part, Joe didn't find it so exciting. He was gambling that he wasn't being watched. Even so, he had no choice but to go through with it, and got down to business, moving up behind to help her off with her wrap. As he folded it across his arm, she tilted her head to one side, and he dutifully kissed her cheek. She purred with pleasure, then turned around and gave him a look of reproof.

"You've been avoiding me," she said. "How long has it been since we last visited?"

"I don't remember," Joe began to stutter. "It must be . . . um . . ."

"It's been at least six months!" May Ida scolded him.

Joe looked appropriately abashed as he hid his astonishment. It had been closer to two years. He wondered if she knew who he was, and began to worry that this was a mistake.

"I've been out of town," he said gamely. "Traveling on business."

"Is that right?" she said. "Well, I'm glad you decided to reply to my message."

Joe blinked at the sudden change in her tone from warm to cool. It was as if she'd thrown a switch.

At the same time, she was taking mincing steps in the general direction of the bed. As she sidled along, she reverted back to her giddy self, chattering about this and that: the weather, Christmas coming, and how the help she was getting was not—

"You said there was something you wanted to talk about," Joe broke in. He didn't have time to listen to chatter.

She stopped in the middle of her sentence and treated him to a keen look. "Yes, I did, didn't I?"

Though she now stood at the foot of the bed, there was nothing in her face or posture that told Joe she was eager to make use of it. Quite the contrary; something feral was lighting up her face and eyes, giving her the look of an animal seeking prey. She was nothing like the daffy woman he remembered from the liaison at the Dixie so many months ago. But who could tell how living with the Captain had affected her?

He watched her for another few seconds and decided it would be wise to take her seriously. "Please, have a seat," he told her.

She settled on the bed, gazed at the mattress for a bemused moment, then turned back to him, her hands folded primly in her lap. "What happened to your face?" she asked him.

"I got a beating." He paused, then said, "It was your husband's idea."

"My—" Her mouth set in a hard line and he thought she was going to spit. She said, "I'm sorry to hear that."

"He had me picked up and thrown in jail yesterday."

Her brow stitched. "Why?"

"He thinks I'm holding out on a crime."

"The theft of jewelry?"

He studied her more closely. "That's right. You know about it?"

"I read the papers," she said vaguely. "And I hear things. Did you steal those goods?"

"I didn't. But the Captain thinks I know who did."

"Well?" Her eyes danced as if she was playing with him. "Do you?"

"No," he said. "Do you?"

She smiled like a lazy cat and curled her back, giving her bosom a prouder forward thrust. "I know what I know," she said deliberately.

Joe drew his eyes off her bustline and raised his eyebrows with appropriate curiosity. Now he could imagine her flicking a forked tongue.

Though there was no one else in the room, she whispered. "He's been talking and I've been listening," she said. "He doesn't think I understand, but I do. But just to be sure, I wrote some things down. It's quite a story, all right." She batted her eyes, feigning a helpless look. "I want to share it with someone, but I don't know who I can trust."

Joe couldn't miss her meaning; his sharper instincts came into play. He went into action like the sneak thief he was: quietly, slyly, at odd angles, and with the same sleek stalk that served him so well when he invaded a house.

He began the gambit with a sincere look, murmuring words she wanted to hear. *Can't that wait? It's been a while since I've seen you. We can talk later . . .*

Meanwhile, he edged close, and with a gentle, unhurried motion, removed her hat, letting his fingertips brush her ears and neck. She swooned a bit under this treatment, her flesh flushing a shade darker. As soon as he dropped the hat on the bed, she took his hands in hers, kissed them both, then placed them to her breast, as if giving him an offering. She closed her eyes and sighed with pleasure, her face so ardent that he had to stifle a laugh.

"Oh, I've missed you so!" she breathed as he began undoing the top buttons on her dress, echoing the words from a movie card. This was the May Ida Joe knew. He pushed the fabric off her round shoulders to find she was wearing a white, lace-trimmed chemise that was about one size too small for her girth. If he fell into that cleavage he might never get back out, but he was willing to take that risk in the service of saving Pearl, Sweet, and himself from the vile clutches of her husband. He sighed, thinking he truly was a rat.

He now cupped her elbows and brought her to her feet. As she stood up, her dress dropped the rest of the way to the floor.

"It is rather stuffy in here," she said with a little gasping laugh.

Joe laid light hands on her upper arms to urge her back down on the bed. As she tumbled down, she said, "My, my. Whatever is on your mind?"

He went at her hard, giving her all the pleasure he could in the limited amount of time. It helped that May Ida responded with an instant ferocity. She huffed and moaned and cried out like a crazy woman. She wasn't Pearl, who would respond with a fierce energy that would all but break his back. This one dug her nails into the mattress and held on as if his assault might send her off the bed and through the wall. He knew he could work her until she was ready to turn over everything, including the keys to her house. There wasn't time for that. So he pounded her flesh pink then red and wet, until she finally broke down into a drunken heap. Her expression was clownish with sated desire.

A few moments passed, and quite abruptly her face dissolved into a mask of sorrow and she began to weep. Joe, at first startled by this outburst, felt a pang in his own chest, as her hurt and loneliness came seeping out. What a life she had led, a good person who was first scorned for her appetites, then had jumped from one man to the next until she was yoked to a crude and heartless man like the Captain. Who had now earned her revenge in return. He didn't know what to say, so he just held her tighter.

That moment passed soon enough, and she drew away just a bit, a sign that told him she didn't need his sympathy. When he looked at her again, the sorrow was gone and the carnivorous gleam was back in her eyes.

Now it was her turn to deliver, and she knew it. She reached over the side of the bed for a piece of paper that had fallen among her clothes. With a smile that hinged on wicked, she stretched languorously one more time, then settled herself.

"Well, to begin with," she said, waving the page like a fan, "the man can't handle his liquor."

It took her only a few minutes to go through it, and when she finished, he lay there in such a befuddled state that she had to poke him to get his attention.

"I didn't think anything could surprise a man like you," she said.

She had surprised him, and then some. As she had explained it, he passed through puzzlement, disbelief, and anger to arrive at a grudging amazement over the design she described. The pieces fell into place, the beginnings of a picture.

He lay there for some moments, then came out of his brooding to go at May Ida one more time, as if to brand their connivance into her very flesh. It was over in a hurry, and when he was done, she looked stone-dazed with pleasure. Joe felt another twinge of shame that came and went.

Once they both caught their breath, he asked her to run it down once more, posing a question here and there, until he was satisfied that he had everything. She let him look over the paper for himself. It was some slick business, worthy of a moll.

Their time was up. Gently, he explained that he had to move on the information right away. She nodded, though he could see regret in her eyes, as if realizing that they'd never meet like this again.

He left her to get dressed and hurried down to the street to whistle up a taxi, sending the driver around to the rear entrance.

May Ida appeared at the door and passed by him without a word, keeping her head low as she got into the car. She watched him with a cool and steady gaze as the taxi pulled away.

As Joe stood there in the cold doorway, a sudden sense of loss and loneliness crept up to worm its way into his brain. It was the same cloud that came over him whenever he considered what a fraud he was, and how the roles he played—the detective, the sneak thief, the lover of women like May Ida Jackson—were empty charades that had nothing to do with a real life.

He could have had that. He was clever and could have done something worthwhile. Instead of that, he made a living by stealing things that belonged to other people.

He stood there for a while longer, with a chill in his bones, looking at nothing. He knew the feeling was temporary and he always managed to chase it away. Though this time it had an uncommon weight. Or maybe he was just tired.

He had come to Atlanta with nothing on his mind except another stop in his wandering. As always, he would stay a few weeks or months, make a score or two, dally with Pearl until she got too deeply under his skin, then move on. Something was always happening somewhere.

It wasn't working out that way. He was up to his neck in trouble. He thought about poor Jesse giving up the ghost, poor, frightened Robert Clark shot down in the rail yard, a beating for him, and jail for Pearl and Sweet. It was a crazy disaster any way he looked at it. And now May Ida Jackson, the wife of his tormentor, had pushed into the middle of it. Beneath that sweet flesh and inside that foolish mind some other kind of creature lurked, a coiled serpent that had been waiting for a chance to strike.

With all that, Joe knew there was nothing to do except move, and so stepped back into the lobby and crossed to the telephone booth to call Albert Nichols at police headquarters.

Quietly, Joe told him what he had found out without mentioning the source. Albert listened and when Joe finished, he didn't say a word. Joe felt like he could hear the gears grinding over the line.

Nichols got it; he was not a stupid man. "What the hell's wrong with you?" he blurted fiercely. "Have you lost your mind? There's three people dead already. You want to be next?"

"I might be anyway, if I don't figure a way out of this," Joe said. "So I'll take what I can get. However I can get it."

There was a pause and then they both laughed a little.

Albert said, "You really are a lunatic."

"I can bring his lousy ass down," Joe said.

"Bring him *down*? You poke a bear like him with a stick and he'll take *you* down. You and your sweetheart and her brother, too."

"That's why I need you."

"Why, so I can go down with you?" The detective fumed for a second. "I don't need to be in the middle of this."

"Who else?"

"What about your friend Collins?"

"He works for the Captain."

"That's not his choice." Albert was quiet for another few moments, mulling. "All right, now what?" he said.

"You need to get out of there so we can talk. But first I want you to go check on something."

"I'm on a desk."

"Get off it, then." There was no reply. "Come on, Al."

The detective huffed with exasperation. "Check on what?"

"Any arrest reports from the last couple months that involve Jesse Williams."

Al didn't say yes and didn't say no. What he did say was, "And then what?"

"Then come out and meet me."

The detective paused, and Joe thought he was going to tell him to forget about it. "You know the place," he said, sounding gruff.

"When?"

"An hour. Maybe a little more. Just wait." He clicked off.

Joe put the earphone in its cradle and stepped out of the booth. He glanced over toward the desk, to see the clerk who had been staring at him quickly look away, and wondered if there was anyone in the city of Atlanta who wasn't in his business.

Albert Nichols felt eyes on him as he pushed the telephone set away. He glanced to the other side of the detectives' section to see Lieutenant Collins lounging with his feet up on his desk and gazing at him with an expression that seemed absently curious.

Collins sat forward as if he was about to say something, then seemed to think better of it and returned his attention to the papers in his hand.

Albert did not look in the direction of Captain Jackson's office. Though there hadn't been a sound from that dim cave, he could feel the Captain lurking like an alligator in a swamp, half submerged and waiting for its next meal. He reached out to pull another dusty file from the endless pile and opened it to study a crime that had been committed more than a decade ago and would never be closed, no matter how long he sat there.

When Pearl finally reached Lyon Street, all but staggering the last few paces along the broken sidewalk, she found the front door of the house hanging open on its hinges with the cold air blowing inside. Stepping closer, she saw that the frame had been splintered and the lock broken off with it, likely by the kick of a heavy boot.

She looked up and down the street. No one was about, and the shades in all the neighbors' windows were drawn down tight. It was as much a signal as if someone had shouted it out. The police had paid a visit, and no one around there wanted any part of that kind of trouble.

She crossed the threshold to find that the house had been tossed from one end to the other. All the furniture had been upended and every drawer pulled out with the contents dumped across the hardwood floors. Pictures lay facedown on the floor, the glass shattered. The lamps had been knocked over, too, and one was in pieces. Clothes and papers were strewn from wall to wall.

In a daze, she wandered through the bedrooms to find that they had received the same rough treatment. It looked like a hurricane had blown through, and she felt a moment of dizzy weakness that welled up to force a quivering sob from her throat.

Standing among that wreckage, she knew who had done it, and why, and swore that same somebody was going to pay.

At the same time, she knew it was her fault. Her wild ways had brought this calamity to their door, and the only good news was as far as she knew no one else was dead. Sweet, God bless his good soul, had been right about everything. She should have listened to him, right from the beginning. She should have stayed away from the speaks and the rounders who frequented them. She should have left the whiskey and the cocaine be. She should have lived a life on the right side of the law. And she never should have laid down with Joe Rose, the white man or Indian or whatever he was.

She mused for a few moments, and decided that she wasn't quite sure about that last one.

Detective Nichols pretended to work for another hour and a half, until Captain Jackson finally stepped out of his office, stalked through the detectives' section, and went out the door. When another quarter hour went by and he didn't return, Albert got up and ambled into the hall without telling anyone where he was going, taking one folder from the hopeless mountain as camouflage. From his desk, Lieutenant Collins glanced at him but said nothing.

The detective descended one floor and made his way along the corridor to the Records Room. He had spent enough time there doing bits of research on his dead files that the two clerks barely lifted their heads when he walked in.

The room was arranged into rows of two types of file cabinets. Down the middle were cases of drawers that contained four-by six-inch index cards, upon which officers had noted the bare essentials of particular incidents: crime, perpetrator, victim, date, and location. The more detailed reports were kept in the full-sized cabinets that lined all four walls, except for gaps for the doorway and the clerks' desks in back.

Albert knew his way around and soon found the card drawer that matched the dates Joe had mentioned. He went about his work, reminding himself every couple minutes to look over his shoulder, and keeping the bogus file close at hand. At one point, he asked to use the telephone set on the clerk's desk.

A half hour later he slipped out of the room, leaving the dead file he had brought with him in the basket. Down on the first floor, he located a patrolman whose initials were attached to one of the reports he had found. He asked a few questions, then thanked the cop and hurried into the hall to leave the building by the side door. Crossing Decatur Street, he jagged from one corner to the next until he reached Mississippi Alley. He had left his coat on the rack to complete the deception and now kept his hands in his pockets and moved at a quick pace to ward off the chill.

He found Joe huddling in the space between two buildings, and the two men walked in silence to a doorway at the end of the alley. Joe rapped a knuckle, and after a few seconds the door opened and they stepped out of the cold afternoon light and down a few steps into the dark refuge of a speakeasy, one of those that was closed until dusk except for certain patrons.

They were the only customers in the low-ceilinged basement with its damp stone walls. A bar made of slat wood took up one side and some mismatched tables were pushed against the other. From the back corner, a squat, cast-iron woodstove threw out dry heat and an orange glow. A smaller room behind the bar held supplies and an icebox containing some vittles. Two ship's lamps threw faint swaths of yellowish light. It smelled of tobacco, rusted pipes, and stale beer.

Without a word, the short, fat, and bald fellow who went by the nickname Pudge relocked the door, leaned his broom, and went behind the bar to fetch two whiskeys for his visitors, who had crossed the floor to slouch against the bar.

Albert quaffed his drink in a quick swallow. He cracked the glass down on the bar and Pudge poured him another one.

He waited for the bartender to go back to his sweeping to turn a baleful eye on Joe. "Are you crazy calling me like that?" he fumed. "Jackson was sitting twenty feet away, for Christ's sake!"

"You think he knew you were talking to me?" Joe said.

"In case you haven't noticed, you got a damn bull's-eye on your back," the detective said. He took a sip of his drink and stopped to snicker darkly. "He seems to think you're the cause of his troubles."

"He's just the suspicious type," Joe said.

Albert wasn't amused. He went into his coat pocket for his cigarettes and offered one to Joe, along with a light. He took a drag, then coughed. Catching his breath, he said, "You know your lady friend was released this morning."

Joe stared at him. "When?"

"'Round about eleven thirty." The detective saw something come over his friend's face and said, "What?"

"Nothing," Joe said. "What about Sweet?"

Albert shook his head. "They'll keep him for as long as they need to. And use him, if they can." The detective puffed on his Chesterfield.

Joe frowned, pondering this. "What did you find out about Williams?" he said.

Albert glowered. "You know, I had to sneak out of there like some goddamn—"

"Yeah, okay," Joe said impatiently. "What did you get?"

"I found the card," Albert said. "Williams was arrested and booked on a gambling charge in November. I talked to one of the beat cops who was sent to break up the game. He said he was surprised because as far as he knew, Williams had always paid up. No reason to bust him."

"Did he say who gave the order?"

"He told me he didn't remember. He just didn't want to say."

Joe said, "The Captain."

"Could have been," Albert said. "But that's all I could get. I could tell I was making him nervous, so I let it be."

"What was the date?"

"November twelfth. But when I went looking for the file, it wasn't there. No record of the disposition of the case."

"Then he destroyed it." He saw Albert's wry expression and said, "What?"

"I telephoned over to the Tower. Got hold of someone who remembered Williams being brought in. I had him check the papers. He was released the next day."

Joe said, "Anything else?"

"I went through Williams's other arrest records. Did you know he was picked up as a suspect in a burglary?"

"I just heard about that this morning," Joe said.

Albert waited for him to take a sip of his whiskey. "It sounds like your research was more interesting than mine. So let's hear it."

Joe put his glass down. "It was Jackson set up the Inman Park job," he said directly. "But you probably already figured that."

Albert said, "I've had suspicions."

"You didn't tell me."

"You're not a cop, remember?" The detective puffed on his cigarette. "Christ! So he's got the stones?"

"No," Joe said. "That was the plan, but it didn't work out that way. Something went wrong."

"Do I really want to hear this?" the detective said. "I mean, considering the source." Joe shrugged. Albert hedged for a second, then said, "All right, go ahead."

"The whole idea was to make sure the mayor and Chief Troutman couldn't get rid of him," Joe said.

Albert nodded. "They were about to kick his ass out the door. The word was January first and he's gone."

"Yeah, well, before they could do it, he set up a burglary during one of the most important social events of the year. The richest people in Atlanta were there. It really did take some damned
gall, but I guess he was desperate." Joe laughed shortly as he conjured the scene in his head. "He must have been planning it for a
couple months. He had his officers break that game Jesse was
running so he could toss him in jail. Then the charges were
dropped and he was let out."

Albert said, "So he could burglarize the mansion."

"They must have made a deal and the Captain told him what
he wanted and how he wanted it done."

"He thought he was smart enough to pull that off?" Albert
said.

"Wait a minute," Joe said. "The plan is once it's done, he'll
come to the rescue. He breaks the case, delivers the jewels back
to the Paynes, and he's got his moment of glory. He'll have his
name in the paper. There's no way they can fire him. He'd be a
hero. Maybe even get chief of detectives."

Albert grunted dismissively. "They'd never give him that
job."

"Well, that's what he was after," Joe said. "He thought it was
all set. But right away things started going wrong."

"What things?"

"First of all, he got crossed."

"By Williams?"

"No, not by him." Joe kept still for a few seconds. "By Pearl."

The cigarette fell from Albert's mouth, bounced off his overcoat, and tumbled to the hardwood floor with a small shower of
sparks. "Pearl!"

Joe crushed the burning butt under the toe of his shoe. "Jackson planned it right down to telling Jesse to find her and tell her
to go down and get hired on for that party. And she did."

"Why would—"

"Because of me. Jesse must have made up a story that he was setting up a caper and that I was in on it. Or maybe he didn't even have to say it. She'd think of it herself."

"So she gets hired for the party . . ."

"That's right. And when the night comes, he gets someone, maybe Baker, to hand this other girl a note to give to Pearl. It's signed with a *J.*"

"As in 'Joe.'"

"Or 'Jackson.'" Joe grimaced. "His idea of a joke. Anyway, she goes down and unlocks the cellar door. When I don't show, she leaves it open. He figured she would. And that it would put both of us in the middle of it."

"He wanted you that bad?"

"He's never been able to lay a hand on either one of us. Sounds like a solution, what do you think?"

"I think he's not bright enough to pull it off."

"He's not bright at all," Joe said. "He made a fucking mess of it from the start. Pearl probably caught on right away." He stopped to sip his whiskey. "Hiring Logue to get rid of Jesse was another mistake."

The detective blinked in confusion. "What?"

"The Captain's the one who paid Logue the two hundred dollars to kill him," Joe said. "That was part of the plan, too. Jesse was just another damn rounder, and he'd never talk if he was dead. So he set him up to get in and grab the jewels and then paid Logue to shoot him once it was done." He sipped his whiskey. "Except he picked the wrong man and Logue didn't finish the job. Two nights later, he sent Baker out to kill Logue. Or he did it himself."

"Wait a minute," the detective said. "You came up on Williams after he was shot." He raised an eyebrow for emphasis. "That was some *coincidence,* pal."

"Not really," Joe said. "I heard about it out on the street. I went over there and found him and Willie. That's all." He finished his cigarette and stubbed it out in the ashtray. "That should have been the end of it. Except that Jesse lived. And there was a witness."

"Robert Clark."

"He ran off, but he couldn't keep his mouth shut. The word got around that he saw. I had been looking for him when he was killed. Baker probably did that one, too. The Captain figured that would be the end of it, but there were already too many loose ends. No way he could put it back in the bottle."

"Well, goddamn," Albert said. "That's some story." He thought it over for a few seconds. "So where are the jewels?"

"Pearl might be holding them," Joe said. "Or maybe Jesse stashed them somewhere. If he did, they might never turn up. What I do know is that the Captain doesn't have them."

"So he's in a hell of a corner," Albert said.

"He thought he had the whole thing figured out," Joe said. "He didn't."

The detective drummed his fingers on the bar, then leaned back and waved to Pudge for another round. After the bartender had poured their drinks, he said, "The person who gave you this . . ." He made a point of not mentioning her name. "Why'd she do it?"

Joe shrugged. "She hates him, she wants to fix him good. That's why."

Albert tilted his head thoughtfully. "And it sounds like Pearl wanted to fix you, Joe."

"I don't know what she wanted."

"So why didn't Williams go ahead and tell you?"

"I guess he was waiting for the right time." Joe was quiet for a few moments, thinking about Jesse in his last hours. He heard Willie's tenor voice echo in his head as he sang the lines he had composed for Little Jesse.

*Boys, I got to die today . . .*

He was about to tell Albert about the song when another line came into his head. *What broke Jesse's heart . . .*

"I'll be damned," he said.

"What?"

"He tried to."

The detective frowned and said, "What, now?"

"He tried, but I didn't catch it," Joe said. "Right before he died, he said something about how a woman can do you wrong. He was pointing me to her. And I missed it."

"Why didn't he just come out and tell you? He knew he was dying."

"He thought he could last. That goddamn doctor said he had a ways to go. He didn't."

Albert drank off some more of his whiskey, then gave Joe a sidelong glance. "So what's Pearl's play now?"

Joe shrugged and said, "If she's got the jewels, then she and the Captain are in a standoff," he said.

"And if she doesn't?"

"Then I don't know."

"And what about you?"

Joe gazed into his empty glass. "I'm a side problem. That's all."

Albert regarded his friend with some sympathy. "I thought she had it bad for you."

"Not bad enough," Joe said quietly. "And if she had to choose between her brother and me, that's no choice at all."

The detective said, "What's that line . . . 'hell hath no fury . . .'?"

"Yeah, I know."

Albert called to Pudge for one more round. The drinks were poured and Joe sipped deeply. The warm glow the whiskey sent into his brain made him wish he could just stay there and never go out into the cold again.

"So now what?" Albert said, breaking into his musing.

Joe came back to the present. "I'm going to need your help."

"And what do you think I'm going to do?" the detective said

sharply. "Drag the Captain into a room and grill him until he confesses? How about I give Baker a good beating? That might work."

"You'll think of something," Joe said. He smiled slightly. "You break this, you'll get a promotion."

"You think so? More likely I'll get a bullet in the head." He muttered something under his breath, then drank off the rest of his whiskey in a fast swallow.

"So?" Joe said.

Albert frowned pensively. "So . . . I'll see what I can do. But you better find her. I mean today. And get her to give up the jewels. Maybe we can finish this. But we need her to do it."

"I know."

Albert pointed a hard finger. "Listen to me," he said. "Don't go calling me at work again. No matter what. Come by my house tonight and we'll see what we've got. And what I can do with it. Until then, you lay low." He eyed his friend bleakly. "I mean it. I can't protect you, so watch yourself."

"I understand," Joe said.

"Seven o'clock." Albert turned away and left without another word.

Joe spent a minute dawdling over his drink, then asked Pudge if there was anything in the icebox. The bartender went in back and came out with some beef and cheese on a roll that looked none too fresh, but Joe hadn't eaten anything since his mediocre breakfast at Lulu's.

As he ate, he thought about what he'd told Al, which added up to a handful of pieces that he had tied together by guessing. If confronted, Captain Jackson could deny everything. Nothing his wife said could be used against him, even if she did come forth. Nichols was right: Without Pearl, they had nothing.

Then Joe considered the possibility that he could be wrong. What if he had jumbled the pieces? What if May Ida had been mistaken or was playing him to get revenge on the Captain?

What if he was putting Albert Nichols in the middle of some-thing for no reason? What if, what if, what *if* . . . That was al-ways the question without an answer.

The other question was *why,* and with the whiskey stirring in his veins, bitterness over what Pearl had done blackened his heart. Though he still wasn't sure what he could blame her for. Not for Little Jesse's death, nor J. R. Logue's, nor Robert Clark's. Those were all the Captain's doing. Not for landing her brother and him in jail. Not for the beating he himself had taken, nor any of the danger he faced just walking the streets of Atlanta.

None of that was her fault in any direct way. He believed that she had betrayed him, led him to wander around like a fool, aim-less, harassed, and edging into treacherous water, and never said a word. Still, he knew her well enough to understand that what-ever she had done was not out of malice. She must have believed that there was no other way. And once she started down that road, she couldn't turn back.

Joe wouldn't know for sure what was in her mind until he found her again. With that in mind, he thanked Pudge, dropped a dollar on the bar, and went out the door into the gray light of the December afternoon.

Albert Nichols ran into Lieutenant Collins coming down the stairwell.

"Captain Jackson's been asking after you," Collins said. It wasn't an accusation, more like fair warning. In fact, the lieu-tenant sounded a bit concerned.

"I was feeling poorly," Albert said. "I thought stepping out-side might help."

"Sorry to hear that," the lieutenant said. He didn't comment on the lapse of more than an hour for a breath of fresh air.

"Is he in his office?"

"He's gone out again." Collins smiled absently. "He's busy

these days." He seemed to be waiting for something. When Albert didn't speak up, he smiled blandly and continued down the stairs.

Albert mounted a step, then stopped. "Lieutenant Collins?" he called down. "Could I have a minute of your time?"

Joe walked along Fort Street and turned west on Lyon. He didn't remember which one of the frame houses belonged to the Spencers. He had only been there once a few years back, and since that time it had been off-limits because Sweet had come home and found him in bed with his sister.

He located it by way of a front door torn apart and a lock broken off. Feeling his pulse quicken, he stepped onto the porch, tapped and called, and got no response.

From the corner of his eye, he caught sight of a woman in the next house leaning a cautious head outside her door.

"She was here, but she done left out," the woman said, plainly puzzled to see his likes standing there.

"When was that?"

"Hour or two ago, maybe."

Joe gestured toward the door. "What happened?"

The woman shook her head. She had given up all she cared to share and went back inside.

Joe stepped off the porch, walked another two blocks to Houston Street, and headed into town. He spent some of the time wondering where she had gone, nursing a hope that when he got to his room, she would once again be waiting there, ready to tell him that it was a mistake and that she had fixed it, and it was all over now.

As it turned out, it didn't matter. Pearl wasn't in the lobby and she wasn't in his room. He couldn't decide whether to be heartbroken or relieved when he remembered that he hadn't even made the bed from May Ida's visit. Anyway, his gut told him if he knew Pearl at all, she had gone into hiding.

He took a quick sip from his bottle and then headed out again, wondering if he had already seen the last of her.

The two officers descended to the basement, exchanging not a word all the way down the four flights of steps. It was dark there, a long corridor lined with closed doors of heavy oak, behind which were storage closets and records and property rooms. Along with these were narrower passageways laid out like a puzzle or a maze and leading to closets. Cool and damp even in summer, the basement was illuminated by four bare bulbs so dim that candles would have thrown the same light.

Albert had heard rumors about the basement rooms having other uses. The word was that certain officers made a habit of bringing women who couldn't pay bail down there to work out a trade for their release. Then there were stories about stashes of opium and whiskey for the use of upper-echelon officers. He had heard other whispers about degenerate criminals who arrived there and were never seen alive again.

As he reached the bottom step and gazed along the cavernous space, he noted that it would be a fine location to hide things from the light of day—a place for secrets. A murder in that place would never be detected.

These thoughts spooked him, and when Lieutenant Collins cleared his throat, he turned around a little too quickly. The lieutenant took a startled step back. Albert waved a dismissive hand and went for his cigarettes. The lieutenant did the same. Two matches hissed and flared, and the two men leaned against the cold stone wall.

Momentarily, Collins said, "What's on your mind, Sergeant?"

Albert watched the burning ember. "I figure you already know some of this or we wouldn't be down here," he said. "We could talk anywhere."

"I suppose that would be correct," the lieutenant said carefully.

Albert heaved a breath. "I've got something on Captain Jackson, and I don't know what to do with it," he said, and gazed directly at the lieutenant. "Do you know what I'm talking about?"

"Maybe," Collins said.

Albert shook his head, faintly amused by this dance. He gazed along the corridor for a few seconds, then said, "The Captain had a hand in the burglary at the Payne mansion. And in the deaths of Officer Logue and two Negroes."

It had come out in more of a blurt than he'd intended and it sounded odd to him, like he was a crazy person talking; and even though he had whispered, the words echoed off the walls and ceiling. He was relieved to see that Lieutenant Collins did not look surprised. As usual, his face didn't show much of anything.

"Where do you get your information?" Collins inquired. "From your friend Joe Rose?" When Albert didn't respond, he said, "He's up to his neck in it, isn't he?"

"He's got trouble, yes, sir," Albert said. "But I don't believe he's guilty of any crime."

"Do you—," the lieutenant began, then stopped. He peered sharply into the shadows.

"What is it?" Nichols said.

"Nothing," the lieutenant said. "Just rats." Then he looked at Albert and said, "What do you want me to do?"

"The Captain's guilty, sir."

"Based on what Rose said?"

"It all points the same way. And most of it fits."

"How did he manage to dig all this up in so short a time?"

Albert saw the look Collins was giving him and figured that he'd given away enough. "He's a sharp fellow," he said. "I think he's got something."

"Is there any hard evidence?"

"No," Albert admitted, grudgingly. "The Captain covered his tracks pretty well. That doesn't mean it's not there."

Collins didn't look convinced. "I don't know about this, Sergeant," he said.

"All right, then," Albert said. "We can forget we had the conversation."

The lieutenant frowned and flicked some ash from his cigarette. "What's your next step?"

"Right now Rose is trying to track down someone who does have evidence. And then he'll bring it to me."

"Is that Pearl Spencer?" Collins saw the look of surprise on the detective's face and smiled slightly. "I've been paying attention." He considered for a few seconds, then said, "When do you expect to hear from Mr. Rose?"

"Later on tonight," Albert said, going back on his guard.

The lieutenant stayed quiet until he finished his cigarette, tamped it out against the wall, and field dressed the butt, letting the shreds of tobacco and paper flutter to his feet.

"What if you're wrong about this?" Collins said. "You know what that would mean? You'd be finished. And I would be, too, if I went along with it."

Albert said, "I've known Rose for a long time. I say what he's got is good. But if you think otherwise, I'll drop it right now."

Lieutenant Collins stared at him without speaking.

# TWELVE

Joe gave up on looking for Pearl when the sun went down. She had not visited any of her few haunts, and no one he spoke to had seen her. He was enough a creature of the streets to sense when someone didn't want to be found. It was a matter of becoming transparent, and not everyone had a gift for it. He was one of them, and so was she. And Albert Nichols had been in his criminal days.

Maybe Jesse Williams once had the ability, but he had been too wild, too much a character. That likely helped put him in the ground. He just couldn't lay low. On the other hand, no one would ever write a song about Joe Rose. That was something. Not the same as being alive, but something.

If Pearl was hiding, his gut told him she hadn't left town. So he wouldn't find her until she was ready. He would have to show up at Al Nichols's house empty-handed, and unless the detective had something they could use, it would go no further. The Captain would survive and Joe wouldn't be showing his face in Atlanta for a good while.

In any case, there would be no reunion and no resolution in that room. So he poured himself a drink and waited for the darkness to fall so he could go meet Albert. If the Captain won the game, then Pearl would have to disappear, too. What other choice would she have, if she couldn't ransom her brother from jail?

Sipping his whiskey, he understood more. A creeping feeling had come upon him in slow ebbs that there was something between Pearl and the Captain, a whispering presence lurking just on the edge of his vision. He was all but cut out of it, the price he paid for neglecting her so.

At six P.M. Sergeant Nichols cleared the last file and got up to fetch his coat and hat from the rack. The detectives' section was quiet. He was the last one still there from the day shift, and all the evening-shift detectives were all out on cases. The only other person remaining was the officer on the desk. Albert wished him a good night and stepped into the hall.

Outside, it was a pleasant enough evening, cool, with only a faint sprinkle of winter rain, and he decided to walk rather than take the Number 10 streetcar heading north. His wheezy lungs could use the work, though it was hard to believe that breathing Atlanta's rank and sooty, gritty, smoky air did them any good.

As he crossed Five Points and started up the gentle Peachtree Street slope, he thought about the fix he was in, courtesy of Joe Rose and his own foolish self.

For all the scrapes and jail time he avoided, Joe had always been a magnet for trouble, or maybe more a compass or dowser. The same second sense that led him to nice scores in cities from New York to New Orleans also got him tangled in messes, and usually with women. This one, with a burglary and three men dead, was definitely the worst. Not content to throw himself into the middle of a bloody puzzle, he had the good grace to drag his crony Albert Nichols along with him.

Except the way Joe described it, there wasn't much of a puzzle left. Captain Grayton Jackson was guilty as sin, and all that was lacking was evidence or a solid witness. It was true that most criminals were stupid, and Captain Jackson was no exception.

He thought himself a mastermind who would save the day and claim the glory that went with it. Unfortunately, he had overlooked the hazards of a smart Negro woman, a drunken beat cop, a vindictive wife, and a former police officer and detective who was at least part Indian.

And it had all come to nothing. Without the stolen jewels in hand, the Captain had to be feeling that there was quicksand under his feet. If Joe got to Pearl before he did and she talked or delivered the trinkets, Albert would make sure it all got into the right hands. He would turn everything over to Collins and let him decide how best to destroy Captain Jackson's life. It was going to be an interesting twenty-four hours.

The detective was not so lost in these musings that he failed to notice the automobile parked a half block down Hunnicutt, a black Chevrolet four-door that looked like it had seen better days, the engine idling with a nasty rattle as it belched black smoke from the exhaust pipe. The same sedan had been parked at the corner of Mills Street when he crossed that intersection and had now reappeared two blocks farther on. Though it all seemed harmless enough, his mind registered it automatically. He tried to get a look at the occupants without being too obvious, but saw only shadows.

He rounded the corner onto Baltimore Place as the half-moon, just rising, cast blocks of slate-colored shadow on the cobblestone street. His rented digs, one of three in a row of shotgun houses, was dark and quiet. The middle unit was vacant and the one on the opposite end was leased by a brakeman on the Georgia Southern who was rarely home.

He climbed the steps to the low porch, unlocked his door, and stepped over the threshold. The streetlight coming through the windows illuminated spare quarters that were exactly what might be expected of a bachelor cop. The few women who had visited him there had eyed the place critically, and one had even set to tidying until he made her stop.

He walked through the living room and bedroom and into the kitchen, where he turned on the overhead bulb. Dropping his coat on the table, he went under the sink for the bottle of muscadine wine he kept there. He poured a glassful and was taking his first sip when the light blinked and then went out. He tried the lamp on the table. It didn't work any better.

He let out a grunt of frustration. Interruptions in the power were common all over the city. Then he happened to glance out the back window to see that the lights in the house across the back alley were fully on. It wasn't the first time that had happened, either. The building was old, and when it rained the damp shorted the fuse box.

He took another swallow of his wine, put the glass on the sideboard, and stepped to the closet. He had just put his hand on the knob of the closet door and pulled when a sudden tingle ran up his spine, telling him that something was wrong. Before the thought connected, the door squealed and flew open, the edge catching him in the chest and forehead with a stunning jolt that threw him back against the bathroom door. He was groping for his pistol when a searing pain shot through his chest, sending him staggering sideways over the kitchen threshold. As he clawed at the side of the icebox, another sudden shock slammed him to the floor.

Lulu's was closed, but Mr. Heeney told Pearl she could stay while he finished cleaning up. The manager was plainly puzzled by Sweet's sister showing up after he'd locked the doors. At first he thought she had come by to plead for her brother's job. She didn't say anything until he asked, though, and then she told him he could expect Sweet back to work in another day, two at most. She was sure. Other than that, she just wanted a place to stop for a few minutes. He shrugged, too worn out to worry about it, and went back to work.

Pearl stood by the window for ten minutes, watching the Hampton until she saw Joe come out and head off at a quick pace, dodging traffic as he cut diagonally across Ivy Street. She drew back when he turned his head her way, then realized he couldn't see her. She fought an urge to rush outside and call his name, and instead let him go on. Once he had disappeared from sight, she buttoned her coat, pulled on her hat, thanked Mr. Heeney for his kindness, and went out into the night.

Joe hurried around the corner from Spring Street onto Baltimore Place, a few minutes late for the appointment.

From the long nights they'd spent drinking, playing cards, and telling lies, he remembered Al's address as the left end of three shotgun houses connected under one roof. As he drew closer, he saw Al's door standing halfway open, though not broken down like Pearl's had been. Peering inside, he glimpsed only murky darkness.

"Al?" he called as he stepped on the porch. "Al Nichols!" There was no response. He looked at the other houses that lined the narrow street. No one was about.

"Al Nichols!" he called again, raising his voice.

The silence spooked him, but there was nothing he could do except plunge in and hope he wouldn't run into something. He drew a steadying breath and threw the front door back the rest of the way so that it hit the wall with a force that sent an echo through the house. He listened for a half second and heard nothing. Slipping a hand inside, he felt for a light switch, found it, and turned it around. There were no lights.

He bit down on his panic, ducked inside, and crossed the dark front room. At the next doorway, he found the bedroom also empty. Beyond it was a short hallway with a closet on one side, the bathroom on the other, and the kitchen beyond.

The back room was bathed in moonlight, and as soon as he

stepped in, he saw the body slumped on the linoleum floor. With a groan, he stepped close and crouched down. The detective's eyes were open and quite still as if they had settled on something far away.

Joe, choking on the words, said, "Al . . . goddamn . . . Al . . ." He sank the rest of the way to his knees and felt a wetness seep into the cloth of his trousers. He noticed the black stain on Al's shirt and, clenching his jaw, ripped it open on a gaping hole, two inches tall and a half inch wide. A second gash had pierced Al's side below the ribs. Joe had seen wounds like these before, on a street in Philadelphia, done with a heavy knife and most often fatal. The pool on Al's other side had spread all the way underneath the kitchen table.

Joe drew back and didn't move for a half minute, his brain in a spinning rage. It was his fault. He had done this. He had led his friend to this slaughter. It took another long minute before he could reach out and close Albert's eyes.

He was rising to his feet when he saw something gleam between the clenched fingers of the detective's right hand. Bending down, he pulled the fist open to reveal a policeman's silver badge. He plucked it free, stood up, and turned it into the pale light through the window. At that angle he could make out the engraved words ATLANTA POLICE DEPARTMENT above the city emblem, and LIEUTENANT below it.

Joe burst onto the porch and ran over to the house with glowing lights, pounding on the door until the owner appeared. He told the startled gentleman to call the police and report the homicide of one of their officers just across the street.

He stood on the sidewalk, unable to move any farther. Another victim was dead, another man he had called a friend. He felt something terrible rising from his gut into his throat, burning and blinding him. He stood there until he heard the faint wail of sirens. Then he moved.

Pearl, watching from the shadows a half block down, saw Joe come out the door of the row house and half stagger across the street. She watched him step back down to the sidewalk and stand there, his body trembling. Then, suddenly, he turned and stalked away.

She knew where he was going, and didn't try to follow. Instead, she waited for another minute before beginning a slow walk back to town. She was on the corner of Peachtree Street when the first sedan crested the rise at Ellis Street with lights flashing and siren howling.

Plum Street was eight blocks due west once Joe turned off Spring onto Pine, and he covered the distance in less than ten minutes. Though he had never been to the address, he knew the street was only three blocks long, and his choices would be few.

When he got to the intersection, he saw a police sedan parked at the curb in front of a frame house halfway to Carroll Avenue. No one was behind the wheel. He shifted his gaze and saw a man slouching next to the front door of the house. There was no mistaking Corporal Baker's thick body and block of a head.

He waited a few seconds until he saw Baker look the other way, then crossed over in a quick sprint. Once he reached the other side of the street, he cut down the well-traveled alley that ran behind the house. Standing at the back gate in the cold and dark, he heard voices that he couldn't make out, carrying from inside the house and across the yard. It sounded like two men and a woman engaged in some kind of an argument. Shadows moved across the kitchen windows, blown up to monstrous proportions.

Joe stole a quick glance up and down the alleyway, then opened the gate and crept along a flagstone path until he was at the back door.

Though the three voices were still muffled, he could now make out two of them, the Captain's gruff snarl and his wife's soft soprano. He was doing most of the talking. May Ida tried to cut in, along with the other voice, but apparently the Captain wasn't having any of it. Another man's voice jabbed in every few seconds.

Joe heard the Captain say something about "lying" and "bitch" and the words "behind my back." It sounded like he was describing May Ida's little plot to betray him; or maybe Pearl was the subject. He figured he'd be hearing his own name next, and as if he had conjured it, the Captain's voice went up as he snapped out "—fucking Rose and that goddamn whore!" To which May Ida made some indistinguishable plea. Then some object was slammed or a body was hurled against a wall.

Joe ducked around the side to the narrow space between the Captain's house and the one next door. He couldn't hear much of anything now. He waited another few seconds, then slipped to the front of the house.

He saw the police sedan at the curb with the driver's-side door propped open a few inches and a large head silhouetted through one of the side windows. Lazy smoke drifted up and over the roof. Tired of standing around, Baker had gone to wait in the car.

In a silent creep, Joe reached the sidewalk and stood next to the trunk of a bare apple tree. When nothing happened, he stepped into the street and saw one thick wrist holding a short cigar draped over the windowsill. He crept closer, making no sound until he got to the rear fender, when he said, "Hey, there!"

Corporal Baker jerked and pulled the arm off the sill. His head came around, and when he saw Joe, he grimaced in surprise and started to say something. Before he could get it out, Joe grabbed the doorframe with both hands and threw it closed using all his weight, crushing Baker's head against the body-work. The corporal let out a sharp grunt, and his eyes rolled up as his derby popped up like in a stunt from a comedy routine. His arms waved about in a weak and clumsy effort to fight back. Joe was on him, though, driving his right fist first into the corporal's snout and then into each of his eyes with quick jabs he remembered from his boxing days. His knuckles collided with Baker's brow, and he felt a blade of pain shoot up his right arm.

Baker grunted some more and tried to pull himself up. Joe let him make a few inches of progress before slamming the door on him again, this time catching him full in the face. Baker's nose blossomed with blood and he crumpled back, falling against the steering wheel and then slumping across the seats with his legs still hanging down over the running board. Joe made sure he was completely out before moving away.

As he strode up the walk, he heard voices from inside, rising in jagged peaks, the two men's and one woman's. When he reached the front porch, he found the door unlocked. He opened it a foot and slipped inside.

The voices were coming from the direction of the hallway that was on the opposite side of the front room. Joe slipped to the arched doorway and perked an ear. He could make out the Captain's gruff growl and May Ida's twittering soprano. The third person wasn't speaking.

He poked his head around the corner. Shadows played at the other end, cast in the bright kitchen light. Halfway along the hall was an open doorway to a bedroom. Under the cover of the blustering shouts, Joe crept the five paces to duck through the doorway and lurk in the darkness, listening.

"You think I'm going to let this alone?" the Captain was demanding. "You understand what she done?"

May Ida whimpered, "Grayton . . . stop . . . please."

"You need to let her go, Captain." It was Collins, his voice steady, a man working for calm. Thinking of poor Al Nichols with the badge clutched in his hand, Joe wanted to rush him at that moment. He kept still, though; now wasn't the time.

"Why's that?" Jackson barked. "You been fucking her, too? Along with everybody else in town?"

"We need to stop this before it goes too far," Collins said.

"Already gone too damn far."

There was some movement and May Ida cried out.

"You think I didn't know?"

May Ida whimpered again, and Collins said, "Captain—"

"She'll spread them fat legs of hers for any-goddamn-body! You think I don't know? I know! I know everything!"

*Not quite,* Joe thought as May Ida's voice went up in a keening swoop.

"You shut up!" the Captain growled. "Now, what'd you tell that fucking Rose?"

There was a second of stunned silence. May Ida wailed, "What?"

"What the hell did you tell him?" the Captain bellowed.

"That's enough!" Collins barked.

"I'll say when it's enough," Jackson grunted. "And you can drop that weapon right about now, too."

Joe peeked from the doorway, saw Collins's silhouette cast against the white enamel of the icebox. A shadowed hand extended and a shadowed pistol dropped to the floor with a thump. Joe could just see the tip of the barrel, a few inches from the threshold.

"All right, it's gone," the detective said. "Now why don't you put the knife down?"

"You giving orders now?"

There was a thick pause. Joe thought he heard Collins whisper *Don't!* and then a thin dark scream from May Ida. Collins's shadow bolted suddenly and there was the sound of a wild scuffle, chairs rattling, glass breaking, the two men huffing and cursing, May Ida's shriek going up and down like a siren.

Joe covered the two steps to the doorway and snatched up the detective's pistol. He yelled, "Stop!" before he could fix on the tableau in the kitchen and untangle body from body.

The three of them froze, stunned by the intrusion. The Captain and Collins were locked in a grapple, their arms around each other's necks in a violent dance, Collins's hand grasping the Captain's right wrist. Above the wrist, Jackson's hand held a kitchen knife. May Ida had crumpled to their feet and was grabbing at one side of her throat, where blood seeped from a short slash.

Joe understood. The Captain had been holding his wife and had taken the moment to try to cut her throat. It hadn't gone deep enough to do fatal damage, though, and Collins was on him before he could finish the job.

"You!" There was a mad glitter in the Captain's green eyes, and his lips curled into a half smile as he realized that someone else wanted in his clutches was standing a few feet away.

Joe saw it coming. Jackson took advantage of those seconds of surprise to throw Collins back against the sideboard with a low grunt. Then he reached down to snatch May Ida by her curls and wrench her head back at an angle. He was bringing the knife down, muttering the words, "Now, you fucking whore . . ." when Joe pulled the trigger.

The Colt barked and flashed in that small space, and the Captain twisted around in a spasm that sent him backward into the corner. The knife tumbled to the linoleum. Jackson started to slide down, staring at Joe, his eyes spitting hate. He grabbed his chest where the wound was bleeding, his crazy eyes fixed on the man who had shot him. He managed to snarl, "I'm a *police* officer, goddamn you!" He slid down to the floor. "I'm a . . . a . . ." He sputtered, as if he had forgotten what he wanted to say.

Joe was gazing in wonder at what he had done when, behind him, he heard Collins say, "No!"

May Ida came spinning from her crouch on the floor, took two strides, snatched up the knife, and drove the blade into her husband's solar plexus. He let out an animal groan as she leaned her weight against it.

"There," she said in an eerily calm voice. "There." She straightened and let the Captain topple over on his side. She held the red-stained knife dangling idly at her side.

In the stunned second that followed, Collins stepped up to lift his pistol from Joe's hand. Joe jerked it away and drew back, leveling the weapon at the lieutenant.

"You went to Al Nichols's place," he said. "You were there."

The lieutenant nodded carefully. "He told me to come talk to you. Someone got to him first. He was still alive when I came in. He couldn't make it, though. Not with a wound like that." He took a grim pause. "My guess is Baker did it. But I was with him when he went down."

Joe dropped a slow hand into the pocket of his jacket. "He grabbed this," he said, holding up the badge.

The lieutenant looked down and spotted the faint trace that Albert's hand had left on his coat. He looked at Joe again. "May I have it?" he said. "And the weapon, please."

Joe glanced at him and saw a face that had gone cop blank, the mouth set in a line and the eyes cool and flat. He handed over the badge and the pistol. The lieutenant placed them on the sideboard. Before he did, though, he grasped the pistol firmly by the grip, erasing any trace of Joe's handprint.

May Ida turned around, again assuming the pose of the helpless girl that was her mask and shield. She held up the knife. "What shall I do with this?" she asked simply.

"Just lay it on the table," Collins said in a steady voice.

May Ida did as she was told, then dropped her hands to her sides, standing a little stiffly, like a small child about to be dressed down over some mischief. She looked between the detective and Joe, her eyes wide and expectant.

"Both of you stay where you are," Collins said. "Don't touch anything and don't try to leave. Please."

He walked out of the room. May Ida gave Joe a sweet, absent smile, then cast a pensive gaze out the window. In the silence, they heard the lieutenant crank the telephone and then start speaking in a clipped voice.

Momentarily, he came along the hall and stepped back into the room to address Joe. "Do you know what happened to Corporal Baker?"

"I laid him out across the seat of the car," Joe said. "He might come around in an hour or so."

A hint of a smile twitched at the corners of Collins's mouth. He said, "In that case, you may leave, sir."

"Wait a minute," Joe said. "What's going to happen to him?"

"To who?"

"Baker."

"Oh. He'll be prosecuted. I'll see to it."

"He needs to be put to sleep."

"I'll take care of it, Mr. Rose."

"What about Sweet Spencer?"

"I'll have him released. Most likely tomorrow."

"Tonight, Lieutenant," Joe said, softly insistent. "You know what kind of place that is."

Collins paused. "All right, sir. I'll make the call."

Joe nodded, mollified. There was nothing more for him to do there. He looked over at the Captain, crumpled glassy-eyed on the floor. He shifted his gaze to May Ida and she smiled at him fondly, but with a vexed expression, as if all this bedlam had her puzzled.

"Mr. Rose?" Collins said. Joe looked at him. "If you happen to see Miss Spencer, tell her it would be smart for her to return those items that were stolen. If she has them, I mean."

"If I see her, I will," Joe said.

"And then you'll want to think about your own plans."

Joe understood; it was a warning to get out of town.

He left them there, stepping into the hall, through the living room, and out the door, closing it behind him. When he got to the sidewalk, he saw that some of the neighbors had come out of their houses, alerted by the gunshot. Little huddles formed at certain doorsteps, arms crossed in the chilly evening as they whispered back and forth. A few of the men were moving cautiously toward the sedan, peering in at the body slumped across the seat.

Joe made a quick escape around the corner of Pine Street and past the Luckie Street School, and turned south toward town. As he reached the edge of the city, two police sedans whizzed by. Though they were moving at a furious clip, neither employed a siren. Joe thought he saw the face of Chief Troutman in one of them, but they went by so fast that he couldn't be sure.

Willie opened the door without asking who was knocking, as if he knew who was calling. Joe was relieved to find him home and some of the tension he had been carrying blew away.

"Joe," the blind man said in his soft voice. "Come on inside."

Joe stepped in and closed the door behind him. It was a simple, tidy little space that was warm, close, and rather homey. An iron-frame bed occupied the far wall. The twelve-string Stella reposed there, as if resting before the night's performing. To the right was a chest of drawers. Opposite it was a washstand and in the corner next to the door was a worn easy chair with a lamp next to it. A picture hung on each wall, cheap art in cheap frames. Joe smiled at that; not that Willie would know. Or maybe he did.

Willie said, "Take the chair, Joe." Joe sat, sagging onto the brocade cushion. "You want a drink?"

"Not right now."

Willie crossed to the chest of drawers, leaned against it, and cocked his head as if hearing some wayward echo. "Something happen tonight?"

"A lot happened tonight," Joe said. He was quiet for a few seconds. "My friend Albert Nichols was murdered. The cop I knew from Baltimore? Him. I got there too late. So I went to Captain Jackson's house. And while I was there, he tried to murder his wife. And I shot him."

The blind man was stunned. "You shot *the Captain*?"

"Not a half hour ago," Joe said.

"He dead?"

"Dead as he can be," Joe said.

Willie said, "But you're not . . . well, my Jesus. Since when do you carry a gun?"

"I don't," Joe said. "This lieutenant named Collins was there, too. I picked up his pistol. The Captain was taking a knife to his wife and I put one in him."

Willie's brow stitched. "I ain't following. This have anything to do with Little Jesse?"

"It has everything to do with him."

"You want to explain it so a poor blind Negro can understand?"

Joe rolled his eyes at this quip. Then he said, "The Captain paid that cop to kill Little Jesse."

"Because why?"

"Because Jesse was working for him. He had him rob those jewels so he could produce them and make some hay out of it. He wanted Jesse out of the way."

"Good lord," Willie said.

"Logue made a mess of it, so he had to go."

"The Captain hunted him down and shot him?"

"Or another cop, a corporal named Baker."

"What about Robert Clarke? Him, too?"

"He saw what happened. That was right before you came along. He should have kept his mouth shut. But he didn't. Baker got him, too." Joe sighed, steadying himself. "I got Al Nichols involved in it. He dug something up. The Captain found out and sent Baker to his house tonight to make sure he didn't use it. I found him there. And after that I went to Jackson's house."

"That wife of his in the middle of it, too?"

"She was. She's lucky to be alive."

Willie mulled all this. "Why the hell didn't Jesse just say what was going on?"

Joe settled back. "I suppose he didn't want to tell me what he'd done. Or maybe he was protecting Pearl."

"He was sweet on her?"

"Maybe so." He smiled sadly. "Hey, there's a song for you."

Willie straightened from his slouch, crossed to the bed, picked up his guitar, and sat down on the edge of the mattress. Idly, he began strumming the strings.

"And what about the jewelry?" he said. "That ever gonna turn up?"

"I hope so." Joe hesitated, then said, "I have to find her first."

Willie went back to strumming, though his touch on the strings was so light Joe could barely hear it. After he had played a few bars, he said, "You sure you don't want a drink? It's in the top drawer." He tilted his head.

Joe got up and went to the chest, where he found a short bottle of rye and two short glasses. He poured one full for each of them, then carried Willie's to him. Rather than sit, he stood in the middle of the floor, pondering all that had transpired. At one point he laughed a little, and Willie cocked his head quizzically.

"What's funny?"

"I just realized that the Captain's wife will probably get some kind of widow's pension from the department."

Willie was quiet for another long moment. Then he said, "You going on the run now?"

"I'll have to leave pretty quick, that's for sure."

"They won't want you for shooting a policeman?"

"I don't think so," Joe said. "The Captain was as dirty as can be. They'll make up a story. Maybe say someone came after him, like some criminal he arrested. So it would be a revenge matter. And the wife isn't going to say a word."

He drank off the rest of the liquor and placed the empty glass atop Willie's dresser. "I've got something to do, Willie."

"Sometimes it's best to just let things be," Willie said. "You know that."

"Sometimes, yeah," Joe said. "Not this time."

Officers had been assigned to block off Plum Street and chase the nosy neighbors back indoors. Chief Troutman arrived in the second car on the scene. A reporter who had received a telephone call about a possible shooting at Captain Jackson's residence came rushing along, hanging on the back of the Pope motorcycle that the photographer used to buzz around town. The reporter was promised news as soon as it could be released. When he got pushy, a burly patrolman was assigned the task of placing him on the seat of the motorcycle and standing by until it roared away.

The medical examiner, a veteran of thirty-odd years who had seen every imaginable kind of bloodshed, was collected from his home and rushed to the scene. Neither he nor anyone else was all that surprised to see the Captain on the floor with a bullet hole high in his chest and a knife wound in his gut.

Joe knocked on another door that night. It creaked open and he felt a mixture of relief and the old familiar fear to see Sweet's hulking form standing there. For all he knew, Sweet would now grab him by the throat, drag him inside, and murder him on the spot. No matter that his little sister had been much to blame for what had happened. Joe was her willing or unwitting partner and that might be enough.

And yet, he saw that Sweet's face wasn't at all hard. It was sagging with resignation, in fact, and the big eyes looked dog tired. Behind the big man was a mess that he had begun to put back the way it was.

"She ain't here, Mr. Joe," he said. His voice was heavy, too.

"You know where she went?"

"I suppose she's out lookin' for you." He let out a baffled

sigh. "You know I never could keep her in line," he mused. "She always went her own way. I guess I should be pleased she ain't dead." He regarded Joe curiously. "You have anything to do with them letting me out?"

"A little bit. I asked someone to take care of it."

"Uh-huh." He paused, and when he spoke up again, some of the edge was back into his voice, though more fretful than angry. "I don't want her disappearing for good," he said. "She's all the family I got. You understand?"

"I do," Joe said. "I don't think you need to worry about that, Sweet."

"Go on, then," Sweet said, and closed the door.

When he got back to his room, he found her there, sitting in his one chair, slouched down, a hand over her eyes to keep out the light. An old carpetbag valise was at her feet, and her coat was draped over her lap. She didn't look up at all when he came in.

After a moment's pause, he said, "I guess you heard what happened."

"I saw," she said. "I was on the street when the police cars went by, and I got a taxi and went to that house. I saw all those coppers and everything. Then I saw you come out and walk away. And I figured it was all over."

"It is."

She drew the hand away from her face and said, "I'm glad about that."

"Yeah, I guess you would be." He glanced down at the bag at her feet. "Where are you going?"

"Away," she said. "I don't know where. Once I get to the station, I'll catch whatever's leaving."

Her words brought a soft blow to his chest. "Don't wait," he said. "That lieutenant will come for you. For the jewels."

Her eyes flashed. "You want me to go right now?"

His eyes flashed right back at her. "You started all this, Pearl. So don't play wounded."

"I didn't *start* nothin'," she said. "I got dragged in, just like you."

"You could have backed out any time."

"Yeah, I could have, but I didn't."

She glared at him for another few seconds, then sagged a little, dropping her eyes. "I knew as soon as Jesse came by the house to tell me I needed to go get hired on for that party that something was going on. I thought it was you." She shook her head slowly. "He should have known he was getting set up. He thought he could be some kind of a big-time rounder. He wasn't nothin' but a pimp and a gambler. And a fool."

"When did you see him?"

"I watched the back stairs. I didn't see when he went up, but I saw him coming down."

"Is that when he gave you the jewels?"

"That's right."

"Why didn't he just turn them over like he was supposed to?"

"He thought he could run a game on the Captain. I told him if he was going to do that, they'd be safer with me. That way he could make his deal and they couldn't touch him." She shrugged. "I didn't know he was going to get shot."

"He was a dead man the minute he threw in with Jackson."

Pearl stayed quiet, brooding. Her gaze shifted and she stared at his feet. "You've got blood on your shoes." She raised her eyes. "And your . . ." When he didn't say anything, she sat up, her hands fidgeting. "What the hell did you do?"

"Don't worry about that," he said. "It's done. And you'll be in the clear. As long as you don't try to run with the jewels." He paused, then said, "Where are they?"

She didn't respond right away as a strange smile worked its way from her eyes to her mouth. Then she reached up and began undoing the buttons of her blouse. Joe watched, transfixed in spite of himself. Once the third one was undone, she pulled open the blouse to reveal a gold chain from which a single green stone dangled. Joe's practiced eye widened.

"And what about the rest of it?" he said.

"All safe," she said.

He didn't have to open her valise to know what that meant. "You've got to give everything back. It's the only way."

She paused, then nodded and absently began to put her dress back together. When she finished, she stood up.

"I'm going." She pulled on her coat and hat and picked up her bag. She didn't look at him. "So, you think I betrayed you?" she said.

"You did. And look what happened."

He wanted to hear her explain it, but she didn't say a word. Whatever she had done, the truth was she owed him nothing. He came into town, used her body for his pleasure for a few months every year, and then went on his way. He had never stopped long enough to let himself care for her beyond a good time. So when it came down to a choice between him and the brother who did love her and had tried to protect her all these years, there was no question what she would do.

"I'm sorry I caused you this trouble," she said. "And I'm sorry about your friend. It wasn't me killed him, though."

She walked to the door. Now she was standing next to him, though they both kept their gazes averted. There was nothing to say. She waited for him to reach out, turn the knob, and open the door. She stepped outside and he closed it behind her.

He heard no footsteps fading down the corridor. After a moment, he turned toward the window and saw a few snowflakes were coming down, fluttering white. Beyond that was a cold and dark blue night that seemed to stretch on forever. He opened the door and found her standing there, her head bent and her hands clasped before her, a posture that was almost prayerful.

"Come back inside," he said.

She gave him a small, puzzled, hopeful smile as she stepped over the threshold.

"I'll tell the clerk I want the room for one more night," he said. "In the morning, we can pack up and leave."

She watched his face as if she was searching for something.

"We?" she said.

# ACKNOWLEDGMENTS

My thanks to those at Harcourt who help turn humble words into modest legacy: Jenna Johnson and Sarah Melnyk in New York, Cathy Riggs, Kelly Eismann, and Sara Branch in San Diego, and Debbie Hardin and Dan Janeck.

To my readers: family, friends, and strangers, knocking on my door with kindness and support.

And to Dion Graham, a partner in crime.